IT WAS A MEETING SHE HAD NOT PLANNED, WITH A MAN SHE HARDLY KNEW . . . AND SUZANNAH FELT THE FIRST STIRRINGS OF PASSION . . .

It was a wonder to each of them that fate had caused them to meet in this way. They had everything in common, it seemed. Travis had not imagined that he would ever meet a young woman whose thoughts so perfectly harmonized with his. As for Suzannah, her meeting with Travis in this way was sufficient to erase all bitter thoughts of what had occurred at the Shawns. Even her terror of Crazy Edythe was gone. . . .

"The rain has stopped," she said regretfully, at last. "I must go home. My family is sure to worry." She stood up, brushing the hay from her skirt.

"In the future I shall regard this hay barn as a kind of shrine," Travis told her, completely in earnest. Helping her on with her cloak, his hand brushed her throat. She caught her breath. "Miss Hopewell. . . ."

Suzannah turned to him; their faces were but inches apart. In the hollow of her throat, the pulse beat wildly.

"Miss Hopewell . . . Suzannah!" He drew her into his arms.

Suzannah sighed against him and reached up, her fingers intertwining behind his neck. Her eyes closed, their lips touched and for an instant Suzannah lost herself in the sweet sensation of her first kiss. . . .

Broken Promises

Drusilla Campbell

A Dell/Banbury Book

Published by
Banbury Books, Inc.
37 West Avenue
Wayne, Pennsylvania 19087

Dell ® TM 681510, Dell Publishing Co., Inc.

ISBN: 0-440-00837-9

Printed in the United States of America

First printing—March 1982

This is for Blackacre

PART I

Chapter 1

Amoset, Massachusetts—1832

She awoke to the song of birds. A mockingbird, perched in the colored maple outside her bedroom window, welcomed the first light of day. From somewhere else—an eave or gable, or the topmost point of the brass weathervane—a lark competed with full voice.

A pleasant, late-September chill lingered in the bedroom. Savoring the morning, Suzannah Hopewell pulled her lace-trimmed bed cap down over her ears and snuggled deeper beneath the goose-down comforter.

But she didn't sleep. She could have slumbered an extra fifteen minutes or so before one of the maids—Victorine probably—would knock to say that breakfast awaited her downstairs. But sleep was impossible on such a day. The sky was the color of the sapphire earrings she had received for her eighteenth birthday. Sunlight flashed from the amber, red and gold maple leaves that still wore a sheen of dew.

The first thought that occurred to Suzannah was that Talleyrand Shawn could celebrate his ninth birthday outdoors on Cooper's Mountain as planned.

Recalling her part in the picnic surprise that she and Lucy Shawn had organized, Suzannah threw back the bedcovers. She recoiled only an instant as her bare feet touched the cold floorboards, then hurried to where she had hidden the boy's gift. The Hopewell house was full of Irish servants and Suzannah had been taught to distrust them. The precious enameled tin of Swiss chocolates was hidden deep in her wardrobe where even Victorine would not find it.

The tin was brightly colored enamel and the lid bore the painted likeness of a boy and a dog. The boy wore a blue suit fitted with snug pantaloons and a lacy collar. Suzannah smiled, thinking how Talley Shawn would laugh at the picture of a dandy. He was a wild cub of a lad, willful and competent beyond his years. But like all children he had a sweet tooth that was rarely satisfied. With one polished oval fingernail, she pried the lid open, breathing deeply of the aroma that rose from the chocolates. Though the candies were wrapped individually in shiny paper, their sweet smell escaped, filling her nostrils. For an instant, Suzannah was almost overcome by sensations—the brilliant day, the song of birds, the delicious aroma of chocolates. She was short of breath, filled with joy, certain that on this day something wonderful would happen.

"Are you awake, Suzannah?" It was her mother, Sarah Hopewell, a note of nervous energy unmistakable in her quivery voice. "Answer me, Suzannah! Do you hear?" The door opened before Suzannah could hide the chocolates again. "What have you there?"

At forty, Sarah Hopewell had the appearance of a younger woman. Her hair was a pale mass of silvery blonde waves. She was still pretty, though years of nervous agitation had left lines in her forehead. When she relaxed, her expression sometimes had a dismal cast, bespeaking loneliness and despair not expressed in words.

"I bought them for Talley," Suzannah explained as she handed over the tin of chocolates. "Remember, you told me I could go? It's his birthday."

Sarah looked confused. She could not recall ever having said such a thing, nor could she imagine giving permission for an outing that was certain to enrage her husband. Still she knew that she was often forgetful—Suzannah was an honest daughter. Independent and spirited though she might be, Suzannah was not inclined to take advantage of her parent's absent-mindedness.

"You told me last week that I might spend the whole day with the Shawns. We were in the sewing room finishing the handwork on Valentine's new shirts for Divinity School. Victorine was there and I said. . . ."

Sarah put a hand to her forehead and cried, "I know, I know, I know! My Lord, girl, was there ever such a memory?" She bit her lip and shook her head. "Just don't let your papa see you go. You know how he feels about Yankees like the Shawns. I hate to think what he would do. . . ."

Suzannah dismissed Sarah's worries with a laugh. As her mother helped her dress in a heavy cotton gown with a short woolen jacket, Suzannah asked the question that had so often been on her mind. "How can Papa disapprove so awfully much when he himself sent me off to spend my summers with the Shawn family?"

"That was different. You were ill. You needed the country air—that kind of life. . . ." Her mother broke off.

"But why would Papa let me go there if he hates Yankees?"

"Mmmm?" For a moment, Sarah lost her hold on the thread of conversation. She put her hand to her forehead.

"Are you ill, Mama?" asked Suzannah, touching her mother's hand gently.

"What? Oh, no. Well, just a little. My nerves." With a sigh she sat on Suzannah's bed.

"Lie down, Mama. I'll fetch your tonic."

"I haven't any. I sent Victorine to the apothecary but the foolish slattern has not returned. I wonder why we let the Irish into our homes when we can't even trust them to run a simple errand."

"You know what Valentine says."

"Yes, he always speaks ill of the Irish. And somehow, I always listen to him." Sarah stopped and sighed. "Now why is it I can recall his silly slander when everything else drops right out of my mind?" She began to fidget, then cried out, her voice strident, "Where has Victorine got to?" She always behaved this way when she was forced to do without Dr. Whitaker's Nerve and Stomach Tonic. This time she had asked Victorine to get her two large bottles.

"Rest here, Mama. I'll go look for the girl. When did you send her?" Suzannah pulled the laces tight on her ankle-high walking shoes.

"An hour ago, maybe less. I don't know."

"That's more than enough time to walk to Amoset and back. She's probably forgotten her business and stopped to gossip in the kitchen. I'll see to her on my way out." Suzannah stopped for a moment to glance at herself in the mirror. Her dark curls were tied at the nape of her neck with a pale green, velvet ribbon that matched the color of her eyes. Her fair skin was flushed—yes, her excitement showed.

"Don't forget to bid Valentine Godspeed." Tears welled in Sarah's eyes at the thought of her darling twenty-year-old son. "The boy's so young! How will he fare, so far away from me?"

Kneeling beside the bed, Suzannah tried to comfort Sarah. From prior experience she knew that when her mother was agitated and without her tonic, she was apt to weep, sobbing uncontrollably, unable to explain her grief. "Dear Mama, Boston is less than a day's ride. We'll see Valentine often, I'm certain." She kissed Sarah's flushed cheek. "Anyway, you still have Eben and me."

"You'll understand when you're a mother. It's just not the same. No matter what I do, I still look at Valentine and see a little lad with hair falling over his eyes and holes in his pantaloons." She snuffled and reached inside her sleeve for a lace-edged handkerchief. "Valentine was such a perfect little boy. Such a joy to me."

Sarah's eyes were closed and she did not see the look of irritation that hardened Suzannah's features as she thought of her older brother. It was no wonder Eben was a strange man. All his life, he'd been forced to compete with Val's perfection. A part of Suzannah wanted to reprimand her mother for choosing a favorite son so blatantly. But Suzannah had been well schooled in deportment and she dismissed the impulse as quickly as it came to her. Guiltily, she kissed her mother a second time. Clutching the tin of chocolates, she said good-bye and hurried from the room.

Suzannah's bedroom faced a long, dark hall that ran the length of the big house. On the floor below were the drawing rooms, the dining room, the pantries and the sitting room. On the second floor were the bedrooms. Servants' quarters, a library and a ballroom occupied the third and fourth floors.

The kitchen was attached to the house and an open passageway led to the wash house, where the laundry was boiled clean in huge copper drums. Suzannah imagined she would find Victorine somewhere between kitchen and wash house, chatting with the laundress or the cook. From what Suzannah had observed, Victorine cared very little for her ailing mistress.

As a rule, Suzannah made a conscious effort to think kindly and deal fairly with the dozen servants who cared for the house and family, but on this particular morning she felt increasingly bad-tempered. It would take her an hour to walk to the Shawns' and most of the way would be uphill. If she stopped for breakfast, her arrival would be delayed another hour. She would have only a short time to visit before she would have to hurry home again. Yet she had to say good-bye to Valentine. There was no way out of it if she wanted to keep peace with her mother.

In her present mood, she did not bother to knock on the door to Valentine's room, but barged in. Her fury was growing. Clearly, the day's events were conspiring to ruin her outing and Talleyrand's birthday.

But her emotions changed the instant the door swung open. She stood in the doorway, her hand on the brass knob, struck dumb with amazement.

Valentine was kneeling on the bed, wearing only his linen shirt. She recognized the shirt. She had made it for him and, even from the doorway, she could see the crooked hem she had struggled to sew properly. Apart from the one garment, he was naked, and in the dimly lit bedroom his buttocks glowed like half-moons. Beneath him on the bed—her skirt and grimy ruffled petticoat hiked up, her fat white thighs exposed—was Victorine the Irish maid.

No one moved. From the bed Victorine and Val stared at Suzannah while, frozen in the doorway, she stared back. On the floor beside the bed were two amber-colored bottles of Dr. Whitaker's Tonic.

Suzannah wheeled and ran down the hall. Her legs felt weak and her heart beat so furiously it seemed to grow larger with each thump. She had to stop! She could scarcely breathe!

"Sister Suzannah!"

It was Val, of course, coming after her. She knew she could not look at him. She dared not, for fear of the terrible thoughts that might overwhelm her. "Stop, Suzannah! Hear me out!" She was on the landing by the time he reached her. His hand clutched her elbow, pinching painfully. She tried to shake him off but he only held her more tightly. Pulling her close to him, he forced her to look at him. His face was inches away. Suzannah smelled spirits on his breath.

"You've been drinking!" she cried incredulously.

"Didn't anyone ever teach you to knock?" His bangs of hair were disheveled. His eyes resembled pale blue stones. "I suppose you're on your way to tattle like a schoolgirl." He shook her. "Well?"

"I won't say anything. I promise, Val. I only came in to say good-bye." He let her go and she stood, still and fearful. "Mama needs her tonic."

"What?"

"Victorine has Mama's tonic. I was going down to see if she was in the kitchen with it and I wanted to say good-bye to you."

He ran his hand through his unruly hair. "All right, all right. So you did. I guess you saw more than you reckoned on."

"I won't tell, Val. I swear. I'll make any oath you say."

He shrugged. "You're such a child, Suzannah. Don't worry. I believe you. You're shocked. I have offended the sensibilities of the little mill town princess." Before she could reply, he went on. "Well, it isn't what you think. You're a child and don't know what you saw."

She nodded emphatically. Like everyone in the family, Valentine had a quick temper. She knew he would be unkind to her unless she mollified him somehow. She repeated her promise to keep silent. Then, despite her fear of his anger, she could not help asking the question on her mind.

"Are you still going to be a minister, Val?"

His laugh was a hoot. "Indeed I am, little sister. You might say that this morning I have prepared myself for the onslaught of sanctity." She stared at him in innocent confusion. "Even a man of God deserves a bawdy memory or two, Suzannah. Goodness means little unless it comes as a matter of choice."

She nodded in mute acquiescence to his logic.

He laughed again and grabbed her roughly, pulling her against his chest so tightly she could feel his heart pound. Or was it her own? She was frightened by her brother, trembling with the desire to escape.

"You're pretty, Suzannah—a flower grown from this rocky New England soil." Suddenly he kissed her. His mouth, open and wet, pressed against hers. She struggled, beating her hands against his chest. His body was shaking. Even as he forced his tongue against hers, she knew that he was laughing at her. "Soft little Suzannah is not so little anymore, eh? You'll make almost as good a memory as Victorine."

He let her go and she raced down the stairs, pursued by his unkind, hooting laughter. When she reached the wide front hall into which the staircase descended, she did not look back. Her one thought was to escape the house, to forget the ruin of the morning. Outside she knew the air was crisp and clean, the birds still promised joy. She wanted to be with the Shawns on Cooper's Mountain. She wanted to be a little girl again, with nothing on her mind but catching butterflies and joyfully setting them free. She wanted. . . .

Suzannah did not see the three men until too late. Rushing toward the front door, she careened into their midst. She almost fell. A hand caught her. The enameled tin flew from her fingers, hit the marble floor and crashed open, spilling a dozen brightly wrapped Swiss chocolates across the floor.

"Suzannah!" Martin Hopewell's bellow filled the front hall. The stone house, the marble floors and the oaken paneling almost rocked with the sound of his fury.

Held in a stranger's arms, Suzannah trembled as she saw the final ruin of her perfect day.

Chapter 2

"What are these?" Martin pointed at the foil-wrapped chocolates that littered the black and white marble floor. "Where were you going with those?" He took her brusquely from the arm of the young man whose quick action had prevented her from sprawling on her face. "Speak up, girl. What's the meaning of this display?"

Beside Martin Hopewell, Travis Paine and Foster McMahon surveyed with interest this unexpected domestic dispute. For young Paine the moment was particularly pleasant. It occurred to him that he had never seen lovelier eyes or a shapelier, more temptingly innocent mouth.

How old is she, Paine wondered. Her behavior was that of a disobedient child caught in a prank. But her figure, though slight, was clearly that of a woman.

Martin gave his daughter a little shake that seemed to bring Suzannah to her senses. Her voice was clear and musical as she replied confidently, "Today is Talleyrand Shawn's birthday, sir. The confections are for him."

"Shawn? You were going up the mountain?" Martin Hopewell's hand tightened on her arm.

"Yes, sir," she answered, squirming.

"On whose permission?"

Suzannah paused too long before she answered—long enough for Martin to guess that she was lying. "I had no permission, sir. I thought I could go up the mountain and get back without my absence being noticed. I meant no harm."

"I am opposed to this friendship, Suzannah. You know that well."

"But, Papa, Talleyrand's a little boy. He doesn't understand such things and he's expecting me. I gave my word I would bring him something special." Again, Travis Paine noted how her green eyes shone. The perfect mouth pouted charmingly. "Please, Papa?"

Foster McMahon, the unattractive man standing near Travis Paine, coughed once or twice and shuffled his feet, bringing Martin Hopewell's thoughts back to the business of the day. He didn't want to involve strangers and employees in his family affairs and this episode with Suzannah was embarrassingly prolonged. "Very well, Suzannah," Martin decided suddenly. "You may go up Cooper's Mountain one last time. Never again. You understand me? Regardless of who gives you permission, you may not visit with the Shawn family again." He glared at her, his angry eyes shadowed forbiddingly by thick grey eyebrows.

Cowed, Suzannah nodded without speaking.

"We'll talk of this later." Martin turned to Travis Paine and Foster McMahon. "Now I have mill business to attend to. There will be no more interruptions, I trust." He turned to leave the house with his associates. But before his hand twisted the crystal knob, Suzannah flew into his arms.

"Thank you, Papa!" she cried, kissing his cheek. "You're a wonderful father."

Embarrassed, Hopewell pushed her away and glanced at Paine and McMahon. Always acutely con-

scious of what he feared others were thinking of him,
Martin feared that Suzannah's daughterly affection
might give the men the wrong idea—that he was soft
or easygoing.

"Mind your manners, girl!" he demanded gruffly.

Suzannah dropped an abashed curtsy toward her
father, taking in Paine and McMahon with the same
gesture. She noticed the handsome young Paine for
the first time. When their eyes met, her blush returned. She looked away quickly.

"You must not forget the chocolates, Miss Hopewell," he said with a smile as he stooped to gather
those that had fallen near him. Returning them to the
tin, he handed the gift to her. "They make an excellent
present. Your young friend will be pleased."

A moment later, when they were gone, Suzannah
ran to the window and peered out after the three-
some, watching as they descended the hill into town.
Then, humming softly to herself, she clapped her
hands together. She was almost dancing as she made
her way out the back door and started up the road
toward Cooper's Mountain.

Martin Hopewell was a large, overfed man in his
early fifties, with thick wavy grey hair and a
mustache that drooped almost to his chin. His face
preserved a glum expression regardless of his frame of
mind. He affected a formal, dark and unadorned style
of dress that he thought befitted his elevated station
in the world of hard industry. Scarcely a moment
went by that Martin was not fully conscious of who
he was. The importance of his position in Amoset
might be ignored or overlooked by some but, to him,
his station was always of the greatest significance.

He was particularly self-aware this morning as
he, McMahon and Paine descended the gentle slope

from his house to town. The path was lined with fire-thorn bushes already heavy with ripe berries. Beyond, on either side, were meadows and woods alive with colors of gold and red. To the west, beyond the house, rose the mountains from which the Amoset River rushed in wild cataracts.

Stopping the men midway in their descent of the hill, Hopewell pointed out the details of Amoset. It was his town. Without him, he knew, the land would still be in the hands of Indians and sanctimonious Yankee farmers.

"That's Hopewell's over there, of course." He pointed northeast of the small city. "When I came here sixteen years ago, built the factory and first boarding houses, there was nothing in Amoset. Now—well, you can see for yourselves. This city rivals Lowell in importance. Now there are twenty other mills along the river, as well as a tannery, a box factory and a scythe factory." He pointed to a distant cluster of dark brick buildings. "That's the musket factory. We have a little hospital, a theater. I would say that Massachusetts can be proud of Amoset."

"Indeed it may, sir," said Paine. "What is the city's population?"

"Six thousand at nearest count. It could be more but certainly no less." Hopewell eyed Paine speculatively. What was this Yankee thinking? Like most of his New England kin, Paine had a reserve that Hopewell had never learned to ignore. He always sensed some condescension in the Yankee manner, as if he, Martin Hopewell—a Georgian by birth and long heritage—were inferior by nature. "Plenty of work for an architect like yourself with enthusiasm and energy—eh, Paine?"

The younger man nodded. "Indeed there is, sir. When I first met your son Eben at Yale and heard of

Amoset, I set my mind on coming here. I am sure I shall not regret my decision."

Hopewell cleared his throat gruffly. He did not like hearing about Yale. Such talk only made him aware of his own lack of education. Despite his need for Travis Paine's services, Hopewell already disliked the architect and, in his thoughts, applied to him such adjectives as arrogant and affected. Travis' demeanor was uniformly quiet and unassuming, and yet there was something about the young man that Hopewell did not like.

McMahon was much more to his liking. They understood each other, though Hopewell could not quite forgive McMahon for being Irish. Probably because of his peasant background, McMahon was a man who knew the meaning of authority and the responsibilities of those who serve. As Hopewell's new general overseer, the supervisor of dozens of other overseers and hundreds of operatives, McMahon could be tough, hard-driving and productive.

As they continued their walk down the hill, Hopewell spoke of his plans for Hopewell Mills. "These factory girls have some idea that the working life is meant to be a pleasure, McMahon. I trust you'll disabuse them of that notion." Hopewell thought he read disapproval in Paine's sideward glance and he was quick to add, "Not that we want them ill-treated or grossly overworked, mind you. Hopewell's has a name for fairness and I mean for us to keep our reputation. We need these girls as much as they need us—although, of course, it wouldn't do to tell them so."

In 1832 there was a shortage of labor in Massachusetts. Only by wooing the daughters of Yankee farmers could the mills remain open. In some ways these young women—most of them highly literate, descended from the soldier-patriots of the Revolutionary

Army—made a perfect labor force. They believed in work as something almost holy. Progress, exemplified by modern factories and the newest, most efficient machinery, was greatly admired by them. Martin could not fault the factory girls' diligence. In spite of himself, he admired them. After working from dawn until past dusk, most of them attended the Lyceum in the evening for lectures on philosophy and art. Or they belonged to the many self-improvement circles that they had organized on their own.

There was only one problem with these hardy young women. Like his own daughter they were given to independent thinking and seemed to believe they actually had a right to control their lives for themselves. They arrived from farms and villages all around New England to work at Hopewell Mills, but despite the efforts made to train them and board them, they never stayed more than two or three years. They earned the money they needed to pay off the family farm or finance a brother's expensive education and then they left, forcing Hopewell Mills to train new operatives constantly. To entice new workers, Hopewell's "black wagon" went as far north as French Canada. Every year, recruitment became more difficult.

"These girls have to be happy here in Amoset," he told McMahon, "but that doesn't mean Hopewell's is a charitable institution."

McMahon laughed at this. "Never worry, Mr. Hopewell. We'll up production and the young ladies will never know what's happened. You can trust me, sir." McMahon had a hungry face. With close-set eyes, gleaming like black beads, a sloping forehead and a receding chin, McMahon's threatening appearance filled Martin Hopewell with confidence. It was the face of a man who would do everything he could to gain favor from his employer.

They were almost to the base of the hill when, without warning, a man leapt from behind the bushes and blocked their way.

"I must have a word with you, Mr. Hopewell." The speaker was thin and raggedly dressed. There was a wild glint in his eyes, and a narrow, tormented sneer twisted his mouth.

Hopewell's response was automatic. "Get away from me! How dare you . . . !"

McMahon grabbed the stranger's lapels and lifted him off the ground. "You heard what the master said!"

The man twisted, showing an energy that contrasted with his frail and shabby appearance. "Master!" He spat on the ground disdainfully. "You had me blacklisted, *Master* Hopewell. There's no work for me or mine in Amoset. The gates are barred. What right have you . . . ?"

Now Martin recognized the man. It was Ephraim Grace, whom he had fired months before. The man was a notorious labor organizer.

"I have a family. Seven children call me Papa. They're hungry. They cry, they beg for food. What can I tell them? That the great Master Hopewell. . . ."

McMahon's hand slammed across the man's face. Ephraim Grace squealed.

"That's enough, McMahon." Hopewell's voice was sharp.

"This kind of matter is best left to the overseer, sir," complained McMahon.

"Perhaps. But you must understand that physical violence is the last resort." Hopewell turned to the thin, dirty figure. "Grace, I regret that your family must suffer. Nevertheless, you knew the risk when you agitated against me. Get out of Amoset if you desire honest labor. I'll not send word to owners outside this town." Hopewell turned to his new overseer. "Let him go."

McMahon did so reluctantly. For an instant after his release, Grace stood without moving as if he could not believe he had been dealt with so moderately. Then, slowly, he backed away, his wary eyes shifting from McMahon to Hopewell and back to McMahon. Travis was reminded of the wolves he'd once seen traveling in packs in northern Maine. Their eyes were as cagey as this laborer's.

When Ephraim Grace had withdrawn some distance from the men, he turned and glared at Martin Hopewell, undisguised hatred in his eyes. "You'll pay," he threatened just audibly. Then he whirled and plunged through the bushes into the thick woods.

Later, during the tour of Hopewell Mills, the scene on the trail troubled Travis Paine. Though he recognized the necessity of strong management and strictly enforced rules, the treatment of the former mill operative seemed harsh.

That's why you're an architect and not a manufacturer, he told himself. An architect could afford scruples; a man of industry could not.

Hopewell Mills was a proud, six-story brick building with a sharply peaked clerestory roof and many windows. The factory, machine shop, carpentry shop, furnace and yard were enclosed behind a high spike-topped iron fence. The only entrance was through an iron gate which was opened and closed by a grim gatekeeper. Once that gate clanged shut behind Travis, he felt an illogical urge to kick the bars and demand his freedom. The factory gave him a sense of claustrophobia that never went away, even when he entered the bright, pleasant spinning room where the open windows let in the sunlight and cool

autumn air. Around the windows of the spinning
room were freshly laundered cotton curtains, and the
sills were like gardens crowded with potted plants.
Most of the female operatives smiled affably and said
good day as if they enjoyed this intrusion of
strangers. Travis noticed a number of pretty faces
among them.

The weaving rooms were less pleasant and the
operatives too busy to waste more than a fleeting
smile. Here the windows were tightly closed and the
rooms unpleasantly warm. Children sprayed the air
with water frequently to maintain the high humidity
necessary to keep the threads from breaking.

"It's here I need your help," said Hopewell to
Travis. The mill owner had to shout to be heard. The
long, broad room shook with the buzzing, hissing and
clanging of pulleys, rollers, spindles and flyers.
Hopewell pointed to the female operative nearest
them. She was constantly in motion, moving back and
forth between two giant looms she supervised, alert to
any trouble. At the first sign of an empty bobbin or a
broken thread, she leapt forward to attend the shuddering machines.

Hopewell drew the men aside to a corner where
the roar was softer. "There is wasted space up here.
With one or two structural changes, we could double
the number of looms on this floor."

"In Lowell the girls supervise three or four looms
at a time," contributed McMahon. His small eyes were
narrowed, and Travis could see that the man was
seeking out the lazy, the incompetent and the trouble-
makers in the room. His gaze fell on a young woman
who held a Bible in her hand as she paced before her
looms. She appeared to be memorizing passages from
the book. As she worked, her lips moved. From time
to time she glanced down at the text for verification.

"I would forbid the reading of books. Even the Bible," said McMahon. "These operatives put such high store by learning that they forget what they're about."

Hopewell nodded. "Of course, McMahon. Do whatever is necessary. What about you, Paine? Can you see how to double the capacity of this room?"

Travis could not. "It isn't the room, sir. Nor is it the heavy work of the young women that concerns me. But, sir, this floor simply won't support the added weight. The building wasn't meant to carry so much heavy machinery on this story."

Martin Hopewell displayed his impatience at this explanation. "You're the architect. Shore up the place. Make the building stronger."

Travis shook his head. "I'd like to say it's as easy as that, Mr. Hopewell. But the problem is more than just the building. It's the land."

"What's wrong with my land?"

"It's merely an engineering problem. This close to the river, the ground isn't solid enough to support a massive structure like this mill. As a matter of fact, even without additional weight on the top floors, it seems to me that the building is unsafe."

"Are you telling me that—"

McMahon interrupted. "Sir. If you'll permit me. I've seen dozens of mills built at riversides like this, and I never saw one of them collapse." He smiled thinly at Travis Paine. "Perhaps the young man is being a trifle overcautious? I think I could safely double the number of looms here without altering the structure of the mill in the slightest. If you'll permit me, Mr. Hopewell, I believe I can save you the trouble of an architect altogether."

"McMahon, I must protest. . . ."

Hopewell ignored Travis. "You mean to put the looms up here anyway? Crowd 'em?"

McMahon nodded.

"If you do that, Mr. Hopewell," Travis interjected, "you are risking a dreadful tragedy. I must warn you. . . ."

But it was too late. Hopewell listened until Paine's futile protests died out in the thunder of the looms. Then, with an expression of forgiving condescension, the mill owner turned to his overseer. "McMahon, you order those new looms tomorrow. Let the girls know we intend for each of them to supervise three or more machines. And you're right: no books permitted within the gate."

Then he turned to Travis. "Well, Mr. Paine. I must say I had hoped we might work affably toward the betterment of this mill. However, to my mind you're an altogether too cautious young man for this business. You might do better designing houses for rich folks in Boston or New York."

"Mr. Hopewell, as a Christian and a man of conscience, you must know and care that this mill is. . . ."

"Good day, Mr. Paine. I am sure you can find your way out." Martin Hopewell's expression was frozen.

"This is criminal, sir. You cannot possibly. . . ."

"Out!" bellowed Hopewell, pointing toward the stairwell. "There is no further business between us!"

"I protest, sir!"

Hopewell jerked his head toward his new overseer. "McMahon!" was all he said.

The Irishman stepped forward, threatening. He did not bother to conceal his pleasure. He reached for the collar of Travis' jacket, but the young architect was too quick for him. With a quick blow, he knocked

McMahon's hand aside and crouched, ready for the overseer's attack. Startled, McMahon looked up at Hopewell for orders. The mill owner shook his head.

Travis Paine took two steps backward, came erect and dusted off his collar where McMahon had touched him. "Fine men you choose to work for you, Mr. Hopewell. Very fine men, indeed."

Bowing sardonically, the young man turned on his heel and left the room.

Chapter 3

Making her way up Cooper's Mountain, Suzannah scrambled up the steep path that led to the Shawn farm. In previous years, before Martin Hopewell had forbidden her visits, Suzannah had traveled this way often. There was an easier route, but the way was longer and the path lay somewhat to the north of Amoset.

Suzannah had first become acquainted with the Shawn family when she was eight. She had been troubled in childhood by headaches and during the summers she had difficulty breathing. Her malaise resulted from the summertime humidity and heat, or so the doctors told her parents. They said that living near the river was bad for her and they prescribed a cooler elevation. Dr. Lewis, in Amoset, suggested that the Shawn family on Cooper's Mountain might be pleased to take in Suzannah during the summer months if Martin Hopewell would finance her care.

Since then, Suzannah had often wondered at the perversity of her father's decision in accepting such an offer from a man he despised. But now, at age eighteen, she was almost accustomed to her father's perversity. Martin Hopewell had a way of behaving out of character. She did not understand his impulses, but she at least respected his perversity and perhaps even loved him for it.

As she hurried up the narrow trail, she carefully avoided Crazy Edythe's derelict cabin. It was located in the midst of the stump-littered clearing, halfway up the mountain. Suzannah remembered summers filled with laughter when she and Lucy had played like fauns on the mountain. Lucy's brother and sister, Talleyrand and Ingrid, had frequently accompanied the two girls on their fantasy-filled jaunts through the forest. The vast, wild world made a backdrop for the heroic stories they wove out of history. Recalling damsels in distress, revolutions fought and liberties won, Suzannah was saddened. Gradually her pace along the overgrown path was slowed by melancholy.

At thirteen her ailments had disappeared. After that, she was forbidden to spend summers on the mountain or to play with Lucy and her family. Sarah could only tell her, "It's because he hates them. Hates them all like poison." Martin directed his animosity toward all Yankees, making no exceptions for the sake of gratitude. In his perversity, he managed to utterly disregard the hurt feelings of his daughter.

Though she was normally obedient, Suzannah could hardly tolerate this separation from loved ones. It was lonely growing up in the big Hopewell mansion. Her only companions were Eben and Valentine, who were too self-important for her games, and her mother Sarah, who was distant and distracted. Now she went as a fugitive up Cooper's Mountain. Deceit caused no pangs of guilt. Suzannah loved her father, but experience had taught her to act with independence despite the risk of scenes like the one that had taken place in the foyer that morning.

She had dared not confess to her father that her mother had given permission for today's visit. If he

knew, Martin would berate his wife until the whole
house reverberated with the force of his displeasure.
Suzannah could remember a lifetime of parental argu-
ments. After each bout her mother seemed shrunken,
as if Martin Hopewell were some wasting disease that
gradually robbed Sarah of her health.

Beneath Suzannah's heel a dry stick cracked like
a musket shot. To her left she heard the crash and stir
of wings as an autumn-colored turkey lifted up in
fright. She watched it move, admiring the grace of
the great wild creature. A pair of turquoise jays
scolded her intrusion. Forgetting her father and
family, Suzannah laughed aloud at the birds' audac-
ity. Wrapped warmly in a russet cloak to match the
season, Suzannah felt a buoyant happiness, a sense of
belonging that dispelled her earlier melancholy.

Farther up Cooper's Mountain the trees
brightened. Suzannah trod a path spread with leaves
of gold as the sunlight flickered, dancing in and out
through a canopy of amber, orange and vermilion.
Ahead, on the exposed eastern slope of the mountain,
most of the trees had lost their foliage and stood bare,
heaped like dry kindling mounted against the hearth
of heaven.

The Shawn farm occupied a high valley divided
by a serpentine stream. It was a fertile plot of land,
ideal for growing vegetables and corn, and for grazing a small herd of dairy cattle. But Suzannah knew
the farm had never yielded enough to support the
Shawns. On the slopes above the valley were stands
of pine and oak, maple and gum. Descending through
this growth, Suzannah skirted the wild hedge of
blackberries, almost ripe for picking, and hurried
through the kitchen garden toward the cabin.

Halfway across the clearing she halted, stopped

by the sound of an argument that was taking place inside the steep-roofed house. Suzannah hesitated, suddenly uncertain of her welcome, yet unwilling to walk away.

"If you go down there, Lucy, you're not my daughter anymore," James Shawn was saying. "Martin Hopewell thinks you girls are just so much machinery like his looms and spindles and what-have-yous!"

"Papa, there are advantages in Amoset!" Lucy Shawn was pleading.

"A lending library? Lectures? You'd sell your freedom for those things?"

"You don't understand." Suzannah was forced to smile at the familiar stubbornness in Lucy's voice.

"Indeed I do not understand. That's white slavery down there in Amoset, my girl. You sign on with him and you'll work like a Negro from sunup 'til dark. Believe me, you won't have a stomach for lending libraries and lectures after such days as that. And what'll you get for it, Lucy? Blood knots in your knees, half-blindness, backache. You'll kill your youth and beauty down there."

"There's nothing for me here on the mountain, Papa. I have to go. I'll send you back money for the farm and Ingrid, and I'll come to visit often."

"You know I don't believe in keeping freedom from anyone, but if I have to set down rules to keep you home, I'll do it."

"You want me to rot up here?"

"You've been talking to that silly Suzannah Hopewell. Don't deny it. She's been filling your mind with a rich girl's nonsense."

Hearing her name mentioned, Suzannah felt a guilty curiosity. She was eavesdropping, but could not restrain herself.

"Suzannah has nothing to do with this," said Lucy quickly.

"I don't believe you! She's been gossiping in your ear about parties and fancy dresses and you think if you go down there you'll get a taste of that high life." Shawn's voice went hard and mean. "Is a daughter of mine so easily misled? Use your good common sense. If you go to work in the mills, Suzannah won't have anything to do with you."

Suzannah stood with her burning forehead pressed against the rail of the porch, listening to James Shawn malign her. The tears stung in her eyes but she could not turn away; something held her, forcing her to listen.

Helen Shawn spoke up. Her voice, in contrast to her husband's, sounded sweet and reasonable as she explained to her daughter, "You're only sixteen, Lucy. Wait another year before you decide you have to go. These things bear considering, you know."

"The longer I wait, the harder it will be for me to learn."

"Talley and Ingrid need you. I need you, girl." The mother's words were simply spoken, as if she only declared the facts of life.

"Mama, think of the money I can send you!"

"I don't want any more talk of money!" declared James, angrier than ever. "You've got these high ideas of playing Lady Bountiful to your poor relations. Suzannah's been encouraging you. Helen, I don't want that girl in the house."

"She's harmless, Jamie. Just another flighty young woman. Why do you always blame . . . ?"

"Lucy, you are forbidden to see her again."

"Jamie. . . ."

Shawn ignored his wife's interruption. "If I hear

any more about work at the mill, I will lock you in the house until you come to your senses."

"That's not fair, Jamie. You've never in your life been so unreasonable."

"Keep out of this, Helen. I want my feelings known and no argument." There was a long pause. "Well?"

"I can't just cut her off, Papa. I have to explain. . . ."

"You're asking your daughter to be unkind, Jamie. That's not like you. What gets into you every time Suzannah Hopewell's name comes up? I swear I don't understand. . . ."

"Nothing gets into me, Helen. I simply want our girl to get her values straight. I don't want her sacrificing her youth. There's plenty for a young lady to do here."

Suzannah heard the sound of a chair being pushed across rough floor and footsteps approaching the front door. "You may say this land isn't much, Lucy. But it's yours. Just remember that. This land is yours and having it makes you free. You need be no man's slave."

The heavy oak door swung open. Suzannah and James Shawn stared at one another.

He was a tall, handsome man. His strongly featured face was unlined, tanned to a deep gold by the summer sun. He wore his sandy hair long, tied at the back with a dark cord. The eyes that bored into her appeared blue-black in color. He stared at Suzannah so long she felt the blood rise in her cheeks. She bit her tongue to keep from saying something she knew she would regret. As he stared at her the tears rose—he saw them—and Suzannah tried to wipe them away with her sleeve. She would not shame herself before this man who hated her.

"What is it, Jamie?" Helen asked as she came to the door. The moment she saw Suzannah, she cried, "Sweet Heavens!" and hurried down the steps to embrace the girl. This act of kindness came as such a surprise to Suzannah that she wept unrestrainedly and rushed into Helen's comforting arms.

"You're a brute, James David Shawn. A cruel, insensitive. . . ."

"I am nothing of the sort, woman. And well you know it!" The door slammed shut.

Helen led Suzannah away from the house, back through the garden to the path that led down the mountain. There she stopped, and placing her hands on Suzannah's shoulders, looked deep into the girl's eyes. "I don't know what you heard, but from the tears I'd guess it was too much. It's a cruel way to learn how folks feel, but perhaps it's better this way."

"Why . . . why . . . does he hate me? He used to call me Little Pigeon. He taught me how to ride the pony." The gentle memory brought fresh tears. Suzannah shook her head in pain and confusion. The childhood summers had been happy, but now James Shawn's bitterness made her doubt. Had she been misled in those days?

"Did he hate me when I was a little girl?" she asked aloud.

Helen shrugged her thin shoulders and an expression of deep weariness crossed her face. While James had retained his youth and vigor, Helen had aged quickly. Scarcely thirty, she stooped painfully when she walked and her light brown hair was tinged with drab grey. "I don't know what gets into him, Suzannah," Helen replied. "It seems I know my man less well as years go by. There's something about you and your family that riles him, but I don't know what it is. The reason hardly matters since his attitude never will change."

"It's my family then?" asked Suzannah, trying to understand. "Not me?"

Helen laughed gently. "Oh, it's you. I would like to pretend it's otherwise, Suzannah. But the truth is, you rile my man as much as your papa does."

Suzannah swallowed. Her voice broke when she inquired, "Then I may not come here again?"

Helen nodded. " 'Tis for the best." She tried to smile as she stroked Suzannah's hair, almost unconscious of her motherly gesture. "You'll get over this soon enough. You'll be going to balls and attending sociables. You won't have time to think of us."

Determined not to cry, Suzannah took a moment to control herself before she responded. When she did, she sounded angry, though she felt a deep sorrow and loss. "You think I have nothing on my mind but entertainment. You agree with Mr. Shawn, don't you? I'm a bad influence on Lucy."

"Now did I ever say that, Suzannah?"

"You didn't have to." She tossed her head proudly. "Well, you can think what you want, Mistress Shawn. In the meantime, you need not be concerned that I will invade your privacy. I won't return where I'm not wanted. But the time will come when you will know how badly you misjudged me."

Helen shook her head sadly. "Forgive us our cruelty, Suzannah. James never meant. . . ."

The words were lost on Suzannah, who turned away and began to run down the path. The leaves clouded about the hem of her cloak, then fell softly behind, covering her footsteps as if she had never passed that way at all.

She walked a long way without noticing her surroundings. At first her sight was dimmed by tears. Later, when her vision cleared and her sobs subsided, she trod wearily, her eyes fixed upon the path immediately before her, glancing neither right nor left.

She felt knocked down and kicked about by what had been said. Her stomach hurt and the pulse in her forehead beat painfully with every step down the mountain. Beside a chestnut tree laden with spiky-shelled nuts, she stopped at last. Resting her forehead against its rough, reassuring bark, she wept again.

"Suzannah." It was Lucy's voice behind her.

"Go away."

"I am so sorry, Suzannah. Forgive my papa. He's. . . ." Lucy sighed as if she knew words alone could never mend the damage. "Shall I walk with you a little way?" she asked tentatively. Suzannah nodded and wiped her eyes.

The trail curved up above the valley. Rounding the opposite slope, it crossed a steep, narrow meadow of wheat grass and wild rye decorated with parasols of Queen Anne's lace. From the trail the girls could look over the peaceful valley all the way into Amoset. From their vantage point high on the mountain, it appeared a miniature town, its harsh realities softened by distance and by the blue autumnal mist.

Lucy said, "It isn't you. Not really. Papa makes a big fuss about our friendship, but it isn't that which bothers him." She chewed her lip a moment, her head bent in earnest thought, as if she had to solve some complex problem. Looking up, trying to catch Suzannah's eye, Lucy continued. "I think my father feels left out of things. The Amoset Valley is changing so quickly, filling up with towns and factories and people. Some of them don't even speak English. Nothing seems the same as it was. He's a good man, my papa. But he hates being poor and powerless."

Suzannah did not reply. Lucy's sharp-featured, intelligent face was tense with concentration. "When Papa was a boy, he knew everyone in the valley," Lucy continued. "Shawns have always been simple folks, but we're proud of who we are and what our family stands for. My great-grandfather fought in the war and, according to all stories, he was a hero. But that doesn't count for much these days, unless you're some fancy Boston family. Papa can't get used to the way this town has changed. He says nothing counts any longer except making money." She stopped and took Suzannah's hand. "Do you understand? Can you forgive him for being so unkind? He envies your world as much as he hates it."

"You're my best friend, Lucy. If I don't have you, it's the same as having no one." Suzannah waited for a reply, but when Lucy said nothing, she continued, "Do you think I'm silly and superficial the way he does? Tell the truth, Lucy."

"You're the way you are because of who you are. I'm me because I'm James Shawn's girl. Let's not label one another."

Suzannah's expression hardened and a faint sneer curved her lips. "In other words, you do agree."

Embarrassed, Lucy laughed. "You only seem silly because he doesn't know you. He hears you going on about dresses and parties and. . . ."

"You think I'm silly. Say it."

"Let's not fight, Suzannah. I came to say I'm sorry." They had stopped walking again and now they stood facing each other on the path. In the pocket of her russet cloak, Suzannah felt the tin of chocolates she'd brought for Talleyrand.

"Here," she said, thrusting the tin at Lucy. "It's for Talley's birthday."

Lucy waved it away. "I can't take it, Suzannah. Papa would be furious."

"Take it, I said. Take it. They're just chocolates—just a gift. Can't I even . . . ?"

"Oh, stop it!" snapped Lucy. "It's just this kind of thing that makes Papa feel so bad toward you. Can't you understand? How do you think he will feel when I bring this tin home? Why, just look how pretty the tin is—all decorated! Why, just the tin costs more than he could ever afford, and the chocolates! I don't suppose he's eaten chocolate more than once or twice in his whole life. Perhaps he's never. . . ."

"Hide them from him. Enjoy them. Don't punish me for being able to buy a special gift for someone I care about."

Lucy glanced anxiously at the sun that lit the crest of the mountains. "I must go, Suzannah."

"When will I see you again?"

Lucy shook her head.

Suzannah persisted. "Next month is the Harvest Bonfire. Will you be at the knoll?"

"I suppose so. Yes, of course. We always go."

"Promise we will meet then."

"I've got to leave. He'll notice. . . ."

"Promise, Lucy. Promise! You know you can do it if you want to. You do want to be my friend, don't you?" Suzannah grabbed her friend's wrist.

"You're hurting me!" Lucy wrenched herself away and rubbed her sore wrist.

"Will you meet me?"

"I don't know. It isn't so easy." Lucy waved her hand. "I have to go, Suzannah. I'll try to see you, but. . . ." She was breathless, eager to be off.

"What about the chocolates?" Suzannah called after Lucy, her voice shrill with frustration. "The chocolates!" she screamed, almost hysterical at being defied. Raising her arm above her head, she hurled the enameled tin, flinging it far into the woods. Sobbing, she turned and ran down the mountain.

Chapter 4

As she neared Crazy Edythe's cabin, Suzannah became aware that the weather had changed. Gone were the blue skies and the warmth of the afternoon sun. Towering, plum-colored clouds boiled up from the west, casting dense shadows that darkened the woods long in advance of evening. Wind riffled the tree tops, lifting off golden leaves that fell to the forest floor with a delicate, dense patter like soft rain.

The wind was rising. Above Suzannah the trees swayed and groaned, creaking against each other as if to protest the storm to come. At any other time, Suzannah would have taken the usual detour to avoid Crazy Edythe's ramshackle cabin—squat and dark and windowless amidst juniper and sweet fern. Like most other children in Amoset, Suzannah feared Crazy Edythe and half-believed the exaggerations told of spells and charms and premonitions. But heartache and anger—with the pressing threat of a storm—made her brave this day. Hiking her cloak, skirts and petticoats almost to her knees, she darted into the open, across the rough clearing.

"That you, Suzannah Hopewell? Edythe sees you!" The voice came as a screech, emanating from some point alongside the cabin.

Suzannah glanced up quickly and saw the old woman lurking beside a bank of cages meant for animals and birds. She was hunkered over a walking stick, long, matted grey hair flying about her withered face.

"I would have words with you, Suzannah Hopewell!" Edythe rattled the end of her cane along the cages, creating a rapid-fire sound like bursts of ammunition.

Running faster, Suzannah leapt over a rotting log; her cloak snagged on a limb and she sprawled forward, face down in the dirt. Digging her nails into the soil, she struggled to her feet only to find her cloak snagged firmly by the limb. Twisting awkwardly, she tried to extricate herself as Crazy Edythe hobbled up to her.

"No need to fear, Suzannah Hopewell. I do not hold thee responsible for what was done to me and mine."

"Keep away from me!" Suzannah cried. "Our Father, Who art in Heaven. . . ."

Crazy Edythe only laughed. She raised her cane as if to strike Suzannah. There was a crack of lightning. With one desperate lunge, Suzannah tore her cloak free. She staggered, regained her footing and ran, the mad, scratchy laughter pursuing her.

She did not stop running until she reached the base of the hill, where the trail intersected the town road. In her flight from Crazy Edythe, she realized she had taken a wrong turn. Now she found herself a mile from home with the rain pelting down in earnest.

She glanced around her. Just off the road was a hay barn where she sought shelter. Under its protection, shaking with cold, she slipped out of her wet cloak and spread it on the bales to dry. It was dark in the barn and the only sounds she heard were the skittering of mice. Far above, the discontented hoot of an owl echoed among the rafters. She had begun to recover from her headlong dash down Cooper's Mountain, but she could not help shuddering at the recollection of Edythe's words. "I do not hold thee responsible for what was done to me," the woman had said. What did it mean?

Suddenly, there was a hiss of footsteps on straw, coming from the corner of the barn. Suzannah spun around just as a man stepped out of the shadows.

"It is Miss Hopewell, is it not?" Travis Paine stepped forward. After her first start of surprise, Suzannah relaxed, recognizing the young man she had seen earlier that day. "I did not mean to frighten you, miss. We met this morning. I am Travis Paine, the architect your father was to have engaged."

Suzannah's short laugh expressed her relief. "I suppose one should expect to find architects in old barns?"

"But rarely manufacturing heiresses." Travis Paine bowed formally. "Like yourself, I was caught by the rain. I expected the weather to clear soon."

Suzannah peered toward the barn door. "I fear we will have some time to wait." She tried to sound calm, but her heart beat alarmingly fast. She told herself she should leave the barn soon, regardless of the rain. The situation would create a scandal if the young man were to tell anyone. She looked at Paine surreptitiously. Would he do the gentlemanly thing and go for help?

"I'll be off then, to fetch a wagon," he said, as if reading her thoughts.

"Oh, don't." She spoke without thinking. Instinct seemed to rule her tongue, driving away discretion. "That's hardly necessary," she added hastily. "The weather is impossible and there isn't a house for at least a mile."

So much had happened to Suzannah that day that she craved the distraction of his presence and she welcomed the musty quiet of the hay barn. The slightly risqué encounter with Travis—sure to shock her family and friends—began to seem like a thrilling adventure. She had never before spent more than a few moments alone with any young man near her age, other than her own brothers. Now it appeared that she and Travis Paine would be together for some time. She could not help marveling at the fortuitous encounter, as if there were something more than chance in their meeting.

"Perhaps the clearing will come as suddenly as the rain. It is sometimes so with autumn storms." Suzannah looked about for a place to sit.

"Permit me," said Paine hurriedly, arranging a comfortable seat for her on a hay bale. He found a comfortable place for himself a discreet distance away and leaned casually against a soft bale. For a moment they did not speak.

"And what did you and my papa . . . ?"

"Did you enjoy your visit . . . ?"

They spoke simultaneously, then laughed. There was another pained silence.

"You were saying, Miss Hopewell?"

"I was only asking what you and my papa decided. Are you planning marvelous innovations at Hopewell Mills?"

Paine shook his head. "Alas, Mr. Hopewell and I could not agree." He did not wish to go on. A young beauty like Suzannah would only be bored by business. But she pressed him to explain himself, and so he did, warming to his subject. In the most inoffensive terms he could muster, he explained that Hopewell and McMahon would do quite well without him, that he was perhaps a trifle idealistic for the business of mill design, and that he hoped her father understood he meant nothing personal when he refused the job.

Though he made a gentlemanly effort to conceal his true opinions, some of Travis' dislike for Martin Hopewell became apparent to Suzannah. For the second time that day she was hearing her father maligned; but somehow, when it came time to defend him, she could not speak. She loved him but had guessed that in affairs of business, he was hard and somewhat unscrupulous. She accepted this with unquestioning equanimity, assuming that such characteristics were virtues in the world of manufacturing and business.

Unfastening her damp hair, she let the soft curls fall about her face. "You know my brother Eben?"

"Indeed. It was he who encouraged me to move here to Amoset."

"And now you will have to leave because you failed to strike a bargain with my father?" She was aware of sorrow at the thought of his departure. Her eyes having grown accustomed to the dimness, she found herself studying Travis closely. She had to admit she admired his firm good looks and his proud manner. His eyes sought hers as he shifted position on the hay bale.

"Amoset is booming. Already I have the prospect of commissions to design homes and shops. There are plans for a theater and I believe I have a good chance of being commissioned for the job."

"I'm sure you will be," Suzannah responded enthusiastically. "I remember that Eben spoke about a fellowship of some kind. Do you plan to study abroad?"

"Indeed I do, Miss Hopewell. I am pleased that you remember. I will spend part of this winter in The Eternal City."

She clapped her hands. "How wonderful! Rome is a magnificent city—isn't it? Though somewhat in ruins, of course!"

Paine laughed at her attempted worldliness. "The ruins are what make the city so magnificent, Miss Hopewell. It is those very monuments, the living remnants of past civilizations, that I will study in order to learn the essentials of symmetry and design."

Suzannah listened intently as he went on, and her interest encouraged him to speak of Rome and of what he hoped to learn. As Travis spoke, Suzannah was distracted by thoughts that might have caused the young architect to blush. She admired the fine, loose waves of his brown hair, the way he used his hands to emphasize the vivid pictures his words created. It seemed then, in the twilight atmosphere of the barn—separated from reality by the rain that kept them here, together—that she had never met a more handsome or more completely admirable young man than Travis Paine.

"You bear a famous name," she said later, when there was a shy pause in the flow of his conversation.

"A name I am proud of," he responded, "though I must confess the line between myself and the patriot is indirect. He was a second cousin."

"You are too humble, I think, Mr. Paine. The blood of patriots runs in your veins." It was not difficult for Suzannah to imagine Travis Paine defending liberty with the sword of justice and honor. He was handsome, thoroughly admirable, a man who rose in her estimation with every passing moment.

It was a wonder to each of them that fate had caused them to meet in this way. They had everything in common, it seemed. Travis had not imagined that he would ever meet a young woman whose thoughts so perfectly harmonized with his. As for Suzannah, her meeting with Travis in this way was sufficient to wipe away all bitter thoughts of what had occurred at the Shawns. Even her terror of Crazy Edythe was gone. Though the barn was bathed in a somber silver light and the rain beat noisily on the roof, Suzannah felt as she had that morning when she had awakened to the melody of birds and the brilliant promise of a clear blue sky.

The boy and girl laughed foolishly at one another's jokes and Travis soon forgot that Suzannah was the daughter of Martin Hopewell. Suzannah appeared to possess such gentleness of nature, such delicacy of thought, that she could not possibly be the daughter of the manufacturing tycoon.

"The rain has stopped," she said regretfully, at last. "I must go home. My family is sure to worry." She stood up, brushing the hay from her skirt.

"In the future I shall regard this hay barn as a kind of shrine," Travis told her, completely in earnest. Helping her on with her cloak, his hand brushed her throat. She caught her breath. "Miss Hopewell. . . ."

Suzannah turned to him; their faces were but inches apart. In the hollow of her throat, the pulse beat wildly.

"Miss Hopewell . . . Suzannah!" He drew her into his arms.

Suzannah sighed against him and reached up, her fingers intertwining behind his neck. Her eyes closed, their lips touched and for an instant Suzannah lost herself in the sweet sensation of her first kiss.

A nicker from the barn door startled the lovers' moment. Guiltily, they jumped apart. Silhouetted darkly in the doorway was a large figure on horseback.

Chapter 5

It was her brother, Eben.

"Come home, Suzannah. Our father has been worried." He had a voice like ice, edgy and chilling.

She hurried to explain. "I was up on Cooper's Mountain, Eben, and Crazy Edythe started chasing me. I took the wrong turn. I had to stay in the barn until the rain stopped." She stepped farther away from Travis, praying Eben would forget what he had witnessed.

"I don't want to hear about it." From the way Eben glared at her, Suzannah knew he would never forget the secret kiss he had interrupted.

Travis knew it too. "Come, come, man," he said. His voice, though calm and reasonable, showed a hint of agitation, revealing his concern for Suzannah's reputation. "I know it's tempting to jump to conclusions. But I assure you. . . ."

"Your assurances are not necessary," replied Eben as he dismounted. He did not glance at Travis as he helped his sister up onto the saddle. "I have spoken with my father about what transpired between you at the mill. You have offended him and our family. When I urged you to come to Amoset, I did not intend for you to become our critic and censor. But it is too late to mend the damage you have done. You've lost your chance, Travis. I suggest you leave Amoset now to spare yourself the humiliation of being ostracized."

Paine was incredulous. "You can't mean it, Eben. I did not insult your father or your family. He asked my advice as an expert and I told him frankly. . . ."

Eben looked at his former companion at last, bitterness in his eyes. "You have contradicted the most important man in Amoset, Travis. There is nothing here for you now."

"I have commissions. I am to design. . . ."

"Your commissions will be canceled. You will design nothing in Amoset." Eben remounted, sitting behind Suzannah in the saddle. "I am sorry, Travis. We might have continued our friendship in Amoset if you had cooperated."

Travis listened in silent dismay as Eben continued to lecture in his cold, passionless voice. Was it possible that the prospects Travis had described to Suzannah only moments before could be so easily shattered by Martin Hopewell? Did the man possess the power to ruin Travis' life? Travis saw himself maligned, forced to leave Amoset in shame. And what of Suzannah? Moments before he had felt her warm, young mouth against his own. Her soft, swelling breasts had yielded to the pressure of his body. Now . . .

All at once she seemed more important to him than all the commissions and designs that Amoset might have offered a luckier man. Kidnapped from his embrace by a harsh brother, she seemed a princess held captive.

"Don't leave Amoset, Mr. Paine," she called out boldly as Eben turned his horse toward the road. "Don't let them frighten you!"

"Be quiet, Sister!"

"I will not!" She twisted around, attempting to dismount. Alarmed, the horse reared and pawed the air. The riders held their seats precariously. Uttering an angry epithet, Eben hooked his arm tightly about Suzannah's waist, holding her still. The action infuriated her. She struggled against her brother's clasp, refusing to be silenced. "Please don't leave, Travis Paine!" Her cry rang out again as the horse trotted away through the high, wet grass onto the dirt road. "Don't go!"

Martin Hopewell sat behind the desk in his study. Despite a blaze in the fireplace, the darkly furnished room was cold and damp. As Suzannah stood before her father, she trembled, feeling the room's chill and her own nervousness in equal measure.

Wearing a maroon smoking jacket and somber cravat, Martin waited with his hands folded neatly before him, his expression composed. The outward show of calm frightened Suzannah. She and her brothers had inherited fiery tempers from their father. Knowing her own temperament as well as that of her brothers, she could recognize signs of concealment. She knew her father's apparent composure disguised a terrible rage. In such a mood, she understood and feared that he might do anything.

She glanced at her mother. Sarah Hopewell's eyes were puffed and red-rimmed. Her pale, nervous hands fluttered mothlike over the needlework that lay in her lap, and from time to time she sniffled softly.

Eben was at the sideboard pouring himself a brandy. He spoke without turning. "I found her in the hay barn opposite Denton's property."

Suzannah waited for Eben to say he had seen her kissing Travis Paine. But her brother withheld this information, adding only, "Crazy Edythe chased her down the mountain—or so she says."

"Thank you, Eben." Martin's composure was terrifying now. "That will be all."

Dismissed, Eben raised his brandy glass to Suzannah with a dark smile. Bidding his mother good evening, he left the study.

"Now, my girl," said Martin. "You and I must talk about today." Tilting back in his chair, he pressed his finger tips together, his hands resembling a long-legged spider perched on its own reflection. "Rather than argue before strangers this morning, I gave reluctant permission for you to visit the Shawn family. But you lied to me. You did not say that your mother had already granted her permission for the excursion." He gestured toward his wife. "I have spoken to Mrs. Hopewell and I believe we now understand each other. Do you agree, Mrs. Hopewell?"

Sarah nodded but did not look up from her embroidery.

"Let me hear you tell your daughter, Mrs. Hopewell." There was a pause. "Well?"

"You are forbidden to visit the Shawns," said Sarah quietly, still looking at her needlework.

"And what else, madame?" He resembled a hard schoolmaster forcing a reluctant student to recite. Suzannah despised him completely at that moment. Her heart went out to her mother, who seemed so small and vulnerable in the shadow of her husband's wrath.

"Should you again wish . . . ," Sarah's voice broke but she controlled herself, looking at her daughter. "Should you wish to make an excursion, you must beg your papa's permission." She glanced at Martin, her eyes pleading.

"There is more, Mrs. Hopewell. Continue."

"Please, Martin, don't make me. . . ."

"Are you unconvinced, madame? Even after our discussion of the matter, have you doubts?"

Sarah's eyes clouded with tears. The trembling of her hands was so extreme that her nervousness was visible to Suzannah from across the room.

Suzannah rushed to her mother, embracing her impulsively. "You are a cruel man, Papa. Can't you see that Mama is. . . ."

Sarah pushed her daughter away. "He's right. I am not fit to be your mother. That's what he wanted me to tell you and it's true. I am too nervous, too. . . ."

"Thank you, Mrs. Hopewell. Admirably stated." Martin rose from behind his desk and joined his wife. She grasped his offered hand, and leaning on him slightly, allowed herself to be led from the room like a feeble old woman.

Suzannah sank down on the settee, burying her face in her hands. Filled with despair, she tried to erase from her mind's eye the memory of her mother's hopeless expression. A storm of guilt raged within the daughter's conscience. She had known full well the heavy price Martin would exact if he knew she visited the Shawns with her mother's permission. Suzannah had known her mother's position and yet had gone her own way, intent on her own pleasure. Sarah seemed utterly beaten. Her husband's words had battered her down until the woman believed she was incapable of mothering. And now Suzannah blamed herself for her mother's punishment.

Long minutes passed before Martin Hopewell returned to the study. "Now, Daughter, I hope you're satisfied with the terrible fruit, born of your willfulness. Is it now clear that you may not visit. . . ."

The bitterness spilled out of her. "It may surprise

you, Papa, but the Shawns no longer wish to see me. Under the circumstances, you have my word that I will not visit there again."

"And your friendship with Lucy?"

"Papa. . . ."

"It is terminated, girl. Lucy Shawn is the same as dead to you."

Suzannah stared at her father, hating him in a way she would not have believed possible. For eighteen years she had been spared his full anger and she knew that even now he was trying to contain it. She should have been thankful. But something inside Suzannah refused to submit to his arbitrary control.

"Why do you hate the Shawns? What have they ever done . . . ?"

"Done?" Martin roared at her. "What has passed between the Shawns and myself is none of your concern. How dare you question my authority?" A man six feet tall, weighing over two hundred pounds, his mere physical presence should have been enough to silence Suzannah. But she had seen what acquiescence did to her mother. Sarah was cowed, timid. Suzannah began to understand that if she gave in to this man too readily, he would use her weakness against her, and in time she might become as weak and frightened as Sarah.

Standing up before him, she said, "I am eighteen years old, Father. Old enough to. . . ."

His hand slapped hard against her cheek, and she was thrown back against the cushioned settee. She touched her face and felt the skin burning.

"How could you?" she cried, eyes wide, not really able or willing to accept what had just occurred. It was not only the pain of being slapped that wounded her. She felt betrayed by her father. For eighteen years he had tricked her into loving him—and she had

done so, always overlooking his harshness. She had
been willing to forgive him anything, but this was too
much.

She tried to sit up but he hit her again, the blow
ringing across the ear. "No!" she screamed at him,
clutching her aching head in her hands. "You cannot
do this!"

"You are my daughter. I will do as I please with
you—whatever it takes to make you dutiful!"

"No!" She struggled to her feet and stood bravely
before him, arms akimbo. "I have done nothing to
deserve this. I have loved you as my father all my
life—always—in spite of what people said about you."

"Suzannah." She heard a touch of regret in Martin's voice.

"You have betrayed my love." Her body shook
with rage and the risk of her words.

"You must not question my authority, Suzannah.
I ask only that you respect my wishes. Is that so
much?" There was faint pleading in his voice as if he
recognized in his daughter a will to match and perhaps best his own.

"You hurt me." In spite of her determination to
be hard, tears gathered in her green eyes.

At this first sign that Suzannah was relenting,
Martin put his arms about her. Though she cringed at
first, he held her tight. "Don't move away, Suzannah.
Forgive me. I have been so worried all afternoon,
with you up on the mountain in the storm." He rested
his cheek against her sweet-smelling hair. "You are
my daughter—do not forget that I love you as such,
Suzannah."

"You hurt me," she sobbed. But the pain had
gone, and against her face his woolen waistcoat
tickled as it had when she was a little girl held in his
arms for a goodnight kiss. She smelled the lavender

water he habitually used and heard the ticking of his gold watch. Though a part of her demanded vengeance, she ignored it. She was a little girl once more, held and protected by the strongest man on earth. "I forgive you, Papa," she murmured, clinging to him. "It doesn't hurt anymore."

But later, in her own room, she stared at herself in the oval looking glass that was mounted on her cherry bureau. She could see the mark left by the heel of his hand and her ear was swollen, tender to the touch. The ringing in her head had subsided, but in its place was the pain of a cruel headache. The constant, dull throbbing would not permit her to forget what had been done to her.

Had she not felt the physical signs of argument, she might have denied that it had happened. Already, Martin's terrible rage had taken on the dim unreality of a nightmare remembered at dawn. She forgave him. To do otherwise was unthinkable. But she could recall her own fury and it frightened her. Better to forgive the beating and forget the anger. Better to learn a daughter's place than risk the potential of that awesome emotion of righteous vengeance.

But what about Travis Paine? She wanted to obey and please her father, but she also knew she could not give up Travis when they had just begun to know each other. On impulse, she leaned forward and kissed her reflection in the glass, thinking, as she did so, of the warmth of Travis' mouth and the soft blossoming of warmth she had felt at his touch. For that feeling alone, almost any risk was worthwhile.

Her troubled reverie was interrupted by a soft rapping at her door.

"It's me, Eben." Without waiting to be invited, her brother opened the door.

Eben was a handsome man in his early twenties. He was dark-haired and, though his eyes were as green as Suzannah's, the similarity was not immediately noticeable. Heavy, scowling brows darkened the luster of those eyes and lent his face a brooding, angry expression.

"What do you want?" Suzannah demanded angrily, tightening the belt around her fawn-colored satin wrapper.

He reached out and touched her marked cheek. Smiling thinly, he said, "Even Papa's favorite must be taught a lesson, I see."

She pushed his hand away. "Did you come here to gloat, Eben?"

"I was about to offer my condolences." He sprawled in the cushioned chair near the window, and crossing his legs at an angle, leaned back comfortably as if he meant to stay a while.

"I'm tired," Suzannah told him.

"What I have to say will not take long."

"It's about Mr. Paine, isn't it?" She had been expecting a visit from her brother. He was too cleverly devious to miss an opportunity to expand his power over her. From the outset, she had thought it peculiar that he did not report to their father what he had seen in the barn.

"Speak your mind, Eben. I am exhausted."

"Poor Suzannah," he mocked. "You've spent a busy day disobeying, haven't you?"

"Why didn't you tell him?"

"Because I need your help."

"Are you threatening . . . ?"

"I am. I am indeed!" He laughed and, like his voice, the sound was hard and cold.

Suzannah stared at her brother a moment. What had become of the young man who once had loved and cared for her, helping her face the minor tragedies of childhood? She wondered now if Eben had ever truly felt a warm emotion. Was he even capable of love? Suzannah thought not. Though he emulated his father in all things, she suspected that Eben did not even love Martin.

"I'm sorry for you, Eben."

He laughed as she had known he would.

"What do you want me to do?"

"You are to arrange a meeting for me with your friend, Miss Lucy Shawn." Eben took a pearl-handled file from the pocket of his waistcoat and began cleaning his fingernails.

"You know how Papa feels. I am not to speak to her again." Remembering, Suzannah touched her bruised cheek. "He'll hurt me. Do you want that?"

Eben frowned bitterly. "Frankly, at this point I don't much care. You've been the darling of his life for so long, it only seems fair that you should get a taste of his temper for a change." His lip curled unpleasantly. "All those years, I was breaking my neck to please him and prove I had what it took to handle mill affairs—and all he ever noticed was his little poppet! Valentine was Mama's precious and you were Papa's. Old Eben had to get along on the dregs. Well, now maybe you know what it's like." Eben looked at her forbiddingly. "You don't *really* know—not yet. Believe me, you wouldn't want me to tell Papa what I saw in the barn. So I'm sure you'll arrange for me to be alone with your friend."

Suzannah sighed; her shoulders sagged with defeat. She was exhausted, and even if there had been a way to dissuade Eben, she would not have had the strength to do it. Nevertheless, she did not submit immediately. The pace of her thoughts quickened, and she wondered if she might somehow turn Eben's bargain around to her own advantage. Was it not possible that Mr. Paine, like the rest of the residents of Amoset and environs, would attend the Harvest Bonfire?

"I will not see Lucy for a month. But we made arrangements to meet at the bonfire on the thirty-first."

"That will do," said Eben, rising from the chair and tugging officiously at his snug waistcoat. In the dainty feminine bedroom, among the flounces and floral arrangements, the crystal atomizers and delicately framed miniatures, Eben seemed larger and more threatening, as if his hulking frame threatened to shatter the delicate world surrounding him. With dawning horror, Suzannah saw herself surrounded by such men as Martin and Eben, in a place where there was no hope for her. Unless she could become as cleverly self-seeking and as hard as they, she was sentenced to do their bidding, learning, like Sarah, to cower at the very sound of their steps.

"I can wait a month. But no longer." Eben jabbed a threatening finger at her. "In November Papa and I are going down to Grandfather's in Savannah on business. I want to go with memories of Lucy Shawn fresh in my mind."

"Very well." Suzannah opened the bedroom door.

As he passed into the hall, Eben patted the top of her head condescendingly. "A beating has made you quite agreeable, Sister. I have never approved of using force on the gentler sex. But like everything our father does, his treatment of you was wise. Very wise indeed."

Chapter 6

For Suzannah, in the solitude of her room at the top of the big stone house, the days and nights of October passed in fantasies of love.

A week after their fateful meeting in the hay barn, Travis Paine sent a message to her. Fortunately, the letter arrived when Martin and Eben were away at the mill and it was delivered to Suzannah by hand. In the letter Travis told her he had determined to stay in Amoset until the time of his departure for Rome. "When can we meet?" his letter asked, as if this were of more concern to him than his career. She replied, "at the bonfire," her fingers trembling as she penned the cryptic message.

Travis—his face and form, the sound of his voice, the touch of his lips—filled her mind like a drug. She rarely thought of Lucy, except to wish she had her old friend as a confidant. She tried not to brood about James Shawn, Eben's callous bribery or Valentine's scandalous behavior. Sometimes she even found it possible—in her remote, girlish chamber furnished wth chintz and cherry—to forget her father's brutality.

Somehow, by trick or cunning, she would find a way to steal an hour or so with Travis at the bonfire.

Her heart would not heed the small voice of reason that occasionally intruded on her dreams, cautioning her with warnings and presages of doom. She refused to believe that there could be anything wrong in such a rendezvous. When the inner voice of duty reminded her of her father's admonitions to behave correctly, she dismissed it, drowning the whisper of caution by recollecting Travis' warm lips and embrace. She would be a good daughter, but in this . . . ah, in this she would have her own way because her heart told her she must.

Suzannah spent the greater part of every day in her room, reading and writing in her journal, dreaming of Travis Paine. Sometimes she sat for hours amidst the cushions on her window seat, watching as the season turned to winter. It was a blustery autumn, marked by short, violent storms. High winds stripped the trees, prematurely bringing the bony arthritic look of winter to the woods and hillsides. All the summer past, the coppery sunlight had filtered through the broad-leaved maple outside her window, filling her room with warm gold. Now that warm glow was replaced by a flat white light filtered by the mists and fogs that shrouded the countryside at dawn.

It had always seemed to her a sad time, this dying of the old year, and the season made her think of ancient peoples faced with winter—people who had no certainty they would live to see another spring.

She wrote in her journal one day: "I feel this winter marks the end of everything as it was. Nothing will be the same again; none of us will be as once we were."

Every autumn, for as long as Suzannah could remember, she and her brothers had been permitted to join the crowds of mill operatives, farmers and townspeople for the celebration of the Harvest Bonfire on the bare knoll east of town. The event was part agricultural festival, part pagan tradition and perhaps part whimsy. Whatever the reason, no one seemed to recall the first bonfire or remember who had begun the tradition. But during the years since the region had first been inhabited by white settlers, the Harvest Bonfire had grown into a festive occasion almost as eagerly awaited as Christmas.

For children it was an opportunity to run about wildly, noisily chasing one another through the dark without fear of adult reprimands. For the young and flirtatious, it was a time of stolen kisses and promises exchanged in the glow of firelight. It was a time of fiddle music, rough country dances and boisterous fun. Farmers from the countryside rode into town in wagons piled with logs and corn shucks, the seats of their buckboards shared by broad-bosomed wives holding baskets bursting with food. Each brought along breads, pies, cakes and stone crocks filled with fruit preserves—a bounty to share with friends, with extra to trade for applejack and corn liquor.

When the long-awaited day arrived, Suzannah was jumpy as a kitten as she tried to pass the hours until dark. She tried on half a dozen dresses before deciding on a simple, green wool frock that fitted snugly at the waist and was decorated with broad lace at the collar and cuffs. She tried arranging her hair in imitation of the styles she'd seen pictured in modish quarterlies—but, ultimately, she simply tied it back with a piece of lace, fearing Travis would not like it any other style than the way she had first worn it.

Travis, Travis! Her heart sang his name as time and again she saw his face and figure in her mind. By the time the sun had set and a medallion moon had risen over the barren landscape, she was flushed with excitement. She was so eager to be off that she feared her father might notice her agitation and, taking it for some sign of illness, condemn her to remain at home.

"Now, remember," Eben told her, his hand tight on her arm, "you find Miss Lucy Shawn and make arrangements for our meeting."

She nodded without looking at him. She dared not think what would happen if she did not find Lucy or if the girl refused Eben's invitation. Somehow, some way, she must do as her brother wished, for only then would she be able to steal time with Travis.

Their steps quickened as they came within sight of the knoll, which was already crowded with town and country people. On their way they stopped to gather loads of dry twigs and branches. Arriving at the site, they tossed their contributions on the massive pile that rose ever higher on the summit of the knoll.

To approach the pile, Suzannah and Eben had to push their way through the hordes of mill operatives who were laughing and calling to one another gaily. Many of the girls, Suzannah noted, were just her age or younger. It was women like this—hardy Yankee farm girls—who made up the work force in the Amoset mills and in the other manufacturing towns around New England. For them the mills offered the chance to become more independent and sophisticated than their rural brothers and sisters. For girls of their age, mill work paid well. The wage for weaving and spinning was considerably higher than that paid for teaching. And the work was certainly less demeaning than serving as a domestic. Suzannah found herself observing these industrious young women closely. This was the army of labor that Lucy Shawn ardently wished to join.

If I were such a young woman, Suzannah

thought with a touch of envy, I could come to the bonfire and meet Travis without fear of discovery. I could spend the whole night talking with Lucy and no one would scold me for it. To Suzannah it seemed ironic that she, the child of a wealthy and influential gentleman, should be less free than these simple daughters of the countryside.

She saw Travis watching them. He stood a little apart from a crowd of dandified young gentlemen, his hands thrust deep in the pockets of his greatcoat, a soft hat pulled down to shadow his face. He took a step or two forward, but Suzannah made a quick, sharp gesture, warning him to stay away.

"Did you see her?" Eben asked, seeing his sister's movement.

"I thought so, but I was mistaken." She urged Eben ahead nervously, hoping Travis knew to be patient. Her heart drummed crazily. She knew she would die if anything kept them apart this night. You must be here, Lucy, she thought over and over, as if an incantation could bring her friend. You must be here and help me.

But another desperate quarter of an hour passed before Suzannah saw her friend at last. Lucy was accompanied by Talleyrand and Ingrid. James and Helen Shawn were nowhere to be seen.

"Let me speak to her alone," Suzannah said, extricating herself from Eben's strong grasp.

"I'll wait for her behind those wagons."

"What if she refuses, Eben? Lucy is an independent girl. She doesn't like to be told. . . ."

"She's your friend, isn't she? Tell her if she stays away, you'll suffer for it. That's true enough, I guarantee!"

They parted with this threat in Suzannah's ear. Eben was quickly hidden by the crowd. Immediately,

Travis was beside her, his hand on the shoulder of her cloak.

"It is not safe," she whispered, turning to look into his eyes. Those eyes were full of moonlight, like her own, and suddenly the knoll was empty—empty, but for them and the glowing moon that hung over them.

"Suzannah!" Travis whispered passionately. "I have waited a lifetime for this moment."

Her heart was pounding so she could not trust herself to speak. But in that moment they had little need for words. The sympathetic communion of two young minds and bodies reaching out for one another took the place of ordinary speech. Yet they smiled shyly, like awkward children, and they blushed nervously, their embarrassment concealed only by the night.

At last Suzannah managed to speak. "Eben must not see us, or he will surely tell tales to Father."

"We must be alone. This month apart has been an eternity for me."

"For me as well." Suzannah leaned toward him. "I have a plan. First I must find my friend Lucy Shawn, as Eben has instructed me. When that is done I will join you by those boulders where the boys and girls are playing."

"Do not disappoint me, Suzannah."

"I promise."

Reluctantly, they parted. Suzannah hurried to where she had last seen Lucy, but her friend was gone. Talleyrand and Ingrid had also vanished. It was some time before Suzannah found the Shawns again. They were sitting on the back of a wagon, eating apples and chattering impatiently as they waited for the monstrous fire to be ignited.

"I was afraid you would not come, Lucy."

"I promised I would." From her high perch Lucy peered down at her friend. "Is something the matter? You look strange."

Though Suzannah had not planned it this way, the good news just spilled out of her all at once. "I believe I am in love, Lucy. And only you can help me!"

Lucy looked wary. "I dare not talk to you for long, Suzannah. My father. . . ."

"I was beaten! And all for visiting you!"

Lucy jumped down from the wagon and embraced Suzannah. "I am so sorry but it does not surprise me. Your papa's dislike of Yankees is well known." Lucy looked around furtively. "Are you sure we should be seen together?" When Suzannah nodded assertively, Lucy turned to Talleyrand and ordered, "Keep a sharp eye out for Father, Talley. Give us warning if he comes." She turned again to Suzannah. "Now what is it? How may I help you?"

"Eben has been begging for a rendezvous with you, Lucy. He's around the other side where the big wagons are drawn up. He sent me to find you."

Lucy's expression clouded. "Why should I do that?" she demanded crossly.

"So that I can meet with Travis. Oh, please, Lucy."

"You expect me to act instantly, just because you have some . . . whim!" Lucy folded her arms firmly across her chest, her expression turning belligerent.

"Not a whim, Lucy. Truly, if you fail to do this, Eben will punish me by telling father about Travis Paine." Lucy said nothing. "It is he I love, Lucy. We must have this time together. Please be my friend." In the very act of pleading, Suzannah despised herself. But she could think of no other way to win Lucy's cooperation.

Her old friend shook her head in disbelief. "You are remarkable, Suzannah. What gall it takes to make such unreasonable demands." She laughed unpleasantly. "I see you are truly Martin Hopewell's daughter. I have been defending you to my father these several weeks, but I know now that it was wasted breath. You are exactly like all the Hopewells, wishing to use others to your own advantage!" Lucy spun on her heel, making her way back to the wagon. But Suzannah's hand touched her waist, stopping her.

"I have never before asked anything of you and will not again. But I fear my life is ruined without this one favor from you."

Lucy stared at Suzannah with an expression of anger and disbelief. "I know you overstate, Suzannah. You forget how well I know you and your gift for melodrama."

"I beg you, Lucy."

Lucy hesitated. "Very well," she finally sighed. "But I will foil your wretched Eben and take my brother and sister with me!" She lifted a hand to Ingrid as Talley leapt from the wagon. Then Lucy added, "We are two very different people now from what we were in childhood, Suzannah. Back then, it was possible for friendship to bloom between us. No more, I am afraid. Good-bye, Suzannah."

If Travis had not been waiting for her, Suzannah would have argued with Lucy. But she could see that the girl had turned against her, now deaf to all entreaties. Burning from the unkind words, she stumbled away. Only Travis could make it up to her; only he could restore her happiness once more.

The knoll swarmed with life. Hundreds of voices were raised aloud, calling for the fire to begin. The chant was picked up by all, growing to a roar. Everyone but Suzannah joined in. She ignored the noise;

only Travis existed for her. Pushing through the throng, she did not see the farmers with their torches held high. She was so distracted that she did not even look around at the sound of a hollow *whoosh* of flame, as the blaze shot upward, roaring through the high, piled wood and dry kindling. Above Suzannah the sky was suddenly full of fiery stars, a billion of them thrown like jewels against the blackness. A tumultuous cheer went up from the crowd, and everyone moved back as the first waves of heat rolled out from the source, singeing the icy night air. At last, through the noise and confusion, Suzannah found Travis, eyes fiery with the reflected glow.

"Look, Suzannah!" he shouted, vibrant with animal energy. He turned her around so she could see the flames rising in the sky. There was another deafening *whoosh* as the corn shucks ignited. The heat of the blaze was ferocious.

"Hold me, Travis," Suzannah cried, clinging to him, oblivious to the crowd. "Never let me go!"

PART II

Chapter 7

Savannah, Georgia

For as long as he could remember, Eben had dreamed of going south alone with his father. The anticipated excursion had, over the years, taken on a significance that exceeded the mere prospect of a trip. To Eben the journey almost signified a rite of passage, his entrance into manhood. Though he tried to still his expectations, fearing ultimate disappointment, he believed that by journeying to Savannah he would, finally, feel his father's love for him.

With so much at stake, it was no wonder he was excitable and clumsy during the coach ride from Amoset to Boston. His father declared him a rubber-fingered lummox after Eben dropped a box of quills, breaking the tips off half of them. Matters were even worse on the ship south. The weather was stormy and wet, and Eben was seasick two days in a row. He had to take to his bed like a woman.

"I wish to hell I'd left you home!" Martin exclaimed one night as he watched his white-faced son clutch a spit bowl, a line of dribble falling from Eben's mouth to the vessel. "You disgust me!"

Martin left him finally but the self-loathing remained. Eben felt like killing himself. How could he blame his father for treating him badly when everything he did was either too much or too little, stupid, awkward or incompetent? Eben opened the porthole in his cabin and let the spume frost his face with salt. His eyes stung, but he enjoyed the pain. He would have inflicted any suffering on himself if, by doing so, he could guarantee perfect, flawless, exemplary behavior ever afterwards. As the creaking ship tossed him roughly from side to side on the narrow bunk, he swore that in Savannah everything would go smoothly. No matter what efforts were required, Eben swore to please Martin Hopewell.

After dark, the sky cleared and the sea grew calm. When he went up on deck to refresh himself, Eben stared at the sky. The stars seemed to hover close together, making a silver strip across the night. At the Harvest Bonfire Eben had tried to engage Lucy Shawn in conversation by pointing out and naming the constellations. It still stung him to recall her rejection. She had simply ignored his friendly efforts.

What's the matter with her, he wondered. He was the mill owner's son. She had nothing to gain by rebuffing him—absolutely nothing. She ought rather to be grateful for his attentions. But the night of the bonfire she had acted as if he smelled bad. He might have worn a sign about his neck proclaiming QUARANTINE for all the attention she had paid him. He ended up spending the evening telling Talleyrand Shawn about city life and watching Lucy from the corner of his eye.

"Stupid chit!" he said aloud and spat downwind.

Yankees are all alike, he thought. Lucy Shawn, Travis Paine. . . . He remembered Suzannah kissing Paine in the hay barn. Eben recalled how he had

used this information against her and now he was
ashamed of his behavior. Suzannah was the one person who had always loved him without question—or
so he believed. Now, surely, she would reject him too.

Well, it didn't matter. Nothing mattered now except the success of the Savannah trip. It was his great
opportunity! Though he had never spoken of his
dreams to anyone, Eben's imagination was full of
business schemes. Perhaps he would have a chance to
tell Martin about one or two of his grand ideas. Staring out across the rippled sea, he imagined how his
father would praise and admire his son's cleverness.

Almost twelve years had passed since Eben's last
visit to the Southern city where the Hopewells had
started their bank. Since that visit, slow but definite
changes had occurred in the pretty port on the Savannah River. In places, the town still seemed like open
country. The frank-faced Georgian houses, built of
grey rock or sandstone, were spaced well apart, separated by gardens and arbors. Behind the river man-
sions, velvet green lawns curved down the slope to
the waterside. Squares and commons with wide,
paved walks connected the elegant residences. Each
public square was a generously landscaped, miniature
park where exotic trees, such as mulberry, pomegran-
ate and palm, grew beside the taller, homelier natives
of oak, sassafras and bay.

But in the center of town the shops were packed
side by side with scarcely a lane between. Merchants' names were frosted on windowpanes or painted on wooden plaques that swung from hooks over
the doors. Behind a high iron fence, the Hopewell
Bank of Georgia presented an imposing façade. The
solid-looking, grey stone structure was situated at the
end of a block with a common before it and the river
behind. A building of stark, Georgian design, com-

pletely without ornamentation, the bank seemed like a part of the earth. It was as if the structure had risen from the ground itself and would remain there, like the rock of Gibralter, for all time.

As Eben and his father stepped from their carriage to the porticoed entrance of the bank, two smartly dressed doormen saluted briskly and opened the door for them. Inside the dimly lit bank, employees formed a line on either side of the front door, their shoes shined and hair slicked down with Turkish oil. Eben saw respect and fear in their eyes and it seemed to him that his heart might almost burst with pride as he contemplated the awesome responsibility that came of being a Hopewell, scion of such an honored Southern gentleman as his grandfather.

At the end of the receiving line stood the bank owner himself, Theron Hopewell. In a less dignified environment, Eben would have thrown down everything to run into his beloved grandfather's arms. But he managed to feign a cool, unruffled composure as he extended his hand and his voice was almost formal as he said, "Good morning, Grandfather."

At nearly seventy-five years of age, Theron did not believe in standing on formality. He was, quite simply, overjoyed to see his grandson and had no reason to hide his happiness. With a huge, theatrical gesture, Theron Hopewell enveloped Eben with his arms, almost lifting his grandson off the ground.

"Father," Martin admonished, glancing at the employees uncomfortably.

"Go on, all of you!" cried Theron to them imperiously. "Back to your work. No need to gawk at an old man's softheartedness!" He looked at Eben and nodded his head with satisfaction. "God bless your pretty mama, Eben lad. The injection of Welsh blood has certainly improved the looks of the Hopewells.

You're a handsome lad! Isn't he, Martin? Eh?" Few people could have guessed that Theron Hopewell was three-quarters of a century old, for the slender, sinewy man crackled with energy. From his thick head of snowy hair down to his impatiently tapping toes, he was the picture of robust health.

"You look wonderful too, Granddaddy. After all this time, I thought maybe. . . ."

"I'd be an old man doddering about on a cane, half-blind, deaf as a stone. Eh? Is that what you thought?" Chuckling, Theron led his son and grandson into the executive offices at the rear of the bank. As he slipped into the chair behind the desk—assuming a position that gave him a clear view of the river—he asked, "What about you, Martin? Are you distressed to find me looking well?"

"Father, there is no need. . . ."

Ignoring the response, Theron said to Eben, "And are you ready to get married? We've got a fine young lady lined up for you. A dandy little Georgia peach!"

Struck dumb by the unexpected question, Eben looked toward his father. Martin shrugged. "I meant to speak to you about it on the ship, but you were so damn sick all the time."

"So tell him now, Martin. Sit down, Eben. You look like you might pass out!" Theron Hopewell laughed with pleasure at the image of Eben fainting dead away. Martin frowned at his father, but the old man didn't seem to care one bit. "Tell him!"

"Very well," Martin acquiesced. "However, you will permit me to say, Father, that discussing Eben's future is something we might leave until after banking hours."

"Yes, I permit you to say that. Now hush up and tell Eben about Mandy." Theron beamed at his grandson as he rubbed his hands together with delight.

"Amanda White is the only daughter of Gregory White, the owner of another large bank here in Savannah. A marriage between the two of you would be of the greatest benefit to both our establishments. Georgia is on the verge of economic expansion, and a merger between our banks would provide us with the kind of capital we need."

"Forget about business for once in your life!" Theron interrupted. "Amanda White is a little blossom, Eben. That's what counts to a lusty young man. You'd be getting someone mighty special. She's young yet. . . ."

"How young?"

Theron looked slightly uncomfortable, but he recovered his composure quickly. "Not quite fifteen. However. . . ."

"You want me to marry a fourteen-year-old girl?" Eben didn't know whether to laugh or pretend to be outraged at his grandfather. Images of dollhouses and tea parties came into his head.

"Of course not!" Martin answered curtly. "Her father will not let her go at this age. But she'll be ready at sixteen. You can have her then."

"Now don't look so stricken, Eben. Once you get a look at her, you'll adjust to the idea well enough. We all do when the time comes." A shocking thought occurred to the old man. "You do like the ladies, don't you, son?"

Eben coughed. "Of course, sir."

Theron pretended to mop his brow. "Well, now, that's a relief!"

During this play, Martin had grown increasingly impatient. "I don't see what this has to do with business, Father. I want to discuss the mortgages on those new places out West. And what about the Grissom place? Is it ours yet? I need to know what kind of a season this is going to be. After all, the way I run my mill depends on what kind of shipments I'm getting from Savannah. Now. . . ."

"Ever had a woman, Eben?" the old man asked.

"Father!" roared Martin, incensed at being ignored. "This is important!"

Theron's fist crashed down on his desk and the old eyes flashed with life. "At my age, don't you think I know what is important and what is not?" Theron shook his finger at his son. "You come down here, and I know what's in your mind. You want to run things your way, and to hell with what the old man thinks! You have some idea I'm half-senile. Well, you listen to me: maybe I am and maybe I'm not! It doesn't really matter because until the day I die, no matter if I entirely take leave of my senses, I am still the owner. My word is final at this bank. Do you understand me, Martin?"

"Yes, sir." Martin turned away, his face crimson with restrained fury.

Theron seemed satisfied. "Very well. Glad we understand each other. Now, Eben, what about you. Ever had a woman?"

Beet-red, Eben shook his head.

Theron didn't laugh. "Now don't be ashamed, Eben. There's a first time for everyone. Just be glad yours is coming up."

"Sir?"

"End of the week, Martin, I want you to take Eben out to Miss Aimee's with you. I'll make some arrangements for him." He grinned at Martin and winked with ancient deviltry, his anger now completely past. "I know you won't mind making the trip out there. Question is, can you wait?"

Chapter 8

At the very moment when Theron Hopewell was making plans for his grandson, Felicity White was speaking to her daughter.

"Now, Mandy," Felicity cautioned, "you are to mind your manners and remember you're a young lady now and not just a child. Eben Hopewell is coming to court you this evening, and your daddy and I want everything to go perfectly smoothly. Do you hear?"

Amanda nodded sulkily, her lower lip pouting. She looked about her with an angry gesture of defiance, kicking at the dolls that were lined up on the floor. She had been playing school with them before her mother came into the nursery.

"For shame, child!" cried Felicity. But Amanda ignored the remonstrance and kicked again, more viciously. A doll with a china head and azure, open-and-shut eyes cracked as it hit the parquet floor.

Beginning to cry, Amanda flung herself onto the cushions in front of the fire.

"Oh, darling, it's all right," her mother comforted, rushing to Amanda's side quickly and enveloping her daughter in a tight embrace. "Mustn't cry! Nasty tears will make your eyes all red and radishy."

"She was my favorite doll." Amanda's lower lip pouted again.

"Papa will buy you another when he goes to New Orleans in the spring." Felicity dabbed at Amanda's cheeks with a handkerchief. "Now, are you better? Why not run downstairs and ask Cookie for a nice big piece of chocolate cake and a cool glass of milk? Wouldn't that taste fine? You watch—all those tears will just disappear like magic! Are your hands all spicky-span?"

Amanda stared at her childish hands, then quickly rubbed them several times on her pinafore before holding them out for inspection.

"That's just fine, baby. You are my good little girl, aren't you? And you will be nice to Mr. Hopewell when he comes. I've heard he's a very handsome young man."

"Would I have to live far away?"

"We'd just see about that. I think probably if you were just as sweet as could be to Eben Hopewell, he'd live anywhere in the world just to be with you." Felicity believed completely in what she told her daughter. To her, Amanda was an exquisite, utterly irresistible child. Her glossy yellow curls, pouty rosebud mouth and prominent blue eyes composed the very picture of a tempting young lady who was sure to win the heart of any normal young man.

"Can I keep my slaves? Please, Mama! I want Biddy and Dora to come with me, no matter what."

"I don't know about that, baby. It's up to Daddy to. . . ."

"I won't be nice unless you promise."

"Honey, I can't promise. It's up to your daddy." Felicity felt herself growing nervous. Pretty and winning as Amanda could be, she also had a stubborn streak running right through the middle of her. She

had a will of iron and could be completely intractable
when she chose to be. Lord knew, Felicity had done
what she could to eradicate this flaw from the temperament of her otherwise exquisite daughter. But the
mother had not been at all successful.

"I won't do it, then. You can't make me!" In a
whirl of gingham and sparkling crinolines, Amanda
flung herself into a chair and crossed her arms across
her tiny breasts.

"Stop behaving...."

"You want me to go somewhere far away and be
all by myself with some horrid man and not even
have Biddy and Dora to take care of me. You don't
love me. You and Daddy can't wait to get rid of me.
You both love Hiram best!" Amanda's lip trembled violently, but her eyes were dry and calculating.

It was Felicity who began to weep. Her daughter's accusations were so unfair, she thought her heart
would break from having to defend herself. "Baby,
we do love you. Your Papa and I would do anything
to see you happy. Of course, we don't want
you...."

"You promise I can have Biddy and Dora? Can I
have their papers?"

Amanda's demands sometimes amazed her
mother. Papers! Documents of ownership! Felicity
was shocked, but secretly she was rather pleased to
realize that Amanda was a fledgling businesswoman.
Still it would not do to let on that this was so. Particularly not around Mr. Eben Hopewell, who might be
offended by such a masculine characteristic in an otherwise enchanting doll of a girl. But Felicity knew
that a strong business sense was not a bad thing for a
woman, providing she controlled her urge to mix in
men's affairs. At least no cheating storekeeper would
ever take advantage of Amanda!

"Well?" Amanda demanded.

"I'll speak to your father. That's the best I can do, Amanda."

"Promise I can have Biddy and Dora."

"I can't. You know. . . ."

"Promise!"

Felicity sighed and gave up. She nodded. Compared to Amanda, she had no strength at all. "Very well. You can have both those silly girls. And their papers."

Amanda jumped up from her seat and threw her arms about her mother. Covering her cheeks with kisses, Amanda cried, "You are the very best mama in the whole, wide world!"

Eben did not know what to expect that evening when he called on Amanda White. The girl's parents owned a house with splendid white pillars and balconies on the river road a quarter mile from town. Eben rode out on horseback in the early evening. All along the way, he told himself he would do anything, even marry, to please his father. But this resolve was badly shaken as soon as he met Amanda.

He disliked her instantly. Perhaps if he had not contrasted the girl with Lucy Shawn, he would have felt differently. As it was, however, Amanda suffered greatly by comparison. Both Lucy and Amanda were blondes, but it seemed to Eben that Amanda's curls were painted yellow, so bright and hard was the color. And her large, round eyes disturbed him, for he perceived little intelligence in them and too much of the sly coquette. No matter how Lucy felt about him, Eben knew that he could trust her. Deception was foreign to Lucy: she could not be other than forthright. Amanda, on the other hand, made Eben think of lies and cruel secrets whispered in the dark of night.

"Sit down, Mr. Hopewell. Do!" Felicity White smiled radiantly at Eben as he entered the drawing room. "We are so happy to have you in our home at last. Your granddaddy is one of our favorite people, and he just talks and talks about you with so much fondness." She paused breathlessly, brushing aside a wisp of greying brown hair from her plump, rouged cheek. "Will you have a cordial this evening? Perhaps something stronger?" She turned to her husband, who had just come into the room. "Mr. White, will you do the honors?"

Gregory White was also eager to have the match between Amanda and Eben settled. In the last few years he had made a great deal of money in Georgia's burgeoning cotton industry. He was far-sighted and knew that with enough capital for investment and speculation there was virtually no limit to the profits he could draw from the state. He was already overextended, however. He needed Hopewell's Bank of Georgia even more than it needed a merger with Merchants & Planters.

"Let me pour you a tot of our cherry brandy, Eben. Made on one of our farms upcountry near Macon." He handed Eben a small crystal glass filled with the ruby-colored liqueur. "You ever been up Macon way?"

"No, sir, I haven't."

"Well, now," White clapped his hand on Eben's back, "you just ought to do that. Fine country. Fine farm land." White was a handsome man in his late thirties. Obviously prosperous, he still preserved some manners of the farm boy—manners that Eben found attractive.

"I don't like Macon," declared Amanda fiercely, as if this were something she wanted clearly understood from the outset. "There's nothing to do up there and no one to look at but darkies."

Gregory White laughed indulgently. He winked at Eben and clapped him on the back again. "Women! What do they know about business, eh? Regardless of what my little darling thinks, central Georgia is going to boom one of these days."

"It's virtually inaccessible, isn't it? I've heard there's a strong need for roads to haul out the tobacco and cotton." Roads and transportation were Eben's favorite topics of conversation and he'd picked up a good notion of the situation in Georgia. He began to feel more comfortable in the Whites' drawing room as he sipped the potent cherry brandy and continued to speak of roads and railways, riverboats and canals. It was just this sort of conversation he would have liked to have with his father. Gregory White was impressed by Eben's knowledge of the countryside and of the commercial needs of farmers and planters. Eben knew that he was making an excellent first impression and he only wished his father could be there to witness his son's success.

"I'm not going inland until every last one of the Indians is dead," stated Amanda suddenly. Clearly she was tired of the men's conversation, which for some time had made no mention of her. Seated on the piano stool, she had her full, floral skirts spread around her, creating a pretty pink and blue composition that harmonized with the bouquet on the grand piano. "You can put in all the roads you want, but until the Cherokee are wiped out, I'm not going anywhere." Amanda leaned forward, her china eyes growing wide. "Did you know there was a whole town massacred up the Ogeechee? Not a soul was left alive!"

Gregory White smiled fondly at his daughter.

"That's just one of those stories, Amanda. Nothing to worry your little head about."

"Hiram told me and he swore to God it was gospel truth, every word."

"Hiram is Amanda's older brother," Felicity told Eben. Privately, she wished her daughter would not pout so elaborately whenever anyone disagreed with her. Mr. Hopewell might get the wrong idea about Amanda's disposition.

"Speaking of that boy, where is he?" White glanced out the window. A wide sweep of lawn decorated with tulip trees stretched to the road.

"He'll be along presently, Papa. He went up the road a piece to try the new gig. He says the balance...."

"Isn't right. I know. I know." White laughed, adding in a confidential tone, "Children are a great advantage to a man, Eben, but they have one drawback. They think they know better than their elders."

"I'm sure Mr. Hopewell isn't interested in your theories and opinions on family, Mr. White." Felicity smiled to mask her tone of criticism. "I know he'd like to hear our Amanda at the piano, though. You do like music, don't you? Go on, Mandy. Sing something pretty for your guest."

Delighted at being restored to the center of attention, Amanda complied quickly. As she played a medley of light Scottish airs, singing to her own accompaniment, Eben watched from beneath his scowling brows and wondered at the strength of his aversion to her. Inexperienced though he was, he knew enough of human nature to recognize a woman who was spoiled and pampered, impossible to satisfy. If they married, he knew Amanda would do her very best to make him miserable, if only to please herself. Eben was seized with a sudden compulsion to run out of the house. The Whites aimed to capture him for their daughter. Like one of those Cherokee braves hounded by settlers and soldiers, he felt his days were numbered.

Chapter 9

Near the end of the musical interlude, the door to the drawing room opened and a short, stocky young man strode in. His boots and clothes were caked with mud.

Without waiting for Amanda to stop playing, he began at once to talk over the sound of her singing, finally forcing her to stop. "I told you that damn gig was off-balance. I got thrown into the road taking the curve out near Miss Aimee's." Though he spoke to Gregory White, he stared at Eben with undisguised curiosity.

"Hiram, don't mention that place in this house. There is an innocent young woman in this room and if I've told you once, I've said it. . . ."

"Are you all right?" squealed Amanda, leaping up from the piano stool and hugging her brother tightly.

"Your clothes, Amanda. Step back, for heaven's sake!" Felicity made a little face. "That road smells of I don't know what, Hiram. Run off and change. Then you can meet our guest and be sociable."

Hiram ignored his mother. "I'm Hiram White," he said, extending a broad, workingman's hand to Eben. "Glad to know you, Hopewell. Amanda told me you were coming." He hugged his sister possessively.

"What do you think of this little picture book, eh? Pretty nice?"

"Hiram!" Amanda shrieked in delighted embarrassment, but her protest only made her brother laugh and squeeze her all the tighter.

"She's young, but she's coming along nicely."

"That will do, Hiram," admonished Gregory. "Do as your mother asks. When you're fit, come down and you can have a glass of brandy. Git!"

Felicity stood up. "You go with him, Mr. White. I'll just step into the sewing room to make sure that darky isn't stealing us blind. She's been at the sewing so long, she must be up to no good. Amanda, why don't you show Mr. Hopewell some of your pretty little sketches? I had Dora bring the book down and it's set there by the window." She smiled at Eben benevolently. "So nice to have you with us. You just make yourself at home. It's just like you were family, Eben."

When Eben and Amanda were alone, they quickly found they had nothing to say to one another. Again the image of dolls and tea parties came into Eben's head and stuck there. He looked at Amanda and saw a child far from womanhood. The bodice of her pastel flowered dress, slightly smudged with mud from her recent embrace with Hiram, appeared too flowery and ornate for the slight, blonde girl. She stared at the floor, biting her lip. Eben shuffled his feet uncomfortably. More than anything, he wanted to be far away from Amanda White.

But he had been well-schooled. He tried to smile and, finally, the right words came to him. "Show me your drawings, Miss White. I am a great admirer of artistic talent, having none of it myself." Though he kept his tone light and friendly, a mood of dark melancholy had descended over him during the course of the evening. He found it difficult to disguise his gloom with enforced casualness.

The drawings of garden scenes and posies in a vase were, like Amanda's artistry at the piano, adequate. They were no better and not much worse than others Eben had seen in young ladies' sketch books. They were boring. And Eben resented Amanda's attitude, which told him as clearly as words that he should be more exuberantly appreciative.

"I have the best drawing master in all Savannah. He is French and he says I have real talent."

"This is a pretty view."

"You like it? Really? I did it here, looking from this very window. During the summer the sun is too hot for delicate skin like mine, so I stay inside most of the time, and last August I sat right here and stared and stared at that tulip tree until I knew I could paint it. . . ."

"Who is that?" Eben pointed out the window toward a woman who was just leaving the house, following a gravel path that led past the drawing room windows. She was carrying a large brown-paper package. She wore a dark blue cloak and her head was covered by a hood. As she came nearer, she began to run and the hood slipped back to her shoulders, revealing a delicate face with fine features.

Amanda shrugged. "It's the seamstress, I suppose. Why?"

Eben replied without thinking. "She's very beautiful."

"Her?" Amanda looked again but the girl had passed out of view. "How can she be pretty? She's a darky."

Eben was surprised. "She didn't look. . . ."

"You should see her sister. She's as white as you

and I. Of course, I'm not supposed to know anything about her!"

"I beg your pardon?" Amanda's childish chatter made little sense to Eben.

"Never mind! Never mind!" Then, coyly, Amanda urged, "Take back what you said!"

"About what?"

"Her."

"The seamstress?" Eben could not recall having said anything worthy of either owning or denying.

"Take back what you said about her being pretty." Amanda stood primly before him, her eyes bright and eager.

All at once Eben realized what was required of him. He thought of his father, of pleasing him, and then he spoke. "She is pretty, Miss White. I cannot take that back. But for fairness, her beauty certainly cannot compete with yours."

Amanda beamed at him. "Why, thank you, Mr. Hopewell. May I pour you a little more cherry brandy? It does make you say the nicest things. . . ."

When Eben got home that night, it was almost ten. As he entered the house he heard his father and grandfather arguing, but the disagreement ceased abruptly when Eben entered the study.

His grandfather seemed glad to see him. "Well, what do you think of that little darling, Eben? Isn't she the prettiest thing you ever laid eyes on—all that curly blonde hair and those big, blue eyes?" Without waiting for an answer, Theron strolled to a massive walnut sideboard and poured a large glass of brandy for his grandson, who accepted it reluctantly. He'd had so much cherry brandy that his tongue felt oiled with the sweetness of it.

"You didn't answer your grandfather," observed Martin. "Did you like her?"

Eben tried to smile enthusiastically. On the ride back to town he had grown increasingly depressed as he contemplated a life with Amanda White. But not once did it seriously occur to him to refuse the match offered by his father. If this was what it took to make Martin proud and happy with him, then Eben resolved to endure the courtship. But he hated the thought of marriage to Amanda with a fervor that alarmed him.

"Well?"

"She is as lovely as Grandfather says she is. And her family seems quite nice as well. I had an interesting conversation with Mr. White on the subject of the Georgian economy." This much, at least, was true.

Martin laughed. "White must really want this wedding to come off if he's willing to waste his time talking business with a pup." Still laughing to himself, Martin put his glass down and rose to his feet, stretching luxuriously. "I've heard all I need to. Soon as that girl's sixteen, Eben, you wed her and bed her and start producing me some grandsons. Gregory White and I need to get on with the business of making money in Georgia." At the door of the study, Martin had an afterthought and he turned to his son. "Day after tomorrow, I want you to go upriver and collect some mortgage money for me. Tomorrow, you can do what you want."

"I'd like to work with you if I may, Papa."

Martin laughed shortly. "Thank you for the offer, Eben. But you'd just be in the way. Besides, you need to save your strength for Aimee's!" Laughing to himself, Eben's father left the room.

Eben stood in the center of the carpeted study,

staring after his father. A great sense of loss came over him, smothering the last flicker of hope.

"What's eating you, Eben?" Theron asked. "You don't have to drink that brandy. Put it down and tell me what's the matter. You remind me of my first son, Percival. Before he got himself killed by the Cherokee, I saw the same moody spirit in him. Never could learn to hide his feelings, that boy."

Eben blushed, mortified that his hurt feelings were so obvious.

"No sense keeping it all inside," Theron advised. "I've been alive a long time, three-quarters of a century, and by now I know what's worth doing, and what ain't."

"Granddaddy. . . ." Eben began. But he could not go on.

"First off, it's my guess you don't like Amanda White any too much. Am I right?" Theron's sparkling blue eyes seemed full of wisdom at just that moment, as Eben met his grandfather's gaze and nodded.

"She's so young and . . . silly."

"Give her time. Maybe it's a mistake setting the thing up while she's a kitten, but we need the alliance and so do they. Couple of years from now, she'll have some polish and charm. You'll like her fine."

"Maybe." Eben tried to smile. "I like her father a lot. And the brother, Hiram, too. We talked about business."

"You like talking about money, Eben?" Theron asked softly.

Eben nodded, thought a moment, and then burst out, "Why won't Papa listen to some of my ideas? I've got good ones. I know how to make us rich if he'll just give me half a chance. Gregory White listened to me! He told me I had the kind of sound judgment he respected in a partner."

The old man shook his head. "You're never going to get Martin to say anything like that. You ought to know that by now, Eben."

"But why? I'm his son. I love him." Eben's voice almost cracked with shame as he realized that he might weep from sheer frustration.

"And I'm his papa and I love him, too. But do you think that makes any difference to him?" Theron drained his glass. "I know you admire him. You'd like to be just like him, wouldn't you? You're a good son, and that's normal right behavior." Thoughtfully, the old man traced a pattern in the carpet with the toe of his boot.

"What is it, Granddaddy?"

"He's my only son now, so might be I shouldn't say this. Still. . . . Don't try to be too much like him, Eben. Martin's a cold man, born with ice in his heart and blood. You be like him and you'll think only of making money and using people to get what you want." With a sudden movement Theron gripped his grandson tightly by the shoulders, giving him a brusque shake. "Your papa can't love. Doesn't know how. Don't be like him, Eben. You have to love someone or you're half-dead."

Chapter 10

The next evening after dark, Eben and his father drove out along the river road past the White plantation to Aimee's establishment. They went in a closed carriage and did not speak to one another beyond saying a few necessary words. For once, Eben did not mind his father's silence. He had much to think about and he felt his heart weighted with a terrible burden of worry.

Having resolved to trust his grandfather's advice about Amanda, Eben told himself that the old man knew better than Eben how a shallow, spoiled little girl might become a charming woman. Eben would have liked to tell his granddaddy about Lucy Shawn but, when he considered speaking, he realized that he had nothing to say about the Yankee girl. His admiration for her was hardly returned. Lucy cared for him not at all. Why pursue a hopeless love? Accepting Theron's wisdom, Eben told his heart to adapt to Amanda White.

But Eben's frame of mind was further shadowed by thoughts of his father. If only Martin could be made to understand that his son would do anything he asked. Winning a father's affection did not seem an outrageous goal. And yet Theron had told him Martin was incapable of giving love. The idea that his father would never love him, no matter what he did to ingratiate himself, was too horrible to consider. The inevitability of living with this constant disapproval or—worse still—indifference, threw a cloak of gloom across Eben's life. Blackest midnight descended upon his soul.

They drove on through the drizzle of a mild Georgia night, past stands of hickory, ash and bay. In places by the river the trees had been cleared, and Eben saw the Savannah flatboats, lit by swinging lanterns, being poled downriver by slaves. To Eben, in his tortured frame of mind, there was something both sad and sinister about the sight. There seemed to be hidden forces all about him. Riding in the carriage, he slouched against the leather cushions and thought of what lay ahead of him in the night.

Aimee's was a large, elegantly maintained residence set far back from the road. The Georgian facade was fronted with a wide, marble-pillared verandah stretching the width of the house, festooned with gaily colored lanterns. As the carriage approached, driving up the long straight driveway between rows of fruit trees, Eben saw through the open front door a hallway blazing with light. The sounds of laughter, music and voices greeted him the instant he stepped from the carriage.

The area in front of the house was crowded with handsome carriages, tended by black coachmen and footmen wearing livery. As Eben passed them, he imagined those attendants all knew the purpose of his visit and were laughing at his innocence.

Martin and Eben were met at the door by a strikingly beautiful woman wearing a bright-red satin dress ornamented with crystal baubles. The dress was cut so low in the bodice that Eben caught a glimpse of dark nipple when the woman bent near him.

"Martin Hopewell, it has been a time since we last saw your handsome face. Too long," she said. Her Southern drawl mixed with an accented, foreign cadence Eben could not identify. "I'm glad you sent word you were coming. Marie Celeste is waiting for you. She's been excited as a bride all day." The woman hooked her arm through Martin's. Then, turning to Eben for the first time, she said, "And you are the elder son." She smiled at him appreciatively. "I am Aimee. Your grandfather told me you were much a man, but I had no idea how truly he spoke."

"My grandfather?" Eben blurted out the question in disbelief. A blush rose like fire in his cheeks as Aimee laughed gently.

"Such a man that Theron Hopewell is! Like a young buck! You are fortunate to have such a family."

Escorting Eben on one arm and Martin on the other, Aimee entered the large central hall. Immediately, they found themselves in the midst of a festive gathering of obviously affluent men of all ages. Beautiful women, scandalously clad in brilliant-colored satins and silks, sparkling with jewels and bubbling with quick laughter, looked after the men attentively. Eben was so taken with the surroundings that he forgot his father for a moment as he stared about him.

Off the wide, bright central hall that ran the length of the house were a half-dozen gaudily decorated rooms furnished with game tables, chairs and couches. In these rooms guests were occupied with cards and dice games. While the women enticed them with flirtatious conversation, the men drank heavily, drawing from the well-stocked bars in every room. Eben heard piano music and the words of a bawdy song followed by hearty, male laughter.

Though he had been offered many opportunities, Eben had never visited a brothel. He could not be certain of his reasons for abstinence, but somehow he had never been tempted to call on the many fancy houses supported by the student population of New Haven. The young men he lived with always returned from their bawdy excursions with vulgar stories. But Eben detected a faintly shamefaced manner behind their bragging—and he found that he neither envied them nor particularly wished to accompany them.

Now, suddenly, he was at Aimee's. He had no choice but to go through with the plans that were made for him.

"Where is my father?" he asked his hostess. Rapt in fascination, Eben had not even noticed his father's departure.

"Back there. Near the game table."

Eben looked where she pointed. He could not have been more astonished by what he saw. Martin reclined on a couch against a wall. Beside him lounged a red-haired woman, smoking a pipe studded with tiny gemstones. Her bodice was open to the waist and Eben could see her breasts.

"You see that pipe?" whispered Aimee, slipping an arm around Eben's waist. "Your papa gave that to Marie Celeste last time he came here on business. He's very generous, your father."

"He comes here . . . often?" Eben asked incredulously.

"Every time he comes to Savannah." Aimee looked at Eben quizzically. "You did not know? You find this strange? Your grandfather likes Marie Celeste, too, you know. She is a great favorite with the Hopewells. Perhaps you would like. . . ."

"No!" Eben spoke so loudly that several boisterous couples nearby turned to stare at him. Quickly he lowered his voice. "I mean, I think my father is happier without me just now." Eben tried not to look, but his eyes were riveted on the incredible sight of his father, the Amoset manufacturer, with his hands groping beneath Marie Celeste's full, emerald green skirts, his mouth nuzzling her breast.

"Come with me," whispered Aimee. "I think you will like it better upstairs."

Eben allowed himself to be led up the curved staircase to the second floor. Though a part of him was revolted by the indecently sexual atmosphere of Aimee's, he was aroused too and nervously eager.

"I have selected someone very pretty for you, Eben. My very own sister." Aimee stopped before a closed door. "She is young, but wise. I give her to you on your promise that you will be gentle with her."

Eben's palms were moist. He rubbed his hands on his pants leg.

Aimee smiled at him affectionately. "Marianna is lucky, Eben. So many old men come to Aimee's! Few that are so young and virile as you. If you do not find the little bird suitable, I would be pleased to entertain you myself. If not tonight. . . ." She reached out, loosened his cravat and unfastened two buttons at the top of his shirt. ". . . perhaps another night."

A shudder of excitement went through Eben and Aimee laughed throatily. "Lucky little Marianna," she whispered as she opened the door for him. "Take as long as you like."

The room smelled sweetly of a fragrance that suggested tropical flowers. The aroma contrasted so strongly with the vulgarity downstairs that Eben was taken by surprise. He had the odd sense of being somewhere very different from Aimee's. A single candle, mounted on a table beside the bed, scarcely illuminated the room. Gradually, however, Eben's eyes became accustomed to the gloom.

He was alone. But a thin ribbon of light glowed from the base of a door across the room. Restless and discomfited, he perched on the edge of a chair and cleared his throat noisily. He was mildly aggravated when a soft, musical voice urged him to be patient. He had not really wanted to visit Aimee's establishment in the first place. Now, to be kept waiting seemed an outrageous affront.

Eben occupied himself by looking around the room. Like the delightful floral perfume he had smelled on entering, the furnishings in the bedroom seemed out of place in a brothel. All the pieces—the bed, two dressers, a chiffonier, a pair of tables and a chair—appeared to belong to a set that was of French design. All the furniture was elegantly wrought, suitable for any wealthy home in Savannah. Though everything about the room pleased Eben, he was disturbed by the contrast between this room and the ones below.

When the door at last opened, Eben glimpsed a small, slim figure silhouetted against the lighted dressing room. Instantly, he had the impression that he recognized the woman. But the impression passed as he told himself that recognition was impossible.

Eben stood up, feeling suddenly clumsy and stupid. "I am Eben Hopewell. You are Marianna?" His words sounded embarrassingly stiff and formal to his own ears.

"I am she." Marianna did not move from the doorway. As he cleared his throat, Eben sincerely wished he were home.

"You suffer from catarrh? May I pour you some wine to soothe your throat?" she inquired. Not waiting for a reply, Marianna hastened to the table and poured wine into a long-stemmed glass. Accepting the glass, Eben saw Marianna's face clearly for the first time.

"You're the seamstress!" He remembered her vividly. The night before, standing beside Amanda White at the window, he had obtained only a quick glimpse of the seamstress. But that was enough. She was indeed extraordinarily beautiful. Even in the revealing gown of bronze satin, cut low, fitted snugly over her hips, Marianna's aura was somehow demure and ladylike. She appeared as refined as the subtle fragrance she wore. Though Amanda had dismissed Marianna's beauty by observing that the woman was black, it was impossible for Eben to say whether this was true or not. As he faced her in the dimly lit room, her skin appeared dark rose, her eyes like amber. Her small face was framed by dark, glossy waves of hair.

"Why are you here? Aimee said you are her sister." With the recognition that Marianna was no ordinary harlot, Eben felt all his sexual excitement disappear.

"She told you that? I am surprised. It is a confidence rarely shared. You see, we have the same father, but my mother was a slave." She spoke with a slight accent as Aimee had.

"Where do you come from?" He could not stop looking at her. Marianna's beauty had a dreamlike quality. Eben almost feared that if he looked away for a fraction of a moment, her delicate presence would alter in some way.

"I come from Martinique. You know the island perhaps?" she asked hopefully.

He shook his head. "No. I have only heard the name." He paused, then asked, "You are free?"

Marianna laughed softly, sipping her wine. "In a sense."

"What do you mean?"

"Who of us is really free, Mr. Hopewell? There is always bondage. If not the body, then the mind. Even the heart may be held captive."

"You don't belong here." Eben paused to wonder why he said this. What was it about Marianna that he found enchanting? "You are too beautiful." The explanation sounded feeble even to his own ears. Something in his tone made her laugh aloud.

"Beauty is a requisite at Aimee's. You have described what my sister deems my greatest asset."

"But you're different from the others. You are well educated. I can tell by the way you speak."

"That is true. My father was an enlightened man. I was educated in his house by the same governess who attended to Aimee. But unlike her, I was also given a skill so that I might survive . . . in the white man's world." She raised her glass in a mocking toast. "Ironic, is it not?"

"And the things in this room, the furnishings, are they yours?" Little by little, the pieces of the puzzle began to fit together and make sense to Eben.

"My father gave them to me before he died. As to their current use, I fear he would not approve."

"Do you . . . do this often?"

"From time to time." Marianna tilted her head beguilingly and smiled at Eben. "Do you want me?" She began to unbutton the bodice of her gown.

"Don't do that!" His hand stopped her roughly and she shrank away. "No! Don't be afraid. Please, I won't hurt you. I'm just. . . ." Suddenly, he reached into the pocket of his trousers and withdrew a large fold of bills. He threw the money on the bed. "Take it!" he ordered.

"So much? For nothing?" Fear and curiosity were

mingled in her eyes as she glanced first at the money
and then at Eben.

"I don't want you to do this anymore." He
grabbed her by the shoulders and shook her until she
begged him to stop. There were tears in her eyes. As
he embraced her, feeling the slender, vulnerable
body, it occurred to Eben that he was behaving
madly, irrationally. But he didn't care. All that made
sense was keeping Marianna out of the arms of paying strangers. "Whatever you need, I will get it somehow. But promise, promise me truly, you will not . . .
sell yourself again."

She pulled away from him. "Why do you care?"

"I don't know."

"I am no one to the grandson of Theron Hopewell, the son of Martin."

"You know my father?" A terrible thought occurred to Eben. He grabbed Marianna's wrist. "Do
you?"

"I will answer truthfully without being hurt."
With her free hand, she touched his hand, signaling
him to free her. "Please, Eben."

"I'm sorry." He stepped back. "Forgive me,
but. . . ."

"I do not know your father in the sense you fear,
nor your grandfather. But I have known both men by
sight since coming to Savannah. Martin Hopewell is
known at Aimee's for his . . . robust appetites."

"I am not my father!" Eben heard himself declare
ferociously.

"You do not care for women? Is that it? If so, I
do not. . . ."

"Of course I care for women! Why must it be assumed that because I will not pay for what is laugh-
ingly called love, I am, therefore, effeminate?" He
stared at the lovely woman before him. It would take

so little, he knew, to make her come to him. And he
desired her; he did not bother to deny this to himself.
But the urge was diluted in some way, and he knew
he could never touch her in a place like Aimee's, with
money on the bed between them. In another world,
another life, the attraction he felt for Marianna might
have grown to become a strong and permanent at-
tachment. But Eben was too rational to consider seizing her and running away with her. He could not
take her as she was. Hence, he reasoned, she was des-
tined to remain forever out of reach.

"Do you promise not to do this again?"

Her expression showed clearly that she was mys-
tified by him. "I cannot swear such a thing to you.
Aimee will not keep me here for free and there are
times when my customers do not pay for the needlework I do. Then. . . ." She made a wry little face and
shrugged her shoulders. "It is as I have said, Mr.
Hopewell. We are none of us truly free."

On the long ride back to Savannah, Eben continued to hear her final words repeated in his mind.
Glancing at his father asleep in the corner of the carriage, the smell of Marie Celeste heavy on him, Eben
realized that he had never been at liberty to be himself. Always, Martin had watched over him, nagging
Eben with his demands, setting ever-new requirements for the affection that was never forthcoming.
Eben thought of his sister at home. She was not free
either. As soon as possible, Martin would marry her
off to someone who would increase his business in
some way. Valentine, off in Boston, was devoting himself to religion and Eben felt sure that his brother
would never be free of the church, now that Valentine had committed himself to the ministry.

Was there no hope, then, for any of the Hopewells? Was liberty an illusion created by philosophers and promoted by politicians in order to tempt impoverished spirits? In the midst of his depression Eben found it easy to believe so. But there was still in him a glimmer of hope that flared valiantly against the deep night of his despair.

Marianna was wrong. He would somehow prove it to her and to himself.

Chapter 11

The next morning found Eben once again on the river road, but he passed by Amanda White's house without stopping. When he came to the pillars marking the entrance to Aimee's, he spurred his horse on, looking neither right nor left.

About a mile past Aimee's, he turned south, away from the river, following a narrow, unkempt track through dense scrub and pine woods. It was still early -morning and the trees were alive with birds. A magpie screamed and dove at him as he rode by. But Eben, intent on family business, scarcely noticed the raucous attack. After the drizzle of the night before, the woods smelled pleasantly of sweet, damp earth.

Under normal circumstances, Eben would have been in fine spirits. But the net of melancholy still held him entwined and every thought that came to mind seemed to bring new sorrow, anger or despair. He had not been able to sleep the previous night for thinking of Marianna and her terrible resignation. He had alternated between the extremes of acceptance and harsh denial until, by dawn, he had no idea what he really believed. That morning Theron had joked with his grandson, teasing Eben about his manhood and, to save face, Eben had gone along with it all. Now, riding along the river road, Eben recalled the entire, shameful scene.

"What was her name?" Theron had asked, as they sat down to a breakfast of grits, ham and piles of eggs whipped up with cream. "Or did you stop to ask? I know how it is with you young colts. I was one myself once, you know."

"Marianna." Eben did not look up from his plate. He had lost his appetite suddenly.

"Well, good for Aimee! I told her to choose someone special for you and, by golly, she did. That little flower is her sister, did you know?"

"She mentioned that." The eggs were dry as sawdust.

"You might have been happier with someone a mite more experienced, of course. Still, young people don't need much encouragement." Theron tapped his patent leather boots on the patterned hardwood floor. "Marianna! Well, fancy that. And her a seamstress in all the best homes! I might just drop in at Aimee's myself one of these days and see if that little flower is available. . . ."

Eben shoved back his chair noisily. "She says she's not doing it anymore." He almost ran for the door.

"Where are you going, my boy? You've not finished your meal!"

"I have a long ride ahead of me. I'm going out to Grissom's to collect the mortgage money." Eben could not look at his grandfather. The thought of the old man and the rose-skinned girl sickened and enraged him.

"Go easy on Grissom. He's had a hard time."

Now, reflecting on the breakfast conversation, Eben understood what his grandfather meant by those final words. As he approached the Grissom farm, Eben observed that the outbuildings all were dilapidated and in need of paint. The fences were ramshackle. The house itself—a fine, large edifice on a little rise with a stock pond to the rear and what once were formal gardens in the front—seemed unoccupied, abandoned. The shutters hung aslant against the scarred masonry and many of the glass windows were broken. The front door was open. Leaving his horse in front, Eben walked onto the verandah and called down the central hall.

"It's me, Eben Hopewell. Are you here, Mr. Grissom?" At the sound of his voice, a pack of tricolor hounds tumbled around the corner of the long verandah, yapping and howling, their teeth bared. A man not more than thirty years of age was right behind, calling them back.

"I'm glad you got here! I thought they were going to take a bite out of me!" Smiling, Eben offered his hand. "I'm Eben Hopewell."

Grissom frowned and ignored the extended hand. "I know who you are."

"Who is it, Gris?" A young woman, hardly more than a girl, came around the corner and saw Eben. "Oh." She stopped dead in her tracks.

Eben shifted uncomfortably. "Excuse my manners, ma'am," he said, removing his hat. "I called out because I didn't see anyone about."

"We sold our darkies last month," replied Grissom.

Eben turned the brim of his hat nervously. "You're all alone here, then? Makes a lot of work for just two of you, doesn't it?"

The woman let out an unexpected shriek of laughter. The sound sent a chill through Eben.

Unconsciously, he stepped back, drawing nearer to the verandah steps.

"Work?" the woman asked. "What are you talking about work? Aren't I healthy, strong? Isn't my man fit for anything?"

"Shut up, Clarie."

"Mr. Grissom, clearly you've got trouble here. Believe me, I am very sorry to intrude." Eben ran a hand through his thick hair. "But you understand. I have to collect the money owing Hopewell's Bank."

"We don't live in the house now," said the woman. "If you want to find me and Gris these days, you should come out back to where the darkies used to live. That's home now." She made a vague gesture toward the empty mansion. "Only mice and cats live in there now. The whole place stinks of cat. . . ."

Eben wanted to interrupt but he couldn't think of anything to say. He had only one purpose in being here, and that was to collect money. But despite Eben's silence, Clarie Grissom continued to talk. All the while, her husband stared at the broken, rotting planks of the verandah beneath his feet. Nearby, the hounds panted noisily and scratched at fleas. "Used to be, the house was real nice, Mr. Hopewell. I grew up here." Clarie pointed to a corner window on the second floor. "That was my room up there. It was just as pretty and delicate as could be. Just the thing for a belle. I was a belle then, wasn't I, Gris? Hands so soft. . . ." She was distracted for a moment by her memories. "Then, when Daddy died and Gris and me got married, we thought we would expand the farm into cotton. . . ."

"So we borrowed from Hopewell's Bank." The farmer stared at Eben with undisguised hatred in his eyes.

"Mr. Grissom, I realize you've had some bad

luck. But it will change. It always does." Eben hated
himself for speaking such pap. He was not so innocent that he did not understand what had happened
to the Grissom farm. And he knew perfectly well the
part his family had played in the ruin of this man and
woman. But he reminded himself he had a job to do.
"I have to collect the money, Mr. Grissom. Do you
have it for me?"

Grissom and his wife stared at each other.

"Mr. Grissom?"

Silently, Clarie Grissom held out her left hand to
Eben. It was not the hand of a belle, though once it
may have been. Now the hand was dark from work
outdoors, and the palm had deep cracks in it. Around
the chipped, torn nails, the shingled cuticle was red
and raw.

"Ma'am?" Eben did not know what was expected
of him. He looked at Grissom.

"Take the ring," the man said. He turned away,
unable to watch Eben slip the thick gold band from
his wife's finger.

"Isn't there some other way? Have you negoti-
ated with my grandfather? Perhaps. . . ."

All at once Grissom was on him. Eben felt himself
hurled to the floor of the verandah and, in an instant,
the farmer threw his full weight on top of him. Grissom's hands were strong. Eben felt their grip on his
neck. His head was lifted, then slammed down. Eben
thought his skull would crack. Dizzy from the impact,
nauseated, half-blind with pain, he reached for some
hold on his opponent. But the shattering pain in his
head blurred his vision. Grissom tightened his hold.
The dogs were snarling and snapping about Eben's
head and shoulders, confusing him with their wild
yapping. He struggled for air as Grissom's thumbs
pressed hard on his windpipe. Eben struggled and

groped with his hands, losing all hope, feeling himself utterly smothered.

Then, distantly, he heard the sound of a woman's screams. His vision cleared. Clarie Grissom was over him, dragging at her husband's back to pull him away. Eben began to breathe again, coughing for air. With the hope of survival came the horrid rush of fear. He had to escape, to get away from this killer. Still on his back, Eben kicked violently, throwing his feet into Grissom's chest with all the power he could muster. The man cried out as the air was driven from his lungs. He fell back, Clarie staggered behind him.

"Take it!" she screamed, throwing her gold band off the verandah. The ring spun through the air, landing in the dirt beside Eben's horse. Her husband tried to rise but she held him down.

Eben did not argue. Waving his arms to keep the dogs away, he staggered off the porch and grabbed the ring. Finding strength in despair, he managed to pull himself into the saddle.

"Get off my property now!" On his feet again, Grissom threatened Eben with upraised fists. The man's face was contorted with rage, blood-red and terrifying. His wife, clinging to his waist, screamed and cried out wildly.

As he galloped from the yard, Eben heard her shrieking, the sound rising shrill above the din of yapping hounds. "God damn you Hopewells! God damn you to hell!"

At the stream a mile distant from the Grissom farm, Eben stopped to cool his face in clear water. His cupped hands trembled so violently they could not hold the water. His bruised and aching head seemed ready to explode. He took a drink, gagged and vomited into the sand beside the stream. Closing his eyes, he lay back and tried to think.

It was difficult to say with whom he was most angry—Grissom or Martin Hopewell. Slipping his hand into the pocket of his waistcoat, Eben removed the simple gold band that had been Grissom's payment on the mortgage. It was enough, Eben supposed, to pay for another six or seven months on the property. Then what would become of Clarie and her husband? Eben expected they would go to a place where they were unknown and there make a life for themselves working another man's property. Somehow, the more he thought about the Grissoms' plight, the less anger he could find within himself. When the man had tried to kill Eben, he had only been doing what his bent and broken pride demanded. Wretched though it was, the tattered farm was all that Grissom and Clarie could show for their freedom.

It was his father who was most at fault, Eben concluded. Though he knew none of the details of the transaction between the bank and the Grissoms, Eben understood that the treatment of this man and wife was inhumane. Why had it been necessary to mortify the Grissoms? Why could the bank not have been lenient when one bad season followed another?

Eben knew the answer. Business was business. A hundred times, he had heard Martin say that there was no room in banking for individual cases, repeating the phrase like a maxim. All people must be treated alike, in Martin Hopewell's view. In the past, Eben had always been quick to agree. But now, as he lay on his back staring at the blue sky beyond the stitchery of pines, he seemed to see clearly for the first time that human beings did not remain anonymous. Just as each pine needle appeared to him minutely etched, perfect in every detail, so the mark-

ings of his life were clear as well. He knew that he
wanted no part of banking or manufacturing. He did
not know what work might someday claim him, but
unless he could make his own rules, he wanted nothing to do with the Hopewell empire.

Though it was growing late, Eben rode slowly on
his return to Savannah. He was not eager to announce
his decision to Martin. He knew his father would ridi-
cule and despise him for being softheaded, an ingrate.
Yet he felt a strong resolve, even to endure his father's disgust if it came to that. In the last few days
Eben had witnessed too much of buying and selling;
he had seen too much that was good go bad.

His father. His beloved father would not understand. But, perhaps in time. . . .

He realized it didn't matter any longer.

It was well after dark when Eben arrived in
Savannah, his head and body aching from the encounter with Grissom. Not wishing to disturb the
stableboy, Eben took care of the horse himself, then
entered the house through a side door. It was his in-
tention to go directly to bed, thus avoiding an unpleasant scene. But as he entered, he heard the sound
of angry voices coming from the study. He lingered
outside the study door, wondering whether he should
go in. But there was something in the sound of the
raised voices that made him hesitate. Eben bent down
and peered through the oversized keyhole, wondering
at the scene that greeted his eye. He had a clear view
of his father and grandfather standing face to face in
front of the fireplace, arguing fiercely.

The old man's face was livid. "If you foreclose, I
will not be able to hold up my head in this town!
There is a limit to what you can do. . . !"

"This is business, Father. Dollars and cents."

Martin shook his finger in Theron's face. "Those are the only limits I know."

Eben saw Theron Hopewell spit in disgust into the fireplace. "I thank God your poor mother didn't live to see what the love of money has done to you."

At this, Martin laughed viciously. "You taught me, Father. Don't forget that!"

"I taught you to be a human being! I taught you to add and subtract columns of figures and to calculate percentages. I never sent you off to be a usurer. I pity the poor little girls who work in your mills. You must drive them like slaves!" Again Theron spat into the fireplace.

"So. You don't like me. You don't approve of me. You pity those who have dealings with me. All of that means nothing to me. Nothing. You cannot bend me with disapproval. I'm no soppy little boy like Eben. Your ranting holds no weight with me. You're just an old man with an addled brain. You've got one foot in the grave and I wish to hell you'd fall in!"

Astonished at the venom in his son's voice, Theron stepped back. Eben saw how white his face had suddenly become. He tried to speak, but the words caught in his throat. If he were caught like this, listening, his father would beat him unconscious.

"Martin, my boy. You don't mean. . . ."

"I mean every word!" hissed Martin. Striking as quickly as a snake, Martin grabbed the old man by the lapels of his smoking jacket and threw him hard against the rough stone fireplace. Once, twice, a third time, the old man's head knocked against solid rock.

Eben watched the head hit, the eyes roll into the skull, the mouth fall open. He saw his grandfather slide limply to the floor, leaving a trail of blood against the stones. He collapsed at his son's feet.

Eben could not move. For what seemed a long

time, he stood rigid, staring heedlessly at the whorled grain of the oaken door. His mind was totally empty, like a man whose feelings had been excised. Then, from the distant corners of his consciousness, there began in his head a terrible screaming, a monstrous howl of rage and impotence and betrayal. Putting his palms to either side of his head, he pressed hard against the temples to drive away the sound. But even as he shut out all light, sound and sensation, a horrible image burned in his consciousness.

Eben saw his father staring down at the lifeless body on the floor. The father was utterly transformed in his son's eyes. No longer the father to love and emulate, he was disfigured beyond recognition, turned into a monster by the evil of this deed.

"No!" Eben whispered. "No! No! No!"

And suddenly fear returned, fear for his own life. What if he were found, discovered here, outside the door, a witness to everything? He had to flee, to get away from that man. . . .

Stumbling drunkenly through the dark, deserted hall, Eben fled. Down the steps and across the cobbled yard, he lurched like a wounded bear, blinded by its own blood. A misty rain had begun to fall. It touched his face like cool silk and mixed with the tears that nearly blinded him as he saddled a horse. Heaving himself up, he galloped out of the yard.

The screaming in his head was much louder now. Each ranting cry was a knife point that drove into the membranes of his heart. The screams drowned all thoughts. And so, in a way, he was protected for a time from the full realization of what had occurred. As the horse galloped through town, following its own head out to the river road, Eben rode like a man pursued by the wraiths of hell. Only the speed of his

mount and the shield of screams protected him from
the deadly peril of self-annihilation.

Like a man in a dream, Eben listened, hearing
the sound of frantic hammering. It took him several
moments to realize it was his own fist he heard,
pounding at the door of Aimee's. He had no memory
of the long ride into the country, no clear idea of why
he was there, or what solace the place could offer.
The house was dark and silent, but eventually an eye
appeared at the peephole in the door and someone
said, "We are closed tonight."

"Let me in!" Eben roared, beating the door with
a force that threatened to split the timbers. Tears
coursed down his cheeks; his throat was dry and rasp-
ing. "Let me see her."

"This place is closed!" the firm voice repeated.
There was a warning in it that Eben did not heed.

"I must see Marianna now!" In his pain and rage,
Eben's sobs came in noisy, choking gulps.

The door opened, and a huge black man dressed
in a dark suit came onto the verandah. He towered
over Eben. "Ain't no one named Marianna here."

"You're lying. I was here last night. I was with
her. Let me in!"

As Eben tried to push past, the huge man's fist
drove into his stomach. He doubled up and staggered,
hurled across the verandah by the sledgehammer
blow. He felt himself being picked up like someone's
toy. Tossed from the porch, Eben crashed face down
in the dirt. He wanted to fight back, he wanted to kill
the man who had attacked him. But the will had gone
out of Eben. He gave in to unconsciousness,
crumpling like a man utterly stripped of his defenses.

When he came to, hours later, he was lying in
the dirt beside the river road. Through the trees

above him the moon, like a medal of honor, hung against the shroud of night. At first Eben remembered nothing of what had transpired during the preceding twenty-four hours. Then it all came back to him. The Grissoms. Marianna. The blood of his beloved grandfather smeared on the stone fireplace.

The screaming in his head was silenced at last, but in its place came a new, crueler madness. Images of death, pain and degradation crowded in upon each other, driving him down as he crouched in the dust of the road. He was impotent. He could not move to stop the murder he was doomed to relive. Each moment of the day it came to him over and over until, at last, when he thought his mind bent and twisted by an intensity of pain he could tolerate no longer, he hurled himself to his feet. The tears had dried in streaks on his dusty cheeks. His eyes were bright, fierce and wild.

Shaking his fist at the heavens, Eben screamed. "God damn you, Martin Hopewell. God damn you to hell!"

PART III

Chapter 12

Amoset, Massachusetts

Sarah Jones Hopewell rapped softly three times, then pushed open the door to Suzannah's room. It was empty. On the canopied bed were a number of discarded winter afternoon dresses.

Victorine should have hung those back up by now, thought Sarah irritably. The lazy slattern was getting worse each day. Sarah picked up one of Suzannah's dresses, a warm brown velvet, and looked around for somewhere to hang it. Then, with a sigh, she let the garment drop back onto the bed. It was all just too much trouble. Chewing her lower lip and twisting her gold wedding rings around her finger, she paced the room.

Why did she go out on such a cold day? Where had she gone? Sarah knew the answers though she could scarcely bring herself to face the truth. She knew that Suzannah was with Travis Paine. Her daughter was probably in love with him!

Dear God, what would Martin do when he found out? Sarah's lower lip began to bleed and she dabbed it absent-mindedly with icy finger tips. Martin was sure to find out. Suzannah would refuse to conceal her romance with the Yankee. If Sarah knew her daughter, Suzannah would not long be able to tolerate the play-acting, the sneaking, the lies. What would Martin do to punish her?

The worst of it was that to Sarah, Travis Paine seemed a nice young man. She had met him twice during Martin's absence in Savannah, when Travis dared to call formally at the house. He was good-looking, and, from what she could gather, he faced an excellent future in architecture. Under most circumstances, he would have been considered a fine choice as husband for a woman like Suzannah. But to the Hopewell family—why, why did Martin always insist on the hard way, the contrary view?

Before his departure, Martin had told his wife, "See that Suzannah minds her ways and keeps to home. There's to be no gallivanting up Cooper's Mountain or idling in hay barns. One misstep and she'll be answerable to me. You understand, Mrs. Hopewell?"

But no sooner had Eben and his father departed by carriage for New York than Suzannah was out of the house. For hours at a time she went walking, rode her horse or sat sketching by the river. There was no way, short of making the most extreme effort, that Sarah could keep control of her daughter. Though she despised herself for being a bad mother, she now realized it was too late for her to take control, even if she had been capable. Suzannah was running wild; there would soon be talk of her around town. A scandal was possible. Still, Sarah could do nothing. Time and the tonic had robbed her of the little determination fate had accorded her. Sometimes it seemed she watched herself from a great distance. She saw herself as a vague and fluttery woman faded almost to invisibility. Was it really she? Had all her passions, her pride and her spirited demands come to this?

Gladwyn Jones was pleased to have Martin Hopewell as a house guest. The year was 1808 and in all of England there was no more highly acclaimed manufacturer than Gladwyn Jones. Visitors came to see his perfect factory village in action, most of them doubting what they'd heard of the workers' extreme diligence and the orderliness of the village's daily life. Visitors came, observed and generally went away converted, although there were always those few timid men who refused to accept the truth—and the truth was that men, women and children had to be made to function as parts of the machinery if industry was to make a profit.

Among the visitors to Crompton Village were a good number of eligible men. This pleased Gladwyn Jones. As the father of two daughters, he longed for agreeable sons-in-law and grandsons to whom he could recite the poetry of progress. True, one of those daughters seemed an unlikely candidate for marriage. Gladwyn's eldest, Bronwyn, was a restless, wild, importunate girl. But the younger daughter, Sarah, seemed in all respects the model of dutifulness.

In the year 1808 Martin Hopewell was almost thirty, fourteen years Sarah's senior. He was broad-shouldered and as handsome as a hawk. He frightened Sarah a little, though she thought he was attractive too, and he presented such a novel figure, with his Georgia drawl and his stories of life in Savannah.

"You would enjoy my city," he told her one afternoon as they walked along the ridge of hills overlooking Crompton. It was a grey fall day, windless and damp. On either side of the ridge, the hills fell away gently into the blur of a dismal mist. "We have many fine homes and excellently appointed public buildings."

"And red Indians?" she teased. Her eyes were as grey as the day. "I should hate to be scalped." With unconscious coquetry, she tossed her blonde head and smiled up at him through thick, fair lashes. All the countryside was talking about the attention Mr. Hopewell from America showed Sarah Jones. Only sixteen, she was already the envy of half the county.

"There are no Indians in Savannah, Miss Jones. And if there were," Martin added gallantly, "I would fight each one single-handedly for your sake!"

They stopped at a place where a bit of old rock wall was crumbling. Sarah could not climb it without assistance. As Martin put out his hand, she took his fingers hesitantly. Her eyes, searching his, saw in the depths of his gaze a look of rapt appreciation.

"You are breathless, Miss Jones." He did not release her hand though she tried gently to pull away. "Perhaps you should rest a moment."

"No. They will be expecting us for tea."

"A moment, Miss Jones. Only one." Bending down, he took her face between his hands and pressed his lips against hers in a kiss that lasted forever, leaving her terrified. It was as if a door had opened on a forbidden room, revealing unspeakable treasures, a wealth of emotions that would destroy Sarah Jones, so greedy for their possession.

Later, in the privacy of her room in her father's house, she paced for half the night. She wished with all her heart that Martin Hopewell would disappear from Crompton, taking his impetuous kisses with him. His kiss had introduced her to a morass of confused feelings, undiscovered in her previous experience. She did not even like him, really. He made her feel uneasy. He was too large and took up too much room beside her. She felt trapped when Martin stood near her. But his kiss had been thrilling and totally unexpected. Though the adventure had begun and ended in a moment, the waves of sensation continued hours later, surging within her. The next day, when he asked her to walk with him again, she opened her mouth to refuse and heard instead an eager voice answering, yes.

Her parents encouraged the match. Once or twice, she tried to tell her mother that Mr. Hopewell was not her first choice, but Janet Jones refused to understand her daughter.

"He is very wealthy," the older woman reminded Sarah at every opportunity. Whether folding linens before the press, sorting the plates or gathering fall chrysanthemums in the Jones' splendidly wild garden, Sarah's mother would speak of the man without provocation. Out in the garden, snipping the heads off the chrysanthemums that had gone to seed, Janet Jones declared, "Mr. Hopewell's family is excellent. For an American."

"He is not a gentleman." Sarah held the basket into which her mother carefully placed the long-stemmed cuttings.

"Stuff and nonsense, girl! Where did you get such an idea?" Janet peered at her daughter accusingly.

Sarah feared to confess that several times Martin Hopewell had kissed and held her. She knew what her mother's reply would be. Janet Jones would retell the old horror stories of what had happened to Cousin Vinia and that distant aunt who disappeared mysteriously. She would blame Sarah for permitting such liberties and defame the man who dared to take them. Besides, if Sarah once convinced her parents of Martin's unsuitability, they might send him away from her forever. Despite the discomfort and confusion he caused her nerves, Sarah did not think she wanted him to go away. At least not yet—and certainly not forever.

Still, she told herself she was relieved when he left for Savannah just after Guy Fawkes Day. That year, the holiday season for Bronwyn and Sarah was more than usually festive. Sarah danced with dozens of admirers, went ice skating in the long winter twilight and sat through musicales at neighboring homes and estates. The young men making eyes at her, vying for attention, all seemed rather boring, however. In the midst of their conversations she caught herself wondering about their kisses. She would redden then and stammer foolishly, as if she believed that her scandalous thoughts were instantly transmitted through the air to their curious ears.

When Mr. Hopewell returned the following summer, she was eager for him. He seemed to have grown still larger in the months they were apart and he was boastful of his accomplishments in Massachusetts. Determined to prove his independence from his family, he had bought two thousand acres along the Amoset River. Near the falls, a modern textile mill was being built with the name Hopewell emblazoned across its front portals.

"You would be wise to consider him," urged Janet Jones as she walked with her younger daughter through the garden at Crompton. The swinging tassels of her blue satin parasol hung down around Janet's head, and Sarah could not see her mother's face. "It's not every young girl that has the chance of a real man. Boys are one thing, but Martin Hopewell is a man. He knows what he wants."

And he wants me to share his bed, Sarah could have told her mother. But she had given up pretending that a revelation of this kind was possible. Things had gone too far now. Pacing the geometric brick pathways between beds of crysanthemums, roses and azaleas, Sarah smarted at her unseemly eagerness to be with Martin Hopewell. He was not a nice man, most certainly not a good or particularly honorable man. He was not the man she cared to spend her life with. But she had given up trying to understand the attraction and she no longer tried to stay away from him. Waking or sleeping, she dreamed of his kisses. When his arms were about her, she no longer pushed him away but melted against him, succumbing to his demanding lips.

Sarah Jones Hopewell stood in her daughter's room, idly rolling the multicolor hair ribbons that careless Victorine left untidily strewn in the basket. Her thoughts were of a day twenty-four years past. Mr. Hopewell had taken her into Mayberry Fair in Gladwyn's gig. She had worn navy-blue hair ribbons that hung down below her dark straw bonnet, curling like satin ringlets. It was late summer and, after a midnight thunderstorm, the world was sweet and green.

Martin stopped to water the horse and, helping Sarah down from the chaise, he suggested that they walk awhile to give the animal a rest. The morning was humid and as they strolled along the track among high, damp grass, the world was noisy with the singing and clicking of insects and the drone of diligent honeybees. They stopped in the shade of an elm and Martin helped Sarah remove her hat and coat. Beads of perspiration clung to her fair skin and when she sighed, the warm, moist drops trickled down between her breasts, making her pleasantly conscious of the sensation on her body.

When Martin Hopewell kissed her and pushed her back into the tufted field grass, she struggled just a little. But by his touch he had set a part of her in motion as if she were one of his machines. When his hands pushed inside her bodice and touched her breasts, her nipples grew hard, eager for his touch. She did not stop him for it seemed hypocrisy to deny her all-consuming ardor. The flesh of her thighs tingled as his hand stroked upward, and without resistance, opened her legs to his hand and his probing fingers. Without alarm, now expecting everything, she raised her skirts to help him enter her. Like a field wench, a country maiden out behind the haystack, she moved her body naturally in response to the ancient rhythm that overwhelmed her with its insistence.

Eben was conceived on that day, on the way to Mayberry Fair. A quick and shameful wedding followed. Sarah did not love Martin. She did not even like him. But her body operated by certain laws, and those had taken control. She was helpless, seduced by her own passionate nature.

Now Sarah wondered if the same, inevitable passions had taken hold of Suzannah and Travis Paine. Was her daughter's body alive beneath this young man's touch? Had the forbidden treasure been revealed to Suzannah as it had been to her mother so long ago?

Martin would be home from Savannah in a matter of days. If Suzannah was in love with Mr. Paine, the father would soon learn of it and be quick to punish her. And he would punish Sarah, too. Irritably, she threw down the pink ribbon she had been rolling and resumed her pacing. Just now it was imperative that Martin not have cause to be angry with her. She needed all his good will if she was to be given permission to visit her sister.

Bronwyn was dying.

The letter had come just the day before she had heard from Martin. Bronwyn had written from Palermo, Sicily, where she had lived for many years. Bronwyn had what she discreetly termed a "special relationship" with an Italian duke whose family controlled much of the land on that island. And now Bronwyn was dying. She had written her sister:

> Come to Palermo and remind me of our girlhood. It has been so many years and I have forgotten what it all was like. I am not afraid, Sarry, but I am lonely for you.

It was hard to imagine Bronwyn as anything but lively, gay and beautiful. Whereas Sarah was pale and delicate in her coloring, Bronwyn favored Janet Jones' Norman grandmother. She was dark and her opulent mouth faintly sullen. Sarah recalled a vibrant young woman who laughed often and could never be intimidated. More than twenty years had passed since they were last together. Logic told her that Bronwyn had changed just as she, Sarah, had been altered in many ways. Time had etched its marks upon her body and heart, and she could hardly recall the young woman of promise who had taken the hand of Martin Hopewell.

I must be with my sister, Sarah told herself, forgetting Suzannah for the moment. Martin *must* permit me to be with my sister now.

And if he did not? What then?

Sarah wrung her hands together and her pale face wrinkled with worry. To argue with Martin was unthinkable. Over the years her husband had grown in wealth and confidence, while she seemed to herself to have become smaller, less substantial, like a moth fluttering through a black and monstrous cavern.

Chapter 13

"They've come, Suzannah. Papa and Eben are home!" Sarah's tremulous voice rose up the stairwell, feigning joy.

"I see them!" the girl responded from her sentry post at the landing window. "They're coming awfully fast!" The team of four raised dust clouds as it galloped up the road.

"I fear there's trouble." Sarah spoke to herself. She had taken her dose of tonic and now, when she looked at her hands, it gratified her to see that they did not tremble. Still, she was edgy. Anything out of the ordinary—like the excessive speed of the arriving brougham—was sufficient to set her heart beating irregularly.

Suzannah, raising her skirts and petticoats as she bounded down the stairs, joined her mother and stood breathlessly beside her. As the carriage swung into the half-moon drive between boxwoods and broad ellipse of manicured lawn, Suzannah's heart, too, was beating wildly.

The day before, she had made a promise to Travis Paine as they walked near Amoset Falls. "I'll make him change his mind about you. I'll arrange everything so you're allowed to come call on me. Trust me, Travis. After his trip, he'll be sure to grant me a favor—just this one!"

With Travis beside her and Martin still many miles away, it had seemed the most likely thing in the world that she could persuade her father to accept her point of view. Now, however, the grey reality of Martin Hopewell's expression as he descended from the carriage told Suzannah the futility of her situation. If he knew she had spent many hours during the last several weeks in secret rendezvous with Travis Paine, Martin would not only punish Suzannah, but Sarah as well. As Suzannah embraced her father, his touch reminded her of what she had firmly banished from her mind weeks before. This man had hit her. And more than once.

Sarah was saying, "I trust you had a pleasant. . . ."

There was a noise from within the carriage. Out stumbled Eben. He shoved past them and stalked up the stairs. Suzannah caught a glimpse of his expression. His handsome face was tormented. He seemed to have aged decades since his departure only weeks before.

"Eben!" Suzannah reached out to touch her brother as he passed. Ignoring her gesture, he stormed into the house.

Suzannah and Sarah looked to Martin for some explanation.

"The boy's useless; no backbone." As the women followed Martin into the wide foyer, they heard the study door slam.

"What's happened to him, Papa?"

Suzannah and Eben had been close to each other throughout childhood. There were many moments when he had comforted her, had seemed to understand. But in recent years, with profound sorrow she had watched him set aside the gentler aspects of his nature to emulate Martin's stern rigidity. Now, as she realized that the trip had wrought some great change in Eben, her sympathy for her brother was strong and protective. "What happened to him in Savannah?" she asked again.

"I told you—the boy's useless. A coward. Let him be." Martin looked piercingly at Suzannah. "Your mother has no complaints of you, I trust?"

"No, sir." She dipped her head, avoiding his eyes. She had promised Travis she would speak with her father immediately. But, clearly, now was not the time. "May I go to Eben? Perhaps I can talk to him. . . ."

"Leave him be, I said! Tell me how you spent your time." The foyer where they stood was brightened by the winter sunlight that spilled through the stained glass over the door. The man who faced the two frightened women was dappled by the soft colors. The moment felt more like a military inspection than a family homecoming. Suzannah was terrified of saying the wrong thing. Sarah, fortified by tonic, answered for her.

"She walked a lot and helped me in the house. Suzannah is a good girl, Martin. You've only just got home. Don't agitate yourself." As always, Sarah's words were timid. She used caution to protect herself from Martin. Sarah looked uneasily at the paneled study door. From inside the study came the mutter of angry words.

"What's he saying, Papa?" Suzannah asked bluntly.

For reply, Martin strode to the door and pounded with his meaty fists. The house trembled with the power of his blows. "Boy! I've had enough! I won't allow you to disrupt. . . ." Martin grabbed the brass knob and shook, but to no avail. Eben had locked the door tight. "Let me in!"

"No!" screamed Eben. His defiant word was followed immediately by hysterical laughter. "I'll never come out. I'll rot here." His laughter rose in pitch. "See how you explain that!" There were tears in his voice and this, more than anything, sent an anxious quiver of alarm through Suzannah.

"What does he mean about explaining?" Sarah, large-eyed and timid, begged her husband. Receiving no reply, the nervous woman turned to her daughter. "Suzannah, dear, get me my tonic, will you? All this fuss. . . ."

"Sit down, Mrs. Hopewell. You too, Suzannah. I have some bad news for you."

"Oh. . . ." Sarah's hand covered her mouth.

"Is it about Eben, Papa?"

"In a manner of speaking. First, I regret to tell you that your grandfather, Theron Hopewell, is dead."

Suzannah understood immediately. "Eben was Granddaddy's favorite."

Digging in her sleeve for a lace-edged handkerchief, Sarah asked softly, "How did it happen, Martin?"

She had always felt a deep fondness for her father-in-law. She recalled him as a gracious and gallant old gentleman, a character who sympathized with people—in marked contrast to his hard-headed, materialistic son.

"He slipped and hit his head. He had been drinking heavily."

"Granddaddy?" Suzannah shook her head, puzzled. "That wasn't like him, was it?"

Martin eyed her sharply. His reply was clipped and final. "It was not. Nevertheless, that is the case.

For some reason, he drank too much that night, slipped, and died from a blow on the head."

"A blow?" Suzannah persisted.

"His head hit the mantel," said Martin. Suddenly, he turned on Suzannah. "Are you quite finished interrogating me, Daughter? Perhaps you wish me to sign a written statement?"

Sarah rested against the banister, shielding her face with her hands, sobbing quietly. Martin, having silenced Suzannah, addressed himself to his wife.

"The boy's been unstrung since it happened. Found him out on the river road raving all kinds of nonsense. He was so pitiful, I couldn't even have him with me at the funeral."

"But what can we do, Papa? Let me. . . ."

"Send one of the servants for Reverend Strickland, Suzannah." He glanced dismissively at Sarah. "Your mother obviously is not going to be much help."

"May I speak to him later? He might let me help him, Papa."

Martin studied Suzannah a moment, then nodded his head. Crossing to the stairs, he stopped for a moment, thinking. "Your appearance is uncommonly bright and healthy, Daughter. Have you, by chance, been to Cooper's Mountain recently?"

"I swear I have not, Papa." At least Suzannah could say this much honestly!

He nodded his head again. For the first time since his arrival, his weary face wore a look of satisfaction. "That's good. I'm glad you're learning to behave as your place in society dictates."

"Yes, Papa."

Lying did not come naturally to Suzannah, yet she found herself doing it easily. Where Travis Paine was concerned, the ease alarmed her more than the substance of the lie, for she saw how dissembling might in time become a habitual way of avoiding difficult truths. It occurred to her that lies might be a little like her mother's nerve tonic, an easy way to escape responsibility.

She had promised Travis she would speak to her father, but Martin had been home scarcely ten minutes before she realized the difficulty of keeping that promise. With her father far away, Suzannah had succeeded in forgetting Martin's true nature. She had romanticized him, creating once again the heroic figure who had dominated her childhood, a knight capable of winning any battle and satisfying her every wish.

Now, as she watched from her bedroom window for Reverend Strickland's carriage, Suzannah's guilt blossomed. She almost wished she had never met Travis. This jungle of deceit, she knew, was dangerous and filled with treachery. Some day, she was sure, she would have to pay for her deceit.

In her conscience there was a simple equation, a measure of punishment in retribution for each measure of duplicity. For every misdeed, for each unworthy action, she felt a person must pay, sometimes very dearly. When Martin inevitably hears she is in love with the architect, he will be furious. She will be punished. It was the geometry of life. Unless. . . . Despite her certainty, she continued to wonder if there might be some way to get what she wanted.

The Reverend David Strickland arrived and retired with Martin to the downstairs sitting room. After half an hour they emerged, both stern-faced, with a solution to the problem of Eben.

"Cartland House is not a hospital, not an asylum," the minister assured Suzannah. He was a tall, thin man with forgettable features and a propensity for beige-colored clothing. "The couple in charge of it are simple, good Christian folk who know that from time to time the most upright individual may need to be apart from family and the press of business." Strickland patted Martin's back in an awkward attempt at sympathy. A man just past thirty, he was still uneasy in his role as pastor, except when dealing with those he believed to be his inferiors, morally or materially. "I know Eben will feel better after a few weeks on the Cape. He has suffered a painful loss but he's young and time heals. The weather on the Cape is of great therapeutic value; strong winds and bracing salt air will help improve his temperament."

Martin seemed only partially convinced. "I don't want him home before he's completely well. These people won't be intimidated by him, will they? I fear what he may say to them, and how he might prey on their kindheartedness."

Strickland shook his head. "We'll make arrangements for him to be released only on your permission."

"It sounds like prison," Suzannah ventured. She was troubled by the thought that Eben could be confined for an indeterminate length of time, merely at his father's behest. Eben was moody and decidedly bad-tempered sometimes; nevertheless, he was her brother and she felt a strong affection binding them together. "May I try to see him?"

Martin would have denied permission instantly, but Strickland interrupted, "A woman's gentle presence might assist in calming him, Mr. Hopewell. I suggest we let her try."

"Very well," answered Martin, but Suzannah could see that he agreed reluctantly.

The two men watched her go to the study door and knock softly. "Eben," she called gently, "it's me, Suzannah. Let me in."

"I don't want to see anyone."

"Only me, Eben. Please let me in."

"Is he out there?"

"Papa?"

"Well, is he?"

"Yes, but he won't bother you. I'm the only one who wants to come in."

Eben's maniacal laugh began again, strident and jarring.

She raised her voice. "Just let me be with you a moment, Eben. Only me. I swear."

The response was silence.

"I'll stay only a few moments and then. . . ."

"Why should I trust you?"

"I love you, Eben. You know I do." She lowered her voice, facing the doorjamb as if the solid oak could respond to her plea. She imagined her brother on the other side, his ear pressed to the wood, listening for any sound that might indicate betrayal. "Reverend Strickland is here, Eben. You don't want him to come barging in instead of me, do you? You know Papa could force the door if he wanted to. Why not just let me in?"

Again there was silence. But a few seconds later the door opened just enough for Suzannah to see into the study. Eben moved away as she peered in. At first she saw only shadows laid upon shadows in the dark room. No fire burned in the grate. The air was cold and dank, like a tomb long closed. She pushed the door open another few inches and slipped inside.

"Lock it again," Eben ordered. She obeyed.

It took some time for Suzannah's eyes to become accustomed to the darkness. Eben had seated himself in Martin's tapestried wing chair beside the cold grate. Like a small boy, he had his boots on the cushion, knees tucked up under his chin. His arms were over his head so she could not see his face. As he muttered something, she stepped closer to hear.

"What do you want?" he challenged when she was almost upon him.

"Why have you done this?" She pointed around the room where Martin's private papers and documents lay scattered like leaves on the carpet. The dead grate was piled with them.

"I wanted a fire."

"With Papa's business papers? What can be the matter with you, Eben?" She was now close enough to touch him, but when she did so, he pushed her away roughly. "When he sees what you've done, he'll be furious. There's no telling what he might do!"

Eben laughed horribly.

"Stop it!" she cried, covering her ears.

"Why do you care what happens to me? You're Papa's darling baby girl, aren't you?" Eben looked up at her like a child abandoned.

"I am your sister. And no matter what, I care for you. Believe me. I want to help."

The crazed laughter began again and Suzannah had to cry out over the sound. "They're going to send you away. They will lock you up and throw the key into the sea unless you prove your sanity." She fell to her knees before him and pressed her cheek against the cold leather of his boots. "Whatever happened down there in Savannah, I know it must have been terrible. But it's over now. Granddaddy's dead and nothing can bring him back. I know it hurts you, Eben, but you must be strong. He wouldn't want you to sacrifice your life for him."

Her pleadings were interrupted by Martin

pounding at the door. "Come out of there immediately, Suzannah."

At the sound of his father's voice, Eben's laughter faded. He stared at his sister. When he spoke his voice was controlled.

"Have you seen that architect?" he whispered, clutching his arms tightly about his legs. It was as if he feared he might fly apart without warning. "Don't think I've forgotten Travis Paine."

"Don't tell Papa, Eben," she begged. "I'll do the telling, but in my own time. You know how Papa can be."

He looked at her. Even in the near darkness of the study, she could see the wild flame in his eyes. He needed no fire to warm him; there was white, hot anger burning behind his eyes. Suzannah could feel the intensity and she recoiled in horror.

"What is it? What happened down there?" Her voice was a whisper.

A smile like the squirm of a reptile shaped Eben's mouth. He caressed her head with an icy hand. "I'll tell you in my own time," he whispered, almost as if he spoke to himself. "You know how Papa can be."

Chapter 14

During his employer's absence, Foster McMahon had instituted several important changes at Hopewell Mills. Most significantly, he had crowded new looms into the weaving rooms on the top floor, and now each operative tended three of the clacking monsters. A privileged operative might even be given more if she could handle the responsibility. Initially, a few young women complained of the extra work. But when McMahon threatened to dismiss them, they quickly adjusted to the new regime.

Though most of the operatives thought McMahon was ugly and unpleasant, they misjudged him when they called him stupid behind his back. McMahon was far from stupid. As his employer had been quick to realize, he had a decided talent for managing a female work force. Because the women often underestimated him at first and left themselves unguarded, he found it easy to uncover a weakness and take advantage. The fact that McMahon was a master of intimidation meant that the girls in Hopewell Mills eventually learned to fear him.

Martin Hopewell was definitely pleased with the changes that had taken place during his visit to Savannah. McMahon had proved himself an able, inde-

pendent and firm-minded general overseer. Martin
Hopewell gave him a salary increase and granted him
permission to move with his wife and son into a fine
company house situated above the river path just beyond the mill.

But even with an excellent overseer to relieve
him of some of the burden of running the mill, Martin
never felt easy when separated from his work. In the
days after his tempestuous homecoming—as Sarah and
Reverend Strickland prepared to accompany Eben to
Cartland House—Martin arrived at the mill before
dawn and stayed until after dark. He patrolled the
floors by lantern light, his hooded eyes quick to note
any infraction of the rules. Any hint of idleness or
inattention brought a fierce reprimand from the mill
owner. And all knew that if Martin Hopewell noted a
second infraction of his strict standards, the guilty
employee would be fired immediately.

Martin had felt immensely relieved the instant
that Eben and Sarah departed for the Cape. His children were distractions from his real concerns. Martin
was intent on matters of finance and management and
now mill affairs consumed him. He scarcely noticed
Suzannah.

Suzannah was free to spend long hours of every
day with Travis Paine but, after each of these clan-
destine rendezvous, guilty feelings assailed her. She
longed for a confidant, an adviser and friend who
could help interpret the confusing emotions that
sometimes seemed to threaten her sanity. It never occurred to her to confide in her mother. To Suzannah,
Sarah was a bland, even pitiful creature, devoid of
sexuality. She seemed leagues away from the thrilling
game of love that occupied all of Suzannah's waking
thoughts.

She might have ventured up Cooper's Mountain

to make her peace with Lucy Shawn, but a growing sense of rebelliousness forbade it more forcefully than her father's command. No matter how she considered the situation, she could only feel that her oldest and dearest friend had wronged her. Based on mindless prejudice, Lucy's false accusations and challenges had stung Suzannah, hurting her more bitterly than she cared to admit. Better to be alone, she knew, than risk more attacks.

She could not deny who she was. I am Martin Hopewell's daughter, she repeated to herself. I am Suzannah and I will not be ashamed.

But her growing sense of identity did nothing to help her interpret her feelings for Travis. Did she love him? Was this feeling, this thick, humid warmth that suffused her when they walked or talked or stood together, almost touching—was this what poets called love?

Lying awake at night, her eyes fixed on the stars visible through a gap in her bedroom curtains, she tried to imagine a permanent life with Travis. She tried to see him as the father of her children, the man whose name she would proudly bear. She tried to imagine a lady named Suzannah Paine being introduced at society dinners, prayer meetings and socials. Somehow, the dream of love that set her thoughts churning never survived the monotony of the ensuing years she could picture all too vividly. A part of her declared, I don't want any one man *forever*. But she forbade herself to heed such a declaration, which contradicted all she knew of right and wrong. The idea of wanting to love more than one man was surely put in her mind by the Devil! She knew her mother had never entertained such a sinful thought.

Very late at night, when her eyes burned with fatigue and she ached with restlessness, Suzannah imagined herself damned for unclean thoughts. She prayed hysterically and swore never to see Travis Paine again. In her head she composed a dozen letters of parting that were neither written nor recalled at dawn.

Eventually, she reasoned, there was but one solution to her moral dilemma. She must marry Mr. Paine as quickly as possible and be done with doubt and wondering. Marriage, he assured her, was what he most wanted.

"Every time we meet like this, in secret and alone," he told her, "I risk compromising you. Given half a chance, the gossips would ruin your good name—with pleasure."

They were downriver some distance from Amoset near the ruins of a century-old stone mill. Their horses nearby grazed amidst the rubble. A few pale grasses that had survived the bitter cold poked up in tufts among the fallen stones. The lovers walked in silence, without touching. Since that first, importunate kiss in the hay barn, Travis had showed perfect decorum with Suzannah. He had apologized repeatedly for that one, chaste, stolen kiss. At last, wearying of his sincere apologies, she had told him not to trouble his conscience. But the memory was vivid to both of them. Between them the moment of pleasure hung like a threat and a promise.

"I love you, Suzannah," Travis said, keeping his eyes on the river. "Life holds no meaning if I cannot have you for my partner."

She stared at the stern, handsome profile without responding. Was this the face she wanted to see through all her tomorrows? She supposed it was. Certainly Travis was the man she wanted to hold, to caress her. Was that longing the same as love?

Of course it was! Why must she continue to entertain sinful doubts when he was strong and sure enough for both of them?

"I will tell my father that you wish to speak to him."

"You promised that a week ago."

He sounded petulant and Suzannah was momentarily annoyed with him. It was easy for Travis to sulk: Martin Hopewell was not his father.

"I will do it tomorrow after church," she said. "I promise."

"Suzannah. Dearest girl!" He took her hand and kissed her fingers fervently. Her heart and body cried for more than this chaste gesture, but she told herself to be grateful for Travis' respect. If he could read the passion that filled her thoughts, she knew, he would think much less of her.

During Reverend Strickland's absence, the Unitarian service was conducted by his young assistant. Suzannah realized, the next morning, that the assistant minister was gifted with an even sterner frame of mind than his superior. In a sermon lasting almost an hour, the young Unitarian excoriated his parishioners thoroughly, urging them to wipe their minds clean of ungodly thoughts and to empty their days of ungodly deeds. As he droned on, in the stuffy, overcrowded stone church, Suzannah tried to imagine her brother Valentine preaching this way. He wrote from Boston that his religious studies were going well, that he grew daily in theological understanding, but Suzannah was not sure she believed any of it. Whenever she had dealings with the servant girl Victorine, she blushed, recalling the scene in Val's room the morning before he left.

Thinking then of Travis, Suzannah fidgeted on the hard maple pew that was marked with the

Hopewell name. A glare from Martin stilled her. She tried to follow the minister's order and cleanse her mind of unseemly thoughts, but the harder she tried, the more resolutely her sensuous imaginings persisted. She thought she would die from love—or something very like it.

The service ended near one o'clock. After church, Suzannah and Martin idled away some time in friendly conversation. As Martin became involved in discussion with another manufacturer, more than half an hour passed before Suzannah finally escaped. When Suzannah and her father climbed into the gig at last, she said, summoning all her courage, "Let us take a ride to the Falls before dinner, Papa. The day is fine and clear."

"You have forgotten your stomach, Daughter." Pulling out his pocket watch, Martin glanced at the time. "Esther has been waiting dinner. That preacher is too long-winded for my taste."

"May we go afterwards, Papa?"

"I'll be going down to the mill then." He peered closely at her. "You would do better resting than gallivanting. You look a little peaked."

It is lack of sleep, because you won't let me marry Travis Paine, she wanted to scream. But she kept her peace and they were silent for a time as the horse jogged peaceably towards home.

"A young woman must take good care of herself if she wants to attract a marriageable gentleman." He looked at her appraisingly. "How old are you, Daughter?"

"Eighteen, Papa."

He nodded as if he had guessed correctly all along. "It won't be long before you're ready to marry. Your mother was just eighteen when I brought her here to Amoset."

"Yes, Papa."

"You're a very pretty young woman; and although I know it is an old-fashioned sort of idea, I intend to settle a significant dowry on you, enough to make you extremely eligible. Then, of course, you have money from your grandfather's estate. You and Eben both do. I tell you, I'll feel that much happier when Eben's well and married to Amanda White and you are. . . ."

Suzannah could bear the tension no longer.

"I believe I am already in love, Papa," she cried. Then, before he could speak, "Can't we drive up to the Falls? Just for a few minutes. We could talk. . . ."

Before she had finished her suggestion, he reined in the horse and turned on her with the fury of an attacker. Other carriages returning from church slowed as they passed the Hopewell carriage, and the curious passers-by peered at Martin Hopewell and his daughter. Stopped in the mud at the side of the road, less than a quarter of a mile from home, they presented a strange sight.

When the crowd had passed, Martin grabbed Suzannah's wrist. "What have you been about, young woman? I told your mother I didn't trust you. It's that Lucy Shawn. She's introduced you to some stuffed-shirt Yankee farmer, hasn't she?" He shook her hard.

"Stop it, Papa. You're hurting me! He's not a farmer and Lucy doesn't know him. Please let me speak. I swear I have done nothing to be ashamed of!"

He laughed. "You're a she-dog like your mother! Making a fool of me, trapping some poor man. . . ."

Not listening, making no sense of his words, Suzannah grabbed his hands before he could strike her, and covered them with kisses and tears. "I beg you to hear me, Papa. Please believe me. I have been a gentlewoman and done nothing to shame you. Travis has been. . . ." The look on Martin's face froze her tongue. In that instant, Suzannah knew the full error of having spoken that name aloud. Her father was an unforgiving man. Only a miracle would make him accept Travis Paine in the family

"You love the architect?" He pronounced each syllable venomously, as though the mention of the architect brought bile to his lips.

"I think so, Papa."

"You think so? What does that mean?" Never had her father looked more terrible to her than at that moment. The vapor of his breath clouded the icy air between them in the little gig.

"I know you had some difference of opinion back awhile, but really he is so fine. And from an excellent family. Do you know his people are related to Thomas Paine?" Suzannah talked fast, searching in panic for protection, paying little attention to what she said. Her mention of the patriot was utter folly. Her father's loathing for Yankees surely included the Revolutionary War hero. But if she could just keep talking. . . . Her frantic protests were interrupted by Martin's command.

"I won't have him! You must tell him. . . . No, I forbid you to speak with him! I forbid you to have anything to do with him. I'll send you away!"

"Away?" At the prospect of separation, Suzannah's love lost all uncertainty. All at once she knew that she loved Travis as no woman had ever loved before. To be parted from her beloved was agony. Yet what was the use of argument? She was her father's property. What he told her to do was law.

"Your mother's sister, Bronwyn, has written to say she is ill. She wants your mother to be with her in

Palermo. I do not approve of the voyage and I find Bronwyn immeasurably offensive. But now that this has come up, I think I'll send you both away." Martin Hopewell smiled narrowly. "We'll see if that doesn't cool the young lovers."

He snapped his whip and the horse broke into a steady trot. Father and daughter rode home in silence.

PART IV

Chapter 15

It was a cold, wet day when Suzannah and Sarah Hopewell left for Europe. Their carriage lurched through the muddy streets of Amoset, its wheels throwing off an arrogant arc of spray that left pedestrians wet and angry.

Lucy Shawn, at that moment, was leaving her new boarding house in the company of her sponsor and housemother, Mrs. Quinn. The hurtling carriage splashed mud on their boots and coats. When Lucy grumbled, Mrs. Quinn shushed her, cautioning that she must be careful whom she criticized in Amoset.

"That's Mr. Hopewell's carriage," Mrs. Quinn confided. "He'll be your employer soon. A more honorable, God-fearing gentleman you'll not likely meet in this life."

"Was that Suzannah, then?" Lucy turned to see, but the carriage had already disappeared around the corner.

"You know Miss Hopewell?" Mrs. Quinn asked, a trifle awed, as they resumed their walking. Lucy explained. For many years, she said, Suzannah had been a summertime guest in the Shawn home on Cooper's Mountain. The older woman harumphed loudly in response to Lucy's explanation.

"It won't do any good to put on airs here," she lectured. "None of my girls has fancy connections, but they are all perfectly fine young ladies."

"I know they are, ma'am," Lucy replied meekly. "That's why I asked you to sponsor me at the mill. I am most grateful to you for your kindness."

Mrs. Quinn cleared her throat again, but this time, the sound indicated pleasure. Hannah Quinn liked compliments. A gaunt woman of indeterminate age, her plain and simple style of dress was adopted as a matter of principle as well as necessity. She had sharp, curious eyes and a thin, disapproving mouth that years before had lost the knack of smiling. She thought of herself as a good woman, certainly of value to the community of Amoset.

Quinn's boarding house was situated between other identical establishments of brick and stone. These unadorned, four-story buildings, square-fronted and steep-roofed, faced directly on the thoroughfare that connected Hopewell Mills to the commercial section of town. Facing the river, Front Street intersected other unpaved roads lined with similar boarding houses. More than four thousand mill operatives were required to make these boarding establishments their homes.

As Lucy and her sponsor made their way along the muddy street, the girl looked about her eagerly as if she were seeing Amoset for the first time. Her mind was full of questions about the new life beginning for her. But she held her tongue for fear of saying something that might reveal her guilty secret and lose her the favor of the very proper Mrs. Quinn. If Lucy had set herself a rule to live by in Amoset, it was that she must obey others and do nothing to draw attention to herself. She was a runaway and knew too well that if

James Shawn learned of her whereabouts, he would fetch her home immediately.

As they approached the high fence that surrounded Hopewell Mills, Mrs. Quinn rang the green brass bell that hung beside the locked gate. This single, barred portal was the only entrance to the mill yard. In a moment an old man hobbled out and came to the gate, a ring of keys jangling in his hand. He limped painfully and leaned his weight on a cane as he walked.

"Here's a new young lady I can vouch for, Mr. Wiggins. Miss Lucy Shawn to see Mr. McMahon."

Wiggins coughed up a glob of phlegm and spat onto the muddy ground between his feet. "Full up. Try Shackley's. I've heard they be needing dressers." Wiggins was a frowning old man, badly troubled by rheumatism in the wintery damp. When he spoke, he spat between the spaces of his rotting teeth.

"You always tell me that, Wiggins, but you know all my boarders are Hopewell girls. Let us in now." As the crippled old man complied, punctuating his movements with coughs and groans, Mrs. Quinn whispered to Lucy, "Wiggins takes his work a mite seriously, but you're well warned. If you are late in the morning by so much as a minute, you'll be docked a part of your pay for the price of opening the gate. And there's no early quitting either. Wiggins doesn't unlock until seven-thirty in the evening!"

As they hurried across the brick mill yard, Lucy looked up and saw that all the windows were tightly closed. At the thought of spending fourteen hours of every day in an unventilated room surrounded by the whir and clang of machinery, she paused to doubt her resolution. She thought of her family's clean and airy farmhouse on the mountain, the graceful passing of unpressured days, her work routine decided by the requirements of the seasons and the needs of the animals. Then she thought of the forty or fifty cents a day that mill work paid. Even after deducting a dollar and a quarter a week for room and board at Mrs. Quinn's, Lucy would make more at Hopewell Mills than she could at any other job. With that money hoarded faithfully, she planned to pay for Ingrid's health care. Maybe she could even save enough to send Talleyrand to school.

"Before we enter," warned Mrs. Quinn, pausing at the double doors that formed the entrance to the mill, "let me describe a thing or two. Prepare you, so to speak." She pointed down at the foundation. "Hear that noise? That's the water wheel in the basement. It runs the place, you might say. The Amoset is a mighty stream and Hopewell's, Shackley's and the others are much indebted to its power. Up here on the first floor are the carding rooms, where the men treat the raw cotton and prepare it to be spun into yarn." She put a handkerchief over her nose, then pushed open the door.

The room they entered was noisy and it was crowded with sweating, grim-faced men. Here and there between the unguarded carding machines ran little boys no older than Talleyrand, each carrying carded slivers, the long strands of cotton that were ready for drawing and twisting. The atmosphere was thick with the smoke of dozens of lamps and with clouds of cotton lint.

Coughing, Lucy covered her nose and mouth with her hands.

"It's not as bad upstairs!" cried Mrs. Quinn, shouting above the noise as she pushed Lucy ahead of her. "And anyway, you'll soon grow accustomed to it. All my girls do."

On the way to the stairs they passed women at

the drawing frames stretching and turning the cotton, preparing it for the spinners on the next floor. The spinning rooms were clouded with stinging smoke that brought tears to Lucy's eyes. But from what she could distinguish, this was where the real manufacturing work was being done. The girls at their spinning frames looked up when Lucy and Mrs. Quinn passed by. Some greeted the boarding house proprietor like a member of the family.

In the counting room on the second floor, Lucy was introduced to Foster McMahon.

"She's a good girl, Mr. McMahon," said Mrs. Quinn. "A hard worker—show him your hands, Lucy—and mannerly. The sort of young lady Mr. Hopewell is pleased to have in his employ."

"There's some of you girls think mill work's a lark," said McMahon, staring at Lucy with his small black eyes. "I'll tell you different right now, miss. You'll start as a learner—what we call a spare hand—upstairs in one of the weaving rooms. You'll be paid fairly. Forty cents a day until your apprenticeship is done, six or eight months from now. Agreed?"

Though her heart sank to hear she would earn so little at first, Lucy spoke up clearly. Yes, she understood. Yes, the terms were fair.

"The yard gate is open between four-thirty and five-to-five in the morning. I expect to see you working when the bell rings at five. Your pay is docked for coming late or leaving early. You bring your breakfast with you to eat when the seven o'clock bell rings. Dinner is a half-hour, starting at noon."

Lucy turned to Mrs. Quinn. "But the boarding house is more than a quarter of a mile away. How can I...?"

"You run or go hungry, miss," McMahon interrupted. "Wiggins locks the gate again at twelve-thirty.

If you don't think you can take the pace, I've got no shortage of girls who desire to work here."

To Lucy it seemed that McMahon took pleasure in exhausting her with details. In that moment, she conceived a deep and abiding dislike for the chief of overseers. Chinless and small-mouthed, with eyes like black beans, he appeared to be a witless bully. She told herself that he was stupid, that she had nothing to fear from him.

"You are required to attend church service each Sunday and follow Mrs. Quinn's boarding house rules without fail. No reading matter in the mill, no gossip, no labor organizing. Failure to comply will result in termination and blacklisting. Is that clear?" McMahon eyed Lucy suspiciously. He seemed to doubt her resolve.

"Yes, sir." The man riled Lucy, but she knew that she was dependent on his good humor and dared not show her aggravation. The money at the mill was much too good to sacrifice on account of pride. In only two or three years she would make enough to help her family. She told herself she could tolerate even McMahon for such a short time.

McMahon left the counting room with Lucy close behind him. She hurried after him, along a narrow aisle of spinning frames and up a flight of stairs to the third floor weaving rooms.

"You'll work with the Frenchy, Leveroux. She'll train you." McMahon stopped on the stairs. Standing several steps above Lucy, with all the advantage of height, he towered threateningly over her. "I'll let her explain things to you today. Tomorrow, I expect you to work quiet, and think about what you're doing. There's no time for dreaming or gossip on this job. We don't want any accidents."

"No, sir," murmured Lucy obediently as they stepped into the weaving room.

This was more what she had hoped for, and she sighed with relief. True, there were heavy fumes from the whale-oil lamps that hung from brass hooks on the loom uprights. And the ubiquitous cotton dust and lint formed a cloud in the air. Nonetheless, the high-ceilinged room was the most pleasant in the mill.

In the spring and summer there will be no need for the lamps and, with the windows open, it will be light and airy up here, Lucy thought. Again she sighed, smiling inwardly. She had the sense that a challenging adventure was just about to begin.

The looms, each about four-feet wide, were painted bright green. Arranged in long, even rows like plants in a carefully laid-out garden, each was tended by a pinafored operative who paced back and forth, watching for tangles or breaks. There were children in the room, running quickly when they were called. The children clutched full bobbins that they deftly traded for empties with such practiced hands that the looms never stopped moving.

An operative several years older than the rest was introduced as Marie Leveroux. Lucy recognized her as a resident of Mrs. Quinn's—someone she had noticed the night before when she first arrived at the boarding house.

"Watch out for him," Marie cautioned as soon as McMahon had finished his instructions and departed, leaving the two young women alone. "He is new, but he knows everything. Should he catch you dreaming, you will be finished." Marie spoke with a thick French-Canadian accent Lucy had not heard before. It took Lucy a few moments to understand what the big, heavy-featured woman was saying as she explained the workings of the mill and detailed the

weaver's duties. "Hopewell Mills—all the *l'argent!* So
much money!" Marie grinned, gesturing. "Why?
Look. *Voilà*, everything is done right here. No waiting. The cotton comes in from the South and M'sieur
Hopewell owns that, too. Downstairs they make
thread, upstairs we make cloth. Out there—on the
canal—barges carry cloth to Boston. And what do you
think?" Marie grinned again. "Some—there—is my
cloth!" She pointed to herself, and Lucy realized that
Marie was proud of the work she did.

Like the sight of the high, wide windows of the
weaving room, this pride of accomplishment encouraged Lucy to venture some hope for her future.
Downstairs, among Wiggins, Mrs. Quinn and
McMahon, she had for a moment doubted her decision
to work in Amoset. Now, as she began the long
process of learning a valued trade, neither the challenge nor the closed noisy room caused her much discomfort. Her confidence returned, fear left as her
hands touched the strands of sturdy cotton and she
hummed to herself as she learned the first steps in her
new trade.

Chapter 16

Though she adjusted well during the weeks that followed, Lucy never got used to the early rising that was demanded of her. Of all the aspects of mill life that troubled her, it was the bells at four in the morning that shattered her the most. With five other girls she shared a room fourteen feet wide by sixteen feet long. There were no chests of drawers, no wardrobes or dressers. The girls' trunks and packing boxes sufficed for these purposes and the luggage also served as chairs and chaise longues in the crowded room. There were three brass-framed double beds arranged inches apart along one wall, one of which Lucy shared with a girl named Barbara Bolton. Shortly before, Barbara had come to Amoset from a small town outside Boston. With the raucous chime of the four-a.m. bell, Barbara rose like a mechanized toy and went right to her toilet while Lucy turned and groaned, struggling to ignore the girls who were waking brightly all around her.

Marie Leveroux told Lucy she would adjust. "Soon we all find a way," the older girl said with a wry grin. "Why do you think Hopewell hires women, eh?"

Sooner or later did not much matter to Lucy

when her early morning yawns and stumblings were very much a part of the present suffering. Not only did she hate the wrenching effort required to rise from her bed when the floor was icy, she also was frightened of the mill and of the looms in the morning. Heavy with grogginess, she feared that a trivial error could cost her an arm or hand.

Within hours of being introduced to mill work, she was told a story that haunted her dreams throughout the first weeks of her employment. Months before, at another mill, a child had been running in the weaving room. She slipped and her arm was caught in the cogs of a loom. As the overseer would not permit any weaver to stop her work, the eleven-year-old girl walked a mile to the doctor alone, her arm in a crude bandana sling. Bones were broken in several places between the shoulder and wrist; the arm mended crookedly and none of the mills would hire the girl after that.

Lucy was not easily frightened by such stories or herself given to complaint and she tried to convince herself she had nothing to fear. As she labored, she refused to think how much her feet hurt. Even wearing the large, loose shoes Marie had given her did not make her feet more comfortable. Lucy tried to ignore her aching, swollen legs and the pain in the middle of her back. But most of all, she tried not to think of the woods and the countryside she loved.

She hated being locked up every day. Marie said it wasn't bad during the warm months when the windows of the weaving room were left open and the operatives kept pots of geraniums and lilies blooming on the windowsills. Now was "lighting up" time, winter, when the whale-oil petticoat lamps—hundreds of them—smoked and sizzled in the cold air. After a few days, Lucy's silver-blonde hair had darkened with smoke and she had to live with it that way since hot water and baths were strictly rationed among the twenty-four girls at Mrs. Quinn's boarding house.

Lucy watched Marie Leveroux and learned the ways of the loom quickly. "Each one is different, of course," the French-Canadian told her protégé. "Like human beings, the looms have their quirks, their personalities. But you learn fast, Lucy. Nothing for you to worry about."

Praise like this was enough to make the hardships of mill work bearable and worth the effort of adjustment. Lucy arranged the details of her past life with a neatness that gave her a clear perspective on the future. She missed her family, the woods and the comparative leisure of her old life, but she would never trade those simple comforts for the exhilarating sense of competence she had acquired in a complicated world. Sometimes she fancied that this outside world was calling her. There was a job to be done, it seemed to say, and she was the only one who could do it.

Still, she hated the clang of the morning bell and feared she would never adjust to its strident demands. By the evening closing bell at seven-thirty, she was painfully weary, scarcely able to lift her legs, and her feet were so cold and swollen they might have been stumps tied to her ankles. Like the other girls, she had eyes that were red-rimmed and puffy, stung by the acrid lamp smoke.

One Friday after Lucy had been at Hopewell Mills for six weeks, McMahon told her to carry a tray of full bobbins to the cart at the end of the room. It was almost the end of the day. In fact, it might have been after seven-thirty, for Marie and some of the other girls had begun to suspect that McMahon was keeping "slow time." It was a method used by unscrupulous overseers to get more work for less money.

Picking up the tray, Lucy turned away from McMahon without seeing him. She walked with difficulty on her numb feet and after she had taken a few steps, her right foot suddenly turned beneath her. She grabbed for a handhold and stopped, her fingers only inches from the loom picks. The nearest operative screamed and pushed Lucy away. The tray of bobbins tilted and rolled to the floor, scattering in every direction, leaving trails of tangled, white cotton thread.

Lucy landed hard on her hip. She was stunned for a moment by the pain. The operative who had shoved her away from the picks helped her to her feet.

It was Barbara Bolton who asked, "Are you all right, Lucy?" It was the first time Barbara had used her name, though the two girls had shared the same bed for weeks.

Lucy nodded. "I hurt." She clenched her teeth. "Thanks to you, nothing is broken."

McMahon was shouting ferociously. "Don't lie there like a debutante. Look about you, Miss Shawn! Look what you've done!" He stopped his tirade only as the closing bell rang. The operatives chattered and laughed as they stopped their looms and dashed for the stairs. "You'll stay," barked McMahon, coming up to Lucy. "Cleaning this mess'll keep you here another hour. On your own time, Miss Shawn. Not Hopewell's."

"I'll miss my dinner, Mr. McMahon." For the last hour, Lucy had been daydreaming of roast chicken and biscuits in gravy.

"An empty belly should teach you to watch your step next time!"

Lucy fell to her hands and knees, crawling between the looms to retrieve the bobbins. The other operatives were already gone. Only one remained. Before she left, Marie Leveroux stooped down and whispered, "Don't worry about dinner. I'll save you something."

Hours later, still in the weaving room, Lucy worked by lamplight. She finally unhooked her petticoat lamp, placed it on the floor, proceeded to crawl about under the looms, tracing the tangled trails that led to the fallen bobbins. When the tangles were impossible to pick out with her cold fingers, she broke the thread and stuffed the ends into the pocket of her pinafore, knowing that she could only get in worse trouble for wasting valuable materials. Her hands and clothes were covered with cotton lint and the dust entered her nose and mouth if she breathed too deeply. She rewound the bobbins by feel, her stinging eyes almost closed. She was shaking with cold by the time she finished loading the tray and she pulled herself painfully to her feet by holding on to one of the loom uprights. Recalling how the ugly picks had come close to stabbing her hand, she pulled back quickly from the machine and stood for a moment, utterly still. All around her she felt the malevolent presence of so many mechanized monsters.

Other girls had told her they felt this way when they first started work at the mill. They were country girls like herself, and the sophistication of mass production by machines was not easy for them to accept. The giant looms made Lucy feel small and helpless, insignificant. The same emotions affected her on entering the woods, but there she rejoiced. In the weaving room she felt like cringing.

The bobbin carts were set at the far, dark end of

the room. Though she could not carry the tray and her lamp at the same time, Lucy had to make her way to the carts somehow. It would be dangerous to disturb the already overloaded carts. She had a sudden nightmare vision of all the bobbin carts tipping slowly, slowly, like a scene observed underwater, and the hundreds of bobbins spinning out across the floor. Holding the tray like glass, she slowly stepped along the aisle between the looms. At the end of the aisle, by the windows, the blackness turned grey from the night sky and she was able to find the empty cart. She put the tray down. Something startled her. She turned quickly.

McMahon stood less than a yard from her. Seen over his shoulder, far down the aisle, her lamp glowed like gold bullion. She took a step back and her hand touched the bobbin cart; without thinking, her fingers closed about one of the long spindles with its pointed end.

"You're done, then?" asked McMahon.

"Yes, sir."

He stared at her, his eyes dark pits in his face.

"I'll dock your pay for extra lamp oil and the time it'll take to wash that thread."

"Yes, sir." Her fingers tightened on the spindle. It seemed to her that the hulking looms were all in league with the overseer. Half-human instruments of torture, they surrounded her, staring down with the same, vacuous, pit-dark expression.

"All right, then. Take your lamp and go down. Wiggins will unlock."

"Yes, sir," she cried, dropping the spindle back onto the tray. She ran past him, grabbed her lamp and flew down the stairs, seizing the banister so she could jump down three and four steps at a time. Never looking back, she plunged through the outer door into the mill yard where she finally halted, gasping with relief. Only then did she look back at the factory, feeling once again the terror that seemed part of its dark expanses and grim walls.

The bricks in the yard were wet and slippery, their slick surface reflecting the lamplight. Choosing her footing with care, Lucy slowly made her way across the yard. But already she was breathing more easily. The unreasonable fear had left her. When Wiggins let her through the gate, she handed over the lamp and thanked him. She was almost composed again as she turned to take a farewell look at the mill.

Without warning, someone stepped in front of her on the road. She started back in fright.

"'Tis I, Sister Lucy. Talley."

She yelped with surprise and delight. Instantly, her exhaustion and fears were forgotten. "Little brother!" she cried. Picking up the nine-year-old boy by the arms, she spun around and around, whirling so his thin little legs flew. He giggled wildly, out of control with excitement and joy.

"But, Talley. . . ." Putting him down firmly, she suddenly grew serious. "How came you here to Amoset? Don't tell me Papa knows. . . ."

"He's gone to Meredith to take work as a woodcutter. Mama sent me down here to find you."

"How is she, Talley?"

"Well. But Ingrid's been poorly. From the mist, Mama says. 'Tis the damp that does it."

As they walked along the road, Talley talked in a steady stream, filling in for Lucy all the family facts and anecdotes she had so missed. The outside world was forgotten. Only the news that Talley brought could make her happy. It was a touch of home, her chance to be a child again.

Chapter 17

Front Street was thronged with strolling groups of factory operatives, all carrying lanterns, all bundled against the cold in their mufflers and shawls. They talked gaily, laughing as they passed by Lucy and Talleyrand, their arms linked about each other's waists companionably.

"Where can they all be going after dark, Sister?" To a nine-year-old boy off Cooper's Mountain, the atmosphere was as festive as bonfire night.

For the benefit of her wide-eyed brother, Lucy pretended to be blasé. But she did not really feel indifferent to it all. After six weeks, Amoset still thrilled her with its crowds and sense of industry. "There is ever so much to do in Amoset, Talley. Why, I myself have already visited the lending library several times." She gave him a sisterly jab in the ribs. "The charms of that are lost on you, no doubt!" Before he could think of a cheeky reply, she went on, "There are lectures at the Lyceum and poetry readings. Not to mention political and historical discussion groups. I tell you, Talley, there is such a thirst for learning among us in Amoset, even you would be affected. I was overwhelmed at first. But now I have joined a self-improvement group that meets once weekly."

As she spoke, Lucy began to feel renewed by her own reminders of the benefits of life in Amoset. If mill work was less rewarding than she had hoped, the town more than made up for the pain of labor. In Amoset she had begun to feel important for the first time. She saw herself as part of a courageous new order of female wage earners, among women who were intelligent, curious and unafraid of challenge.

Lucy grabbed Talley's hand in an excess of affection. He *would* learn to read! Her wages from Hopewell Mills would guarantee him an education whether he wanted one or not. And Ingrid would have the finest Boston specialist. Hopewell money— *her* money—would see to that as well!

James Shawn, too proud to accept his daughter's earnings, was the only thought that disturbed Lucy as she flaunted her new kingdom before her brother's innocent gaze.

"Does Papa ever speak of me?" Lucy asked at last.

"At prayers he always asks the Lord to guide you in wisdom and keep you healthy. That's all."

She sighed. It was enough for now.

"What's that man selling, Sister Lucy?"

Lucy looked where Talley pointed. A swarthy, thick-mustached man was pushing a gaily painted cart along Front Street, a pair of bright lanterns swinging from its vividly striped red and blue canopy.

"Fruit, fresh fruit!" he called, as if Talley's question had reached him through the noisy crowd. He stopped so Talley could peer at his wares: apples, pears and grapes gathered in thick clusters like dusty indigo beads.

"What is that?" Talley asked, pointing to a wizened fruit the size of a boy's fist.

"An orange," his sister told him, proud in her knowledge. She could not resist adding, "If you would only learn to read, you would be less ignorant of such things."

"Where does it come from?" Talley asked the vendor, ignoring Lucy's pedantry.

"South where the snow never goes and the seas are warm as bath water." The vendor smiled as he handed the fruit to Talley. "Smell," he ordered.

Talley obeyed. At the first sniff, he sighed, rolling his eyes, "Sister, smell!"

Sweetly aromatic, slightly fermented, the old orange warmed her palm like gold. "How much is it?" she asked after a moment's consideration.

The vendor smiled again, wider this time, no doubt thinking of his profit on the old fruit. "For you, miss, it is two cents."

Talley gasped. It seemed a great deal to pay for such a small treasure. But Lucy felt expansive, and she was aware of the impression she was making on her little brother. "I'll take it," she declared. "Would you like to pay the man, Talley?" She put her last two coins in his palm. Ah, well, tomorrow was Saturday. Payday.

Talleyrand stood straighter as he held his hand out to the vendor, and Lucy realized he had probably never before paid for anything in coin. When her brother handed her the orange, there was a greedy arrogance in his broad grin, an expression entirely new and not at all boyish. Lucy was uneasy for a moment.

She forgot his look, however, the instant her thumbnail broke the rubbery skin of the orange and the sugary juices streamed down the side of her hand to the wrist. She put the fruit to her mouth and sucked.

"Let me, Sister! I want some!" Talley grabbed the orange away from her while she still held it near her lips. Prying with his thumbs, he tore the fruit apart and gave her half. She watched him drag the pulp away from the skin with his teeth. The juice dribbled from his lips. All at once, she lost her hunger for the orange. It was overripe and the odor nauseated her now.

"Take my half, too," she said listlessly. Talleyrand grabbed her half without thanks.

The crowd in Front Street had thinned considerably. It was now after nine, and in every boarding house window, the lamps glowed, casting a light as orange as the fruit and promising fellowship, ease and protection. Inside those stern houses, there was sure protection from the cold, wet river wind. A pair of girls passed by, dressed gaudily in feathered bonnets and fur-collared coats. The heavy smell of artificial scent wafted after them. Talley spun around to stare and, just as quickly, Lucy grabbed his collar and hauled him right way round again.

"Never mind!" she said firmly, before he could ask her about the fancy women. Even Amoset had its shame, though Lucy did not often think of the low life in town. It spoiled the perfect atmosphere to wonder about the girls who came from the country to work as spinners and weavers—and stayed to lose their virtue when the love of money carried them too far. Lucy glanced at Talley and was relieved to see he had forgotten the fragrant ladies and was once more under the enchantment of the orange.

He took a bite of the skin and quickly spat it out, making a terrible face. "Bitter!" he said, shoving the peel into his pocket. "I've saved the seeds for Mama. Maybe she can use the skin for something too. Imagine, Lucy! Oranges on Cooper's Mountain! Wouldn't Papa be surprised?"

She nodded, unable to explain the heaviness in her heart. Pulling her old cloak more closely about her shoulders, she trudged on, her weariness returning to her. After a moment, she said, " 'Tis late, Talley. You'll not make it back up the mountain tonight."

He shrugged. "No matter. I am not expected. Before I met you at the mill yard, I put my bedroll in a hay barn back yonder. I'll sleep warmly there and be home in time for breakfast."

At the foot of the stairs to Mrs. Quinn's boarding house, they stopped. Lucy reached down and hugged her brother very close.

"I love you, Talley. You know that, don't you?" She held his pale little face between her hands. "And I am only here because of you and Ingrid. I want you to have the best, Talley. If you have an education, you can become someone important. You can. . . ."

He squirmed away from her, restless with a little boy's impetuosity. "I should like to work at Hopewell's and live in Amoset, too. I know that boys are hired. . . ."

Shaking him, Lucy ordered him never to say such a thing again. "You have to go to school, Talley!"

"I don't want to! School is boring!"

Lucy tried to laugh, but her throat was dry. "You're ignorant, Talley. If you come to work in the mills, you'll never know more of the world than you do today. A moment ago you had never heard of an orange. . . ."

"And now I have eaten one!" He did a dance, purposely teasing his sister. "When I have lots of money, I will eat an orange every day!"

"If you don't learn, you'll be dirt poor all your life!"

He laughed at the concern in her voice. "Good night, Sister Worry-mouse. Rest thee well. I will tell our mother you are happy in the land of oranges!"

"Talley!" she called, but he had run off into the night. In the nearly empty street, Lucy Shawn stood alone outside Mrs. Quinn's, her heart deeply troubled.

She was about to go up the stairs to the porch when she heard something—the whimper of an animal, she thought—in the basement well of the outside stairs. She peered over the iron railing, then took a cautious step down toward the darkness below.

A female voice stopped her. "Go away!"

"Who are you?" Lucy narrowed her eyes to peer into the blackness below her. A figure was crouched in the corner, a shawl over her head.

"I said go away! Leave me alone!"

Lucy recognized Barbara Bolton's voice. "It is I, Lucy Shawn. May I help you, Barbara?"

"Go away!"

"But. . . ."

"Leave me, I said. Go!" Barbara was almost screaming. Her voice carried far on the night air. "Let me be! Is that so much to ask?"

The plea stopped Lucy. For a moment she was uncertain whether to interfere with Barbara's solitude. Privacy was a dear commodity at Mrs. Quinn's. Like every other boarding house in Amoset, the place was overcrowded and there was little or no opportunity to be alone. Operatives were seldom permitted the luxury of a solitary moment or a private conversation. But adapting to the constant scrutiny of others was especially difficult for some girls to endure. A part of Lucy wished to honor Barbara's need to be alone, but Lucy was too practical to let deference override other considerations.

"It is cold and damp down there. You'll take a

chill. Besides, there are rats in the cellar. I saw them once myself. Come away, Barbara. If you must be alone. . . ."

"No!"

Above her, Lucy heard a window open. She saw a girl she knew only as Violet looking down at her. "Come inside, Lucy," said the girl firmly. "Leave her alone."

"It's Barbara, my bedmate. She. . . ."

"Leave her and come up. Mrs. Quinn has saved you bread and gravy from supper, and there's a bit of warm cider left as well." Violet was one of the senior girls in the house. Only Marie Leveroux outranked her. She spoke with a voice of authority that could not be ignored. Lucy turned away from Barbara obediently and ascended the stairs.

Inside, Violet and several other girls surrounded her as she removed her cloak, gloves and shawl.

"What was she doing?"

"Was she crying?"

"Could you see how she looked?"

"Was she alone?"

Lucy covered her ears to shut out the meddlesome curiosity-seekers. Looking around her in amazement, she saw that her fellow boarders not only wanted but expected her to gossip about Barbara. Lucy was shocked, but, in spite of her protective feelings for Barbara, she was curious too. What did they expect her to tell them?

Lucy took Violet aside. "She'll catch her death down there, Violet. Let me go to her again. Perhaps if I offer her my cider. . . ."

A girl named Julia mocked her. "I'll drink it myself before I let you waste it on that one!"

These frank words shocked the group into silence.

"Well," demanded Julia, "what are you all looking so horrified for? We all know it's girls like her that give factory work a bad name."

"Hush," chided Violet calmly. "There are some things that never need be said, Julia."

"Is that so! I'd like to know why not! We're all thinking the same thing, and you know it!"

"We needn't say everything we know."

"But I tell you, I *do* know. I saw her in the bath before she had a chance to cover up!"

"Julia!" cried Lucy angrily. Turning to Violet, she announced so all could hear: "Barbara saved my life today. She is my friend, I think. Violet—you must tell me. What is this wild talk? It makes no sense to me. What is it? What is wrong with Barbara?"

Julia laughed. "As her bedmate, I'm sure you'll know soon enough. There won't be room in there for all of you!" Several of the girls snickered, casting sly glances of self-importance toward each other.

Lucy was stunned by the eager nastiness she heard in their laughter. Shaking her head in horror, she backed toward the front door.

"Lucy. . . ."

"Whatever you have to say, Violet, I am sure it can wait. I'm going down to get that girl and I don't care what any one of you has to say. Whatever you think she has done, her offense cannot be bad enough to warrant such cruelty!"

Ignoring the looks of displeasure that greeted her outburst, Lucy opened the door and stepped onto the porch. Shutting the door softly behind her, she stood for a moment to catch her breath and control her anger. She knew she had made an enemy or two among the boarders and she would not soon forget the look she saw on Julia's face as the girl turned away. Those lips turned back in a cunning sneer could speak volumes of gossip, but Lucy told herself she did not care what others thought of her. Only hours before, Barbara had saved Lucy from being horribly maimed. For that, Lucy owed her bedmate a lasting debt of gratitude. She had to defend the girl, no matter how unpopular it made Lucy.

But Lucy was startled to see a couple seated at the bottom of the stairs, two heads bent close together. She recognized Barbara's dark hair and in the scant light from the parlor window—now crowded with the faces of curious boarders—she recognized the young man at her side. She had seen him talking to Barbara at the mill-yard gate several evenings before. Lucy stood watching uncertainly and she was about to return inside when Barbara's voice, growing louder, came to her ears.

"My time approaches! I cannot work much longer!"

Lucy stepped back against the door, stunned into comprehension at last. Barbara's own words explained the attitude of Julia, Violet and the others. And she blushed, embarrassed at being so stupid and innocent. Of course—she should have understood from the hints and cruel words.

Barbara Bolton was with child.

Chapter 18

Lucy could not sleep that night. Lying beside her slumbering bedmate, she was acutely aware of the other girl's body, unable to forget the incriminating words she had overheard.

She tried to understand Barbara's situation. To Lucy, pregnancy out of wedlock was a stupid mistake. Any girl so foolish deserved to suffer. Lucy—firm-minded and rational as she was—could not imagine loving anyone enough to lose physical control. Being swept away by tides of passion was something she associated with romantics like Suzannah Hopewell, never herself. It was incomprehensible, as if someone who could not swim would madly dive into a deep pool on the chance that she might miraculously float.

Lucy chided herself. What did she really know about love? From what she had read and seen, love was enough to make sane people mad, to make the strong grow weak. Hearing the tone of her own judgments, she scolded herself and cautioned her own conscience not to judge those things that she did not understand.

Thinking of love brought to Lucy's mind her last meeting with Suzannah Hopewell the night of the bonfire. Lucy had reluctantly agreed to meet Eben to smooth the way for Suzannah's rendezvous. She wondered what had happened to the great love which shone in Suzannah's eyes that night. And, in spite of herself, Lucy wondered what had become of Eben Hopewell.

As she turned from side to side in the sagging, creaky bed, she remembered how clumsy and ingratiating Eben had been with her that night of the bonfire. She had treated him as badly as she could, abandoning him to Talley's boyish chatter. In the end Eben had offered to buy them all cups of cider and candied apples. Despite Talley's loud complaints, Lucy had been proud to refuse an offer that seemed like outright charity.

At the time, it had pleased Lucy to be unkind. It made her feel superior to one she supposed was condescending to her. With the distance of time, however, she had come to see the situation somewhat differently. Eben had simply been kind that night. He was not at all ill-tempered, though rumor had led her to expect a hard, unscrupulous young man. Though she could not face the troublesome truth at the time, Lucy saw clearly that he truly desired her company. There was no condescension in his manner.

Lucy's stomach growled noisily and she forgot Eben Hopewell. Her bread and gravy dinner had been cold, skimpy and indigestible.

Barbara stirred beside her and murmured in her dreams. When she turned and curled close like a kitten, Lucy smelled her breath. It made her gag and pull back to the edge of the bed. Disgust mingled with fear in Lucy. The breath was not healthy, not of things living and growing. Barbara's breath stank of something dead and putrefying.

Turning her back on the pregnant girl, Lucy

squeezed her eyes tightly shut. She tried to force the girl out of her mind. I *will* sleep. I *must*. Though Saturdays were half days at the mill, the bell still clanged the operatives out of bed before dawn. On the roof above Lucy's attic room, she could hear the rain beginning. She huddled deep into the bed warmth, longing for the sweetness of Talley or Ingrid to hold and cuddle.

After a time, her thoughts returned to Barbara and were sympathetic. No matter what the girl had done—call it sin or foolishness—Julia and her gossipy chums had no right to take pleasure in her trouble. Gossip that delighted in the suffering of others was new in Lucy's experience. The residents of Cooper's Mountain were allied in times of trouble, yet they kept a respectful distance from one another, honoring the privacy of each family. That privacy was valued as a God-given right.

Of course, there's no right of privacy here, thought Lucy bitterly. Though it was true she enjoyed meeting women from all around New England—and the free exchange of ideas filled her mind with new energy—she was beginning to realize the great price she paid in personal liberty. Barbara could not keep her pitiful secret from the prying eyes of girls like Julia. Barbara was not even allowed a place to weep alone. In the boarding house and mill, there was always someone watching.

In the midst of Lucy's reveries, the door to her room opened softly.

"Who's there?" she asked.

"Marie." Her friend crept to her side and knelt near the head of the bed. "You are still awake? Come. I brought you some meat from dinner."

Lucy slipped out of bed stealthily. Grabbing a spare blanket off one of the packing boxes, she

wrapped the woolen around her like a cloak and tip-
toed out of the bedroom onto the landing.

"Here," whispered Marie, handing her a plate
covered with a cloth. "It was all I could find."

Lucy thanked her softly and bit hungrily into the
turkey drumstick. It was overcooked, with a thick,
dry skin, and was difficult to chew, but the taste satisfied her palate's craving. She was grateful for her
friend's thoughtfulness.

It was dark on the landing, but as Lucy's eyes
grew accustomed to the blackness, she could see the
expression of concern on Marie's face.

"Violet tells me all what happened. Tonight you
have done a bad thing, Lucy. Very dangerous to
make Julia your enemy."

"I don't care about Julia. She's a vicious gossip
and I don't ever care to have her for a friend." Lucy
bit into the turkey emphatically.

"*Oui*. What you say is true. And being vicious is
what makes Julia a bad enemy. Now you wait and
see. Pretty soon she find some way to hurt you.
Quinn, McMahon, they all are like Julia. That will
mean trouble for you." She shook her finger at Lucy.
"Promise!"

"Are you saying she's a . . . spy?"

"Shhh!" Marie looked furtively down the stairs to
see if Lucy's raised voice had disturbed the sleeping
house. Midnight conversations were strictly against
the boarding house regulations. When Marie felt safe
again, she answered Lucy's question. "You are new
here, Lucy. You think everybody is so nice like your
family. This is not so. Girls like Julia make life hard
for others so their way will be smooth. How do you
think she got that nice room when Violet and me, we
are seniors here? Mrs. Quinn likes Julia because she
gossips her secrets!"

As she listened, Lucy sat quite still on the steps, her blanket forming a tent over her head and shoulders, the edge turned under her bare feet to protect them from the cold wooden steps. Outwardly she was composed, but her blood was boiling. When Marie had finished her warning, Lucy spoke her mind.

"My family is poor, Marie. Our farm has been in the family since long before the Revolution, but it has never given us quite enough. Shawn men aren't much good at farming, you see, but the land means freedom to them, so they stay on. Freedom's what they care about. My granddaddies on both sides fought the British in the War of Independence. My mother's father was wounded and Granddaddy Shawn lost an arm and leg before he was twenty. But he came back to the land. He and his brothers worked it, had families." Marie tried to interrupt, but Lucy stopped her gently. "When I think of Julia, I recall my Granddaddy and what he would think of someone like her."

"But Lucy, greedy, mean-hearted people are everywhere. Your Revolution didn't drive them all out of Massachusetts. Look at Mr. Hopewell."

"He's a Southerner. A slaver. Anyway, Marie, I don't care how many people you show me who are evil. Perhaps they exploit the helpless by spying and cheating. But there is always someone else—always a Mrs. Quinn who encourages people to spy on one another for their own gain. Barbara Bolton—Marie, we must defend her. There is no one to take her side."

"You are wrong. Mill towns only work if girls stay clean and virtuous. That gives the town, the work, a good reputation. Then girls come from all over thinking mill work will be a decent way to earn a living."

"I'm not saying it isn't. But there must be room

for this—this—weakness." Lucy groped for words, still not sure in her own mind what made Barbara behave as she had. "We can't let Hopewell and Quinn and McMahon turn us into spies against one another." Now she was on firm ground again. Her musings began to come together and make sense. Pounding her fist on her knee, Lucy declared, "It's the system at fault. Not the work. I came here to work and work hard. But not to be spied on!"

Beside her, Marie sighed heavily and covered her eyes with her hands as if her head ached. Lucy chewed thoughtfully on a piece of turkey skin, her anger simmering, but now controlled.

Finally, Marie said, "You are a good person, Lucy. Tough. So I will tell you a secret. There is a group—just a few operatives now but by next year there will be many of us—meeting in secret at Mrs. Randolph's boarding house on Carl Street."

"Near the Unitarian Church?"

"*Oui.*"

"You're organizing?" Despite her libertarian convictions, Lucy was astonished. "That's against the rules. You'll be fired! Blacklisted! You'll never work at another mill in New England if they find out!"

Marie shrugged fatalistically. "Alone we have not a chance. Together . . . maybe. Maybe not."

They were quiet again. Outside on Front Street, a rickety freight wagon carrying produce to Saturday's market hurried past the dark line of boarding houses. On the canal a barge bell rang, reminding Lucy that morning was not far away.

"I have to sleep." She yawned and rubbed her tired eyes.

Marie took the gnawed bone from her. "You come with me to Randolph's if you want to, Lucy. I trust you. Others will, too."

"I need this job, Marie."

"So do we all, Lucy."

It was long after midnight before Lucy slept, and then her rest was fitful, her dreams populated with confused images. Still, she awoke before the four-a.m. bell. Beside her, Barbara was weeping in her sleep and, following a sudden, instinctive impulse, Lucy embraced the troubled girl as a mother would, rocking her gently until the sobbing quieted.

Saturday at Hopewell's was devoted to cleaning up the looms and weaving rooms. One of Lucy's tasks was to push a broad, heavy broom, sweeping up an enormous pile of dust and lint. The children assigned to the room scooped up the pile and hurried to dump it in the furnace in the mill yard. Outside, rain mixed with sleet. After every trip to the fire, the children were soaked and shivering. The sight of their pale, pinched faces and trembling bodies, their lips purpled with cold, reminded Lucy of her conversation with Marie the night before. For once she was not tired despite the lack of sleep. She recalled each word of their talk and her anger kept her warm and wide awake.

At the closing bell, Lucy stood at the window not far from the looms worked by Barbara Bolton. Lucy finished her dusting and hurried to join the other operatives going down to the second floor counting room for their pay envelopes. A word from Barbara stopped her.

"Thank you, Lucy." Her eyes were wet with tears. "You are the only one who has been kind to me but I can never repay you."

"Hush, Barbara!" Lucy put her arm around the girl's shoulders. Barbara was so thin, Lucy could feel the shape of her bones against her hand. "Let's get our pay, then see what Mrs. Quinn has made us for our dinner. Nothing too delicious, I'll wager!" She smiled at the attempted joke. "You're thin, Barbara. You must eat more. I'll give you my portion of bread and butter."

"You mustn't be kind to me, Lucy. You'll only make trouble for yourself." Turning aside, Barbara pushed her companion away. "Go down alone. Don't be seen with me."

Incredulous, Lucy looked at Barbara more closely. The girl's pallor and emaciation were painful to see. In contrast to her thin face, neck and arms, her swollen belly looked particularly obvious. Lucy feared for the unborn child. She knew what happened to spring calves when the cows were ill-fed during the winter: they came out stillborn or crippled and strange-eyed. Lucy wondered if, after all Barbara had suffered, she hoped for the child to be stillborn. Or did she long for this child to live regardless of its legitimacy? Lucy did not know. She was confused about many things, clear about one only. Julia and her kind would not intimidate her into betraying a human being in great need.

When McMahon handed Lucy her money through the counting room window, his fingers stroked the inside of her wrist in a familiar and insinuating way that made her pull back with an abrupt rush of fear. There was something terrible in his eyes, an expression that recalled the night before, reminding her again of the dark weaving room, the monstrous looms.

Taking her envelope from McMahon, Barbara Bolton tore it open quickly as she and Lucy walked across the spinning room. She stopped with a cry.

"What is it?"

"They've terminated me. I'm fired from Hopewell Mills." Barbara fell back against a spinning frame and began to sob. "What will we do? What is to become of us?"

The anger in Lucy was like a spindle turning, twisting in her insides, tearing her apart. She grabbed for Barbara, holding her tightly to keep from screaming her rage.

Down the aisle between the frames, McMahon stood at the counting room window and watched the touching scene. His small mouth hung slightly open, his lips glistening in the lamplight.

Chapter 19

Mrs. Quinn met them just inside the front door. Lucy and Barbara were hanging their cloaks on pegs in the entry hall when she appeared.

"I understand you've been terminated, Miss Bolton."

Lucy answered for Barbara, "And with no explanation!" Ignoring Lucy's interference, Mrs. Quinn kept her eyes on Barbara, thin and pale, who stood before her, utterly helpless and exposed.

"In that case, you will make arrangements to leave my house as soon as possible. Today would be preferable."

"But she's going to get another position, aren't you, Barbara?" Lucy interjected once again. "Hathaway's is hiring weavers now. I'm sure they'd be delighted to get her. How many looms were you working? Three? Four?" Lucy turned to Mrs. Quinn. "She's a wonderfully hard worker, ma'am. Hathaway's will take her on, I'm sure."

Mrs. Quinn's lips formed a thin line of displeasure. She shook her head. "You don't understand the situation, Lucy. Having been terminated, Miss Bolton will not find employment again in Amoset. If she wants to work," the housemother let her eyes appraise Barbara's midriff, "and I doubt if she can much longer, I. . . ."

From behind a damp cotton hanky Barbara murmured, "There is a list, Lucy."

"She's been blacklisted?"

"Precisely." Ignoring Lucy, Mrs. Quinn added, "I would like you out by tomorrow morning at the latest. There are many girls wanting room and board. As you know, this is a respectable house."

"I have nowhere to go."

"I'm sure that is your problem and not mine, miss. You should have thought of that before. . . ."

"Didn't you pay a week in advance as I did?" interrupted Lucy. "Well, there you are! You don't have to leave for another seven days. That's correct isn't it, Mrs. Quinn?" Lucy's voice held a hint of challenge.

"That money will be refunded, of course," responded Mrs. Quinn coldly.

"Why not let her stay on a few more days? It's winter, Mrs. Quinn. She has no place to go." The housemother said nothing. "It seems like the Christian thing to do."

Mrs. Quinn raised her eyebrows a little, smiled thinly. "You are a brilliant advocate, Lucy Shawn. What a pity the law is closed to women." Then, to Barbara, with scarcely disguised loathing, she conceded, "You have until next weekend, miss. Not a day longer. I have my business and my reputation to think of. Lucy," she touched her arm, "I'd like a word with you in my sitting room." Mrs. Quinn's tone was vaguely sarcastic as she added, "Can you spare me a moment?"

The cold, bare room seemed to reflect Mrs. Quinn's parsimonious nature, in keeping with her unadorned clothing and austere hair style. Though a fire burned in the grate of the iron stove, it was underfueled and warmed only a small area. In the unlit corner of the room where Lucy stood, twisting her hands nervously behind her back, it was dreary as dawn. She watched Hannah Quinn anxiously, preparing for her reprimand. Lucy knew she had spoken in a bold, offensive way and Mrs. Quinn had a right to be displeased. Nevertheless, Lucy would not retract her defense of Barbara. The girl was being wronged and nothing could make Lucy change her mind about that.

"Sit down, child. Near the fire. Will you take milk in your tea?"

"Oh, please, ma'am." A warm drink sounded wonderful and Lucy was slightly encouraged by this small show of hospitality. But why had Mrs. Quinn called her in, if not to scold her?

After a long, exhausting morning at the mill, Lucy was grateful for the chance to sit. The settee felt more comfortable than it had first appeared, and the sudden warmth of the fire created a pleasant ache as the heat penetrated the numbness of her feet and hands. The crackling little blaze threw a bright glow on the colorless room and lifted her spirits, though Lucy knew for certain she would pay for these moments with itching, oozing chilblains. When tea came, she drank it down quickly. Now warm inside and out, Lucy felt the knot of righteous anger begin to unravel. For the space of a few moments, her thoughts of Mrs. Quinn turned kindly.

"You're a new girl and naive, Lucy. That's why I take the time to offer you advice about deportment and friendship here in Amoset. I would hate to see you go wrong, but I know what can happen when a girl leaves home to live among strangers, far from her mother. Believe me, though I know my words seem harsh, you will only suffer from befriending a girl like

Miss Bolton. We are all judged by our friends, don't you know, Lucy? Tell me honestly, do you want to be likened to her?"

"She seems a nice girl, Mrs. Quinn. That is why I cannot understand. . . ." The tension was returning. The lulling moment of relaxation was gone. Lucy was on guard again.

"Never mind how things seem. Just do as you are told and everything will work out fine for you here in Amoset." Hannah Quinn smiled pleasantly and raised the teapot. "Another cup, Lucy?"

"No, thank you, ma'am." Lucy stood and dipped her head politely. "I believe I would like to change my clothes before dinner. Will you excuse me, ma'am?"

"Of course." Again that pleasant, masking smile, the artificial upward curve of lips. "I'm glad we had a chance to chat, Lucy. I hope we understand each other?"

Lucy dipped her head again, not able to look Hannah Quinn in the eye for fear the housemother would read the disgust in her expression. Lucy was insulted. Did Mrs. Quinn think her loyalty could be bought or sold for a cup of tea?

When Marie Leveroux invited Lucy to spend the evening with friends at Mrs. Randolph's boarding house on Carl Street, Lucy hesitated only a moment before eagerly accepting the invitation. She had been thinking all afternoon of how she might respond when such an invitation came. She feared losing her job, dreaded that she might be blacklisted for organizing. Nevertheless, the past several days had convinced her that the mill town system, with its boarding houses and regimented operatives, was contrary to all she had been raised to value in life. It was not a decision she came to lightly. Lucy was too serious-minded a girl to flit from friend to friend or cause to cause. She knew that if she joined the small band of labor organizers, she would be committed to them for good. So she weighed and weighed again the pros and cons of the argument until she knew for certain that she would take a stand in favor of what she believed.

As she walked through the driving sleet to the Carl Street boarding house, a covered basket of quilting materials tucked under her arm, it occurred to her with wry amusement that city living was a good deal more complicated than she had ever expected it to be. She wondered what her father would think if he knew his elder daughter was embarking on such a course of rebellious action. At the thought of James Shawn she was suddenly depressed. Almost two months had passed since her secretive departure from her home on Cooper's Mountain. In that time she had heard nothing from her father. Apart from seeing Talley, she'd had no contact with those most dear to her. She longed for her father now. Though she was sure that what she was doing was right, she was only sixteen years old and his reassurances would have strengthened her confidence.

At the door of Mrs. Randolph's she almost lost heart. She feared for her job and her good name. Her family had a reputation for being law-abiding and she could not bear to think of shaming them. But as quickly as the doubts entered her mind, they were followed by visions of Mrs. Quinn, Julia and McMahon, smiling and satisfied, confident in their powers. She hurried up the stairs behind Marie and Violet.

Meeting in the first floor sitting room, that small group of young women named themselves the Spindle

Sisters. Lucy had not known what to expect of this
sisterhood and the appearance of the group disappointed her at first. The sisters sat about a cheerful
fire, like an orderly circle of seamstresses, tea cups
steaming, reciting poetry to one another for amusement as they worked on their quilting. She wondered
if she had been misled by Marie's description of the
group. These country girls with busy hands and open,
happy faces could not be labor organizers!

She was introduced. There were half a dozen
girls in the room, several of whom she recognized
from Hopewell's. Faith Lawrence was, like Marie,
from French Canada. Sophie Stewart and her sister
Margaret came from New Hampshire, while Beth
Wayne was a New Yorker. Kitty Tippits was from a
Massachusetts farm community. They greeted Lucy
pleasantly and made room for her in front of a
quilting frame on which a complicated pattern of
pieces was beginning to take shape. Lucy carried a
basket filled with scraps of calico she had saved.

"What have you brought us?" asked Faith,
smiling as she nodded toward the basket in Lucy's
hand.

A little shyly, Lucy displayed the bits of cloth
she could contribute to the project. "It isn't much, but
I think this maroon is pretty. And these blue
polka. . . ."

A fat, grey-haired woman appeared in the doorway. She was simply dressed in a plain brown coat; a
soft-brimmed hat bedecked with lace flowers was
perched on a head of frizzy hair.

"I'm leaving now," she said. "The house will be
empty for an hour or so." She caught sight of Lucy,
still clutching her swatches of maroon and blue
polka-dot cotton. "Good evening, my dear. You're
Lucy Shawn, I expect—Marie's friend from up the

mountain. She speaks well of you and you're welcome in my house."

But before Lucy could hurry to her feet and curtsy, the woman said good evening to them all and closed the door firmly.

"Who. . . ?"

"That's Mrs. Randolph," said Marie. "A good-hearted woman."

"Though a trifle abrupt. She's always in a hurry, you see." Sophie Stewart jabbed her needle into a fancy heart-shaped pin cushion.

"Remember the story Marie told you about the girl whose arm was caught in the cogs of the loom?" As she spoke, Violet riffled through the contents of her sewing basket. At the bottom she had hidden a leather-bound notebook. "Well, that girl was Mrs. Randolph's daughter, her only child. As you can imagine, Mrs. Randolph supports our movement—though you would hardly know her feelings from her abrupt ways."

"Better than most, she knows the price of mill work," added Margaret.

"We're safe here, but only for a while." Violet looked about her at the circle of young women. "Who would care to begin Lucy Shawn's education?"

"Have you heard of Salome Lincoln?" Margaret asked. "She was only fifteen but she led a strike of mill women in '29."

"The year before, in Dover where we come from, several hundred women walked off the job to protest the company's locking the yard gates when the bell rang," Sophie told her.

Like a chorister, another girl picked up the theme. "The company charged the operatives twelve-and-a-half cents to open it again. Talking on the job was forbidden. . . ."

"Sounds like McMahon's work," joked Marie.

"The blacklist from that turn-out stretched from Dover to Boston and back again!"

"A turn-out was the only honorable response those women had," Margaret told her, "and my, they did it up grand!"

"There were flags and a drum-and-fife band, banners and gunpowder explosions," caroled Sophie, her voice bubbling with excitement.

"Were they successful? Did the owners change the rules?" Lucy almost wished she had not asked the question. The mood of the group abruptly changed.

"No," admitted Violet. "Nothing was gained. There has never yet been a successful turn-out by women."

Marie added bitterly. "We're too easy to replace."

The Spindle Sisters stared at one another dispiritedly.

"Well, cheer up!" cried Violet, opening the leather notebook on her lap. "We will be successful when we are united. Now," she glanced at the book, "Sophie, tell us what you did this week to help the progress of the sisterhood."

"I spoke with some of the girls from Hathaway's. There was an accident there on Wednesday, so most of those I spoke to were receptive. They'll organize for safety, at any rate. And they'd like a shorter working day. Ten or eleven hours."

"At Fuller's everyone complains about the thirty-minute dinner break," said Faith. "For those girls, it's a far walk to their boarding houses."

"What about you, Lucy?" asked Kitty Tippits. "Can you say what troubles you the most about mill work?"

She thought a moment. "The hours are long, but

I have a good constitution and I am told that I will adjust. What troubles me is that we spy on one another. The system encourages us to betray each other. And the blacklisting seems . . ." she sought the perfect word, "immoral."

The others nodded their agreement. The conversation continued, until all had a chance to air their grievances. Lucy was pleased to know that she was not alone in her dissatisfaction. But afterwards, as she and Marie and Violet walked home, she expressed some doubts about the effectiveness of a small group of women meeting in secret to complain.

"Companionship makes the waiting bearable," said Violet.

"But what are we waiting for? How will we know when the time has come to make demands?" Unconsciously, Lucy lowered her voice as they neared Quinn's. The outside steps were crowded with laughing girls who had just returned from an evening of entertainment. Filled with good spirits, they were obviously unwilling to see their Saturday end a moment before it had to.

"Good evening, friend Lucy." It was Julia. How long had she been walking behind them? "You missed an excellent program of poems read by Mrs. Phelps from New York. Shakespeare's sonnets were presented most charmingly."

Before Lucy could respond, Julia's attention was diverted as some friends, approaching from the other direction, called out to her. They had been visiting the other mills and were full of gossip. Feeling conspicuous and guilty, Lucy hurried up the front steps between Marie and Violet.

Their arrival was greeted by a chorus of excited voices from the sitting room.

"It's Barbara, Lucy. She's dreadfully sick and calling for you."

"Mrs. Quinn is with her upstairs."

"Hurry, Lucy!"

"Hurry!"

Chapter 20

The following Sunday afternoon, Foster McMahon lazed away the hours on his front porch. Scratching his belly, he yawned as he idly pushed his heel against the plank floor, steadily maintaining the back and forth motion of the swing. The porch captured only a thin film of sunlight and the air was chill. But McMahon enjoyed the present view too much to go inside. He knew that the dark floors and paneling, shabby furniture and faded upholstery could kill his rosy spirits. Though the interior of the house was of his own devising, he hated its gloom.

Sipping a pewter tankard of hot, fermented cider, McMahon liked to watch the mill operatives strolling arm in arm along the river path after their Sunday dinners. Their animated voices carried on the air like the melodies of early spring. Many of them were Hopewell girls who looked his way demurely and sometimes smiled or waved their colored handkerchiefs.

Was there ever a luckier man than Foster McMahon? He doubted it. Martin Hopewell's general overseer was master of hundreds of young, dependent girls. As he patrolled the floors of the mill, they watched him with a mixture of fear and respect that he found enormously gratifying. Proud son of an immigrant, he wasn't at the top yet—but his feeling of self-importance told him he was quickly approaching a high station in life.

Since coming to the textile mill in September, McMahon had instituted marked changes that increased production and certainly fattened Hopewell's purse. Martin Hopewell responded generously, and rewarded McMahon well. This house, for instance, was the finest McMahon had ever lived in. Though the structure overlooking the river was old and seemed dark during the cold months, it was, nevertheless, the house of a family of substance. This satisfied May McMahon and she preened before the ladies of the town. Such respect was novel and eminently satisfying to a former parlor maid for whom English was a second and difficult language.

And Hopewell paid well. McMahon smiled to himself, thinking few men could afford to send their families to Boston for a week-long Christmas shopping spree as he had done. May and little Simon would return laden with packages, beaming at him, calling him wonderful, generous, a perfect husband and father.

Indeed it was a grand life, and McMahon intended to keep it that way.

He had plans for Simon. The boy had an agile mind and McMahon intended for his son to have the best education, the advantages of travel and the benefit of cultured friends. With such preparations, and with the push of an ambitious father, there was nothing Simon might not accomplish in a free country like America.

McMahon rapped his empty mug against the arm of the swing, and presently a maid appeared, carrying a refill in a steaming pitcher. McMahon scarcely no-

ticed her. Like him, she was Irish. But the maid had
arrived in Massachusetts only three months before
and to McMahon's mind, the wench still bore all the
ugly marks of her peasant upbringing.

McMahon knew all the signs well, though—thank
God—he had never set foot on Irish soil. He had been
born on shipboard. His mother died delivering him in
the overcrowded, stinking hold of a ship freighting
Irish, Scottish and Scandinavian poor to the land of
prosperity and hope. McMahon's father had worked
like a navvy to give his only son the semblance of an
education and he'd died, utterly worn out, at the age
of thirty. McMahon did not intend to let the sacrifices
of his parents be in vain. He had a good life now, but
it was going to get better, much better!

The operatives who were strolling about that afternoon looked as pretty as blossoms in their pink,
blue and white bonnets. Though the girls were
bundled up in heavy coats, McMahon pictured clearly
the shapely young bodies concealed beneath layers of
bulky wool. He knew such thoughts were dangerous
for him, and he tried to put them out of his mind. But
the thought persisted nonetheless. He wondered idly
whether other men were tortured by such lascivious
thoughts and, if they were, how they managed to
stifle their desires.

McMahon understood the risk of his desirous fantasies, but he could not still his impulses. Pretty girls
attracted him. Dreams would not suffice. The imper-
atives in his nature forced him to take risks and he
was not afraid to do so.

Still, there were the memories of bad episodes to
hold him back. In his recent past there were a number of sordid incidents. Only luck had saved him from
ruin. A schoolmaster's daughter in Dover had not
been able to identify him. An operative in Lowell was

too ashamed to speak of what he'd done to her. He had arrived in Amoset determined to control his animal imagination. But he had not been successful.

Emerging from the east, a scrim of high clouds dulled the sunlight on the porch. The bare, grey and black trees along the river bank grabbed at the heavens like the hands of the dead rearing up from the grave. In a landscape drained of color, the operatives were a bright relief. All country girls, they quickly sensed a change of weather. McMahon watched them hurry back to town, chasing and calling after one another with the gaiety of children. Only one young woman continued to walk away from Amoset. She approached the steps that led from the river path to McMahon's house and, to his surprise, turned abruptly toward the house.

It was Lucy Shawn and there could be no doubt that she had come to visit him.

From the bottom of the porch steps, she said, "Beg pardon for intruding on a Sunday, Mr. McMahon. May I have a word with you?" Unseen by McMahon, Lucy clutched her hands together behind her back as though they held a life line. If there had been some way to avoid this meeting, she would have avoided it gladly. Though Violet and Marie had emphatically tried to dissuade her from coming, she had refused to heed their warnings. Lucy felt she had no choice but to petition McMahon for help.

"Come onto the porch, Miss Shawn. What is your problem?" McMahon's usually pasty complexion was florid from the quantities of potent cider he had consumed. His black eyes were red-rimmed.

"It is about Miss Bolton, sir." Lucy did not budge from her post at the foot of the stairs.

"You'll have to speak louder, Miss Shawn. And come up here where I can see you properly." McMahon spoke lazily. Though lulled by an excess of drink, he sensed Lucy's unease and wished to worsen it by assuming an air of indifference.

Reluctantly mounting the stairs, Lucy declared, "I've come about Miss Bolton."

"She's been terminated." McMahon yawned without covering his mouth. "She is no longer my concern."

"But you see, sir, she is so very ill. . . ."

McMahon grinned. "Is that what you call it now?"

Lucy blushed and took a step back. She was as far from McMahon as she could be while still remaining on the porch, but even this arm's-length distance seemed too intimate. "She has nowhere to go, sir. No relatives or friends to care for her. There is a brother somewhere, but we've not been able to find him."

"It's no good playing on my sympathies, Miss Shawn. She won't be reinstated. I have my orders from Mr. Hopewell that girls like that one are to be terminated without notice. You know the rules as well as I." McMahon gulped down the last of his cider. Inside he felt the heat slide down his throat to the pit of his belly. "You're wasting your time."

In the sky above, thunderheads were mounting. The wind had risen and the river beyond the bending trees grew choppy as the waves kicked up. Lucy glanced fearfully at the threatening landscape, then turned to McMahon once again, her words coming quickly.

"Please, sir, I have a family on Cooper's Mountain. They will take Miss Bolton in and make her comfortable. My mother will care for her until. . . ." Lucy left off, embarrassed.

"I see." McMahon was thoughtful, distracted by forbidden thoughts, his emotions stirred by the wind that caught in Lucy's golden hair. Her clear discomfort, her scarcely disguised fear of him, was appealing. He was reminded once again of his great importance at Hopewell Mills. "So you want leave to take her up Cooper's Mountain. Is that correct?"

"May I please, Mr. McMahon?" Strands of golden hair swept across Lucy's mouth and she pushed them back impatiently. "I will miss one day of work, but only that. And I swear I will make it up in some way."

McMahon ruminated, clicking his false teeth unconsciously. Lucy reminded him of that pretty operative in Lowell. They had the same corn silk hair, fine as a baby's. He admired that fineness, the way it twisted away from the pins beneath her bonnet. The wind made it seem alive, like a rare soft thing.

"Mr. McMahon?"

All at once the overseer was cross and edgy. He remembered the blood-dampened hair of the Lowell operative, remembered the blank, cold look in her sightless eyes after he was done with her, and a voice of caution bellowed in his head.

"Sir?"

"Come in the house, Miss Shawn. It is going to rain."

She stepped back, starting down a step. "No. I have to go."

McMahon grabbed her, his fingers easily encircling her delicate wrist. "You're not afraid, are you?"

The question was a challenge to Lucy. She did not dare say yes, that she feared him. She kept silent, staring at the ground defiantly.

"Come along. There will be a fire in the drawing room."

There was not. The room, instead, was dark and cold as a mausoleum. When McMahon rang the bell for a servant, no one came.

"Sit down, sit down," he ordered Lucy. Heavy raindrops exploded against the window glass. Upstairs an unlatched shutter banged in the wind. A bolt of lightning striking the ground a mile away illuminated the drawing room. "Sit down!" McMahon demanded and this time he pointed at a worn love seat in the corner.

Perching on the seat like a bird about to fly, Lucy asked, "May I go up the mountain, Mr. McMahon?" She hoped a direct question might bring an unequivocal response. She would run then—run though the rain fell and the lightning struck her down.

McMahon smiled, showing yellow false teeth. "I'm not sure," he drawled.

Outside the closed drawing room door there was a commotion of voices speaking Gaelic. The Irish maid hurried in, apologizing. While McMahon watched in irritation, the maid laid the fire and lighted it. The wood was damp and refused to ignite. The woman tried again, and once more failed.

Lucy could wait no longer. Rising, she hurried to the door. "I must go, Mr. McMahon. My friends know where I am and they expect me back by now. I wouldn't want them to worry. They'd be sure to send someone after me."

McMahon shoved the inept maid away from the fire and grabbed the matches from her as she staggered backwards. When she scurried from the room, Lucy tried to follow, but McMahon's raised voice stopped her. "You'll get your leave on one condition only."

Forgetting all fears for a moment, Lucy halted, smiling uncertainly.

Closing the door, McMahon turned to face Lucy, blocking her only escape. Her smile fled. "Come here to me, Lucy Shawn." Unwillingly, she stepped toward him. "Closer. Closer. That's better." McMahon's eyes narrowed. Red firelight danced demonically in the depths of their blackness. "Remove your little bonnet, Lucy."

"Sir?"

"Do as I say."

She obeyed with trembling fingers.

"Ah. And now, remove the pins from your hair."

The glistening silver-blonde hair, washed that morning before church, fell like gossamer about Lucy's shoulders. McMahon reached behind her head and drew her close to him. Her eyes inches from his face, she refused to look at him. Her eyes focused instead on the ingrown hairs that pimpled his cheeks.

"One small kiss, Lucy. Don't be afraid. I won't hurt you. I'm too smart for that now. Just one little kiss and you can have your day's leave from Hopewell Mills. Only one kiss."

Perhaps he took her silence for assent. Perhaps he did not care. All at once, his cidery mouth was on hers, his lips apart, his thick tongue probing, pushing against hers. Gasping and gagging, she shoved him away and fumbled at the doorknob. It stuck. Then the door opened suddenly, throwing her off-balance, almost into McMahon's arms.

He was laughing at her panicked flight. As she raced across the entrance foyer and stumbled out onto the rain-washed porch, she heard his voice calling after her, a voice filled with mocking laughter. She raced through the downpour, her silken hair pasted to her face with tears of shame, while the driving storm filled her kiss-poisoned mouth with a thousand tongues of rain.

Chapter 21

Lucy could not forget how McMahon's lips felt against hers. His saliva, mingling with her own, tainted and sickened her. On the embankment halfway home, she knelt to vomit until she was weak and her throat was raw. For hours afterward, she felt occasional waves of nausea. Early the next morning, as she and Barbara walked the eight miles to the Shawn cabin through an icy rain, she still felt McMahon's presence as if his lecherous spirit pursued her. An evil miasma seemed to linger in the hollows and invade the hills of her childhood home.

Beside her, Barbara Bolton trudged like one condemned, never glancing up from the rutted muddy road at her feet. They didn't climb directly up Cooper's Mountain, but took the longer and less exhausting route to the cabin. Yet even the easier trail was agony for Barbara. Though only a girl, the trials of the last weeks had etched lines of old age across Barbara's youthful brow. Thin as she was, she stooped like an old woman. Sometimes she was overcome by weakness and lost even the strength to hold up her umbrella. The handle almost slipped from her grasp before Lucy noticed and helped her. Barbara walked with the sleet driving against the back of her neck, appearing oblivious to the added discomfort.

Somehow, the sight of this pitiful young woman whom she had chosen to defend helped mitigate the shame Lucy felt. She was too ruthlessly honest to hide the truth from herself. She had permitted McMahon's foul kiss in order to obtain permission for a day's absence from the mill. It was a simple equation. She had tarried near McMahon when she might easily have run. In a sense this meant she had complied with him, participating in the bargain willingly. It was a kind of prostitution, and well she knew it.

Though they left Quinn's boarding house before dawn, the two made slow progress up Cooper's Mountain. It was almost noon when they reached the farm. In the two months since Lucy had been gone, subtle changes had come over the place. Or was it only the harshness of the season that made the house and barn look shabby and neglected? The trellis where roses grew over the front windows in summertime was broken. Beside the pump a wooden bucket lay, forgotten, on its side. From the barn Lucy heard the steady thudding sound of someone chopping firewood.

Lucy's heart beat faster; her step quickened. She had not expected to see her father, and though a part of her feared he would be angry, she was eager for the sight of him. Before this moment, she had not dared consider how much she missed his strength and wise counsel. She recalled McMahon, and prayed her father would not read her shameful secret in her eyes.

Grabbing Barbara's hand, Lucy pulled her companion along, calling out as she did, "Mama! Papa! It's me, Lucy! I've come home!"

The door of the little, saltbox-style farmhouse flew open. Helen Shawn stood at the top of the steps.

A lovely smile spread across her face, erasing for a moment all signs of worry and fatigue. She opened her arms. Dropping Barbara's valise, Lucy ran to her mother and was held tightly.

Glancing over her daughter's fair head, Helen saw Barbara standing uncertainly in the clearing. Almost obscured by rain, the girl appeared as a featureless, grey-skirted body left to stand alone.

"Suzannah?" Helen called, mistaking the girl for Lucy's former friend.

"No, Mama. Barbara." Lucy withdrew quickly from her mother's embrace and rushed to help her friend; she was only just in time. Barbara collapsed in Lucy's arms.

In a moment, Helen was at Lucy's side, helping her carry Barbara into the main room of the farmhouse. There was a crackling fire in the stone fireplace. A black iron kettle hung to one side of the blaze, its steam redolent of simmering meat and vegetables. Cooling on the table were loaves of crusty, aromatic bread.

While Helen quickly loosened Barbara's clothing and made her comfortable, her daughter explained the situation.

"She had nowhere to go. I could not. . . ."

"You did right, Daughter." Helen patted Lucy's damp, silver-gold hair gently. Slipping her work-worn hands beneath Lucy's chin, the mother tilted up the girl's face to gaze at the features. "You're a good girl, Lucy. And I've missed you. Are you home to stay?"

Lucy shook her head. "I must be back at Mrs. Quinn's by ten tonight." Helen tried to hide her disappointment. "I'm sorry, Mama. But I must go back. My life is there now."

"Yes." Helen rose slowly to her feet and turned to Barbara. Without a word Lucy joined her mother, and together they helped Barbara onto Talley's narrow bed in a corner. It was the only bed in the room. Nearby, a curtained doorway led to Helen and James' room, and above was the loft once shared by Ingrid and Lucy. Gently, skillfully, Helen prodded Barbara's swollen belly.

"She told you she was with child?"

"No. But everyone knows. There was a young man. . . ."

Helen went to the door and called, "Talley! I need you!" Returning to the bedside, she told her daughter, "She is not carrying a child, Lucy. There is something inside her, though. A growth, I think, in her womanly parts."

Tally burst into the room, bringing rainwater and mud with him. "You've come back!" he cried, sounding so disappointed that, in spite of her worry, Lucy had to laugh aloud.

She cuffed him gently on the chin. "You'll be happy to know that I am not staying, little brother."

He was sheepish. "I only meant . . . I like to visit you in Amoset—don't you see?" He hugged her hard, then stepped back and looked around. "Did you bring me anything? An orange, maybe?"

"You're a greedy no-good, Talleyrand Shawn!" his mother scolded without conviction.

"Aw, Mama. . . ." He twisted his body away from Lucy and pouted, his skinny arms folded across his chest. Thick silvery hair fell into his eyes.

"Never mind that!" Helen said, ignoring the stubbornly set mouth and the belligerent stance. She had seen too many of Talley's sullen demonstrations of displeasure to be much impressed by yet another. "You must run a message for me, down to Edythe Whittington's."

"Crazy Edythe?" Talley jumped back and yelped

as though he had been bitten. "That old bat is a witch! I heard she cast a spell on. . . ."

"Nonsense. She's just a poor old woman who's been cheated!"

"I don't wanna!"

"You're a willful boy, Talleyrand Shawn. You'll do as you're told or I'll take a stick to you." Grabbing him by the shoulders, Helen propelled him to the door. "Tell her there is female sickness bad up here. She's wise enough to know, but tell her to come quickly. Make sure you're polite or likely she won't come. Tell her Helen Hildebrand says please. Can you remember that—Please!"

Talleyrand stuck out his tongue, but it was clear he was satisfied with the importance of his mission. Donning his wool coat and hat, he ran out quickly.

"What may I do, Mama?" asked Lucy when her brother was gone.

"Go up to the loft and change into dry clothes before you come down sick as well. Your old things are in Grandpa Hildebrand's old trunk." As Lucy stepped up to the ladder, Helen added, "Go softly, Daughter. Ingrid's sleeping." She sighed. "That little one is ailing, too."

The loft, only ten-feet wide, was ventilated by a single, small window now closely shuttered to keep out the rain. For as long as Lucy could recall this had been a special place to her. Here, she had slept and dreamed and wondered about the world, speculating what life might hold for her. She knew every inch— the mouse holes in the corner, the section of roof that always leaked no matter how James Shawn repaired it, the fanciful whorls in the unpainted plank walls, where the wood grain took the shapes of horses' heads and fabulous coastlines.

"I thought I heard your voice. Have you come

home to stay, Lucy?" In the corner bed, Ingrid raised herself and rested on her elbows. Hers was a tiny rosebud face, lovely and pale.

Lucy hugged her and almost wept. Had Ingrid's body always been so full of points and edges? When the young girl sighed, her lungs groaned.

"You are supposed to be asleep," Lucy whispered. Pushing the seven-year-old girl gently back against the pillow, Lucy drew the old patchwork coverlet close about her chin.

Ingrid made a little face. "I always have to rest. When everyone is laughing downstairs, I have to stay up here. It isn't fair, Lucy, is it? You didn't rest all the time when you were seven!" Ingrid tried to sit up again but Lucy was firm and her sister had no strength to argue. "Tell me about Amoset, Lucy. Is the mill exciting? You're still wearing your old dress. I thought you would make lots of money and be very fancy." Obviously Ingrid was disappointed that her sister had not been wonderfully transfigured by city influences.

Lucy chuckled softly as she slipped out of her wet clothes. "I have plenty of dresses, Ingrid. But I find better things to do with my money than fritter it away on gowns and such." Dressed only in her woolen shift, Lucy dug through Grandpa Hildebrand's trunk for something warm to put on while her wet clothes dried. She found a heavy sack dress that once had been too large for her. Now it was snug across the hips and short enough to show her ankles. Normally, Lucy would have been too proud to wear such a rag. But it would cover her for a few hours, and she was grateful for the warmth of the heavy cloth. Though the loft was warm enough, she had already begun to shiver. Hastily she dried her hair with a frayed shawl.

"How will you spend your wages?" Ingrid asked Lucy as she finished drying herself.

For an answer, Lucy dug into the pocket of her wet dress and withdrew a little leather pouch in which she had hoarded a few coins. It was all she had been able to save in two months. "These are for Mama."

Ingrid was impressed. "May I hold them?"

But before Lucy could hand them to her sister, Helen interrupted, calling from the foot of the loft ladder. "I hear you two chattering. Come down, Lucy. Bring your wet things or they will not dry. Let the baby rest."

Ingrid made a face and whispered, "Will I always be a baby? Lucy, do you think I will ever grow up like you?"

Lucy hugged her sister tightly. Feeling a deep and boundless affection for her sister, Lucy turned her face away, knowing her expression might contradict her own words. "Of course you will! Everyone grows up, little goose. The only thing wrong with you is weak lungs, and that's why Mama wants you to rest. Rest is the only cure."

Coming downstairs a few moments later, Lucy saw that Helen had placed warm compresses on Barbara's distended belly. Lucy held the girl's head against the crook of her arm as she spooned broth into her mouth.

"There's soup for you on the table, Daughter. And some for your papa as well." Seeing the expression on Lucy's face, Helen added, "No need to be afraid, Lucy. He loves you too much to be angry forever. You have to see him. Take my shawl and go into the barn."

Lucy crossed the wet yard quickly but, just inside the old barn, she stopped uncertainly. The smell

of animals and sawdust and feed were sweet to her.
The hound, Billa, ambled to her side, wriggling her
hind end in paroxysms of joy at the reunion. As Lucy
bent to pat the dog's grey muzzle, James turned and
saw her.

"It's you," he said. Nodding once, he returned to
his chores. Chips of wood flew like white sparks in
the dim barn.

Lucy loved her father so much at that moment
that the hurt of it lodged in her throat and ached. He
was just as she remembered him—tall, strong as a
tree, rangy and blond. Lucy was seven years old
when Talley was born. For all those seven years, she
had been the center of attention, blessed with the full
warmth of her father's care. Those times had given
permanent shape and substance to her love and no
amount of time, no wisdom or disillusionment could
change what she felt.

But she did not know what to say.

"I am not home to stay, Father." She paused, seeking a response that was not forthcoming. "I have
brought a friend, a sick girl named Barbara Bolton
who has no other friends or family."

"Hopewell lets you off on Mondays?"

She was glad his back was turned. When Lucy
was little, she had thought her father could read in
her eyes the deepest secrets of her soul. She had
never tried to keep anything from him because she
was convinced that deceit was impossible. Though
she now knew it to be a childish fancy, she found
herself imagining that McMahon's kiss was a blood-
stain upon her lips. Her father would see it there and
never forgive her.

"It's not so bad at the mill, Papa."

"You're lying. I can always tell." He buried the
ax in a log. "Help me stack this. Then you can take an

armload in to your mother." He looked at her closely, staring until she almost cringed in fear of what he saw.

"You're growing up, Lucy." He spoke without emotion; he was simply stating a fact.

"This old dress is too small."

"How old are you now?"

"Sixteen."

"Your mother was fourteen when I married her."

"I'll never marry," Lucy replied firmly, thinking again of McMahon's kiss.

James Shawn laughed. "Hold out your arms, Spinster-girl," he said and began to load her with kindling. "I'm going back to Meredith tonight. I'll take you in the wagon as far as Amoset if you like."

"Father, yes!" she cried, and so great was her happiness that she let drop her armload of kindling so she could hug him. "You have forgiven me, then?"

He held her away from him. "You're a grown girl, Lucy. You must decide for yourself what you do. But I will always hate those mills. That wretched city is full of wage slaves. . . ."

"We aren't slaves!"

"No?" He studied her, then snorted to himself and said softly, almost as if he had figured out a difficult puzzle, "Of course! Men like Hopewell wouldn't allow you to discuss such questions. Still—" And his voice grew hard, "I cannot respect your willingness to lose your liberty for love of money. . . ."

"I am not a slave and I do not love money!" Lucy knelt to pick up the scattered kindling. "I work for a reason and you should know, Father. Ingrid is sick. She needs medicine that is costly. Oh, you don't want to talk about it, but you know it's true. And what of Talleyrand? He must be educated."

James laughed at the mention of his son and education in the same breath. "That lad? He's as wild as wind and fire, and just as hard to manage! I expect to hear any day he's gone to sea like my brother Willy." Though William Shawn's name inevitably came up in any conversation related to recklessness and wild living, Lucy had never known her uncle. So far as she knew, he had not been heard from during her lifetime.

Just then they heard Talleyrand's voice, as the boy came splashing through the puddles toward the house. "She's coming!" he cried. "Crazy Edythe's coming!"

James and Lucy hurried out into the yard just as the old woman appeared from the woods. Her mass of white hair hung down across her back in two thick braids. Over her body she wore a great, loose garment of dark wool that was both coat and dress, reaching just below the knees. Under this she wore a pair of man's breeches tucked into a pair of huge boots. She carried a small sack slung over her shoulder.

"She's come to help Barbara, the girl who came up with me," Lucy explained to her father. Watching Crazy Edythe enter the house, Lucy asked, "Will you come inside, Father?"

He shook his head. " 'Tis women's business, this." He was about to return to the barn when a thought occurred to him. "As to how you spend your money, I don't want it. You are grown in some ways, Lucy, young in others. You don't know how it grieves a man's dignity to take money from a woman."

With that remark, James Shawn turned to his chopping again. Lucy watched only a moment before she too turned away, trudging wordlessly to the house with her heavy load of kindling.

Inside the cabin, the smell of Crazy Edythe was

enough to make Lucy fall back against the door. Her arms went weak and she almost dropped the armload of kindling again. She could not suppress a little noise of horrified disgust. Helen Shawn, standing at Barbara's bedside next to the old woman, silenced Lucy with an angry gesture.

"What can you tell, Miss Whittington?" Helen asked the old woman.

Crazy Edythe did not answer. As Lucy crept near, she saw the twisted hands, with fingers gnarled as old turnips, kneading and stroking Barbara's belly. When the girl sighed and moaned, Edythe put a drop of potion on Barbara's tongue. The medicine seemed to soothe her pain, but the prodding and kneading continued. Several times, Edythe put her ear to the swollen abdomen as if the girl's ailment could be communicated in some audible way.

After what seemed like an interminable period of diagnosis, Edythe withdrew from the bedside and, without saying a word, served herself a cup of soup from the pot on the fire. Her face, all nose and chin and light, bulbous eyes, was directed first at Lucy, then at Talley cowering, plainly curious, in the corner. The old woman turned again to Lucy and then to Helen.

She shook her head and her lower lip protruded dismally. Her voice scratched the cabin's silence. " 'Tis Death that grows inside her. He spoke to me and said it won't be long."

Chapter 22

Lucy Shawn came down from Cooper's Mountain full of rage. She knew the death growing in Barbara's womb was not related to the operatives' work, yet Lucy could not keep them apart in her mind. Some obscure logic linked the spying Julia, Martin Hopewell, McMahon and Mrs. Quinn. All seemed somehow responsible for Barbara's illness. Coming down from the mountain, Lucy returned at once to the weaving room and life in the boarding house. But now, she felt, she had a cause. Her permanent rage—blind though it might be—sealed her dedication to the work of the Spindle Sisters.

The first big snow came to Amoset in mid-December. In the dense quiet, Lucy awakened before four and she crept from her bed to watch the heavy flakes fall silently on the town. She was consumed with sadness as she thought of her home surrounded by the wild, wide stretches of white woods, the expanses of fresh snow marked only by bird scribblings. To herself, in the most private and protected corner of her heart, she confessed how much she hated the city of Amoset and the work in the mill. In less than an hour, she must be about her assigned tasks though her fingers and feet were so cold they felt numb. Barbara's looms were her responsibility now, and they terrified her. She had been advanced too quickly to do the job well. Several times during her first week minding the looms, she had failed to notice a break in the thread. The old-fashioned loom had clacked-in several tight rows that she later had to pick out with frozen fingers.

The mill work frightened her, but the more she despised it, the more she was determined to conquer its tyranny. Hating the meanness she encountered everywhere, her gorge rose whenever McMahon's pinched eyes glowed at her. But she knew from her friends Violet and Marie that it was possible to rise above the demeaning work and the tenement living, to live her Amoset years in such a way that she would be a better person for the rigorous experience.

She wore her coat all that morning and when the Saturday half-day bell rang at one, she set out to face the bitter cold. Clutching her pay envelope in the depths of her pocket, she trudged home between Violet and Marie. After a midday meal of rabbit and dumpling stew, all Lucy wanted was to huddle by herself, inches from the fire, until bedtime came.

Violet refused to permit Lucy her retreat. "It's your own fault, Lucy Shawn, for not shedding that heavy coat. You can sit by the fire all afternoon, but you won't feel as warm as you will if you come with us."

Violet grabbed one arm, laughing, while Marie took the other. Almost dragging Lucy, they separated her from the fire.

"You said you love to skate," said Violet, helping Lucy into the coat she had worn all that morning.

"Now here's your chance!" Marie chimed in. She wrapped a long, fringed scarf about Lucy's head until only her blue eyes showed. Then Marie handed her a pair of wooden skates. "I found these in your trunk."

Lucy looked at her friends, at the skates swinging from her hand. They were right, of course. She would be happier after skating on the pond. The brisk exercise would get her mind off the cold and the work, and help her tear her thoughts from poor, dying Barbara.

The pond, frosted white, lay in a hollow of low, white hills that rose against a white sky. Branches of leafless trees sketched charcoal scribble-lines against this monochromatic scene, and the clustered pines and firs added pale tints of bluish-green. Around the periphery of the three-acre pond were bonfires. Those who were not skating warmed themselves by the fires and socialized by the heat of the glowing brands. Peddlers were everywhere, offering hot drinks and roasted chestnuts. On the ice the skaters flew by, quick swatches of flying color, like unexpected winter birds.

Lucy strapped on her skates eagerly and glided onto the ice. There had been several weeks of severe, unremitting cold before the snowstorm and the pond was solidly frozen. Someone had swept away the snow from a large area and the ice surface, scarcely cut, was ideal for an excellent skater like Lucy. For just a moment she was a bit unsteady, but her sense of balance returned quickly as she glided along, swinging her arms. She was impatient with the slower pace of Violet and Marie and soon broke from them to do a turn. The fringed ends of her maroon scarf flew. Her cheeks and nose tingled, but inside she was warmer than she had been all day. As the tension of mill work left her arms and legs, her movements on the ice became more graceful. Along the bank the onlookers stopped talking and watched with admiration as Lucy skimmed across the ice. She came daringly close to the far end of the pond where an underground spring, bubbling up from below, made the ice treacherously thin. To mark this dangerous spot, the skaters had set out bales of hay as markers.

"Race you!" cried Lucy, charging forward. Violet laughed. Grabbing Marie's hand, she pursued Lucy down the ice.

Later the ice became too crowded and Lucy had to give up her showy, energetic skating. While she waited for the crowd to thin, she and her friends chatted and laughed with other girls around the fires. The favorite topic of the day was a public meeting being planned at the Downriver Unitarian Church. The great labor organizer and preacher Salome Lincoln would be at the church to tell about her experiences. The operatives all expressed amazement that the owners would permit such an inflammatory meeting to take place.

"To forbid it would be to subvert the Constitution, which permits assemblies," declared Lucy with a confidence that made everyone listen. "The owners must appear law-abiding and agreeable, or they will lose their eager and plentiful labor force. But our numbers are not as great as they would believe. Though the owners say many others could do our work, perhaps there are not so many healthy women who can work thirteen and fourteen hours a day."

A masculine voice commented from the shadows. "The tide of immigrants swells each year. If you are of a mind to bargain, you had best do it now. The poor of Europe, when they get here, will work longer hours and for less pay than you Yankee women." A young man, probably in his mid-twenties, stepped closer to the fire where the operatives could see him. Of medium height and build, he had a scholarly look

about him that marked him as a gentleman decidedly
different from the laboring class. "Permit me to intro-
duce myself. I have lately come here to Amoset from
Pennsylvania. My name is Thomas Kilmaine and I am
a newspaperman." Though he spoke to the group, Kilmaine obviously addressed his remarks—and his argu-
ments—toward Lucy Shawn.

"The conditions in Amoset are as bad as anywhere in New England. Yet the mill operatives here
seem determined to find contentment in overwork and
inhumane conditions."

"If you are encouraging us to turn-out, you waste
your breath, Mr. Kilmaine," Lucy responded. "When
the time is right, mill operatives in Amoset will certainly rise up and state their demands. But to act prematurely, on the prompting of one who has nothing
materially to lose by the action . . . that would be
foolish. Don't you agree, Mr. Kilmaine?" Lucy did not
smile. Since her experience with McMahon, she had
come to the conclusion she did not care for men at all
and, given the choice, she avoided their company entirely. She resented Kilmaine's intrusion on a pleasant
skating party. Glancing over her shoulder, she hoped
to see that the crowd had dispersed. But the ice was
still crowded. Rather than endure another round of
argument, however, she excused herself and made her
way onto the busy pond.

Kilmaine joined her a moment later.

"I fear I may have offended you, Miss Shawn."

"Not at all. However, I came to skate and not to
argue."

Their combined breath formed a single cloud
about their heads. Lucy, constrained by the crowd,
was obliged to skate slowly, and Kilmaine easily kept
pace with her.

"Forgive me for being argumentative, Miss

Shawn. Be assured, I did not in any way wish to offend you. However, argument seems to be an occupational hazard for newspapermen."

"You make your living stirring up trouble. Is that what you mean to say?" Before he could defend himself, Lucy stopped skating and faced Kilmaine steadily. "Make no mistake," she said as if disciplining Talleyrand, "if we move at the wrong time, our organizing efforts will be squashed for good. Mark you the turn-outs that have taken place in Dover and elsewhere. In none of those instances did the owners meet the workers' demands. In some cases, operatives actually returned to work for less pay than before. Can you imagine such a thing, Mr. Kilmaine? Believe me, great are the powers of intimidation in mill towns." So saying, Lucy skated off briskly and disappeared in the crowd, leaving behind a bemused and vaguely disturbed Thomas Kilmaine. But after a moment's thought, he darted after her, his face flushed.

"Miss Shawn," he called as he caught up with her once again, "the operatives are fortunate indeed to have such a perspicacious leader as yourself."

Lucy laughed in spite of herself. "I've only just come to Amoset myself, sir." But the laugh betrayed her youth. Clearly, she could not be more than sixteen, and that realization seemed to startle Kilmaine. He looked at her more searchingly as if doubting what his senses told him. The conversation that ensued resembled an interrogation: he asked questions and she answered him. His manner had become avuncular.

But Lucy, too, was guessing and she finally decided that Thomas Kilmaine was older than he looked. She decided on thirty.

She also discovered she was beginning to enjoy herself with Thomas Kilmaine. His company was a distraction. The worries that had pursued her through every corridor of the past dreary days were banished at last. In some ways Kilmaine seemed like family to her. She heard herself telling him things she might have told her father had he been responsive to her talk about the mill. But always, their conversation circled back to its origins.

"You've been with Hopewell less than a season and yet you grasp the realities of the situation here in a way that others never will. Like it or not, you are the stuff of leadership, Lucy Shawn."

They were sitting on the hay bales at the edge of the skating arena. Lucy tried to ignore Kilmaine's intense expression by looking away, but she could not dismiss his words. Instinct told her his observations were true. Already her outspoken views had enlarged her circle of acquaintances. Operatives from many mills knew her by name, and she was a great favorite among the children who worked in the factories.

"If I can be of any assistance to you, Miss Shawn. . . ."

"There's Eben Hopewell," she interrupted with a cry of surprise. "I heard he had gone off somewhere, perhaps to sea. And look who is with him!"

The newspaperman chuckled, amused by Lucy's girlish exclamation. "Eben Hopewell has been to the Cape, to a special place for people with nervous disorders," Kilmaine warned, trying to draw Lucy's attention away from the young man. Finding that she would not be distracted, he contented himself with playing the role of informer. "The man beside him does not have a name, so far as I know. I've only heard him called India Man."

Lucy clapped her hands together gleefully. Seeing a red-turbaned Hindu right there beside a skating pond in Amoset, Lucy displayed her giddy delight. Kilmaine could not take his eyes from her. The maroon scarf was draped loosely about her shoulders and her bonnet was thrown back. Sunshine-colored hair, thick, long and full of wild curls, haloed her glowing face.

"But what is he doing here, of all places?" Lucy demanded.

"I think he cares for the Hopewell boy." Kilmaine used the word boy with pointed condescension. "The India Man is a sort of guardian or bodyguard, I believe."

Lucy dismissed the explanation with a laugh. "Eben Hopewell needs no guardian. Look there. He's strapping on his skates."

Now that the ice was clear of all but a few skaters, Eben was going to take his turn. Feeling a certain empathy, Lucy realized that Eben wanted to avoid drawing attention to himself. Why come at all, she wondered, if he wanted to avoid the public eye? And in the company of that exotic India Man! She knew the answer to her question, and the knowledge pricked her heart with sympathy. Lonely, he sought at least the illusion of congeniality, even as the party all about him was ending.

"Do you know Eben Hopewell, Miss Shawn?"

"A little."

"Well, he clearly intends to speak to you. Do you wish me to withdraw?"

Without thinking, Lucy responded precisely as she might have answered one of Talley's questions. "Of course not! Don't be so stuffy!"

Lucy's hand clapped over her mouth, and there was dead silence for a moment before she and Kilmaine began to laugh. The scene, as Eben approached, might have been a merry party of old, affectionate friends. But the young Hopewell ignored

Kilmaine altogether as he glided to a smooth, steady stop before Lucy.

"May I have the honor of being your partner on the ice, Miss Shawn?"

Slowly, as if the effort hurt her, Lucy raised her eyes to survey the full height of him. The long legs in well-cut flannels, the dark grey coat, cut away at a slim waist to reveal a snug vest and ruffled shirt front—all were in the lastest, best English style. But it was not the clothes she studied. The broad shoulders, longish dark hair, the sensual, sardonic mouth and the brooding expression of his dark brow held her unwillingly fascinated. She offered her hand and Eben Hopewell drew her smoothly away across the ice.

Eben had changed. Just being near him told her he was fundamentally altered from the man who had tried to keep her company at the Harvest Bonfire. The change unnerved her. She was uneasy, fully conscious of the picture she and Eben Hopewell presented skating on the deserted ice. Over her shoulder she saw Thomas Kilmaine waiting for her by the hay bales. And there, by one of the bonfires, were Marie and Violet. They and a dozen others were staring at her, at Lucy Shawn skating with Eben Hopewell. It was a moment the town would talk about for weeks.

Once, only once, did she dare to glance again at the dark man beside her. He was staring down at her with an inscrutable expression that was a mixture of pain and passion, and something else she did not understand. His eyes were haunted. She could not look away immediately. Something held her, linking her gaze to his. All trace of the boy was gone. The face was now that of a man, full of angles and planes. Lucy sensed he carried secrets in him, like the shadows of a former life. She feared him and yet her sympathies were with him in a way she could not explain.

At last she found her voice. "I have to go." She stared at his shoulder.

"Finish the circle."

"No, I. . . ." She stepped away but his hand still held her wrist. She almost lost her balance on the ice as he pulled her close. At last she gave in. They skated on in silence.

From the hill Foster McMahon watched the scene and even at that considerable distance, he could feel the force of those two wills in opposition. He recalled Lucy's lips and, as she skated beside Eben, McMahon imagined he could see the outline of her thigh against the woolen skirt. As little as this aroused him. But he tore himself away from the pond scene and headed toward home, making an effort to distract himself.

It was unfair, he thought, that Lucy Shawn should have this effect on him. For several months, his life had been progressing smoothly toward security, even prosperity. Now, because of Lucy Shawn, familiar, craven feelings returned to him again. He was excited and the heat of his flesh crowded uncomfortably against his leg. With the heel of his hand he tried to hide this embarrassing display, but even his own touch through layers of cotton and wool was titillating.

For a quarter of a mile he walked briskly, trying to ignore the urgency of his desire. But after a time it became too difficult for him to wipe the sensual images from his mind. He succumbed to feeling and, without a second thought, turned his footsteps toward the crowded town.

It was Saturday evening. Outside the Amoset Opera House a line of operatives stood waiting patiently before the box office. McMahon loitered across the street in the shadow of a shop awning, his hat turned down to obscure his brooding face. Like a small-eyed beast of prey, he stared at every girl, searching for the one he wanted. Needed! He would never be able to rest unless he got Lucy Shawn out of his mind, and he knew only one way to accomplish this. Unsatisfied, he hurried away from the theater to a less populated section of town where girls strolled about unaccompanied, making their way from the lending library to the Lyceum or home to their boarding houses.

The girl he wanted was stopped near a stone wall. She had piled her library books on a low pillar while she stooped to button her boots. McMahon could not see her face but he did not care whether she was ugly or beautiful. She was young and alone, and that was enough. Coming behind her silently, he took her by surprise, covered her mouth with his hand and wrenched her back into the alley by the library. She did not have the opportunity to scream. Struggling was futile against his superior strength. Shoving her against the wall, McMahon wrenched up a handful of her skirt and made a wad of cloth the size of his fist to shove into her mouth. Gagged and helpless, she stared at him. And, before he touched her body, McMahon returned her gaze, relishing the primitive fear in her eyes. His big hand pressed against her throat, pinning her. Before he hurt her, he took a fistful of the poor girl's hair and, pressing his face into the richness of it, inhaled the bouquet of spun gold.

PART V

Chapter 23

Palermo, Sicily

"So you see, my dears, I have miraculously recovered!"

Sarah Hopewell stared at her sister in disbelief. Bronwyn Kirkhaven was laughing. Obviously she was delighted by her sister's dumbfounded reaction. In a modish afternoon dress of rose silk, Bronwyn exuded health and vitality, far from the deathly state that Sarah and Suzannah had been led to expect. A number of guests were assembled in the sunlit room and all seemed delighted at the success of Bonwyn's charade.

"Would you have preferred to find me on my deathbed, Sarah?" Bronwyn chided, her tone softening as she realized her sister's feelings had really been hurt. Suzannah answered quickly for her mother.

"Oh, no, Aunt!" Suzannah hugged Bronwyn quickly. "My mother is amazed, that is all. And so am I!"

Bronwyn smiled at the girl affectionately. "Dear child, you are my bonus. I never expected your father to permit. . . ."

Finding her voice at last, Sarah interrupted. "Of

course I am glad to find you well. How can you doubt it, Bronwyn? But I know you and there is something about this entire situation that prompts my distrust. I expected to find you ailing, perhaps even dead. Instead you are . . . like this. . . ." Sarah blinked back tears and mumbled in confusion. The tiresome voyage from Naples to Palermo had left her with nerves of glass.

Further discussion was postponed by the entrance of a serving maid into the salon. Bronwyn, Suzannah and Sarah turned their full attention to the serving of a sumptuous, English-style tea. All the while, Suzannah gazed about curiously, hardly believing she was actually here and that her aunt had carried off a stunt so entirely in keeping with her reputation. Her mind flashed back to Amoset—to the tense days before their hectic departure. Once Suzannah's father had decided to send her to Sicily, the time had passed in quick, confused planning. Last minute fittings and purchases were made in a flurry of haste. The list of necessities seemed endless and all had to be found in an instant. Suzannah had scarcely closed her traveling box before she was rushed out of Amoset. There had only just been time to tell Travis Paine of her departure. And, instead of taking this as bad news, Travis had been delighted. He would be studying in Rome at the same time, he informed her, and before her departure, they made plans to meet in Palermo.

Suzannah glanced to her right as she opened the heavy damask serviette on the lap of her velvet traveling dress. Her eyes met those of Travis Paine as he pulled up his chair beside her. They smiled at one another and her heart beat so fast she felt the pulse in her tightening throat. She rejoiced at how craftily her father had been fooled. Later, there would be time for worry and guilt. For now, the exhilarating possibilities of the present occupied her. For two weeks Travis would be with her at Villa Dolce; for a fortnight their affection for one another would be free to grow in the permissive environment of Bronwyn's sophisticated, slightly decadent palazzo.

She looked again at Travis as he accepted a small cup of aromatic, Sicilian coffee from Bronwyn. Suzannah's aunt was inquiring about Travis' studies, but Suzannah hardly paid any attention to what they were saying. But something made Delio, Duke of Monteleone, and his younger brother Roberto laugh and Suzannah noted with amazement that Travis turned scarlet. Beside the aristocratic brothers, the Yankee seemed suddenly callow to her.

The thought was traitorous. She looked away, her gaze wandering out the open terrazzo doors to the walled garden. Though the month was December, the rose garden held a rainbow of fat, old-fashioned blossoms, and the doorway framing this exquisite view was itself fringed with the purple blossoms of an old vine that covered the tilted roof of Villa Dolce.

Conversation at the tea table had shifted from Travis to Sarah, and Suzannah's attention was caught by her aunt's flip, satiric tone. Bronwyn addressed her sister.

"Life with the scion of American manufacturing has made you suspicious, Sarah." Bronwyn Jones Kirkhaven was like her sister in appearance and yet very different. Like Sarah, she had faded blonde hair and fair skin. Sarah's fair complexion made her appear vulnerable, doll-like and fragile. By contrast, the same complexion made Bronwyn look haughty and aristocratic. A thin, straight woman, her appearance was saved from austerity by blue-grey eyes that were remarkably large; and though the skin about them was marked with lines, those eyes sparkled constantly with youth and humor.

"Tell me," Bronwyn goaded her sister gently, "would your husband have permitted this visit if I had written to say how wonderfully well I was feeling?" She laughed and reached for Monteleone's hand. "Would you have had the courage to ask his permission for a visit under any other circumstances than those I described in my letter?"

"You were never sick in the first place!" Sarah tried to sound horrified, but in spite of herself, she smiled. She covered her mouth quickly with a trembling hand.

"Do not judge her harshly, Signora Hopewell," suggested Roberto Monteleone, the Duke's younger brother. "To Signora Kirkhaven's credit, she was ill with a cold at the time she wrote. I believe she thought she was dying."

Suzannah heard the laughter round the table. Then Roberto's voice invaded her wandering thoughts like music.

"You are daydreaming, Signorina Suzannah?"

The color in her cheeks deepened. These Europeans habitually addressed their American guests in gently bantering tones. Suzannah felt awkward, gauche.

"You have an exquisite profile, Signorina," Roberto Monteleone was saying. He walked up to her and, taking her chin in his hands, he gently turned her head from left to right. His index finger, displaying a perfectly manicured nail, stroked the line of her jaw. Turning to Bronwyn, he said, "The cheekbones are quite extraordinary. Especially in one so young."

Roberto Monteleone, still in his early thirties, was without question the most self-assured individual Suzannah had ever met. Like all New Englanders, she disapproved of the concept of royalty, but she was utterly intimidated by the man. And in spite of her convictions, she could admit to herself that she was attracted to the Duke and his brother.

"Will you look at me again, Signorina?" There was more gentle laughter in Roberto's voice.

She did as he bade her. The eyes that held her gaze were brown velvet.

"Will you honor me by modeling for me during your visit in Palermo?"

Before Suzannah could answer, Sarah began to fret. "I haven't said we'll stay. I am awfully cross with you, Bronnie. . . ."

"But Roberto is one of Europe's most famous sculptors, Sarah! To be asked to model for him is a great honor for Suzannah." Bronwyn patted her sister's hand. "Look, of course you are going to stay. What would Martin say? Can you imagine the questions, the explanations if you arrived home months earlier than expected?"

Sarah was not to be reasoned with. She rose from her seat and, wringing her hands, began to pace the salon, totally ignoring the others in the room.

Bronwyn looked at Suzannah quickly. Was this kind of behavior usual for Sarah? But Suzannah's face told her aunt nothing. Once again, the girl was paying no attention to anyone but the young architect, Travis Paine. More and more his face resembled Mt. Etna, a volcano that threatened to explode at any moment.

"Sarah, dear," Bronwyn said, grasping her sister firmly by the shoulders, "we must have a word." Turning Sarah away from the gathering in the salon, Bronwyn continued gently, "You're overtired. The trip from Naples is always difficult. You'll be more like yourself after a rest."

"I need my tonic. It is in my traveling box."

"Of course, of course. But let us get you settled in your rooms first." Bronwyn pressed her cheek against Sarah's. "It is wonderful to see you after all these years. When you're rested, we'll have a splendid visit."

"You won't forget my tonic?"

Bronwyn kissed Sarah's temple gently. "Worry about nothing, my dear. Everything is going to be fine." Under a Moorish arch decorated in bright tiles, Bronwyn stopped and turned to the others left behind in the room. "My sister is exhausted," Bronwyn announced easily. "I will just make sure she is comfortable and then come right down. Do you have a little time, Delio? Can you wait?"

"Of course, dearest."

"And Suzannah," Bronwyn's voice was raised a little, slightly sharp, "unless you wish to nap like your mother, why don't you and Mr. Paine step into the garden? It is quite lovely."

Bronwyn's intent was clear. Whatever was troubling the two young people, they were best sent off alone to settle it between themselves.

In the garden, Travis almost trembled with indignation. Grim-faced and somber-looking in his dark New England clothes, he was out of place in the Mediterranean garden and clearly felt it.

"I shall never feel comfortable here, Suzannah. You must understand that an unsavory situation like this. . . ."

"You are being too censorious, Travis. I know I should have warned you about my aunt but, to tell the truth, Mama only explained it to me a few days ago."

"Nothing you can say. . . ." He folded his arms across his chest.

Suzannah tugged on his arm. "Don't be cross with me, Travis. Come over here and sit. Let me tell you what I know and then I'm sure you'll be more tolerant." He let her guide him to a marble bench beneath an arbor espaliered with fragrant lemon branches. Repeating the story, she was reminded of how shamefaced her mother had been as she stammered to explain all that had happened. But unlike the older woman, Suzannah thought the story of Bronwyn and her Duke was romantic.

"The British occupied Sicily from 1806 to 1815," Suzannah began, teasing Travis with an apparent bit of irrelevancy. "They were concerned that Napoleon Bonaparte had too much power in the Mediterranean. The King of Naples and his Court were in exile right here in Palermo most of that time and Aunt Bronwyn arrived in 1814. She came here with her husband, Sir Reginald Kirkhaven, but in a matter of months, he caught malaria and died. After that she fell in love with the Duke."

"And why are they not married? One would think, if they were truly in love. . . ." Travis did not finish the thought. Suddenly he blurted out, "I fail to understand your family! Why on earth—?"

"Oh, Travis!" Suzannah interrupted. "Why must you be so prim?"

"It seems like an important question, Suzannah—a question that any decent young woman would want answered." His mouth made a line: critical, unyielding.

"I know, I know. But you ask it like a preacher full of fire and damnation. Cotton Mather himself would tremble at your tone and expression."

"Surely you don't approve of this relationship?"

"I approve of love!" she cried with exasperation. "Aunt Bronwyn and the Duke love each other, and their love has lasted years and years. He's married to someone he doesn't even like; the marriage was all planned and organized by their parents. But the Duke is not to be blamed for that—and certainly not Bronwyn. It's not their fault!"

"None of this excuses. . . ."

"Oh, stuff and nonsense! Travis Paine, I had no idea you were so self-righteous." Suzannah stormed away from him, following the gravel path between broad-leaved avocado trees. He hurried after her.

"Don't be cross with me, Suzannah. I am a man. I cannot help feeling I should care for you and see you safe!"

"I'm not sure I want to be safe!" She tossed her head and walked faster, listening for the sound of his quickening steps behind her.

"Suzannah!"

She spun around. "Don't sound so shocked, Travis. And tell me what's so terrible about wanting to live life to the fullest?" She confronted him, standing soldier-straight, the lush Sicilian garden giving her a kind of territorial power. "I thought you loved me." Her green eyes flashed, glistening with tears of anger and disappointment. "Why are you trying to make me miserable?"

"I'm not. You must believe I do love you."

"Then don't criticize my family anymore. You don't like my father or my aunt. Sometimes I doubt that you care for me. How can I ever hope to stand against your penetrating criticism if you persist in this way? Perhaps we are not the same as everybody else you've met. So be it! I don't deny my family is . . . different." She saw him draw back and reacted to his movement as if he had spoken aloud. "I don't know why you're so shocked. You've been invited here, treated graciously." To her surprise he embraced her quickly. The impetuous gesture stopped the flow of tears and accusations.

"Say the words," she whispered against his cheek after a moment. "Tell me again."

"I love you, Suzannah. You are all the world to me." Their faces were but inches apart; her warm breath brushed his face, exciting him with a touch more erotic than the pressure of her hands or lips. She felt the tension in his muscles and knew the conflict in him. A part of Travis wanted to draw away from her, was horrified by her eagerness for physical love. It was easy to understand his repulsion. In the portion of her mind that remained aloof and watchful, she knew that there would come a later time—a day, a week or an hour from now—when the desire had become a memory, when she too might be horrified. But for now, the spirit of the Villa Dolce had overcome her reserve, and feelings she had never dared acknowledge held supreme power.

Travis pushed her away carefully, as if a rougher hand might break her. "I am in a . . . painful situation, Miss Hopewell." She knew he resorted to formalities when weighty matters were involved. Suzannah composed herself and prepared to listen. "If I could at this time ask your father to accept me as your suitor, I would do so. You know that, don't you?"

"Of course I do." They were again seated on the marble bench—seated as close as they possibly could be without actually touching.

"I have the greatest, the most profound respect for you, Miss Hopewell." He coughed and fiddled with his lapel. "That is why I think we should not see each other except in the company of . . . others." He looked at Suzannah. His face registered complete despair. "You are so young and innocent; you cannot know the dangers. . . . This place. . . . We must be vigilant."

He looked so unhappy that her heart rushed out to him. "I love you, Travis," she whispered, losing all caution as her words escaped her. "I love you and I need you desperately. We mustn't hide behind the old folks as if we were children. Whatever the danger is, we need not fear." She teased him with a sly smile and drew away from his side. "If you ruin our holiday, I shall not let you kiss me again!"

"Suzannah, you make it very difficult!"

"Anyway, I thought you didn't want my kisses."

"I never . . . said such a thing." Her light tone had precisely the opposite effect on him. He groaned softly and covered his face with his hands. "Forgive me, Suzannah, but I cannot stop . . . with kisses. I am a man, and I cannot deny my corrupt and bestial nature."

"You fear for my virtue, Mr. Paine," Suzannah said softly, as she gently pried his hands from his face and looked into his eyes, "but I do not."

Chapter 24

Villa Dolce was a narrow, pink stucco building several stories high, set in a spacious, walled garden facing the Palermo marina. Behind the villa were the lovely gardens of the Villa Giulia. From the window of Sarah Hopewell's bedroom, it was possible to see the harbor with the ships riding at anchor, the wide strand edged by alternating lemon and lime trees, part of the ancient town and all of the villa gardens. But Lady Bronwyn Kirkhaven, standing at the window, was not paying attention to any of these familiar sights. Her experienced eye was fixed on the two figures walking in the garden, and from their movements and gestures, Bronwyn could almost interpret every word that Suzannah and Travis exchanged.

Behind Lady Bronwyn in the pleasant, airy room, Sarah Hopewell rested on an old-fashioned, four-poster bed that was set three feet off the floor on a platform. Behind the light draperies that hung about the bed, Sarah whimpered in her sleep. Hearing the sound, Bronwyn's thoughts flew from her healthy niece to her ailing sister.

There was certainly trouble to come. For the past fifteen years, Bronwyn had made a constant study of the people who came into her circle, and over the years her observations had been so uncannily accurate that she no longer stopped to question the truth of her assumptions. She knew for certain there was trouble to come between her sister and her lovely niece—and Bronwyn also realized that Suzannah's slender shoulders would have to bear most of the burden.

"Are you there, Bronnie?" Sarah stared up from the pillow. Her eyes were wild and Bronwyn hurried to reassure and calm her sister.

"Don't worry. I am here."

"And my tonic? Where is it?"

"You've forgotten? I gave you some the minute we came into the room."

"I need a little more. I didn't take quite enough to calm me."

Bronwyn considered denying Sarah's request, but what was the point of troubling her sister further? Later, at the proper moment, she would tell Sarah that the tonic seemed to have a deleterious effect on her health. But not now, she thought. Her sister was with her for the first time in twenty years. They would have to learn to know each other once again before Bronwyn could begin to have an influence.

When Sarah was resting quietly, Bronwyn returned to the window. Suzannah and Travis now sat on the marble bench, twin dark heads bent earnestly together. She sighed. It was clear to her that Suzannah, innocent as she now was, possessed the warm-blooded nature common to women of her family. Now, under the shield of inexperience, she appeared merely impetuous and willful, but once she had known not only love but satisfaction as well. . . . Bronwyn sighed again and pitied her. The history of the Jones family was crowded with stories of pretty women too hot-blooded for their own good. Forbidden liaisons, bastard children, suicides and flights by night: she and Sarah had been raised on horror stories of what would happen to them should they lose control of their passions. They had been told stories of aunts never seen again, cousins who took their own lives in shame. There had been occasions when whole neighborhoods and towns turned against some unfortunate kinswoman who dared to love wildly and unwisely.

This Suzannah was one of the passionate tribe. What Bronwyn had guessed immediately was only confirmed by the recent scene in the salon. Bronwyn had overheard Roberto when he asked Suzannah to model. The aunt had seen how the young man held Suzannah's gaze. A look passed between them and Bronwyn recognized the fatal terms of their mute communication. And she had seen the disapproving way young Paine regarded the royal brothers. Villa Dolce and its romantic style of life were an anathema to him. Bronwyn thought of him as a typical rock-jawed Yankee, determined to inhibit all natural affection and spontaneous emotion. Yet he cared for Suzannah; that much was obvious. Looking at her, his eyes glowed like embers and his narrow, condemning mouth lost its hard line when he allowed a smile to pass between them.

The two admiring men were completely different from one another and Bronwyn saw Suzannah as a blossom, unaware of her own beauty, of the fatal nectar that attracted those men. In the garden below, the carmine sunset emblazoned her hair with dark fire. Though Bronwyn could not see Suzannah's face, she knew her cheeks were bright with aroused spirits. Something must be done to prepare the child!

Always in the past, fated Jones women had been allowed to blunder into the truth about themselves and they inevitably suffered for their blindness. Sarah would never have married Martin Hopewell if her reckless behavior had not forced her into the ceremony. If Sarah had known a bit of life, if she had been warned somehow, her destiny might have been very different. But in those days there had been no one to speak the truth about love and sex and desire; there had only been warnings and terrible stories that, in the end, were all too easy to forget in the moment of passion.

Bronwyn's marriage to Kirkhaven had been most fortunate, she now saw. Though many years her senior, he was a virile, attractive man who understood her needs. Kirkhaven had taught her what it was like for a woman to enjoy her body without shame. The old, dark stories of horrendous punishment were eventually forgotten. After his death Bronwyn was desperately lonely for a time. But being attractive and sophisticated, she had soon gathered a crowd of admirers to her company. Discreetly, there had been several lovers. But since meeting Delio, Duke of Monteleone, she had been faithful to him alone.

She had never once wanted to return to England. In fact, she had married Kirkhaven, in part, because he promised to take her far from the grim little island. As his widow, she might have returned to a life of elegance and propriety on his country estate outside London. But Bronwyn—who had long since recognized and come to appreciate her own sensual nature—wanted nothing to do with the sharply confined life of British society. For this rejection her family despised her, cast her out. She supposed that in some branches of the family, mothers now warned their wanton daughters to beware lest they become like Bronwyn Kirkhaven.

As the fading sun glimmered in a gilt-edged mirror to her right, Bronwyn caught a glimpse of herself. What she saw was not displeasing. At forty-four she was still a handsome woman; the lines in her face suggested more amusement than grief. Sarah, on the other hand, reminded her of the old Sicilian women in the village, bent and withered by grieving.

Suzannah's laughter rose from the garden. Looking down, Bronwyn saw her niece leap up from the bench, stretch out her arms to Travis Paine, and then, still laughing, swing away from him, lifting her skirts above her ankles and scampering off with the young man in pursuit.

They have the innocence of children, she thought. But for how long?

Later, downstairs, Monteleone chided Bronwyn gently for being so long apart from him.

"Forgive me if I seem unusually possessive, *Bella mia*, but I must soon depart for Naples. The thought of many weeks apart makes me wish to make the most of such little time as we have together." He poured her a glass of sparkling wine, which she took gratefully. Thoughts of Suzannah and Sarah had disturbed her more than she cared to admit. She drank the wine quickly, hoping it would calm her.

"I wish you did not have to go."

He shrugged. "Of course. But I must. The Duchess asks little enough of me. Certainly I cannot balk at spending the holidays with my children and grandchildren. Besides, I must speak at length with His Majesty, King Ferdinand."

"There is no trouble, I hope."

Again he shrugged. "On our little island, you know there is always trouble, *Bella mia*. However, the King is young, energetic. . . ."

"Not an imbecile like Francis," put in Roberto from across the room.

"Exactly. There might actually be some hope of land reforms with such a man on the throne of Naples. This feudal system of ours cannot do anything but keep Sicilia primitive and poor."

Bronwyn poured more wine for both of them. "But, my dear, is this not what all the royal families have wanted? What can be better for them than a captive province?"

Roberto joined his brother beside the fireplace. They were a tall, handsome pair, both olive-skinned with soft, dark eyes. "We must not forget that Sicilia has provided a convenient place where the rich landowners might conceal their assets and escape taxation."

"But the *tassazione* . . ."

"The *tassazione* is a tax more often evaded than paid. Each year the *gabelloti* become more devious in assisting the landowners to escape it, for they know that if they can save the money, they will be rewarded handsomely." Monteleone paused as a servant entered the salon to light the lamps and fire. "It is growing late," he said with obvious reluctance. "I must hurry away, *Bella*. Will you be all right?"

Bronwyn smiled sadly. They embraced. "Without you, Delio, I only survive."

He nodded without smiling. There was a peculiar lack of irony in the feelings they shared so frankly. "Roberto will keep you good company, and now you also have your sister and niece. Not to mention the prim young man who does not approve of pink palazzi."

"Or those who dwell in them." Roberto grinned. "Never fear, Delio. I will protect Lady Bronwyn from outraged opinion." He made the swordsman's gestures of thrust and parry, then laughed. "I will defend your honor at any cost, my Lady."

Bronwyn tried not to be amused. "I'm sure, Roberto, that if there is anything dramatic to be done, you will do it. However it is not my honor that concerns me." She put her glass down on the onyx table. It was inlaid with Russian amber in a mandala design and, without the least consciousness of her sense of order, she set the glass in the center of the mandala. Crossing to the terrazzo doors, she looked out worriedly. "I wonder where they've gone. It's almost dark." She chewed a nail thoughtfully. The uncharacteristic gesture alarmed Monteleone.

"I think these visitors will be a trial to you, Bronwyn."

"No. A worry, but not a trial." Bronwyn smiled up at him. "Didn't I say it would make my life more interesting to have my sister with me for a while?"

"Indeed you said that. Yet I wonder now. . . ."

"Until I discover what has made my sister so . . . strange, I will not rest easy."

"If I may say, Bronwyn, it is many years since my medical studies in Milan. Still, I have not forgotten what I learned. Your sister seems to be suffering from acute nervousness. . . ."

"For which she douses herself with that loathsome tonic," Bronwyn grimaced.

"It could be that the problem has become the tonic, not the nerves themselves." Again Monteleone embraced his lover. "If there is anything I can do, you must not hesitate to call upon me."

"No, my darling. I will miss you during your long absence, but I shall survive. When you return you will find Sarah a much happier person. And Suzannah. . . ."

Roberto interrupted. "I look forward to having

her as a model. Her features are such an unusual combination. Those strong, mature facial bones and yet the mouth so gentle, vulnerable."

"Perhaps you should not be so ready to put her likeness in stone, Roberto," cautioned the older brother. "Paine did not seem pleased with your suggestion."

"No matter what, I must do her head. That young man of hers will have to accept it. After all," he grinned engagingly and opened his arms wide, "am I not a great *artiste*?"

At the end of the garden, Travis and Suzannah discovered an ornamental iron gate leading into a large, formal park. With a little encouragement, the latch lifted and the gate groaned open. Feeling as nervous as disobedient children, they strolled for some distance into the park, following the broad paths between fountains and flower gardens to a small lake. A dozen magnificent white swans hardly disturbed the surface of the glassy water. At the far end of the lake stood a small summerhouse with marble columns. A bench inside faced the placid scene.

After they had sat in silence for a time, Travis said, "I cannot help thinking that a place such as this—although beautiful in its own way—represents what I most abhor in European society."

"How can you say that?" To Suzannah it seemed he was going out of his way to find causes for ill humor. She thought the formal gardens were exquisite. Though she preferred the wilderness of Cooper's Mountain, that preference did not keep her from appreciating the obvious care and the love of nature that had contributed to the fashioning of the gardens. "Are you so critical of Rome?"

"Of course not. Rome is a magnificent city, a holy place most significant in the history of our civilization. Sicily, on the other hand, is an island full of backward peasants and decadent aristocrats."

"You do not mean the Duke, do you? How can you call him decadent? I have heard only the finest things about him. He is one of the enlightened. . . ."

"You are so sweet and impressionable, Suzannah." Travis reached for her hand but she pulled way, frowning.

Everything she liked, he found fault with. If her opinion differed from his in any way, he blamed her impressionable nature, her innocence. She wondered if he would never permit her an opinion without attributing it to her youth and general ignorance. No matter what, he seemed determined to make her cross with him.

"Surely you would not wish to see America divided into private gardens so that only the rich could enjoy flowers and trees!" He was apparently oblivious to her souring mood.

"Of course I wouldn't, Travis. You know me better than to say such a thing!" She pouted and tears filled her eyes. "You have been so harsh with me today. Despite your words of love, I almost think you do not like me anymore."

He embraced her hurriedly as she had hoped he would. Though not deeply cunning, Suzannah was developing a sense of how to bring this man around to gentler, kinder ways. He held her in his arms like crystal, though; and she recalled how he feared for her honor.

How silly all this is, she thought, trying to nestle her head more comfortably against his shoulder. How jumpy and restless he was! If she had not known otherwise, she would have thought he only wanted to get away from her. Didn't he know that she loved him and that nothing terrible could ever come from a love like hers? As to her honor, well, she respected him for caring, of course, but wished he could understand that she was ultimately responsible.

Against his ear, she whispered, "I love you, Travis."

He jumped away as if bitten.

"What is it, Travis?" At his shocked look, she didn't know whether to laugh or cry.

"I told you, Miss Hopewell. This kind of closeness, this physical intimacy, can only bring trouble upon us. It is for your sake. . . ."

"Oh, stuff and rubbish!" She moved some distance from him and folded her hands primly on her lap. If he wanted some skinny-lipped prude, then she'd be just that!

"Suzannah, believe me. I know what I'm saying! Those years in New Haven, I was a man on my own. I've seen a lot of life. I know that young women who hurry after love are doomed to fall. Certain matters are . . . irreversible."

Refusing to answer him, Suzannah kept her eyes on the little lake. The light was fading now, and in the still surface of the water were reflected the last rays of the red sun. Nothing moved, nothing made a sound. The swans were like porcelain pieces set out for decoration.

"You're angry," said Travis. "I should not have come to Palermo."

She would not look at him. "And why not, may I ask?"

"I do not belong here. I am not at ease amidst this . . . this . . . decadence."

"Decadence! What you're saying is that you are not at ease with beauty. Is that your meaning?"

"The place seems to have affected you strangely, Suzannah."

"I?" She could not resist being interested. "In what way have I been affected?" Travis did not answer. "You must certainly speak your mind, or I will believe you are making it all up."

"You seem . . ." He shook his head and rose. "I do not want to say it, Suzannah."

She stood before him. "You began this conversation, Mr. Paine. I suggest that if you care for me, you will finish it."

"Very well. In Amoset, you were lively and beautiful, full of girlish recklessness. The day we met in the barn, I thought I had never known a more innocently desirable girl." Travis stared at his shiny black boots while he spoke. "I thought that I should die if you were not mine forever."

These words were so pleasant to Suzannah that she wished, almost desperately, that he would not go on. But she was determined to have Travis' complete opinion of her. She waited for him to continue, chewing her lower lip impatiently. He sought the words to carry his thoughts.

"Here you are still beautiful and lively. But I sense an impetuosity that is not quite. . . ." There was a long pause during which the young lovers did not look at one another. Above the pond, a wedge of swans circled, crying to the white, still creatures drifting below on the glassy water. "You do not seem so much a lady here, Miss Hopewell. I think your aunt does not produce a healthy influence on one with such a warm and . . . loving nature."

"I see." She sniffed and blinked back her tears. The words were empty but they were all she could think of to say at the moment. Later she would dream up scorching epithets. Later, she would conjure up ways to hurt him as much as he was punishing her. "I think we had best be going back. It will soon be dark, and my aunt will worry." Disregarding his offered hand, Suzannah descended the summerhouse steps and returned quickly to the gate leading to Villa Dolce. Hurrying up behind her, Travis seized her arm and pulled Suzannah to a stop before him.

"You asked to know the truth, Suzannah. And so I told you."

"So you did, Travis."

"And none of it changes the fact that I love you. I do, Suzannah. I adore you!"

"Yes."

"You do not believe me?"

"I believe you love the image of what you think I should be. As to the way I am—well, that is a little different. You have accused me of being . . . I don't know what. You make me sound like a . . . a . . . fallen woman." She accused him. "That's what you meant, isn't it?"

"Oh, no, Suzannah," he reassured her quickly. Holding both her hands, Travis brought the palms to his lips to be kissed. "You're not a bad person. I never would or could say that. You're just . . . impressionable."

Suzannah burst into tears.

Chapter 25

"Are you warm enough, Signorina?" Roberto asked. "You must sit here in the sunlight. Will you have a glass of wine?"

"At ten in the morning?" Suzannah was shocked at the suggestion.

Roberto did not hide his amusement.

"What kind of wine?" she countered quickly to hide her gaucherie. Roberto had placed a cushion on an elevated platform under one of the large windows. His studio was on the top floor of Villa Dolce and the sunlight flooded over Suzannah's shoulder as she took her place on the cushion.

"Marsala. It is a sweet Sicilian wine, a little like sherry. It will relax you." Though Roberto's expression was composed, there was devilment in his eyes. "I assure you, it's as harmless as mother's milk, Signorina."

"Well, a little can't hurt, can it? Just one."

Roberto handed her a glass of the amber liquid. She sipped and made a face.

"You do not care for Sicilia's Marsala?"

"It is awfully sweet." She smiled and licked her lips. "But nice, I think. Thank you. *Grazie.*"

"*Prego,* Signorina. Shall we begin?"

Suzannah looked around. "Where is the marble?"

"First I must sketch you. Then, months from now when you are once more ensconced in Massachusetts, I will be shaping your features in stone and remembering these happy moments with you." Roberto sat on a high stool, a few feet from her. A sheaf of heavy paper was set on the easel before him and even as he spoke, his hand grasped a stick of charcoal, moving confidently over the paper.

"You mean I will never see the finished work?"

"This disappoints you?"

"Well, yes," she admitted. Her shoulders drooped a little.

"Sit straight, Signorina. There. Just so is perfect. Now, without moving, tell me why you have such a look of regret hidden away. You are young and rich and beautiful. What cause is there for sadness then?"

She was at first reluctant to speak. After a few minutes of Roberto's gentle coaxing, by fixing her gaze on his gracefully nodding head rather than the eyes that scanned her, she began to unburden herself. "It is my friend, Mr. Paine. He does not approve of my modeling for you. I had hoped to have a finished sculpture to show him—so he might appreciate your work."

"Perhaps I will have an exhibition in New York one day. There has been some talk about that."

"Mr. Paine would be pleased. He is a great admirer of fine art, you know."

"And of beautiful women."

Suzannah reddened, coughed and nervously changed her position on the cushion.

"You must not move, Signorina. Each time you do, your profile alters subtly—as well as your expression, of course." In his hand the charcoal moved with bold strokes. She heard, but could not see, the scratch of charcoal on paper.

They were quiet for a while. Then Roberto asked, "Tell me what you think of little Sicilia, of Palermo."

"It's lovely here! The gardens and the sea especially!" She spoke as she stared across the studio to a window that framed an expanse of azure sky. "I thought Naples was awful, so crowded and dirty. But here it is mild and beautiful. Mr. Paine and I walked in the gardens on the other side of the wall. There was a gate and it opened easily, so I assumed it would be all right to go in. Oh, and there were swans!" Moving only a little, she sipped her Marsala. The wine both warmed and relaxed her, and she realized this effect was what Roberto had intended. She was beginning to enjoy herself.

"And did Mr. Paine also like the swans? I think perhaps he saw only his pretty Suzannah."

She blushed again but did not move.

"Well? Do not tell me the young architect was displeased?"

"Not that exactly. But . . . well, it is hard to know how to answer."

"With honest candor, Signorina."

She laughed. "No one has ever before suggested that to me. In Massachusetts, I am forever being reprimanded for failing to censor what I say."

"That is a shame, a great shame. For myself, I value the truth above all things save beauty. If we are to be friends—as I hope we are—you must speak honestly."

"In that case, I will tell you that Travis—Mr. Paine—finds formal gardens and pink palaces too decadent for his taste." She turned to Roberto earnestly, eager to say what was on her mind. "But I like it.

Sometimes I cannot help but compare this pretty place to the drab stone of the place I'm from. Oh, if you could see it! There are only mills and endless rows of boarding houses in Amoset. I feel quite discontented when I think of what awaits me at home. Of course, it is winter there now and bitterly cold. That makes a difference. But I'm sure there is more lacking than seasons and architecture. There is a feeling of openness here that is new to me." She smiled engagingly. "I moved, didn't I?"

"I should scold you, but I will be kind this time. In truth, I believe I can forgive you anything, for if you are a beauty when your expression is composed, you are exquisite when animated." The blushes that met his words were expected.

"You are a flatterer, Mr. Monteleone, Signore . . . sir." Her color deepened. "Oh, bother! What am I to call you? This business of titled persons is so confusing!"

"It is a system intended to confuse. But you must call me Roberto. I am only a younger son, untitled and completely ordinary."

"You mean the Duke gets everything? That does not seem fair."

"I shall not starve, Signorina."

"Even so, it does not seem fair." She tossed her head a little and said proudly, "Americans do not approve of such inequities."

Roberto laughed. "What of Lady Bronwyn's arrangement? Do Americans disapprove of that too?"

Suzannah answered at once, "Absolutely!" But after a minute she added, "Well, Travis does. He says Aunt Bronwyn is a bad influence on me."

"You disagree?"

Instead of answering, Suzannah asked, "You don't think she's a bad woman, do you?"

"Do you?" He was playing with her. She realized that, and yet she was not annoyed. Undoubtedly, he thought such discussions were unfamiliar to a girl from Amoset, Massachusetts. And a practical-minded manufacturer's daughter, at that. Well, she would show him! She tussled with the question, thinking of the implications of her reply.

"No. Not bad. But. . . ."

He stopped sketching. "But?"

"It is immoral, isn't it?"

"To love?"

"To love a married man. A man with children and . . . vows."

"Ah, vows." He nodded his head slowly, as if considering this word for the first time. "Do Americans put great store by vows?"

"Of course they do. Doesn't any civilized society?"

"Your aunt is uncivilized then, you think?" A roguish smile challenged her.

"You know I did not say that, Roberto!" She tried to look cross, but the truth was that this lively discussion of forbidden subjects was affording her more entertainment than she had enjoyed in weeks. "But she is immoral. You must think that. After all, Sicily is a Roman Catholic country. Here you are, practically part of Italy, and the Holy City of Rome."

Roberto's eyes twinkled. He seemed intent on teasing her. "And did you know that Delio and I have a brother who is a priest in Rome?" Tearing off a sheet, he shifted to a new position and, without pause, began another sketch. Though she refused to beg, Suzannah's curiosity yearned to see what he had drawn already. But he did not offer to show her, and his indifference made her petulant.

"I don't care much for Papist ways, to tell the

truth. I hope you aren't offended. But even by Unitarian standards, Aunt Bronwyn is. . . ."

"Let me assure you, Signorina, that despite what your church or Sicilia's might say, your aunt is a wonderful woman, remarkable in many ways. For those of us who love her, she is perfect."

"I did not mean to say. . . ."

Roberto laid aside his sketching materials and helped Suzannah to stand. "It is Lady Bronwyn, not the Duchess or her children, who has given meaning to my brother's life. In a young country like yours, there is a greater tolerance for rules and rigid standards. Here in my Sicilia we have had so many conquerors—Moslems, Greeks, Romans and many others—and each has brought a new set of standards and laws, each offered to us as truth." Roberto shrugged. "Is it any wonder we have learned to ignore most rules, to make our own truths? The old women, the frightened, the children, they pray for the Hereafter. The rest of us have learned to live for today with whatever rules seem right at the time."

As Roberto stood looking at Suzannah, he continued to hold her hand in his own. "Would you like to see the morning's sketches?" He led her to the easel.

She stared at the drawings in silence.

"You are displeased, Signorina?"

"Do I really look like this?"

"You do not recognize the manufacturer's daughter from Amoset?"

"I'm not sure. I don't know." For reasons she could not put into words, the sketches disturbed her confidence. It was as if Roberto looked at her and saw another woman, someone different from the person who returned her gaze in the looking glass each morning.

"You will come again tomorrow?" His hand on her arm was strong, compelling.

"At the same time?"

"Of course."

She nodded and they parted in the doorway. On the outside steps, she stopped a moment to breathe in the salt air and gaze at the Mediterranean. She was glad to be out of the studio, yet sorry the sitting was over so quickly. She felt a buoyancy, an unlikely sense of homecoming, that set her humming. Smiling to herself, she danced down the steps, ready to begin her search for Travis Paine.

A servant told her that Travis had left the villa shortly after dawn that morning, carrying a rucksack and books. The land about Palermo was rich in historic sites and Suzannah was sure he had gone off to explore. Though she wished he had invited her to accompany him on the jaunt, she was pleased to have a little time alone and she welcomed the opportunity to visit awhile with her mother.

But Sarah was deep in sleep and, rather than disturb her, Suzannah returned to her own room. The maid who was cleaning there had a message from Lady Bronwyn. Suzannah was asked to visit her aunt at her convenience, any time before noon.

Suzannah found Bronwyn still in bed, luxuriating in a room that was sumptuously elegant. The few walls that had no windows were hung with fine silk tapestries. Every corner of the tile floor was covered with thick, piled Oriental rugs that glowed with amber, red and gold. The bed, on a platform, was draped in velvet trimmed with gold. For a moment, Suzannah saw it all through Travis' eyes and she was almost offended by the regal opulence.

"You've come, my dear. I am so glad!" Lady Bronwyn Kirkhaven put down a cup of chocolate and leaned back against a dozen satin-covered pillows. Around her the beige satin comforter was covered with swatches and rolls of ribbon. Her nightdress and bed jacket were of pale blue silk, extravagantly trimmed in ochre lace. To Suzannah her aunt looked extremely pretty and youthful in her lace bed cap, with her pale blonde curls peeking girlishly from beneath the ruffles. "I have been planning a new wardrobe for the spring," commented Bronwyn. "It will help to occupy my time while Delio is away." She held out two pieces of ribbon. "Which do you prefer, my dear?"

"Both are lovely." Suzannah smiled. "Must you choose? Why not have them both?"

"Why not, indeed!" cried Lady Bronwyn. "And to think I judged you Yankees to be a frugal lot!" She rang a dainty silver bell beside the bed and a maid quickly appeared. "I will take both the rose and the gold, Felice. You may place the order with Signora Gamboli this afternoon." To Suzannah Bronwyn said, "Sit by the fire, my dear. In the wintertime the rooms on this side of the house stay chilly. I will be with you in a moment."

When she rejoined Suzannah, Bronwyn had covered her nightdress with a dark blue satin morning robe, so lavish in length that the hem trailed several feet behind her. The sleeves and neckline were bordered with an abundance of silvery feathers that floated as she moved. Bronwyn had removed her bed cap and her long, fair hair fell in curls to the center of her back.

As she chatted and sipped chocolate with her aunt, Suzannah realized that such a meeting would be impossible in Amoset. No woman of good health and character would dare remain in bed past nine o'clock.

"I asked you here for a very special reason,

Suzannah. Now, as I speak, I know you will be tempted to interrupt me. I ask that you try not to. Hear me through before you...."

"But why should I ...?"

Bronwyn laughed indulgently. "There you go! I have not begun, and already you are asking questions!" She gently patted Suzannah's lips with her index finger. "You must let me speak. This is not easy for me. Yet I fear that if I do not speak honestly now, there may be great suffering ahead for you. Tell me, Suzannah, have you learned the physical facts about love between men and women? Has Sarah told you what you need to know?"

Suzannah stared at the chocolate residue in the bottom of her cup. She was too embarrassed to look at Lady Bronwyn. When she found her voice it was barely a whisper. "I learned from Mrs. Shawn, the mother of a friend. And Eben, my brother, told me a little, but I think he meant mostly to frighten me."

"You are better informed than I expected. I am glad of that. You say that Eben frightened you. How? You may speak frankly, Suzannah. Do not be shy with me."

Suzannah cleared her throat and bit her lip, longing to be anywhere but beside her worldly aunt. Bronwyn seemed so casual, done up in bedtime silks and satins, sitting in a room that almost shrieked of immoral love. Above the fireplace was a painting of Cupid spying on some naked bathers in a country setting. Suzannah stared at the painting and prayed for escape.

"Speak up, Suzannah. We are just two women here. All that we say will be private."

"He said it hurts," Suzannah blurted out. There was a black servant—a turbaned dwarf—waiting on the women whose voluptuous nakedness was scarcely covered by diaphanous scarves. The picture made Suzannah sick.

Bronwyn did not appear to notice Suzannah's distraction. "The truth is that many women pass their entire lives without enjoying physical love, Suzannah. Eben told you that it hurts. Well, the love of a woman will not hurt him, you may be sure of that! But many women only believe that it is unpleasant. I do not want that to be your fate, my dear. Nor do I wish your emotions to take you by surprise one day, as they so easily might. I have seen the way young Mr. Paine admires you."

Suzannah stood up. "He is a gentleman." Never had she been more grateful for the truth.

"Why, of course he is! A thoroughly admirable young fellow. Sit down, dearest child, sit down. I only wish to say that he is also a man, and everyone of that sex is capable of knavish behavior where women are concerned. If you doubt the truth of my words, you will be much hurt by life."

Suzannah stood up again. "Why are you telling me these things?"

"And why are you jumping up and down like a child's toy? And breaking our agreement with your interruptions? Sit down, Suzannah, and have pity. This conversation is far from easy for me. Let me pour you some more chocolate." A moment later, seeing that Suzannah was composed, Bronwyn continued. "I have risked shocking you, Suzannah, because there is something you must know. There is a characteristic among the women in our family. We are thought to be . . . excessively warm-blooded."

"I am a Hopewell, Aunt."

"True. But I have seen your eyes and noted the expression on your face when you look at Mr. Paine. You might not like what I am saying. You might think such passion taints you in some way, but believe me, it does not. You are as you are and if you are to live a contented and productive life—if you are ever to be truly free—you must acknowledge completely who and what you are." Bronwyn paused, looking closely at Suzannah.

Bronwyn knew the young could be priggish when frightened, challenged or shy. Travis Paine was an excellent example of this tendency. She thought that, in his home environment, given life on his own terms, he was probably quite a pleasant and attractive man. But in Palermo, where nothing was familiar, he was cold and critical. In his rigid spirit, he resembled the old grandmothers who met to gossip near Palermo's public well and spat on the ground when the Duke's mistress passed near.

Bronwyn had lain awake half the night, debating what she should say. And she had wondered whether silence might be best in this situation. But she had only to think of her sister Sarah to know that she must speak frankly to Suzannah, regardless of the consequent strain in their relationship. A woman could protect herself, but only if she understood how.

"No doubt you will marry in a few years, Suzannah. Until you do, you may find yourself wishing for a way to inhibit conception."

Suzannah put down her cup. She was too curious to be shocked. "Is such a thing possible?"

Ah, thought Bronwyn, I have her at last!

"A woman may not conceive at all times. In the days just preceding and following her monthly illness, she is generally infertile. In the middle of the cycle there is great danger."

There was a long silence as Suzannah, staring at the ribald painting, tried to absorb her aunt's startling information. Though she embraced the new

knowledge eagerly, she also felt as if she had overheard some obscene secret that no proper young lady
should know. She recalled Roberto's praise of Lady
Bronwyn. But she was also reminded of Travis' conviction that the older woman was a bad example for a
proper girl. Suzannah glanced furtively around her at
the room, suddenly horrified at how much her aunt
resembled a courtesan.

Travis was right! She wanted him to come home
so she might ask him to forgive her criticism. All this
talk of being warm-blooded. . . . It had nothing
whatsoever to do with her. It was only a decadent old
woman's way of rationalizing her sinful way of life.

"You may ask any questions you wish, Suzannah." Bronwyn spoke kindly. "I will be happy to answer you as best I can."

Suzannah fidgeted, thinking only of escape. How
wrongly she had judged her darling, dearest Travis!

"Nothing, child?"

Suzannah shook her head and stared at her
hands. The company of her aunt disgusted her; she
longed for the predictable uprightness of Travis. She
longed, suddenly, to return to Amoset, where clearly
defined rules governed their lives.

There was a long silence and at last Bronwyn understood that her frank, well-meant words had horrified her American niece. She was not offended by the
rebuff, merely disappointed that she had not accomplished her purposes. She liked Suzannah Hopewell
and felt the strength in her. She cared only to save
her from unnecessary pain, to rescue the girl from
slow destruction at the hands of a narrow-minded society that could prove murderous in its total control
of an impressionable woman's mind and will.

"Never mind, Suzannah." With a sigh, Bronwyn
folded her napkin neatly. "Run along and play. For-

get what I have told you until you need to know. Then, perhaps, you will understand your Aunt Bronwyn a little better."

That night, Suzannah knocked softly at the door to Travis' bedroom. She turned the knob easily. The old door swung open of its own weight and she peered into the dim room. The bed against the far wall looked as if it had been carved of one solid piece of mahogany. Beside it, on a little marble table, was a guttering candle. Travis sat up in bed, holding the sheets up to his chin.

"You should not be here!"

Suzannah entered the room without being invited. It did not occur to her that she might not be welcome.

"No one will see me. Mama is sleeping and my aunt and Roberto have gone to the theater. They asked me to go with them, but I could not." She dropped to her knees beside the bed. "I have been so foolish, Travis. I could not wait until tomorrow to tell you." Suzannah looked into his eyes. "Where have you been all day? You missed supper and worried me."

"I walked to the old castle at Erice. Once there, I was reluctant to leave. The view was extraordinary. If you can imagine—the whole western side of the island—I could see everything." Warming to the details of his excursion, Travis seemed to relax. He loosened his clutch on the sheets and sat up straight in his high-necked, long-sleeved nightshirt. "You should have seen Mt. Etna, Suzannah. I had a magnificent view of it from Erice. Even as I watched, clouds of volcanic ash were rising from the cone."

"I waited for you by the gate all afternoon." This was not precisely true. Suzannah had returned to the gate several times to watch for him, but her mind had been too active to permit a long vigil.

"You should not be here now, Suzannah. What has made you come at such a private hour?"

"I could not wait, Travis. You were right, completely and absolutely right about Aunt Bronwyn." Suzannah sat beside him on the bed and though she noticed that he pulled away from her, she gave no sign. "She is worse than you think. So devious and . . . and . . . calculating. Travis, you would not believe what she told me! No, do not ask. I will never tell you. Just believe me. It was utterly shocking."

"In that case, you must speak to your mother. An older woman can be a great. . . ."

"There's no good in telling her anything. I don't know what is the matter with her, but she's been sickly ever since we arrived. I can't speak to my mother: I would only give her cause to worry. Besides, she loves her sister." Suzannah paused. Suddenly she grasped Travis' hand and kissed it fervently.

He tried to pull away.

"Oh, Travis, I love you so much! You are so strong and good. What would I do without you? What would become of me?" With an impatience that was only part love, she leaned forward and kissed his lips. It was their first serious kiss since the hay barn incident—and to Suzannah that was so long ago that it seemed another lifetime.

Travis alone knew how much he had been obsessed by memories of that charged, importunate embrace. To him the second kiss was electrifying, just as dangerous and volatile as he had feared it would be. He could not prevent his arms from encircling Suzannah, drawing her down to lie beside him in the warm, narrow bed.

"Suzannah, Suzannah." He murmured her name as he held her face between his hands and stared into her eyes. In her robe and shawl, she was discreetly covered. Yet his fancy, that had dwelt through hungry hours upon imagined details of her perfect body, could summon the exact image of her soft beauty despite the clothes she wore. The palms of his hands tingled with temptation and when they kissed again, he could not withstand his urges. He touched her breast and pressed gently. His hand cupped and fondled her, feeling her soft, tender warmth through layers of clothing.

Suzannah sighed and moved against him without thinking.

Giving no warning, Travis pushed her away.

"My God!" he cried. "What am I doing? Get away from me!" He shoved against her and she nearly fell as she stumbled off the bed.

"I'm sorry," she gasped. "Don't be angry with me, Travis. I meant no wrong. I wasn't. . . . Oh, my love, you are so good!" She sobbed into her hands.

"You must be mad for coming here. You know how I feel. You know what could happen between us!" He ran his hands through his long, disheveled hair and began to pace the room in his nightshirt, ranting at her as she huddled on the cold floor. "This place is a sewer, sick with corruption. It gets in your bones. I would never have touched you if. . . ."

"I forgive you, Travis." She reached up to hold his arm, but he brushed her away. "Don't punish yourself, my darling."

He turned on her in fury. "You're the one who should be punished. You're like her, Suzannah. That whorish aunt of yours! Maybe you don't want to be, but you are. It's your nature. It's in your blood!"

Chapter 26

Travis was gone the next day. He left no word of explanation, nor any note of thanks. At first Suzannah was certain there would be some message propped against the mirror in his room. There was nothing. A kitchen servant had seen him at the quay at dawn, shortly before the morning boat departed for Naples. He had been standing there among the fishermen who were bringing in their catch of shrimp and lobster. But later, when the Naples boat had left, he was gone.

Suzannah searched no further. Closing herself in her bedroom, she locked the door and wept into the satin bed pillows until her eyes were as red and inflamed as a millhand's. Abandoned, shamed into numbness, Suzannah cared nothing for sculptors or sketching. She entirely forgot her appointment with Roberto.

Over and over she was tormented by Travis' words. "You are like her!" Like Bronwyn Kirkhaven, a despicable, immoral woman! "You are like her!" Those final words, uttered in bitter anger, were like a curse.

Had there been an element of contrivance in her visit to Travis' bedroom? She examined her motives

ruthlessly, but could find no hint of evil in her soul.
She had simply wanted to be near him, to be reassured by his faithful love. But her simple desire had
been poisoned. This pink palazzo, this dangerously
alien environment, had become purgatory to Suzannah since her aunt's honest disclosures. She had gone
to Travis because his reassuring attitudes reminded
her of home.

Her motives were innocent. How could Travis be
so quick and cruel in his accusations?

Questions, excuses, accusations, condemnations
snarled in her mind like tangled threads of a broken
loom. Nothing made sense. Perhaps she was like
Bronwyn, though not yet fully awakened to her
failings. Perhaps the evil in Villa Dolce had invaded
her bones and corrupted her, as Travis had suggested.
Perhaps. . . .

I must be bad, she thought at last. No wonder
Travis was so eager to leave me!

Still, she could not forget that for a few moments
the night before, the touch of his hand on her breast
had been warm and loving and good. Their embrace
on the bed had been sweet despite Travis' ugly reaction.

"Oh, I am bad!" she cried aloud to her pillows.
Her evil was the worst kind, an evil that would not
even show itself, but must be hidden behind a pre-
tense of innocence.

A little after midday, Lady Bronwyn knocked at
the bedroom door to ask if she could be of any help.
Suzannah did not bother answering, pretending instead to be asleep. But by late afternoon, her well of
sorrow and remorse had dried up. Left without tears,
she was exhausted, now hungry for the breakfast and
luncheon she had missed.

Glancing into the looking glass on her dressing table, she shrank back at the sight of her haggard reflection. She felt as if her life had ended with Travis' departure, yet some trace of self-respect lingered. She could not bear to look so wretched. For dinner, she bathed and changed into a soft, blue velvet evening gown cut low in the bodice. The back was gathered in a bustle set off by a cluster of silk flowers. Suzannah did not summon a maid to dress her hair, preferring to distract herself by doing it on her own. She brushed the thick, dark waves until her arm ached from the effort and her scalp tingled. Then she pinned her curls firmly in place, tucking in some gardenias that she had gathered from a bowl on the dressing table.

Occupied with such mundane and soothing pastimes, she managed to survive the hours before dinner. The puffy swelling disappeared from about her eyes and her nose lost its bright red color. Looking at herself in the mirror, she could not restrain a smile. Despite the sorrow in her heart, her expression was radiant with hope. The glib happiness of her smile horrified her. If dinner had not been so near and she so hungry that her stomach spoke aloud to her, she would have wept again. How easy it was to lie, to escape responsibilities! She knew suddenly that her smile and pretty face could fool anyone into thinking almost anything. With a rising sense of melodrama, she imagined herself smiling falsely for the rest of her life, hiding her broken, evil heart from the world's inquiring eyes.

From Lady Bronwyn's dining room there were several tall, multipaned doors that opened onto the terrazzo. Mirrors reflected the flash and glow of silver candelabra. Brass and gold sconces gleamed in the candlelight, and the diamonds at Lady Bronwyn's throat and ears caught the glow of the small, crackling fire that burned in the hearth.

"You are quiet this evening, Suzannah. You are not ill, I trust." As Lady Bronwyn spoke, she selected a tournedos from the silver platter offered by a servant. Her tone was cool. Reliable intuition told her that of all Suzannah Hopewell desired, concern from her aunt was the least. Travis' abrupt departure had been a shock, Bronwyn knew. But the aunt guessed further that the girl was displeased with her for speaking frankly of intimate matters. Perhaps, she thought, the two events were in some way connected. A younger Bronwyn, more lavishly emotional, might have indulged herself in hurt feelings under similar circumstances. After all, she had taken Suzannah into her confidence, only to be rebuffed by her niece. But time had taught her that regret was a useless emotion. She soothed her ruffled spirits with the knowledge that Suzannah would someday recall her good advice and be thankful.

"I missed you this morning, Signorina," interjected Roberto. "Did you forget our sitting?"

"No!" Suzannah replied without thinking. "I mean yes. Yes, I forgot."

"Perhaps you have reconsidered modeling for me?" A teasing smile lit Roberto's features. He poured a little more champagne into Suzannah's glass. "That would be a great loss for me."

She sighed and smiled falsely. "I overslept this morning. That is all."

Sarah Hopewell put down her glass so suddenly the crystal rang out. Her voice was harsh and intrusive. "Where is Mr. Paine? Why has he gone and missed his dinner once again?" Sarah's eyes had a bright, unhealthy glassiness. A strange rash of pus-

tules had flowered on her cheek along the jawline.
"Go upstairs and get the young man, Suzannah.
Really, I am appalled at his lack of manners!"

Suzannah was painfully embarrassed. The edges
of her bright, artificial smile were strained.

Bronwyn handled the awkward moment with her
customary grace. "But, Sarah dear, Mr. Paine had to
return to Rome."

"How dare he!" Sarah cried indignantly. "He is
your guest! He is Suzannah's. . . ."

Bronwyn patted her sister's arm. "Of course. But
he must think first of his important studies. Isn't that
correct, Suzannah?"

The girl nodded, wondering why it was that, no
matter how she tried, she could never completely dislike her aunt.

But Sarah was not to be put off. "What have you
done to him, miss?"

"Mama. . . ."

"Sarah, calm yourself. Suzannah has done nothing. Mr. Paine has his studies to complete."

"That's what you say. But I know better. She's a
willful. . . ." Sarah glanced down at her hands. They
were trembling violently, and she stared at them almost hypnotized.

"He's gone to Rome as Aunt Bronwyn said,
Mama. He would have told you, I'm sure, but you've
been ill. He did not wish to disturb your rest." Suzannah pushed back her chair, ignoring the liveried servant who hurried to help her. "Excuse me," she
blurted to her aunt. "I have . . . I can't . . . oh, excuse me!" She rushed through the nearest open door
onto the terrazzo. Running across the tiles and down
the wide steps into the garden, she brushed away the
tears of mortification that streamed down her cheeks.

The moon was full. Touched by the sea breeze,

the arbor of citrus trees cast lively shadows on the path before her. She inhaled the fragrant Mediterranean air—the perfume of gardenia, lemon tree and sea bitters—and hated the atmosphere of this place almost as much as she despised herself. She thought of how the woods smelled when it snowed in Amoset and she recalled the noise of the cataracts when the thaw came.

"What shall I do?" she asked aloud. How can I endure this shame? I want to go home, her heart wailed. I want to go back where I am known and where the rules are so simple. I will be so upright then, she swore to herself. No one will ever think me bad again!

"Signorina!" Roberto was standing just behind her on the path. She had not heard his steps. "May I walk with you?"

"I don't think I'll be very good company this evening, sir." She looked away, ashamed of the tears she was even more ashamed to explain.

He locked her arm firmly above the elbow. "Never mind. I will be charming enough for both of us."

She smiled at that. Coming from any other man the words would have sounded arrogant. But Roberto was different and ahead lay the gate into the Villa Giulia.

"Shall we go through?" Roberto asked.

"Perhaps we should ask permission of someone."

"You mean you did not know? The Villa Giulia is our family estate. Giulia was my grandmama."

"The Duke lives . . . next door . . . to Aunt Bronwyn?" The convenience of the arrangement sickened Suzannah. Bad, corrupt, evil: the Villa Dolce was like a harem with only one courtesan. "Why does she permit it?"

"Who? Lady Bronwyn?"

Suzannah stopped. "Of course not. My aunt I understand. But what about the Duchess? If I were married to the Duke, I never would. . . ."

"If you were my brother's wife, there would be no need of Bronwyn or any other woman, I am sure."

"She's a harlot!" Suzannah was stunned by her words and instantly wished she could retract them.

"You don't mean that." There was gentle reprimand in Roberto's voice.

His kind tolerance was the last straw. Suzannah burst into tears and covered her face with her hands. "I don't know what I mean! I don't know anything—not even myself—anymore."

Taking her in his arms, Roberto spoke consolingly. "It is perfectly natural what you feel, Suzannah. You have come without preparation into a completely foreign world. Our ways are different from yours; our values are not American."

She tried to stop crying. "But why doesn't the Duchess put a stop to the whole affair. Why?"

Roberto dried her eyes with his linen handkerchief. "Try to understand. She does not stop it because she does not wish to. Although she doubtless could never say it, the Duchess is thankful to Lady Bronwyn for giving her plenty of time to go to Mass and to gossip with her family. If it were not for Lady Bronwyn, my sister-in-law would be in the family way most of the time. This is a pleasant relationship for everyone."

Suzannah's reply was unthinking, ripe with indignation. "In American we never. . . ."

Roberto was amused. He smiled, and all at once Suzannah was weeping again, sobbing against his satin lapel. "I want to go home," she stammered. "I don't belong here."

"Sweet Suzannah." He held her tenderly, his cheek resting against the silk of her hair. "You are utterly beguiling to me."

"You must not say that," she murmured, pulling away.

But his arms held her confidently, and when she looked up at him, the moon was swimming in his eyes. She suddenly felt as if she were on a ship of night that might sail anywhere, to anything. When he kissed her—as she knew he would—she did not resist, though she told herself she must. His lips were warm and soft, yet demanding. The kiss went on for eternity and yet it ended, and she was breathless and shaken.

"Don't run now, little faun."

"I won't." She knew the best and wisest course was to leave him alone in the garden, but she loved the feeling she encountered in his arms.

You are bad, an inner voice told her. You are bad and this proves it.

"Will you come to my studio tomorrow?" His voice held a new urgency.

"I don't know. I am ashamed." She turned her head away. You do not yet know the worst, she thought. If you knew all that I am feeling, you would despise me as Travis does.

"Ashamed?" he asked. "Because of one, chaste kiss? Suzannah, my American, you are so innocent. Believe me, don't waste your shame on love and kisses. Save it for the sins that count."

"You can say that because you are a man and a Sicilian. I am a girl from Massachusetts and . . . and a Unitarian on top of all." She blurted out the last as if it were the ultimate confession of provincialism— and then thought how silly her protestations sounded. But Roberto did not laugh.

"Is the New World full of tender flowers like yourself?" He stroked her cheek in a way that sent a sweet shiver of desire through her body. "Soft as a rose to the touch, timid as the violet, graceful as the lily."

"Roberto. You must not speak this way and in these tones." She feared he could hear the thunder of her heart.

"Tomorrow you will come to me. Say you promise it."

"I don't want. . . ."

"You do, Suzannah. You do." He stared deeply into her eyes, mesmerizing her with his conviction and desire. "Promise."

She bowed her head and softly whispered, "I promise."

Suzannah sat on cushions in a patch of yellow sunlight. Roberto sketched her face, asking her—from time to time—to turn to another angle. Apart from that, they spoke little. But the silence seemed mutually chosen as the best expression of what could pass between them.

Suzannah had spent the night in strange erotic dreams of shadows and ships and kisses. In some, Travis held her. His fingers bruised her shoulder and when he kissed her, she cried so the tears touched both their cheeks. In the citrus arbor, a lover with no face stung her lips and eyes with kisses, while Monteleone and Aunt Bronwyn watched and Sarah Hopewell, upstairs, stirred and screamed in her tormented slumbers.

Suzannah yawned and shifted on the cushions.

"Rest a moment if you would like, Suzannah. You are tired?" Roberto took her hand and led her to the comfortable chaise longue in one corner of his bright studio. He pulled back the paint-spattered drop cloth that protected the furnishing's velvet upholstery. "Rest here. I will bring you some Marsala. It will either cheer your contemplative spirits or help you sleep a little." He smoothed her hair and held her face between his hands. "The weight of all the weary world rests upon your shoulders, but it need not. There is nothing for you to fear."

He made her comfortable with pillows and brought a light quilt from the cupboard to wrap about her. Sipping the sweet, heavy wine, she felt strangely contented, despite the confused emotions that had troubled her dreams.

As Roberto tucked the quilt about her, fussing like an uncle with a favorite niece, he urged, "Sleep awhile. I will not be far away."

Letting her eyes close heavily, she told herself it would be impossible to sleep. The atmosphere of the studio was too charged; there was too much risk here. . . . And yet, when she opened her eyes again, she saw by the changed quality of the light that morning had become afternoon. Not far from her, Roberto was engrossed in work. He had taken out a large canvas that had stood draped in the corner, and all his attention was concentrated on it. Suzannah liked the look of him, working that way, unaware of being watched. He wore a rough peasant shirt and snug, dark buckskin breeches. His tight hose emphasized the long, slim line of his legs. With his untidy hair gathered at the nape of the neck with grosgrain ribbon, his head bent in concentration, he made the perfect picture of an artist. Suzannah smiled and drifted back into a sweet and dreamless sleep.

His kiss awoke her. It was late afternoon and a red, setting sun poured its wealth of carmine across the chaise longue. The corners of the room were smudged with darkness.

Still half asleep, Suzannah reached for Roberto and drew him down beside her on the chaise longue. For a long time they kissed. His lips and tongue filled her with a soaring tenderness that was sweeter than any feeling she had known before. A warmth spread from her center out to every part of her limbs. It was a wonderfully weak feeling; she lost substantiality and seemed to merge mouth on mouth, tongue twisted about tongue, into her lover. A thought of Travis crossed her mind, but it was like the mention of an acquaintance rarely seen and hardly talked about.

Roberto lifted the quilt away and brought his body close along the length of hers. She felt his masculinity for the first time and was alarmed by the way this touch—forbidden, unthinkable before this moment—excited her.

"I am bad," she moaned. "So bad."

Roberto shook her. Though his hands were gentle, there was anger in his voice. "Do not ever say such a thing about yourself. You are the farthest thing from bad. You are good, so good."

"But . . . this. . . ."

"You desire me, Suzannah. And I desire you. What could be more perfect or more natural? We pleasure ourselves and harm no one." He laughed gently. "It is God's greatest gift, Little Unitarian, and a sin to deny it."

Before she could reply, he was kissing her again, and the hand on her waist moved up to press and stroke her breast. He deftly loosened the buttons on the front of her morning dress.

"Say it, Suzannah. Tell me you are beautiful and good. Say it."

Beneath his hand, Suzannah's heart stopped, the breath trapped in her throat. "I am . . . I am. . . ."

His finger tips were rough on her nipples. "*Bella, Bella,* you are lovely. Say it." From his stroking hands a thousand rays of sensation darted out.

She tried to pull away, though truly she only wanted to be nearer. Nearer. Wrapped and consumed by this man whose hands made music in her veins.

"Be easy, Suzannah *mia.* I will not hurt you. I will help you." Undoing the last button, he slipped the gown off her shoulders and a moment later it lay forgotten on the floor beside the chaise longue.

Beneath her dress she wore a camisole. The soft cotton eyelet interwoven with pink ribbon and a full ruffled petticoat covered her frilly pantalets. The sight of her in this virginal array amused Roberto and he teased her, but with a note of seriousness.

"You dress like a little girl, Suzannah. In Europe a woman wears silk against her body. Its touch is a caress." He smoothed his hand across her stomach, down to the soft, dark triangle and to the hidden place that softened, moistened. "She is aroused by its touch. . . ."

Suzannah was suffused with a melting sensation that warmed her, allowing her no resistance in body or mind. She could only relax; she knew she was made for this.

"Tell me, Suzannah." His finger was inside her, preparing her.

She shuddered as she whispered the words he had commanded her to utter, whispering in his ear, "I am good, Roberto. I am good."

Heeding instinct and sensation, Roberto and Suzannah moved together as one, needing no more questions, words or answers. Later she would think how easily it had all happened. Their bodies fit together perfectly as his tender, questing hands explored and opened her for love.

He felt her arousal. "Soon," he murmured. "Only a little longer now." He tongued her ear and made her moan and twist in his arms and press herself against his hand. He laughed in appreciation of her excitement.

"Please, Roberto." She begged for the mystery, yearned for this unknown, giving herself to this wonderful and awesome new universe of feeling. At his touch, her thighs opened, and she drew him closer, almost weeping with anticipation. Her fumbling fingers trembled at the closure of his breeches. She was no longer Suzannah Hopewell, but a woman in red sunlight at the edge of freedom, prepared to sail into some new and glorious land.

"Oh, yes, Roberto, yes." He entered her at last. Her pressing fingers marked his back with bruises.

There was a flash of pain, a dart of isolated discomfort forgotten in an instant as sensation mounted. Suzannah closed her eyes and felt him moving in her. She gave over her will in that moment and traveled with him toward the keen edge of pleasure that moved, rushing into her view and still rushing on, toward her, rushing so she could not break her fall. And near the end she heard her own voice calling for Roberto; and she leapt out into the darkness; and in waves of motion heated by the inward fire of her infinite longing, she sailed across a sea of stars.

Chapter 27

The affair between Suzannah and Roberto Monteleone gave Lady Bronwyn considerable satisfaction. Of course, it was gratifying when Suzannah came to her and confessed that she had grossly and unfairly misjudged her aunt.

"I knew so little of the world, Aunt. I was a child and quick to censure you. Now I thank you for telling me the truth. I will never forget."

What gave Lady Bronwyn the greater satisfaction, however, was the return of harmony to Villa Dolce. She congratulated herself on the clever falsehood that had induced her sister and niece to spend the winter in Palermo. Far from dying, Lady Bronwyn Kirkhaven had never felt a more healthy pleasure in life.

One day, a week after Travis Paine's unmourned departure, Lady Bronwyn and Sarah were seated together in a sewing room on the third floor of the villa. It was a cool, wet day and the weather called for a hearty fire, closed shutters and drawn drapes. A seamstress had come through the rain to fit Bronwyn for her spring wardrobe and she had dutifully brought along the ribbon trim selected the week before. Signora Gamboli was an old woman whose clever hands had served Palermo aristocracy since the days of the British occupation. She appeared blowzy and untidy. Rimless spectacles pinched the tip of her long nose. A mass of coal black, dense, wiry hair rebelled against the confines of a crocheted net, springing out from her head like Medusa's snaky locks. Wasting no time with formalities, Signora Gamboli quickly fell to her knees at Lady Bronwyn's feet and commenced to pin up the wide hem of a splendid, silver-blue ball gown.

Sarah was seated on a bench near the fire, smocking the bodice of a nightgown with fine stitchery. Admiring the gorgeous gown, Sarah asked almost accusingly, "Where will you ever wear such a garment?"

"You would be surprised by the number of invitations I receive, Sister. Needless to say, the clergy and their toadies shun me like the plague. They are as bad as the old peasant women at the well. But there are others—other titled Europeans—with whom I enjoy an active social life during the season. You must remember that in Europe the aristocracy lives by its own code, and I daresay that code is considerably less strict than you realize." Signora Gamboli made Lady Bronwyn turn slowly so she might check the hem for evenness. "You'll love it here in the springtime, Sarah. There are marvelous parties and dances. You'll feel like a girl again."

"We shouldn't stay much longer. Martin will. . . ."

Bronwyn laughed. "Must I take to my deathbed again?"

"Don't say such a thing! Don't even think it!" Sarah's needle pierced the minute tucks in the linen and pulled the thread through. "It is most unwise to jest about such things."

"Oh, pooh! Sarah, you are as superstitious as an

old Siciliana." With Signora Gamboli's assistance, Bronwyn slipped the silver-blue silk off her shoulders and stepped out of the dress. With deft efficiency, the old woman quickly helped her into another gown.

"Look, Sarrie! Have you ever seen anything lovelier?"

Truly, the gown was extraordinary, Sarah thought. Made of heavy blue cotton appliqued with pale green, braided satin, it was cut low in the bodice and amply bustled. Seeing her in such a gown, looking both youthful and worldly, Sarah stared at her sister with undisguised envy. It seemed to her, in that moment, that in the business of life she had made an unwise bargain. Breaking the rules, Bronwyn thrived while she, Sarah, obedient to all the right conventions, felt burdened with age and infirmities. In such a dress she knew she would be ludicrous, a laughingstock.

As Signora Gamboli left the sewing room bearing an armload of cotton, silk and satin, Sarah hesitantly asked her sister if she had ever regretted the life she had chosen for herself.

Lady Bronwyn shook her head emphatically. "I love Delio and he loves me. I am excellently provided for, between what he gives me and the generous money I have from Kirkhaven's estate. The only regret I have is for the children I might have raised. I would have liked to be a . . . proper mother." She looked away, busily sorting buttons into the sections of a velvet box. After a moment, she asked, "What about you, Sarah? Have you regrets?"

"Only one." They both knew what she meant.

Bronwyn considered her own words carefully before she went on. "We are alike, you know, despite the superficial differences. Alike in our natures."

There was a waiting silence. "I told Suzannah how to protect herself from conception. She is like us too."

Sarah's sewing dropped from her hands. The smocking needle dropped to the tile floor. "How could you? I am appalled. Truly, I am. She is only a child, an innocent. You had no right to poison her mind."

"You were innocent too, Sarah. Surely you cannot call it an advantage."

"I was different." Sarah folded her arms defiantly across her breasts. "When I met Martin Hopewell, a kind of sick craziness got hold of me. I don't pretend to understand it. I only wish it had not happened as it did." She drew a fresh needle from the basket beside her on the seat and tried unsuccessfully to thread it. After a moment, she gave up. With an exasperated cry, she flung the needle out of her hands. Rubbing her eyes, she felt a headache begin. A pinwheel of shattering light occupied her center of vision, blinding her.

"Surely you do not wish your daughter to remain in ignorance when you know so well the terrible price a woman must pay." Bronwyn poured a glass of Marsala for her agitated sister. "Drink this, my dear. I did not mean to give you the horrors. I thought you were strong enough. . . ."

"She must be kept from all this, Bronwyn. She must be upright and pure beyond question. Amoset is different from Sicily." Sarah gulped down the drink and held out the glass for more. "I haven't been a good mother. I've let her run wild. But no more, no more. She must be above reproach in Amoset. A paragon."

"But Suzannah is not like other women."

"Don't say that! She is!"

"She's like us, Sarah," said Bronwyn gently. "Face the truth. It's not so horrible."

Sarah turned on her sister ferociously. "Like you, you mean? She's like you! There's nothing wrong with me. I'm not different."

Refilling the glass calmly, Bronwyn held it out for her sister. "Did you know that she and Roberto have become lovers? That this innocent you speak of is learning to accept the urges of her body and heart?"

Sarah knocked the glass away. The crystal shattered against the stucco wall. "I won't hear that! If you persist in this lie, I will leave here tomorrow!" She squeezed her temples between her hands, trying to force the pain away. With each second, the sparkling wheel of light spiraled wider across her vision. She was almost blind. Soon the nausea would begin.

She gasped, reaching out for support. "You must help me, Bronwyn."

"Anything!" cried her sister hurrying to her side. "What is it you wish, my dear? Ask anything, and it is yours."

"Delio is still at the Villa Giulia?"

"For another few days. But why? You know that we have said our good-byes."

"He is a doctor, Bronwyn."

"He has not practiced in many years. He. . . ."

"You must get word to him that I have no more nerve tonic left when this bottle is done. He will get me something." She tugged at Bronwyn's sleeve. "I must have medication for my nerves."

"Sarah, I cannot do that. Of all things, that is what I am forbidden to do. There is a pact between us; one I honor. I may not disturb him in his home."

"But I am your sister and I shall die without my tonic."

Bronwyn considered her sister's request. Was it possible she might die without the tonic, or was it merely neurasthenic fear that made Sarah speak this way? Bronwyn was torn between loyalties.

"It is unwise to rely so heavily upon medication, Sarah. Delio would tell you the same thing. This tonic has made you more nervous than ever, and your skin. . . ." Bronwyn reached out and touched the brilliant rash on Sarah's face.

Sarah ignored her words, her touch. She dropped to her knees as a child might, clutching her sister's legs. "Please, Sister, I beg you. I shall die. Help me."

Horrified by this abject display, Bronwyn took her weeping sister in her arms. "Dear little Sarrie, sweet little girl. You will not die. Bronnie's here. I shall not let it happen."

For a long time Sarah wept against her sister's bosom. At last, she became tractable enough to be led to her room. And eventually Sarah lay down to rest.

It was much later, long after dinner, when Bronwyn returned to the bedroom. She found Sarah huddled against the wall at the head of the bed, the covers drawn up around her neck and shoulders. Her face was ghastly—her skin, the color of papier-mâché, drawn tight across her nose and cheekbones, stretched the mouth in a terrible rictus. Against this pallor, the lesions on her skin were a prominent disfigurement. Open-mouthed, with eyes wide and glazed, she seemed not to see her sister and she made no sound. But to Bronwyn, it seemed the room was full of screaming. When she stepped nearer, hoping to measure her sister's pulse, Sarah struck out at her with unnatural strength, muttering unintelligible syllables. Bronwyn fell back, grazing her temple on the bedpost, then struggled to her feet, determined to try again. When she stepped near, Sarah snarled at her. Spit dribbled from the corners of her mouth.

Bronwyn stared at the empty tonic bottle on the

bed table. The evidence was clear. In her urgent need to calm herself, Sarah had taken all that was left. And she was mad.

Not daring to turn away for fear that Sarah might spring at her, Bronwyn backed away to the partially open bedroom door. As she slipped out quickly, Bronwyn caught a last sight of her sister. Sarah's eyes had rolled back into her head. Only the whites showed, laced with red veins.

"Roberto!" Bronwyn screamed. She pounded frantically on his studio door.

He opened quickly. "What is it?"

"You are alone?"

"Yes. What has happened?"

"It's Sarah. Come, come quickly!"

Roberto followed her to Sarah's room, tying the sash of his dressing gown as they ran through the dark halls.

The bedroom smelled of filth. In her delirium, Sarah had soiled herself.

"Holy Mary," Roberto murmured. Without thinking, he crossed himself.

"It is the tonic, I think," Bronwyn spoke in a whisper. "She drank almost half a bottle."

Roberto approached the bed cautiously. Sarah did not recognize him. When he tried to touch her, she flailed against him angrily. He stepped back, looking helplessly at Bronwyn.

"Perhaps if we both . . ." she suggested half-heartedly. Unconsciously, her fingers touched the bruise that was swelling from the place where her head had struck the bed.

Roberto shook his head. "She is too strong for us. She must be watched in case she tries to harm herself. Apart from that, there is little we can do." He shook his head. "Why must she poison herself in order to find life tolerable?" There was almost bitterness in his voice, as if he were faced with a rank injustice.

"We cannot let her suffer, Roberto," Bronwyn pleaded. "She is my sister. Just this afternoon, she begged me so pitifully to send for Delio to bring her more of . . . that." With revulsion she pointed to the empty tonic bottle.

"I think I must go for him."

"In the middle of the night? Perhaps there is another doctor?" She tried to stop Roberto in the doorway. Gently, but firmly, he removed her hand from his arm.

"A Palermo doctor could do no good in a case like this. We both know that. They are a superstitious lot. You might just as well ask for a priest or shaman. They would tell you to send for Brother Michael, the exorcist."

"Perhaps there is nothing. It is hopeless."

"Then better to hear it from Delio." Roberto gripped her shoulders firmly. "I know best in this, Bronwyn. Delio would wish to be called. You know him. How can you think otherwise?" He glanced at Sarah. She was oblivious to them, intent on her own private hell. "Stay with your sister. If she becomes dangerous to herself, you must call the servants. The men."

"Roberto, I couldn't. She is so. . . ."

"I know, but her life may depend on it. What the servants think is of no consequence." He hesitated a moment. "There is another thing, however. Let Suzannah sleep. She must know nothing of this."

Roberto was gone less than an hour. When he returned to the villa, the Duke of Monteleone was with him, still rubbing the sleep from his eyes and looking somewhat out of sorts. As the Duke came in the room,

Bronwyn searched her lover's face for a sign that he was angry with her. To her relief she saw no anger. Delio smiled and kissed her forehead.

"I am so frightened, Delio." It was easier to admit when his arms held her securely. "What if she dies? Sarah is all I have but you."

He did not answer but gestured Roberto to assist him. "Stay near the door," he told Bronwyn.

The poor woman on the bed struggled against the two men; but though her strength was augmented by madness, it proved insufficient against their combined power. A groan of rage burst from her throat and Bronwyn's heart grieved for her sister, for the shame of her disability. The examination was mortifying. Bronwyn prayed that Sarah would remember nothing of it when it was over.

After five minutes, Roberto and Delio left Sarah's bedside. As if they took with them the last of her resistance, she lay without stirring, staring at them dumbly.

"There is nothing I or anyone else can do," Monteleone said as soon as they stood in the hall outside the room. "Let us go to your sitting room, Bronwyn. And you must send for a maid, someone you can trust to keep silent about what she sees. Have her do the cleaning. Tell her to make Signora Hopewell comfortable. She must have cool compresses on the forehead and a little heavy wine in an hour or so."

"Isn't she dangerous?"

"I believe that phase has passed. She is too exhausted now. When did she last eat?"

"Before dinner. She did not want her evening meal."

"It is just as well. But she must have food as soon as her stomach can take it."

They hurried along the hall to Bronwyn's room.

Passing Suzannah's door, Roberto cautioned them to silence. Once in the sitting room he urged, "If this can be kept from Suzannah, then I bid you both to do so. She is so young."

"But if my sister is dying?"

Monteleone looked up from washing his hands. "Rest assured, *cara,* your sister will not die. But she will be in great discomfort for some days to come."

"The cause?"

He shrugged, turning away from the walnut washstand. "Medicine is not a science. Or, if it is, it is an imperfect one. And remember, it is many years since I took my studies in Milan. I can only guess that Sarah's infirmity is a reaction of some kind to the tonic she habitually takes in large quantities." Shaking the last few drops of water into the china washbowl, he dried his hands quickly, then accepted the glass of wine Bronwyn poured for him. "She will need patient care during the next several weeks. I know you can provide her with that, my darling. Her heart is strong; so is her pulse. She will survive this attack. But there is one thing. . . ."

"The tonic?"

"*Si.* She must be made to understand that her suffering was caused by the tonic. She will not want to believe you, but it is essential that you overcome her disbelief. Otherwise. . . ." He sighed with fatigue and rubbed his eyes with his thumb and index finger. "Otherwise, she will return to Amoset, purchase more of the poison, and the situation will repeat itself." Monteleone shook his head sadly. "This seizure will leave her weak and badly frightened, I think. When you tell her what happened, spare not a single graphic detail—the vomit, the excrement, all of it. She must also know that a second occurrence like this one might kill her. Terrify her, if necessary." Delio put his wineglass on the mantle and, going to Bronwyn's side, took both his hands in hers. "I leave you with a formidable task, *cara*."

"Must you leave me so soon? Now that you are here, might you not stay for one more glass?" Bronwyn tilted her head coquettishly and smiled at her lover.

But he would not be wooed. "I must go, beloved, before my absence is noted." Seeing her blink to keep back the tears, he embraced her passionately, kissing her until she fell back in his arms, gasping. "Even we must live by some rules, Bronwyn. Even we." He smiled, as if the mere idea of their being restrained amused him.

"I know. We would have nothing without order in the world. I know." She responded with a wry sadness. "So it must be. Thank you for coming. For not being angry. Godspeed you back to me."

"You will be fine." He brushed the light hair away from her brow with the back of his hand. "Nursing your sister will occupy your time until the spring." Despite his earlier determination to be off, the Duke now seemed reluctant to part from her. "Will you walk with me to the villa gate? The night is sweet after the rain."

She shook her head. "It hurts too much to see you go, knowing I may never enter that house. I would rather watch you from the window in Sarah's room."

Another embrace, one more deep kiss, and he was gone. Bronwyn hurried to her sister's room. Sarah had lapsed into a shallow slumber, groaning intermittently as the old servant tended her. Bronwyn paid scant attention. She went directly to the window. Monteleone was standing beneath the villa beside the citrus arbor. When he saw her, he smiled and saluted, touching his fingers to his lips. Through some trick of light or sleeplessness, he appeared to her as he had years before when their love was young—when their passion was so urgent that any parting, however brief or necessary, brought them pain. It was a magic moment, a pocket out of a time past, when her heart beat quickly and she was young again.

Chapter 28

Spring came to Sicily, arriving with a burst of wildflowers. Roberto and Suzannah made frequent excursions into the countryside and wherever she looked
there were blossoms—wild gladioli, a dozen different
daisies, their colors speaking out like abandoned
laughter. Roberto knew them all—blue and white lu-
pin, cyclamens, vetches. He told Suzannah there were
more varieties of wildflowers in Sicily than in any
other place in the world.

One day they had a picnic by a little stream,
moss-banked and secluded, and he confided, "I had
an old nurse when I was very little and she gave me
chocolates for every species I could name."

"Did she make you count them, too?"

"Of course." He caught her by the shoulders and
pulled her gently into the grass. "Don't you believe
me?"

She adored his teasing. To be the center of his attention was to be completely happy. He was her
dearest, her darling, all the world to her. As the bliss-
ful days went on, she forgot that she was Suzannah
Hopewell of Amoset, Massachusetts. Sicily was the
world, she and Roberto the twin stars that shone
upon it.

On a morning in March, Sarah Hopewell and her sister were seated on the terrazzo adjoining Lady Bronwyn's bedroom. Facing the sea, the terrace connected to the front garden by outside stairs. Near Sarah, Bronwyn was arranging wildflowers in a Venetian glass bowl.

"They never last long," she said, "but they are so pretty and seasonal when they bloom."

"It will please Suzannah to see them," commented Sarah. She was seated at the wrought-iron table with a writing case open before her. "She will miss Sicily."

It was true. During the months since she and Roberto had become lovers, Suzannah had developed an abiding affection for the primitive island with its curious, twisted heritage of high culture and wild barbarism. Though the constant stares of the townspeople were disturbing, Suzannah still loved to walk through the little city of Palermo. On such rambles she often felt like a traveler from a distant land come to peek and peer and memorize. But sometimes she might have been a native, going about routine tasks. Her use of the dialect improved and she became familiar with the tradespeople with whom Lady Bronwyn dealt. Signore Potenziani, the water seller, brought drinking water to the door of Villa Dolce in stone crocks. His wife—black-eyed and dark-skinned as a Moor—once tried to prevent Suzannah from entering the Church of Saint Rosalie, the patron saint of Palermo. Signora Potenziani stood in the doorway and glared, but Suzannah was not intimidated.

In English she had told the woman, "How dare you bar the door to me when I mean you and your church no harm?" She added for emphasis, "I am an American." For whatever reason, Signora Potenziani backed away and let her through. Though she could

not have understood the English words, she knew the
tone of voice in which they were uttered. It was the
voice of a woman accustomed to respectful obedi-
ence.

Seated on the terrazzo, Sarah explained, "I am
writing Martin to say we will arrive home next
month. Amoset is exquisite in April. The dogwoods
are out and the crocuses pop up wherever you look.
All the colors!" She closed her eyes as if she could see
it all in her imagination. "Oh, I shall be glad to be
home."

Bronwyn was puzzled. "Why? It seems from
what you have confided in me these last months, you
have every reason to despise Amoset. I dare not mention what I would feel for Martin Hopewell were I in
your place. He is a beastly, insensitive man. I think it
would be better to live a widow than to endure such a
one."

"Oh, Bronwyn, you are too strong. Besides,"
Sarah said, glancing over the terrace wall, "I was
thinking of Suzannah, primarily."

For a moment, the two women watched as
Suzannah, dressed in a light, forest-green cloak and a
small decorative hat plumed like a military man's,
came through the gate.

"I've brought the bread," she called up to her
aunt. "And what do you think? Signora Balsamo has
delivered a son. They call him Prospero. Like Shakespeare! Isn't that marvelous! May I make up a basket
to take to her?"

"Of course you may, my dear. It is a generous
thought. But will you wait to deliver it until after Delio arrives? It should not be much longer and he will
be pleased to see you after so much time."

"Of course. And I will speak nothing but Sicilian

to him." Departing with a little wave, Suzannah hurried off to deposit the long, crisp loaves of bread in the kitchen.

"Why not let her stay with me?" Bronwyn asked Sarah. "She is happy here, quite the Lady Bountiful."

But Sarah was firm. "She belongs at home. In fact, I think I must rush her off before she becomes too comfortable here." Sarah sighed, "I believe damage will be done if she stays much longer."

"You're speaking of Roberto?"

Sarah leaned forward intently. "Both you and I know what kind of man he is. Though I do not doubt his affection for my daughter, I know a time will come when he will tire of her. She is, after all, hardly more than a child. I don't want her hurt by this experience. I think it best that she leave Sicily while he still wants her. It will be painful, of course, but not tragic—only bittersweet. These months with Roberto will be a memory for her to cherish later."

Bronwyn was surprised at her sister's words. "I have misjudged you, Sarah. Because you spent your life in Amoset, I thought you were ignorant of romance. But you are absolutely right about this love affair. Suzannah is fortunate to have you for her mother, I think."

Sarah raised her eyebrows in surprise. "I only wish that were true." Bronwyn tried to interrupt, but Sarah waved her words away. "It is no good trying to pacify me. I know I've failed my daughter. For years I have used the tonic like a sleepwalker wishing to dream forever. No wonder Martin despises me. I've let his daughter and sons grow up wild." Sarah touched Bronwyn's hand. "I will be grateful to you forever for bringing me through these months. And for keeping my addiction a secret from Suzannah. It is over now, thank goodness. I am like one reborn, given a second chance to be strong. I bless you for it."

"But you must not be too hard on yourself, Sarah. You are inclined that way."

"I will be just as hard as need be. I am adamant about this, you see. I hope it is not too late for Suzannah. When she is married and settled with a family, I will be kinder to myself. Until then, I may not rest."

In the kitchen, Suzannah was buttering a piece of warm bread, scooping the sweet butter from a stone crock. Though it was not yet noon, the cook had sauce simmering in a kettle suspended over the cooking fire. As Suzannah munched her bread, she stirred the sauce. The delicious smell of garlic and herbs made her ravenous. She looked around. The two scullery maids in their blue and white uniforms were chopping and scouring, and the cook was in her pantry. No one was paying any attention to Suzannah. Quickly, she reached forward and dipped the fresh bread into the sauce. It came out dripping, and the sauce splattered all over the hearth just as the cook appeared at the pantry door.

"You wretched miss! Out of my kitchen! Away from my fire!" She waved Suzannah out the door with flour-covered hands.

Clutching her sodden bread, Suzannah fled, laughing. Her heart had never been lighter. Everything in her life suddenly fit together. Everything made sense! She loved Roberto with breathless intensity.

At first she had not loved him. She had been seduced by him and she had enjoyed their passionate relationship because the seduction was so clearly of his devising. She took her cues from him and, because he was unashamed, she felt the same absence of inhibitions. Gradually, she came to realize Roberto's kindness and discretion and finally she relied on his good humor and intelligence to balance her seesaw emotions.

She loved him, finally, knowing his feelings for her were less deeply felt. She told herself this didn't matter. She loved enough for both of them; the cliche was never more true.

Suzannah sat on the bench in the kitchen garden, dripping tomato sauce in the dust while chickens crowded about her feet to investigate. Roberto, she knew, had recently taken a commission to do a bronze of Signore Villafranco, one of Sicily's premier citizens. He was upstairs working on it this minute. She felt a little resentful.

She and Sarah would soon be leaving Palermo, and she would never have the opportunity to see the bust he had done of her. It still wasn't finished. In fact, in the press of commissions from Villafranco and others, the sculpture had been shrouded in a paint-splattered cloth and relegated to a table in the corner, where it had remained for weeks.

Suzannah licked the sauce from her fingers, letting her imagination drift into its own favorite province. In her dreamland she and Roberto were married. She was a patron lady in the city, known everywhere for her goodness. Even sanctimonious blackbirds like Signora Potenziani dipped a curtsy to her when she passed. And Roberto? He would spend his time sculpting and being romantic. Suzannah could imagine no life more perfect.

After a time she became restless and the daydream no longer held her interest. Aimlessly, she strolled through the gardens of Villa Dolce, admiring the blooming irises that stood like overdressed old women in their skirts of lurid purple. The orchids and flowering vines begged for attention but, ultimately, nothing could distract her from thoughts of her lover

alone on the fourth floor. It was in the avocado or-
chard that she found a ripe fruit, all the excuse she
needed to intrude on him. Quickly she ran back to
the kitchen and, defying the cook's noisy protestations, seized the rolls and the butter crock. Carrying
her supplies, she hurried upstairs.

Roberto did not hear her when she pushed the
door open. His back was toward the door, his head
bent in concentration.

"Surprise," she whispered, close behind him.

He swung around. "I didn't hear you, Suzannah,"
his voice edged with irritation. "I told you I wanted
to work until my brother arrives."

"And it is almost that hour now. I've brought you
an early lunch, that's all. You needn't leap upon me so
angrily. I found a fresh avocado and here's bread and
butter. If you have some wine, we'll make a feast of
it." She felt a little out of breath and frightened of
Roberto. He could be so stern and armored when he
chose to be. "Oh, don't be grumpy with me, Roberto!"
she cried, when he refused to be enthusiastic. "I know
you told me to stay downstairs. And I did for a long
time. But I missed you, and there wasn't anything to
do but sit with Aunt Bronwyn and Mother. Can you
imagine how dull that would be?" She made a face.

"But I must work, *cara mia*. Villafranco is expecting his bust in a fortnight. I have given him my
word."

"I know all that. And I have stayed away all the
other times you bade me. But this is different,
Roberto. In a little over a week I will be gone. Forever. I want us to have every possible moment together!"

Roberto shook his head but he was smiling, and
his gesture was one of disbelief. "You are impossible
to refuse, Suzannah. It would take a man with a heart

of stone to resist your charming demands." He covered his work and strode to the cabinet. He found a bottle of wine and two chipped china plates. "You see," he said, holding them up, "I must have been expecting you."

He peeled the avocado and divided the green meat between them. Pushing their thumbs through the thin crust of the rolls, they tore the bread apart and covered the halves with butter and slices of avocado. The white wine was dry.

Suzannah had her way. But instead of feeling satisfied with herself, she was depressed and too thoughtful to make conversation. Her silence was unusual.

"There is something troubling you?" Roberto hooked his hand beneath Suzannah's chin and tilted her face up to peer into his. He kissed her gently on the eyelids and cheeks and, last of all, on the lips. "Tell me what makes you sad."

She thought a moment. "Promise you won't be angry?"

"Have I ever been angry with you?"

"Almost. When I brought the avocado."

He shrugged. "That was different. We had a bargain. . . ."

"We also made a bargain that I would not fall in love with you. You made it clear from the beginning that you did not wish to marry. You told me the artist's life. . . ."

"I remember what I said to you."

"Well," she tried to laugh at herself, "can you guess who has fallen in love? Who entertains herself with fantasies of domestic life?"

"Whoever she is, it is best she is leaving soon." He considered his words. "I love you too, Suzannah. You need not think you love alone."

"Then?"

"Nothing is changed. We love each other, but we must still part because that is the way it is meant to be for us. There could be no happiness if you remained here. After a time—a few months or a year—you would begin again to remind me that you are an American. You would be nostalgic for your own landscape and language. You would urge me to accompany you to Amoset. I would refuse. We would argue." Roberto held her face again and looked into her eyes for a long moment. She could feel his eyes almost penetrating her, as if he hoped in this way to transfer the intensity of his conviction. "Do you understand?"

She nodded, resisting the temptation to deny his words. Though love had run away with her, Suzannah had managed to keep a part of herself aloof, fully aware of the facts of the situation. She knew they must part, but she also knew that no matter what became of them, she would always love Roberto, always wish that it could have been different.

When she could trust her voice not to break, she said, "I want to thank you. These months have been the happiest of my life. You have taught me something, Roberto."

"And what is that?"

"That I am not a bad person."

Roberto laughed, but not unkindly. "How could you ever think such a thing of yourself?"

"Travis made me think I was. He didn't mean to, of course. At least I don't think he did. I believe it was just his Yankee way of speaking. But I took it much to heart; I thought it was true."

They turned, hearing the sound of a bell coming from the quay.

"It is Delio come on the boat from Naples,"

Roberto said. "We must go down to greet him in a moment."

The lovers gazed at one another. It was a moment for remembering, a time to store away a dozen impressions of each other. Suzannah was conscious of needing to complete a picture of Roberto in her mind. Someday when she was bitterly alone, destitute of hope, she would draw out his memory and be refreshed and consoled. This man had truly loved her. He said so, and she believed him so completely that she required nothing more.

When they entered the terrazzo off Bronwyn's room a few minutes later, Suzannah found her aunt in a high state of agitation. Bronwyn seemed exceptionally young as she waited for her lover to appear at the garden gate. Her light wool dress was wine-red and the warm color cast a bright light up to her cheeks. In the playful spring wind, her fair hair was untidy, escaping from her excited fingers as she fussed with it.

"Oh, there you are!" Bronwyn remarked, seeing Suzannah and Roberto draw near. "You heard the ship's bell, didn't you? He should be here any moment. Suzannah, run down and ask Felice if there is wine enough. . . . Oh, bother to all that! There isn't time. He'll be here soon."

At that moment, they heard the chain of bells jangle festively. Through the iron bars of the garden gate Suzannah saw Delio, Duke of Monteleone, appear on the path. He waved and started to run.

"You're here!" cried Bronwyn, starting down the stairs.

"Of course I'm here!" he replied, opening his arms.

Her eyes on Delio, cheeks flushed, Bronwyn gathered up her skirts and petticoats in one hand, waving with the other. She did not bother to look down as she descended the steep, familiar stairs. Her flying feet touched the uppermost step—and suddenly her expression changed from delight to horror.

The heel of her shoe slipped on a piece of crumbling masonry. Her legs went out from under her. Her head hit the stairs hard and she rolled, wine-red skirts whirling in a blur, to the bottom of the stairway.

It happened so fast that no one moved. No one screamed until Bronwyn was sprawled at the foot of the stairs.

Delio reached her first. By the time Sarah, Suzannah and Roberto descended the stairs, the Duke was already holding Bronwyn. He sat on the ground, her head cradled in his arms.

"Bronwyn!" gasped Sarah, calling out to the unresponsive figure that lolled in the Duke's embrace. Then Sarah looked at Delio, saw the tears streaming from his eyes and watched his mouth work contortedly as he tried to speak.

"Oh, God, no," Sarah began to moan. "No, no, no." Her moaning, the dry whisper of the spring breeze in the avocado trees and, finally, Delio's dull sobs were the only sounds to break the silence of the now-still island.

In the sudden fall Bronwyn had broken her neck. She was dead.

PART VI

Chapter 29

Amoset, Massachusetts

Early the same April, in the house on Cooper's
Mountain, Barbara Bolton died in Helen Shawn's
arms. James Shawn had already arranged for a plot in
the Unitarian cemetery in Amoset.

That noon, at dinner, Martin Hopewell told his
son, "I want you to attend the services. The girl was
one of our operatives." Martin speared a slab of well-
done meat and lifted the piece from the serving platter. "Pass the gravy," he demanded.

Martin and Eben took their midday meal in
the paneled dining room, amid a wealth of dark, old
furnishings. The long, mahogany table was meant to
seat eight or ten easily, but when the pair dined
alone, they sat in the middle of the table, across from
one another.

"It'll make a good impression," the manufacturer
went on when his son failed to reply. Continuing to
eat, Eben stared morosely at his plate. "She's been up
on Cooper's Mountain with the Shawn family,
McMahon tells me."

"You hate the Shawns," Eben said, his mouth full
of food, not bothering to look at his father.

If Martin noticed this rudeness, he did not mention it. "It's that damn Yankee James Shawn and the likes of him that I hate. I haven't got anything against the daughter. She's up in the weaving room now and McMahon says she's a hard worker."

Eben stared at Martin. "Lucy works in the mill?"

"Of course. She has for some time. I have no particular objection. McMahon says she's quiet and follows the rules. Of course, you can't tell about the silent ones; they keep their secrets only until it benefits them to speak. Still, if the owner's son attends the funeral, it'll make a good impression on the operatives. And for God's sake, don't take the India Man with you. If it comes to it, I think you're well enough to do without him now. I'll send him back to Cartland House and good riddance to the heathen."

"It was you who said I needed a keeper," Eben sneered. His complexion had a winter pallor that intensified the haunted emptiness of his green eyes.

"That was before. You're much improved over the winter. You took your grandfather's death hard; that's all that was the matter with you. That, plus too much to drink. I mentioned just that in my last letter to Gregory White. Amanda has been asking after you, I understand."

Eben rolled his eyes. "I am once again fit to be Amanda's playmate and your emissary. Is that it?" He pushed his plate of half-eaten food away as if the sight of it nauseated him.

"I'll ignore the tone of your voice, Eben. Yes, you are fit. You should be married at your age instead of mooning about the house like a wretched animal. And you will attend the funeral. Is that clear?" Martin fixed Eben with angry eyes.

At that moment Victorine entered the dining room. Fat and awkward, she almost stumbled on the carpet edge as she placed a silver tray beside Martin. There were two letters on the tray, the first from his son in Boston.

He read it silently, then tossed the scrawled page across the table to Eben. His son ignored it. "Valentine is so in love with his studies, he's decided to stay in Boston through the summer. Pity you can't be as interested in the mill as he is in God."

"I tried to share my ideas with you in Savannah, but you weren't interested." Eben remembered with vivid pain the hopes he had once had for pleasing his father. Now he only wished to have as little to do with the man as possible. "Gregory White told me I have a businessman's mind."

Martin chuckled. "Do I have to remind you how much he wants you for his son-in-law? He'd call you Pope if it suited his purposes." Martin handed Eben the second letter. "Your mother writes that after her marvelous recovery, Bronwyn Kirkhaven has killed herself by falling downstairs." He snorted disdainfully. "You will be denied the dubious pleasure of her acquaintance! Your mother adds that she and Suzannah will be back in Amoset the middle of the month."

While Eben glanced at the letter, Martin found himself wondering at the tone of control and competence that was implicit in Sarah's correspondence. There was no sign of the familiar, nervous tremor in Sarah's script, no agitated repetitions of words or thoughts. It was difficult for Martin to believe that his neurasthenic wife was capable of composing such a forthright letter. He almost believed that the letter was written for her by someone else, and yet the style of script was certainly hers.

"Mother sounds well," Eben commented, glancing at the page before him.

"Perhaps. Still, I will make sure Victorine has

purchased plenty of her tonic. She'll need it when she hears we have a murderer and rapist in Amoset."

"It has been months," said Eben. "Whoever committed the deed must be far away by now. He'd be a fool to stay in Amoset."

The murder and rape of an operative from Conner's woolen mill had struck terror in the hearts of the Amoset mill workers. Though several months had passed since the horrible event, the operatives still went about in groups of three or more and some of them were known to carry hat pins for protection.

The reporter Thomas Kilmaine had broken the story of the murder in the *Amoset News*. Some said the reporting was too graphic—clearly meant to shock and horrify the paper's genteel readership—but the *News* sold out for three days in a row as he detailed the terrible story. The young woman had been raped, beaten and strangled with her own blonde hair. The deed had occurred on a Saturday night, in the dark alley beside the lending library.

In the aftermath of reports of the crime, there were mass defections of mill operatives. News of the murder reached even remote homesteads, and country wagons driven by nervous fathers or brothers were a common sight. Drawing up before the boarding houses, grim-looking farmers paused only long enough to load their daughters with their few possessions into the creaking wagons before they set off for the country again, leaving Amoset and its lurking terror far behind.

McMahon told Martin that he feared the operatives might organize, now that they could rally behind a single inflammatory cause. But later, McMahon reported that the crisis had passed, stirring only a riffle of discontent among the young women.

That was months ago. Now, life in Amoset was

beginning to return to normal. With the coming of spring and advent of longer days, the operatives were losing their nervousness. Most felt as Eben did, that the murderer was long gone by now. But Martin was not so confident.

He had missed Suzannah that winter and was keenly anticipating her return, but part of him was reluctant to see her return to a town where a blood-thirsty murderer was lurking. He knew he would have to watch her willful movements—possibly have her guarded. Martin thought it likely that the rapist restricted his targets to the mill girls, that he would not dare touch a Hopewell, even in the throes of the most violent insanity. But still he felt threatened, vulnerable, as if the walls of his particular kingdom had been breached by an unseen assailant. Martin Hopewell considered hiring vigilantes to patrol the streets at night. And once, discussing the case with McMahon, he told the overseer, "I'd kill any man who laid a finger on my Suzannah."

He said the same thing to anyone who chanced to listen to his ruminations that winter. Eben heard the threat countless times; he was sick of the subject. Immediately after the crime, his Indian servant had come under suspicion. But the police were unable to charge him because Lucy Shawn and several others, Kilmaine included, came forward at the magistrate's office to say that, on the Saturday night when the murder was committed, the India Man was on the shore of the skating pond.

"He looked so out of place," Lucy Shawn told the officer, "I could not help but recall his presence."

To Eben the violent events of that Saturday night seemed somehow part of his memory of the charged atmosphere and his own strong emotions that wintry night. Eben's thoughts about Lucy were mixed, confused—the source of great agitation in his mind. He wished that he had never met her. Even seeing her from afar, he felt disturbed, uneasy. The image of her golden hair and shining face, the honest, direct eyes and firm chin, were indelibly imprinted in his mind. And though he knew she despised him and all he represented, he sometimes dreamed of her and awoke sweaty and ashamed, thinking himself no better than his brutish father.

He dressed carefully for Barbara Bolton's funeral. Were it not for Lucy, he knew he would not have made the effort to attend, even though he was ordered to do so. He cared little for the affairs of Hopewell Mills. For Eben, stripped of his ideals and illusions, life in Amoset was purgatory. During his weeks of mental recuperation at Cartland House, he had read books about life in the West, the Ohio Country and beyond. And he dreamed of striking out on his own, facing the forces of nature and primitive savagery with only his own hands and wits to defend him. But each reminder of Lucy Shawn brought him back to Amoset. At Cartland House he often brooded, walking morosely from room to room, filled with anger and unresolved tension. But in the end he could not escape Amoset. He came back because of Lucy and—he was now ready to admit—because he needed to see his sister again.

Just prior to his departure for Savannah, Eben had injured Suzannah grievously. His behavior, he now saw, was unforgivable. His heavy-handed exploitation of the matter of Travis Paine, the extortion he used to get his way, filled him now with shame.

Buttoning the dark vest of his funeral suit, he said aloud to his reflection in the mirror, "I will make it up to you, Suzannah. I swear I will. Somehow."

His gig was one of the last to arrive outside the Unitarian Church where services were being held. There were hundreds of operatives in attendance. They filled every pew and stood pressed against each other in the side aisles. They were so alike in their serviceable dark clothes and starched bonnets that they recalled to Eben the look-alike paper dolls fashioned by one of the mad residents of Cartland House. The women filled the choir loft above and behind the congregation. They stood shoulder to shoulder on the front steps, their heads bowed.

Entering the church, Eben had to push his way through the throng. A murmur spread among the congregation, announcing the presence of the owner's son. Heads turned in curiosity, prayers were forgotten and the girls whispered to each other behind their white-gloved hands.

Eben looked for Lucy but he could not distinguish her from the others in the crowd. He strode down the center aisle to the family pew and took his place, grim-faced, suffering the scrutiny of the women. Bowing his head, he closed his eyes as waves of silent accusation washed over him.

From the corner of her eye, Lucy watched Eben enter and hoped he would not see her. If he did, she knew, he would almost certainly engage her in conversation. Since that night at the skating pond, she had been determined to avoid such a meeting. His dark, melancholic appearance, the brooding intensity of his light-eyed gaze, filled her with discomfort. Since that disturbing night, she could admit to herself that Eben was not a bad person. She saw that her first impression, conceived months before, might be in error. Now her view was more charitable. Yet she was certain that his inexpressible longings and urges were doomed to be thwarted by some fatal flaw of character.

As Reverend Strickland rose to the pulpit to begin his funeral sermon, Thomas Kilmaine, seated beside Lucy, noted her distraction. "Are you ill?" he inquired, touching her hand with affectionate concern.

Though a part of her desired to pull away, she recognized his kindness and only smiled faintly, shaking her head. She kept her eyes on Reverend Strickland.

But her thoughts had wandered far from church, far from the funeral rites for Barbara Bolton. She recalled the organizing that had gone into bringing a full force of operatives to the funeral. She had told the Spindle Sisters that the number of mourners must be enormous to make owners like Hopewell realize that there was solidarity among the operatives. And she had felt a glow of satisfaction as she entered the church that afternoon. The crowd *was* enormous. Hundreds of women had come to pay tribute to their comrade. She was a symbol to them all.

Now, as she bowed her head for the blessing, she tried to think of a way of capturing this enthusiasm and turning it to the advantage of all. They must, if wages and conditions were ever to improve.

After the service, Lucy and Kilmaine parted.

"I must get to work," he told her, again touching her hand with that troublesome affection. "I have a deadline to meet, and have yet to write a sentence."

"Don't apologize," replied Lucy quickly. "I will walk to the cemetery with Marie and Violet. I'll see this thing through."

As she hurried off in search of her friends, a

young man appeared before her. Though he was a complete stranger to Lucy, he stood squarely in front of her in the road and she was forced to notice him. He was rather flamboyantly dressed in a soft-collared shirt and short jacket, and he wore a wide-brimmed hat that drooped over his brow eccentrically. Lucy's first thought was that he could not possibly be a mourner, but the expression on his face belied her thinking. He was clearly suffering, and his reddened eyes proved that he had been weeping in the church.

"Miss Shawn," he said, "I am Joshua Bolton, Barbara's brother."

She was startled. "Where have you been? We tried to notify you, but your landlady said you had moved and left no forwarding address." Lucy did not try to hide her distaste for the man. "The least you could have done was see her before she died. Have you so little family feeling that you could permit your sister to . . . ?"

He held up his hand to stop her words and, even before he spoke, the tears fell from his eyes. He made no effort to staunch the flow. "I know you think me the most contemptible of men and you have a perfect right to your opinion. But please believe me when I say I loved Barbara with all my heart. At the time she was with your family, I was myself in New York and Baltimore seeking help for her among our people. Alas, they had none to give. I became ill myself." Bolton turned away. "It is I who killed her. I am her murderer."

"You might have done better by her. But that hardly makes you guilty of murder." In a town where murder had become a reality, Joshua Bolton's confession struck Lucy with particular horror. She was disposed to dislike him for appearing to abandon his sister in her need. The abject tone of his confession only confirmed her dislike rather than prompting her to forgive him.

"You don't realize," he told her. "I am worse, far worse, than even you, her friend, can understand." Lucy begun to walk again, following the crowd up Front Street toward the cemetery beyond McMahon's house. Bolton kept pace with her.

Irritably, Lucy said, "Mr. Bolton, I know you are most unhappy, and believe me, I understand that your loss is very great. Barbara was an angel. Her goodness became known to us all before she died. But I must tell you that coming now, too late, your caring strikes me as . . . well, I will not say it. I would not insult the brother of a dear friend, no matter what my true thoughts might be."

"Then let me blacken my own name!" He tore off his hat and held it against his chest. "Let me speak the truth so that you at least will know the extent of my sin."

"Oh, really, Mr. Bolton!"

"You do not recall me, Miss Shawn, but I have seen you once. I was speaking to my sister one night. We stood at the foot of the stairs at Mrs. Quinn's boarding house. It was the last time I saw Barbara. She told me then that she was ill and I went to raise money for her care. Until that time, I had been boarding at a residence in Boston and Barbara . . ." He hesitated, apparently overwhelmed by the memories that tormented him. "Barbara . . . sent me her pitiful wages."

Again Lucy stopped. She was thoroughly out of sorts with Joshua Bolton. But when she examined her own feelings, she became angry with herself for judging him so harshly. Still, she was cross. "There is hardly a girl in Amoset who does not send some of her wages to someone: a father to pay off the mortgage, a brother in school, a. . . ."

"But I am none of these. I am an able-bodied man who took from his dying sister in order to pursue a career as a poet. While Barbara was growing weaker, I was spending her money for paper and writing poems. And worse—I was using her wages to buy drinks for my friends and pass myself off as a . . . success." At this point, he broke down and began to weep bitterly, burying his face in his hands.

Lucy stared at him, overcome with loathing. Barbara had spoken of her brother many times and always with the greatest affection and pride. "Barbara used to tell my mother you were someone important," Lucy observed coldly. "Someone special."

"I know. I know," he sobbed. "And I encouraged her attitude. I told her . . . a poet could not be troubled by mundane affairs lest he lose sight of his . . . lofty purpose."

The other mourners had passed far beyond them now, trailing up the road beyond Hopewell Mills and the company houses. Joshua and Lucy stood alone on the street, overshadowed by the grim face of the mill that bore mute witness to their conversation.

Lucy spoke quietly. "I think a poet also needs to experience strong emotions in order to write well. Who knows, Mr. Bolton, perhaps your grief will bring the fame you desire. In that case, it will be said that Barbara did not labor and die in vain. Good day to you, sir." Lucy hurried ahead of him.

Privately, she was appalled by the tone in which she had spoken to the grieving man. Her sarcasm had not been lost on him. Before turning away, she had seen his expression and been struck by a fleeting pang of guilt. Hurrying to catch up with the others, however, she told herself he deserved all her acrimony. Barbara might have loved her brother, but Lucy was under no such compulsion.

Lost in her confused thoughts, Lucy did not hear the open gig at it approached her from behind. She was in front of McMahon's house now, keeping her eyes firmly on the road ahead lest she chance to see the general overseer.

"Miss Shawn."

She recognized Eben Hopewell's voice.

"May I offer you a ride? The hill to the cemetery is steep."

She shook her head and kept walking. Eben slowed the gig to keep pace beside her. "If you fear that others may talk, I assure you, my intentions are completely. . . ."

Abruptly Lucy stopped and turned to him with an angry gesture so quick that he fell silent. In his black mourning suit, he appeared to her—in an uncharacteristic flight of fancy—as the angel of death. She had a sudden vision of hundreds of young women laboring through darkness and light, enduring damp mornings, foul weather and piercing cold so that this young man might ride to the graveside while others walked. In a rush of emotion accompanied by pure loathing, she realized that Eben, like Joshua Bolton, lived off the labor of women. While operatives suffered, he took it as his right to profit from their misery and their wasted lives. When Lucy looked at Eben, she no longer saw a fellow human being, but a mere representative member of a class she despised.

"Miss Shawn?" Eben was about to jump down from the gig to help her in, but the expression on her face halted him.

Putting careful emphasis on her words, but strangely aloof from her own impetuous declaration, Lucy heard herself state, quite clearly, "I would not ride with you, sir, were you the last and only man on earth."

Chapter 30

Jerking the reins furiously, Eben wheeled the gig around and thundered away from Lucy. He did not turn to see the expression on her face as she stood in the dust looking after him. If he had, he would not have understood the peculiar mix of satisfaction and remorse written in her features.

Like an ancient charioteer, Eben stood erect in the gig, reins tightly held in one hand, whip cracking in the other. The spring air knifed him with its chill and he gulped to prevent tears of rage and despair from overpowering him. On, on, he drove, racing down the middle of Front Street past the line of boarding houses, the little shops, the plain-faced churches. Not until he had reached the outskirts of Amoset did he cease to punish the horse. Then, all at once, he was exhausted. The reins dropped from his hands and he sank down to the seat.

There was a tavern called McGill's another mile along the road, a place commonly frequented by bargemen and vagrants. It had an unsavory reputation among the townspeople, but the dark, dissolute place, shuttered and unpainted, suited Eben's purposes. After seeing to the horse, he went in, found a dark table and ordered a bottle of brandy.

The first drink vanished in a single gulp. He poured himself a second and third, which disappeared as quickly as he could force the burning liquid down his throat. With the fourth he became disoriented. The outlines of his memory began to blur.

"Lucy," he muttered aloud, at last purging the hatred from his mind. His voice softened. "Lucy." After another drink, it seemed he could see her more clearly in his mind. Her expression of loathing was vivid; he knew he would never forget it, that his skin would crawl with shame every time he recalled the curl of her lip, the deadly animosity.

Why do you care? he asked himself. Who is she? What does she matter? These were questions he could not answer whether sober or drunk. He remembered the days when he had escorted his little sister to the Shawns' in summertime. He had been enchanted by the blonde little girl. Even at the age of nine she'd had an attractive, determined way about her. He used to laugh at her then, teasing her until she cried and ran away from him to hide beneath the stairs. He was awkward and shy; his gibes and jokes had been unthinkingly cruel. After a time, she no longer ran out to meet his carriage as it lumbered up the steep mountain track, but sometimes he caught a glimpse of silver-blonde hair as she ran to hide from him behind the barn or among the rows of corn.

Though he could never have said it, Eben envied his little sister her friendship with a family like the Shawns, a family so different from his own. While he padded after his humorless father, learning every detail of the Hopewell business, always determined to please, he secretly yearned for the high mountain and the laughing companionship of a friend like Lucy Shawn.

When Suzannah's visits were forbidden, Eben

gloated. In time, he forgot his envy and lost his hope for close, easy friendships. Blind emulation of his father filled his life. He became the perfect son, attentive to business, oriented toward success. Sometimes his efforts were rewarded; Martin occasionally smiled at him and managed a word or two of praise.

At the thought of his father, Eben's hand tightened on the half-finished brandy bottle. A soft sound like a snarl emerged from clenched teeth. Inwardly, he cursed himself. He had thrown his life away admiring a man he knew to be despicable in every way.

"I wish I were dead," he muttered into his glass. The thought of death—endless, empty, untroubled—was dangerously seductive. No one would grieve for him, he was sure. There would be no hordes of weeping mourners as there had been for Barbara Bolton.

He poured more brandy, then held the bottle up to the light. It was empty. Good. He had heard of men who died from drink and he wondered if his luck might change. Would he be fortunate enough to fall dead in the sawdust at McGill's?

"Want some friendly company, mister?" She stood beside the table grinning, her gap-toothed smile beckoning him. A buxom, redheaded woman well past her prime, she stood with hands on hips, swaying lasciviously.

Eben saw her through a blur, his vision registering multiple images. For a few moments, he forgot where he was. He saw the old trollop's flaming hair and thought of his father's woman, Marie Celeste, with her jewel-encrusted pipe.

"Marianna," he muttered, looking around for her.

"Dolly, mister. That's my name and I could really use a drink. How 'bout just a little one for Dolly, eh?"

She winked broadly and her hand went up to brush the thick red hair back from her pocked face.

Eben stared at her, remembered where he was and laughed sardonically. He smelled a dank animal odor beneath the heavy floral perfume she wore. Her cheap fragrance mingled with the odor of ale and spirits, stewed cabbage and piss that pervaded McGill's tavern. This was no Marianna, gentle-eyed and fatalistic. Nor was this Death. But Dolly would do! Eben roared with laughter, attracting the attention of the tavern regulars. A few bargemen and an old woman turned to stare at him. Eben kicked the chair beside him. "Sit down, sit down! Why not? Keeper!"

The owner brought another bottle to the table. Wretchedly drunk, Eben did not notice the look that passed between the barman and Dolly as he threw a bag of coins on the table.

Dolly poured two glasses and downed hers quickly. "Hey!" she said, tugging at Eben's sleeve. "I poured you one. Go on! Drink it!"

Eben downed it in a single gulp.

"That's a good fellow," crooned Dolly, pouring another round. "Now you just keep on. Cheer up! Dolly'll take care of you. Don't you worry 'bout nothing." Her hand slipped beneath the table, touched his knee, then reached between his legs. Too drunk to move, Eben stared at her.

"Don't worry 'bout nothin', I said. Didn't I just?" She licked her lips obscenely, patted Eben and gave a gentle pinch. When Eben hardened slightly, she laughed with satisfaction. "I told you I'd take care of you, mister. Everything's gonna be fine for you and me." She gestured to the tavern keeper who hurried to the table and helped her lift Eben from his chair.

He complained, "I don' wanna. Wanna. . . ."

"Sure, Ducky, sure." Dolly held up the bottle of brandy. "I know two things you want and Dolly's got 'em both. Just come on up to my room. Let Dolly make you happy."

Dolly's room was a cubicle behind a curtain at the end of the hall. "Make it fast," the keeper ordered as he dumped Eben on the malodorous bed. It swayed like a hammock, sagging in the middle as he landed.

The details of the place were lost on Eben. He scarcely knew where he was. When his eyes managed to focus and he saw Dolly clearly for a fraction of a second, he was pleased to see that he had sunk to the most abysmal depths of degradation. What else could one expect from Martin Hopewell's son?

"You know what?" he mumbled as Dolly tugged off his boots. "I'll tell you what—it's hell."

"What's hell?" she asked. She wasn't even slightly interested but did wish to keep him happy a little longer.

"Life. Mine. Yours. All of it. Hell."

She chuckled in spite of herself. "You speak right enough there, mister. But you don't hardly know." She unlaced the flap of his breeches and, giving them a tug, pulled the pants down to his knees. Naked, he was like a small boy, flaccid and unaroused. "You got fine equipment, mister," she said, giving his privates a flicking touch. " 'Tis a pity it ain't workin'."

Eben laughed. "You should meet my father," he mumbled. "His works fine for fat old whores."

Dolly's expression went ugly. "Watch what you say to me. Drink up!" She shoved the bottle at his lips. "Might make you friendlier."

The cheap brandy scalded. He let it spill down his lips onto his clothing. A perverse thrill ran through him as he realized what he was doing to himself. He prayed that he might die unnamed in the tavern. Grabbing Dolly by the nape of the neck, he shoved her face down onto his lap.

"Do it!" he demanded. "Now."

As her mouth touched him and the tears slipped from his eyes, in the middle of a whispered prayer for death, he lost the last weak hold he had on consciousness. His head fell back upon Dolly's soiled pillow and he slept.

Hours later, as the afternoon sun was gilding the eastern summit of Cooper's Mountain, Eben regained his senses. He was sprawled across the leather seat of the gig, which was parked beside the river several miles from McGill's Tavern. A man was shaking him.

"Are you hurt?"

Eben held his head and groaned.

"I saw them bring you here. A man and a . . . woman." The man was a stranger. But as Eben's vision cleared, he thought he recognized something familiar about the fellow. He had seen that soft-brimmed hat somewhere.

"Do I know you?"

The man shook his head. "I only happened to be near, passing along the river trail."

"Where did you come from? Damn it, man, I'm sure I know you." Eben struggled to sit up. He shivered in the cold twilight. "I remember. You were speaking to. . . ."

"Miss Shawn." Joshua Bolton's head drooped. He explained who he was. But as soon as he began to share his remorse and self-hatred, Eben stopped him.

"I don't want to hear that. You have your life; I have mine." As a thought occurred to Eben, he quickly searched his pockets. "It's gone!" he cried.

"What?" Joshua, about to move on, hesitated alongside the gig.

"Did you rob me?" Eben jumped from the gig and grabbed Bolton's lapels. His head thundered with pulsing blood and he gripped Bolton fiercely to keep from keeling over.

The poet pulled away angrily and Eben staggered back against the gig. "You may call me many things, but thief is a name I will not tolerate. What makes you think I would deign to touch your stinking money! Do you think you are anonymous? You're Hopewell. As much as I, you share in my sister's death."

Raising a clenched fist as if to strike, Bolton suddenly changed his mind and quickly strode away, walking toward the river path as Eben stared after him. Too weak to defend himself, even with words, Eben could not take his eyes from the rapidly retreating figure. At the edge of the trees, Bolton turned and shouted, "At least I am not a whoremaster. I have at least my self-respect!"

Alone again, Eben closed his eyes and saw spinning lights.

"Fool!" he cried aloud to himself. Now that Joshua Bolton was gone, Eben understood the situation perfectly. Dolly and the keeper had gotten him drunk, then robbed him of every cent he had. They knew that he would never dare to press charges. Shame, and the fear of public opinion, would certainly prevent his doing so. Like Bolton, they knew who he was. Even in the pits of degradation, he could not escape the bondage of his identity. It was as Marianna had said. No one is really free. Only in death could the chains be sundered.

The Amoset River was high. Fed by melting snows, it roared noisily eastward, passing near the shore where Eben stood. It would be so easy to lose himself in the grey waters. He walked slowly toward the boulders that crowded the river bank and scrambled on top of the highest. The river near his feet was wild and powerful, carrying on its breast the broken limbs of trees brought downstream by the raging spring freshet.

"Why not take me?" he called to the waves.

One step farther, he thought, and I am dead. Free.

He lifted his foot and took a deep breath. He could taste the fresh air, almost as if it were a tangible substance. His lungs inhaled and his eyes closed.

But his foot withdrew. His legs refused to move. All around him the river roared, crashing through the rapids below. And the hard, chill wind that followed the freshet along its raging course seemed to waken Eben, for the first time in months, from the torment of his nightmare.

He regained his footing on the slippery rock and stood a long while, staring into the white rush of water below. But he did not take the final steps. No, it was not yet time.

PART VII

Chapter 31

On the morning that followed Sarah Hopewell's return to Amoset, she awakened early. For a moment, she was seized by a familiar panic at the sight of her room. Its dormer windows were open, curtains pulled wide, and spring sunlight fell in stripes across the dark wood floor. In Sicily, and on the ship crossing the Atlantic, Sarah had been confident of her ability to withstand the pressures of life at home. She had been certain she would not require the nerve tonic. Thinking of Bronwyn's confidence in her, Sarah had been proud of her own strength of character. But now that she was home again, she did not believe she could maintain her abstinence.

Just a little sip of nerve tonic could do no harm, she assured herself, and it would give her strength to face the day. She had so much to do, so many plans to bring to fruition. How could she hope to accomplish all these things if her hands shook and her mind wandered? What if she were overwhelmed by the old timidity?

There was a quick, soft knock on her bedroom door, and Victorine entered bearing a tray. Sarah was shocked by the young woman's slovenly appearance.

"Victorine!" Sitting up quickly, Sarah forgot all

about her nervous condition. "Has Mr. Hopewell allowed you to go about looking like this? What will
our neighbors think?"

Though never a pretty girl, Victorine had at least
been fairly tidy and clean when Sarah left for Sicily.
But during the winter she had gained a good deal of
weight. And as she slumped about the bedroom,
opening windows and fluffing cushions, she looked as
dismal as a woman condemned.

"I am speaking to you, Victorine! Have all my
other servants lost their self-respect this winter? Tell
me!"

Instead of replying, Victorine muttered, "I have
brought your chocolates and the tonic Master Hopewell ordered for you." She kept her eyes on the floor.

The small, tempting bottle stood beside Sarah's
cup and saucer on the tray. Staring at the amber
glass, Sarah was distracted from Victorine's miserable
appearance and ignored the abject woman who
snuffled nearby. The contents of that bottle held her
attention. The amber bottle seemed to hold the elixir
of life. It glowed and called her to taste its goodness.

"Take the tonic away," she demanded finally, the
words rushing out. "I no longer use the tonic."

"But Mr. Hopewell said. . . ."

"Mr. Hopewell has nothing to do with this, Victorine."

The servant looked up, surprised by her mistress'
uncommonly firm tone.

"Now tell me what is the matter with you. Are
you ill?" Sarah inquired as she rose from bed. She
pulled on the light wool wrapper that Victorine had
laid in place over the footboard. "Well? I've heard
you gossip by the hour with the servants. Why can't
you find a civil word for your mistress?"

Victorine sniffed and shuffled. Nervously, she

rubbed her palms up and down the skirt of her stained uniform.

"When did you last launder your clothing? Have you given up bathing altogether?" Sarah took Victorine firmly by the shoulders and directed her to the long looking glass. "Look at your hair! It's a rat's nest!"

Victorine stared at herself in the mirror. Even in her own view she appeared sullen, fat and unkempt.

"Say something!" demanded Sarah.

Victorine began to sob. Her nose ran, but she did not bother to wipe the mucus away.

Sarah was appalled, speechless. She stared at the servant until, finally, Victorine's sobs became so wild that her mistress felt compelled to console her. "Sit down, child. Control yourself and tell me what is the matter."

Pushing her dark, oily hair away from her face, Victorine stopped crying at last. She hiccupped loudly. Sarah could scarcely control her revulsion.

"Unless this stops, I shall be forced to let you go, Victorine. I am perfectly willing to help you if I can, but this revolting hysteria will have to stop. Instantly!"

"I can't help it!" In her distress Victorine's Irish accent thickened. It was almost impossible to understand what she was mumbling.

"Nonsense!" Gingerly, as if the gesture might contaminate her, Sarah gave the girl a shake. "Now tell me what's gotten into you?"

Silence. Then, very softly, "I am these five or six months gone."

"What did you say?"

Sullen brown eyes stared at Sarah. "I am with child, ma'am."

Sarah's hand flew to her forehead. "Of course! I

should have guessed it. You Irish have the morals of
. . . well, never mind that. Who is the father?"

Again Victorine remained silent.

"It will do you no good to try to protect him,
whoever he is. If you want me to help you, you must
tell me everything."

Sarah could not be sure, but she thought she detected a smile that pulled at the corners of Victorine's
mouth. " 'Twas your son, ma'am."

"Eben!" cried Sarah, sinking into a chair. "I
might have. . . ."

" 'Twas Master Valentine, ma'am."

"No!" Sarah almost screamed the word. Her heart
beat wildly. From the corner of her eye, she caught
sight of the amber tonic bottle on the tray.

" 'Tis true, ma'am. He had me several times.
Right in his room." Now Sarah was sure! The girl was
smiling just enough to seem impertinent. She had begun to enjoy the moment and the real pleasure in her
gloating spoke the truth louder than words. "I didn't
know how to refuse him, ma'am—him being the
young master and all o' that."

In a single fluid movement, Sarah was on her
feet, and her hand swung out to slap the servant
across her smirking face. "Don't lie to me, you pig! I
don't know what you expect to win from me, but I
swear to God you'll get nothing."

" 'Tis your grandbaby, ma'am. I swear it, by
Christ's blood."

"How dare you blaspheme in my presence?"

"And by the Virgin, too." Victorine rubbed her
crimson cheek.

"I don't believe a word of what you say. Valentine is a saintly boy, a divinity student. He would
never lay a hand on someone like you. You would disgust him."

"Ah, no, ma'am. There you're wrong." Unmistakably, Victorine was gloating now. "He was quite keen. Once in the cedar closet. . . ."

"Get out! Pack what you have and be gone by dinner time. I never want to lay eyes on you again." Sarah tried to shove Victorine toward the door, but the sturdy servant held her place.

" 'Tis your grandbaby, ma'am."

"I will not believe that! Never!"

"You want to send me and your wee grandbaby out to starve? I have no friends, no family here. I'll sicken. I cannot give birth in a ditch." Victorine narrowed her eyes. "Would you have that on your conscience, ma'am? That you killed your own. . . ."

"It's not true!"

"So you say, but I know different. And all your days, won't you be wondering too, ma'am? What if you're wrong, ma'am? What then?"

Sarah stared at her. What the canny girl said was completely true. Though she could not imagine Valentine and this servant together, she knew enough of the world to realize that such things could happen. In the courts of Europe, it was common indeed, Sarah reminded herself derisively. Masters bedded their servant girls and gave them bastards.

But Valentine Hopewell of Amoset? Sarah shuddered.

"How much wages are owing you?"

"A half dollar, ma'am. Not enough to keep a body alive." Victorine shook her head. "Not enough to care for a babe and that's for certain. There will be little things to buy, a cradle. . . ."

"Spare me the details," Sarah interrupted grimly. Her traveling boxes, as yet unpacked, rested in the corner where the valet had placed them the night before. Sarah opened one of the trunks, rummaged for a moment among its contents and brought out a small wooden box. Lifting the lid of the box, she gazed at the jewelry that rested in its velvet-lined interior.

Bronwyn had died without leaving a will. According to the terms of her late husband's estate, the wealth that had been hers reverted, at her death, to his brother's children in England. Those children had openly shunned Bronwyn after Kirkhaven's death and they had no claim to the remainder of the inheritance. It had been the Duke of Monteleone's idea to divide his lover's jewels between Sarah and Suzannah. Sarah now possessed several valuable gems that Martin Hopewell knew nothing about. Now she removed a long strand of pearls from the jewelry box and held it in the palm of her hand. Her gaze wandered to Victorine.

The serving girl's eyes grew wide. A bright flush crept into her sallow cheeks. Greedy harlot, thought Sarah bitterly. To part with the lovely gems that had once graced her sister's throat caused her an almost physical pain. But it was the only way. Martin would never know and Valentine would be protected.

"I will give you these. You can sell them in Boston or New York for a great deal of money. They belonged to my sister and they are perfect. For a time, you and your bastard will live well. If you are wise, you may even find a way to make a comfortable life for yourself." Victorine's hand reached out eagerly but Sarah held back her gift. "I never want to see you again. You are to leave Amoset today and if you ever return I will deny whatever you say. Should you cause this family another moment's shame, I will see to it that you are thrown into the workhouse and left there to rot—and your bastard with you! Do I make myself clear?"

Smirking, Victorine curtsied. Her hand closed

about the necklace. She quickly shoved the loot into the pocket of her uniform, spun around and vanished from the room without bothering to close the door behind her.

When Victorine had left, Sarah felt seized by a paralysis of will. She stood where she was, staring through the open doorway to the patch of maroon hall carpet that lay beyond. Her mind was entirely blank. Suddenly, with the abrupt clarity of a revelation, she saw her daughter's face swimming before her.

Suzannah! Something must be done about Suzannah before her willful, warm-blooded nature got her into the same predicament as Victorine.

Sarah saw everything clearly now; she knew what she must do and saw how to go about her duty. Tying her wrapper firmly at the waist, she hurried from her room. Without knocking, she entered Suzannah's room and strode to the bed where the girl lay face down, still dreaming under the warmth of her fat down comforter.

"Wake up, Suzannah!" Sarah cried, giving the sleeping girl a shake. "It's late. Wake up! I have to speak with you." She shook the girl again, this time more roughly.

"Mama?" Suzannah sat up, blinking as her eyes became accustomed to the bright room. "What's the matter? What's happened?"

Sarah began to pace. "Get up! Put something on. I have to talk to you and I won't do it while you're half asleep." A quilted robe hung from a hook in the wardrobe. Sarah carried it to Suzannah and dropped the robe over her daughter's shoulders. "Hurry now. I'll brush your hair."

With Suzannah seated at the dressing table, Sarah took up the oval, mother-of-pearl brush that lay

on the glass table top and began to draw it through
Suzannah's tangled hair. Shimmering among the dark
brown strands, highlights of gold caught the rays of
sun streaming through the windows.

"I have just had an experience that has frightened the daylights out of me. And cost me Bronwyn's
pearls in the bargain. I am most fearful, Suzannah,
and mostly on your account. . . ."

"What have I done, Mama?" Suzannah's green
eyes grew wide.

"Nothing. Not yet at any rate. But that is what I
need to speak to you about. Judging from the way
you carried on with Roberto, there is not a moment to
lose."

A look of sorrow disturbed Suzannah's features.
"We've talked about that, Mama. You said—don't you
remember—that you understood."

"And I did!" Sarah tugged at a tangle and Suzannah winced. "But that was in Sicily and we are home
now. In Amoset a very different set of standards ap-
ply. I mean to see you adhere to them."

Suzannah sighed. She stared at her mother's reflection and wondered at the change that had come
over her during the winter months. Gone entirely was
the vague, wispy Sarah Hopewell of the previous autumn. In her place was this energetic woman, apparently filled with conviction, bent on having her
way despite the costs.

"I have decided that you must marry Travis
Paine. The quicker the better! You will write to him
today and tell him. . . ."

"Please, no, Mama. I don't want to marry Travis.
I don't love him." Her heart still dwelt on Roberto;
their parting had occurred long ago, yet the pain was
fresh and raw. Now, to have marriage foisted on her,

seemed like sheer cruelty. "Besides, Papa despises him. He will never permit. . . ."

"Leave your father to me, Suzannah. I'll make him see reason. As to love," she yanked at another tangle, "people get along without love all the time. It is Roberto Monteleone who has given you romantic ideas about love. Well, you'll just have to put them out of your mind. You had your daydream in Sicily, but now it is time to get down to the business of living in the real world. Travis Paine is an excellent match for you."

Suzannah could only remember his cruel rejection of her that night at Villa Dolce. It was a scene that she would replay in her mind for the rest of her life, and a memory that would always have the power to mortify her. "For all I know, he no longer cares for me."

"None of that matters, Suzannah. It is an excellent match, and Travis Paine is too clever a Yankee to turn down a young woman who can make him heir to a fortune. He'll soon care for you again."

Striding to the wardrobe, Sarah pulled out a tired-looking, dark blue dress with long sleeves and a high collar. "Wear this today. And when you've finished dressing, you may go into my room and use my desk for writing your letter." Sarah hurried to the bedroom door, but before she went out, she added, "You know how to make him come back to you, Suzannah. See that you do so." The door slammed, shutting off Suzannah's protests.

Suzannah stared at herself in the mirror. She looked terrible, tired and defeated. Coming so soon after her parting from Roberto, the shock of her mother's orders was almost unbearable. She tried to conjure up Travis' image in her mind, tried to recall the reasons she had once thought herself in love with him, but her efforts proved to no avail. Her months with the Sicilian had erased the Yankee from her mind as if he never existed. Except for her too-vivid remembrance of their last moments together, Suzannah could think of nothing Travis had ever said to her that had stirred her blood. Their relationship, in retrospect, seemed passionless.

Suzannah knew her mother was right, that Travis would eagerly become her husband if Martin Hopewell agreed to the match. Yet the thought of a lifetime with Travis left her strangely devoid of feeling, as if the fount of her emotions had been exhausted in the turbulence of the last months.

Going to her bedroom window, Suzannah looked out across the garden and countryside, down to the river and town. It was midweek. The mills were active. In the still, spring air, smoke rose in white columns from every stack and chimney. The grounds and gardens were green with grass and the azaleas bloomed beside pink and white dogwood. The last of the spring forsythia grew in soft, wavy bustles that gilded the slope to town. But Suzannah saw none of this beauty. Instead, her gaze was riveted on the factories and the lines of drab boarding houses that made up her town.

To Suzannah, it appeared that the drab presence of those buildings was felt everywhere. Ugliness, it seemed, was her heritage and destiny.

Chapter 32

While Suzannah mourned her fate, Sarah went downstairs to confront her husband in his study. Most mornings, before leaving for the mill, he spent a few hours in the study organizing the day's agenda and Sarah knew she could find him there. She did not stop to plan her argument in favor of Travis. If she paused to think, she knew she might lose her confidence entirely and never speak her mind. Though not given to self-examination, Sarah could see that freedom from the tonic was in some way related to freedom from her fear. She feared Martin, certainly, but even more she feared her own opinions and responsibilities. Now, padding softly down the carpeted stairway, she felt prepared to speak her mind decisively.

She found Martin at his desk, poring over papers, reports and legal documents.

He looked up irritably as she entered. "It is you, Sarah. What do you want? I am working."

"I must speak with you about Suzannah, Mr. Hopewell. It is most urgent." In reply Martin Hopewell eyed her like a bear glowering from its lair. But she could not retreat now. And, besides, she told herself, he had to agree with her. Suzannah's whole future was at risk. She only needed to make him understand the extreme gravity of the situation.

"I said I am working. Your concerns will have to wait." Martin was more than a little perplexed by his wife's unusual appearance in the study. Just a few months earlier, she would not have dared to venture into his private retreat unless invited. Her letter from Sicily, telling of Bronwyn's accident, had given him an inkling of the change in his wife. With her arrival in Amoset, his expectations had been confirmed. Gone was the nervous, ineffectual wife who habitually dosed herself with tonic. In her place was this fierce little woman with flashing eyes.

"What concerns me should concern you as well," she declared, astonishing him further. Uninvited, she sat down on the settee across from the big desk. "No, there isn't time."

"Time for what, madame? Pray do not speak to me in puzzles. If you must interrupt my morning's work. . . ."

"She must be married, Mr. Hopewell. And as quickly as possible."

His face reddened angrily as an idea came to him. "What happened over there? Is the girl in trouble? If she is, by God, madame, I will . . ."

Sarah held her hands knotted in her lap, squeezing her fists ever more tightly to stop their trembling. For reassurance, Sarah thought of her sister. Bronwyn Kirkhaven would not have cowered before Martin's bullying. She would have returned his fury with her own unshakable determination, demanding to be heard and respected.

"She is not in trouble, Mr. Hopewell." Sarah cleared her throat. "Nevertheless, because she is of a marrying age, I believe she would be . . . safer married."

He spoke slowly, curling the end of his drooping mustache. "And since you have this all arranged in your mind, Mrs. Hopewell, perhaps you have also cornered a suitable young man?"

Sarah felt drops of perspiration slide down her neck. Her palms were clammy and moist. "An excellent match for our daughter would be Travis Paine."

"Never!" Hopewell bellowed, slamming his fist down on the desk top. "That sanctimonious Yankee will not come near my daughter again. Now, this conversation is finished, Mrs. Hopewell." He pointed to the door.

"No, it isn't. You have to listen to me."

"I must do nothing of the sort! This is mindless women's jabbering you trouble me with." He gestured to his littered desk top. "Look at this. I am a man with work to do. Yet you think I can take my valuable time to listen to. . . ."

"She will shame you, Martin. She must be married, else she will shame you surely." In the silence that followed, Sarah was conscious of the heat of the room closing in on her, trapping her. She remembered the tonic bottle still beside her bed upstairs. It would be so pleasant to drift into the warm, calm pool it offered and leave Suzannah, Martin and all the rest behind.

Martin Hopewell stared at his wife. "Shame me, madame?" The ice in his voice cut through the hot room, sending a shudder along Sarah's spine. The sweat on her body turned cold. "May I remind you, Mrs. Hopewell, that Suzannah is as much my daughter as yours. I am her parent and she will do as I tell her. She will control herself until a suitable young man can be found. She will not marry the architect. Do I make myself clear?"

"Martin, do not be harsh with me. I beg you to

listen. Believe me, for a woman like Suzannah, the only protection is marriage. Let her marry Mr. Paine, forget your objections to him and let the wedding be arranged. If you love her. . . ."

"Because I do love her, I will never permit the union. Do you hear me? Never! I would rather see her dead than married to that Yankee prig." He sat down and ran his fingers through his thick grey hair. "Get out, Mrs. Hopewell."

Sarah reached across the desk to touch his hand. "Please, Martin."

"Goddamn you, never!"

Sarah scurried from the room.

She fled to the sitting room across the hall. Burying her face in her hands, she wept uncontrollably. Her whole body trembled from a combination of fear and frustration. She was right about Suzannah. Somehow she knew that Martin, despite his contrary reaction, understood that she was right. Only his stubbornness made him intractable. It was stubbornness that kept him hating Travis Paine and all other Yankees. It was a pure and simple obstinacy that made him contradict her. Yet Sarah knew that she had spoken the truth and, despite his stubbornness, he would be forced to recognize the veracity of her words.

In the pleasantly sunny room, decorated with furnishings she had chosen long ago in a hopeful time, Sarah should have grown easy. Instead she thought about the tonic and longed for the calm it promised. One drink and she would not care that she was married to a thoughtless brute, trapped in a marriage they both hated. Another drink, and her concerns for Suzannah would drift into the grey background of her life.

She tried to deny the sweet illusion of safety just

within reach. She recalled all too clearly the first
painful weeks at Villa Dolce. Only Bronwyn's love
and patience had enabled Sarah to discover the courage to break her addiction to the nerve tonic. Sarah
closed her eyes and remembered the way her sister
had taught her to clear her mind of stress.

She thought of a flat sea, a broad, boundless hori-
zon. Her mind's eye fixed on that featureless seascape
until at last the terrible trembling passed away. Her
eyes fell shut. And when Eben found her a bit later,
Sarah seemed to be sleeping.

"Are you comfortable, Mama?" he asked softly
from the doorway. Hearing the raised voices of his
parents, he had been drawn to his mother's defense.
Without knowing the cause of the argument, he auto-
matically assumed that his father was in the wrong.
Eben touched Sarah lightly on the shoulder. "Are you
all right, Mama?"

She opened her eyes and stared at her son for a
moment without recognizing him. She thought of Valentine and the servant girl's accusations. Why
couldn't it have been Eben? Her eyes filled with glistening tears.

"Tell me, Mama. What is wrong?" Even to his
own ears, Eben sounded like an outcast child trying
to win the favor of his mother. "Let me help."

"It is Suzannah." His mother wiped her eyes,
then tucked the handkerchief into the sleeve of her
wrapper. "Your father forbids her to marry Travis
Paine. He is so unreasonably opposed to the young
man. Do you approve of Travis, Eben? You were at
Yale together. He was your friend."

Eben reflected before speaking. "He is a fine architect. A bit prim and rigid in his ways, but. . . ."

"Surely we cannot hold that against him. And it
seems to me that a young man with firm beliefs is just

what our Suzannah needs." She took Eben's hands. "Your father is deeply opposed to the match, however."

"Tell me, Mama, does Suzannah love Travis Paine? Does she truly wish to marry him?"

Sarah replied without hesitation. "Of course. In Sicily they had eyes only for each other." Realizing her slip, Sarah covered her mouth like a guilty child.

Eben looked astonished.

"It was only for a little while," Sarah explained hurriedly. "He had to return to Rome to study. You won't tell your father, will you? He would surely make something of it. Promise me? Can I trust you, Eben?"

Eben had neither the will nor the desire to resist the plea in Sarah's faded blue eyes. Impulsively, he embraced his mother. "You may always trust in me. I will speak to Father." He stood straighter.

"He won't listen to you. He is adamant."

"On the contrary, Mama, I think he will listen to me." She began to weep quietly, certain that Eben's interference could only worsen the situation. "Don't trouble your mind any further, Mama. This is men's business now. It stands between my father and me."

At the door to the study, Eben paused to collect his thoughts. For some time he had wanted to make amends to Suzannah for his unkindness to her the previous autumn. Now he saw a clear opportunity. With fleeting surprise, he observed that he was not afraid of his father. He of all people knew Martin Hopewell for what he was and Eben had every reason to be afraid. But Eben had endured much during the winter past, and he knew that to go on hating himself was far worse than enduring his father's wrath.

"May I speak to you, Father?" he inquired, entering the study.

Martin threw down his pen in irritation. "I have had nothing but interruptions this morning. It had better be damned important, boy!"

Eben smiled quietly to himself. "Oh, it is Father. It is."

"What's that supposed to mean?"

"I've come about Suzannah and Travis Paine."

"Damn the man to hell! Has your mother taken leave of her senses entirely? Does she think you can bring me around to her absurd point of view? You?" Martin's derisive laughter was meant to sting.

Eben, for once, seemed unaffected. "It was my idea to speak to you. I am in favor of the match and I think you should be too—for the good of the mill."

"This has nothing to do with business."

"You're wrong, Father." Eben sat down and crossed his legs casually. He was unusually calm in the face of his father's growing displeasure. "I know I do not have to remind you of the stories McMahon has reported lately. The operatives in our mill have become less willing to accept the conditions and pay we offer. They are organizing. They may even. . . ."

"Poppycock! They're little girls. They cannot begin to comprehend what it takes to form an organization with any power. Their sewing circles do not frighten me." Hopewell turned his back on Eben and stared out the window. In the back garden, one of the servants was picking roses under a sky that had turned cloudy.

"You never asked me about Barbara Bolton's funeral, Father. Let me tell you, it was a huge affair. There must have been five hundred operatives there. They were mostly young women, but I saw a few men as well. They crowded the church and many stood in the street."

"So?" Martin turned back to Eben. "What are you driving at? The girl was well-liked. Of what significance is that?"

Eben smiled. The conversation was going better than he had expected. For the first time in his life he was enjoying a sense of power over his father. "The significance is that Barbara Bolton was *not* particularly well-liked. She was a retiring girl who kept to herself. I was much amazed by the numbers who came to pay their respects, and so I did a little inquiring. It seems there was a concerted effort on the part of a small group of socially active workers who organized the demonstration of grief."

"I want them fired, every one of them. Get their names and I'll have them blacklisted!" Martin's face was growing florid.

"That is not the point, Father. If you fire these girls—whoever they are—more will take their places." Eben had no idea who the labor organizers were and had made no effort to discover their names. He did not really care what happened at the mill. He felt a certain respect, in fact, for young women brave enough to take on the owners. "The best way to deal with these young women is to weaken their cause by giving them something."

Martin was exasperated. "What in the name of God has this got to do with Travis Paine and your sister? I am a busy man, Eben, and your fantasies have got me out of sorts." He pulled out his big gold pocket watch. "I am already late for a meeting with McMahon."

"Believe me, Father, you have time for what I have to say. You can appease the operatives somewhat if you bring in Travis Paine with a promise to improve the physical conditions at the mill. You and I both know that during the winter the women freeze, and in the summertime, with all the windows closed, it is a sweatbox."

"Have you gone soft in the head, Eben? Forgotten your economics? Repairs, reforms, rebuilding: it all takes money. We're just getting ahead now after the last recession, but you want me to spend profits on glamorous. . . ."

Eben laughed. "I would hardly describe a small amount of heat and fresh air as glamorous."

"Don't laugh at me, boy." Fully angry now, Martin Hopewell was awesome. He stood over Eben, his voice soft and venomous. "Don't come here looking smug and know-it-all. I am not hiring Paine and I am not letting him near your sister. I told your mother and I will tell you: I would rather see Suzannah dead than bedded with that Yankee."

Eben refused to be intimidated. "Sit down, Father. I have something to say that will change your mind."

"How dare you?" Martin spluttered. But seeing the expression in Eben's face, his father sank into his chair.

"Now listen to me." Eben smiled. "I want to tell you how Grandfather died."

Chapter 33

Upstairs, Suzannah folded the onionskin paper and slipped the letter into its scented envelope. In her careful schoolgirl script, she addressed it to Travis Paine and sealed the flap with wax imprinted with the initials S.H.

It was done.

Propping the letter against the inkstand on her mother's desk, she returned to her own room. For a moment, she stood idly in the middle of the carpet, wondering what to do next. This was her bedroom—where she had spent so much of her girlhood—and yet, strangely, the room felt foreign to her on the first day of her return from Europe. Crossing to the wardrobe, she selected a grey-and-white striped cotton morning dress with long, lace-edged sleeves and a deep neckline. With a pang she recalled that Roberto liked the dress especially. He had said the combination of somber colors and revealing neckline made her his "ardent Puritan."

She laughed aloud at the memory, but her eyes filled with tears. Would the longing, the painful daydreaming continue forever? Always, she missed Roberto, every waking hour.

Once dressed, she wandered aimlessly, picking

up familiar objects and examining them as if she were seeing them for the first time. Looking around her, she saw all her childhood treasures, the souvenirs and baubles she had garnered in a distant time when life was simpler. Though she should have known each item well, she hardly seemed to remember them, and she wondered at the change in herself.

Outwardly, she was Suzannah Hopewell. During her winter in Europe, she had grown more womanly, more self-assured, but otherwise she did not appear altered. It was inside that the change had taken place. Experiences, memories and hidden passions made her a stranger to her own bedroom, her house, her town.

Lifting a comforter from the bed, Suzannah wrapped the down-filled cloth around her knees and sat with her legs stretched out on the window seat. Since dawn, the weather had changed dramatically. Now it was dark and wet outside. The heavy rain almost obscured the vista of Hopewell Mills and Amoset.

None of this will ever be the same for me, she thought. In a winter's time she had shed her Massachusetts upbringing. She had lived by the rules of the European aristocracy. But this was not enough in itself to account for the great change within. What was it then? Trying to understand herself, trying to appreciate all that had occurred, she remembered her painful final days in Sicily.

The grief of Delio, Duke of Monteleone, had been enormous. Unaccustomed to such open demonstrations of emotion in a man, Suzannah had been stunned to see the Sicilian weep shamelessly over the body of his lover. Roberto had tried to calm his brother, but Delio would not be comforted. He hovered over Bronwyn as if by staying with her, touching her, whispering to her, he could bring her back to life.

On the day of the funeral, the Duke appeared to be a man diminished in stature. For the first time, Suzannah was aware of his advanced age. To Suzannah it seemed as if Bronwyn, with her passionate spirit, had imbued him with a youth and vigor that passed away with her death. Suzannah wanted to comfort the man, but his grief was a formidable barrier and so she remained aloof, hurting in her own way.

Roberto left for Naples the afternoon of the funeral. Suzannah had walked with him to the garden gate. Strangely, they had little to say to one another. In the light of Delio's profound loss, their parting seemed almost trivial. Nevertheless, Suzannah wept.

"Your pretty eyes, Suzannah—don't spoil them with tears!" Setting down his portmanteau, Roberto had drawn her into his arms.

"I don't want you to leave. I don't want to go home. I belong here, not over there."

"Suzannah, you are as American as you can be."

"I'm not!"

His body shook with gentle amusement. "Perhaps someday we will meet again, *cara mia*. When you are an old woman, I will come to New York and you will have grown too wise to love me. You will wonder at your girlish foolishness!"

"Never!"

He laughed again but just as quickly became serious. "I ask one thing of you, Suzannah. Will you promise me?"

She nodded, willing to say or do anything.

"When we first knew each other, you told me that you believed you were bad. Do you remember? Well, I ask your solemn word that you will never think such a thought again in all your life. Never, Suzannah. Do you so promise?"

She nodded quickly. It had seemed so easy then.

Now, home in Amoset, with the prospect of marrying Travis Paine ahead of her, Suzannah wondered what that prudish young man would think of her if he knew she had been Roberto Monteleone's lover.

It would be impossible for him to accept, equally impossible for her to reveal.

So, she thought, I will begin my marriage with a secret. Instinctively, she knew it would be but one of many, for she and Travis were vastly different from one another. To some extent it had always been so, but Suzannah's experiences in Sicily had created a chasm where only a small rift had existed before.

Ultimately, it was not Roberto or their love affair that had wrought the changes in Suzannah's heart. It was the love of Delio for Bronwyn that made her comprehend the truth about herself. In Delio's grief, she recognized an emotional bond that lay outside the formal laws of society—a bond that was, nonetheless, equal to any formal, legal contract. The rigid rules under which she had been raised were not inviolate, nor were they the sole measure of virtue. Because of Delio and Bronwyn, Suzannah would never again be made to believe that she was bad because she was passionate, sinful because she believed the prompting of her own heart rather than the voices of moralists and prudes.

On the last day, while Suzannah and her mother were waiting on the terrazzo listening for the warning whistle from the Naples boat, a message had come for Suzannah. Delio, who had sequestered himself in Bronwyn's room since the funeral three days before, sent for Suzannah. Puzzled, even fearful of the grief he would reveal to her, Suzannah went at once to the Duke.

He was standing by the window. Suzannah knocked softly, then entered the room. He spoke without turning to face her.

"When you and your mother have departed, I will have the Villa Dolce boarded up and posted for sale. For me there can never be sweetness here again. My brother is moving his studio to Florence."

Suzannah waited silently, still wondering why he had summoned her. When Delio turned to face her, the ravages of sorrow in his handsome face stunned her. Deep, cruel lines had appeared in his cheeks. Stooped, slow moving, he seemed suddenly frail and elderly to Suzannah.

"Lady Bronwyn sent me a letter when I was in Naples with my family. In it she spoke of her affection for you, Suzannah. She said that she believed you had a special inner strength that would carry you through the difficult times to come." He drew a velvet jewel box from his pocket. "But she said that a woman, however strong in character, needs something of her own—so she will never be forced to rely on the generosity of lovers, fathers and husbands. In that letter she asked me if I would permit her to give something away that was very precious to us both." Delio stared at the velvet box and shook his head sadly. "At the time, I opposed the idea. I thought she was being too emotional. Now it is my wish to do as she would have done." He held out his hand. "But before you open this box, Suzannah, you must promise to speak of this gift to no one, not even dear Sarah, your mother."

"I promise . . . to you and to my aunt." Her voice broke.

"Open it now."

Nested in blue velvet was a diamond pendant. The stone was large, brilliant, extraordinary. A woman had possessed it—a woman who knew no bounds, whose beauty and passion shone. She had given life itself to this man and now he held out the perfectly cut gem for Suzannah to hold. Thousands of facets gleamed. The sight was breathtaking. Even in the dim room it flashed as though it held trapped in its heart the light of heaven.

Reaching under the cushions of the window seat, Suzannah found the amber-beaded reticule in the corner where she had placed it the night before. Carefully, she opened the bag and withdrew the velvet box hidden inside. When she lifted the lid, the diamond blinked its brilliance to her, renewing her astonishment. In the plain world of Amoset, Massachusetts, the gem was more extraordinary than it had seemed in Sicily. It had come to the Monteleone family from Africa long ago; now it was Suzannah's. Delio had given her a document of ownership should there ever be any doubt as to her right to the diamond.

There was a sound in the hall. A maid dusting the silver sconces had brushed against the crystal drops and they tinkled musically. Following the moment of alarm, Suzannah replaced the diamond in its box and slid the reticule under the cushions once more. It was not a good hiding place, but for a day or two it would suffice.

The rain dashing against the panes of the dormer windows made Suzannah feel trapped and she began pacing the room. She had nowhere to go, no one in whom to confide her turbulent feelings.

In the mills below, the operatives were awaiting the sound of the Saturday half-day bell. In a few moments they would run free while Suzannah, trapped in the house her father built, a woman rich beyond anyone's wildest imagining, was held alone, a captive condemned to keep her silence.

Chapter 34

Lucy was certain that Foster McMahon kept "slow time" at the mill. It was Saturday afternoon and her loom had been clean for the better part of an hour. Finished with all her assigned duties, she had simply been making work for herself in anticipation of the one-o'clock bell.

Perhaps it is only that I am excited, she thought. She did not own a timepiece and could not swear that McMahon was keeping the operatives an extra half hour in order to get more work from them. But she did have a sense of time that she had developed as a farmgirl and she could usually trust her instincts.

She looked up from the tray of bobbins she was sorting. Now she was sure that it wasn't just excitement that caused the time to go slowly. All around her she saw other operatives making work for themselves and looking restless. And she thought angrily of her father, now forced to wait for her on the street outside the mill yard gate.

Lucy stood near a window, but there was no use trying to lean out. McMahon had ordered all the windows nailed shut. He claimed the humidity had to be high so the threads wouldn't snap in dry air. But Lucy wasn't convinced that nailed-down windows

were the answer. It seemed to her that the threads on
the looms broke because they were weak or handled
roughly. But her opinion, she was quick to remind
herself, made no difference. She was only an operative, a replaceable part in the machinery of weaving.
It made no difference to McMahon or Hopewell that
the operatives despaired in the hot, closed environment of the crowded weaving room.

Did spindles suffer? Did shuttles care that it was
spring? The more she thought of her confinement, the
more frustrated Lucy felt. She cautioned herself to
keep calm. No good would be served if James Shawn
discovered how unhappy mill life made his daughter.
Nor could she disclose her anger. He would worry if
he knew Lucy was working with the Spindle Sisters
to organize the workers.

Her wages were desperately needed now.

James Shawn's visit to Amoset was not prompted
by feelings of fatherly affection. He had been forced
to bring Ingrid to see the doctors at Amoset Hospital.
Whatever news he had for Lucy, she intended to
promise him all her wages to pay for Ingrid's treatment. Only if James believed she was happy in her
work would he be willing to accept her money.

One of the little boys from spinning tugged at
her skirt. In an accident that had occurred before
Lucy came to the mill, the lad had caught his hand in
the wheel. The homely, squint-eyed child was kept on
to run errands at the Hopewell Mills, working for a
pittance, and the operatives went out of their way to
be kind to him. Squinting up at Lucy now, the little
boy stumbled over his words in his haste to deliver
the message.

"Master McMahon wants to see you, Miss Lucy.
Down in the yard."

Suppressing a spiteful comment that might have shocked the little boy, Lucy thanked him for the information and finished sorting the bobbins on her tray. After locking her looms in place, she took her coat from its peg and hurried downstairs to the yard.

McMahon stood just outside the entrance. Before speaking to him, Lucy glanced up the street in search of her father's wagon. She was relieved when she saw he had been delayed. If he saw her talking to McMahon, he would ask questions—and questions about the general overseer were what Lucy least desired from her father.

"You took your time, miss," McMahon said, examining the line of dirt beneath his fingernails.

"And you are keeping slow time in this mill," replied the girl.

He laughed loudly, but entirely without humor. "You're a clever one you are, Miss Lucy Shawn. A mite too clever, I'd be thinking."

Ignoring the innuendo in his voice, she continued her attack. "You have no right to make us work over our time, Mr. McMahon. We signed agreements with the mill that called for half-days on Saturday. Ask Mr. Hopewell, if you would, why we must keep our part of the bargain while he is at liberty to cheat us!"

"Watch how you speak and what you say, miss. I could have you thrown out of work with all I know."

A chill came over Lucy. "Is that what you wanted to say to me?" The issue of slow time was best set aside. Glancing over her shoulder, she thought she saw James Shawn's wagon approaching on Front Street, just visible through the rain.

"Don't you wonder why I chose to speak to you out here? A day like this, the counting room would be a considerably drier place, to be sure." McMahon did not wait for her to comment. "Well, you see, I wanted our conversation to be a secret. Just between us two."

Lucy could not answer. Her throat was dry, and she was visited by the horrible memory of McMahon's kiss. If he touched her again, she knew she could not remain at the mill. Despite Ingrid's illness and the need of her family, the repetition of such a humiliating experience was too much to bear—even for the sake of a precious weekly wage.

"I could cause a lot of trouble for you, fix it so you never work again. I know it's you and Frenchy been agitating among the other girls for conditions and wages. And you know there's more than plenty of cause for blacklisting you. There's not a mill between here and Boston would hire either of you if they knew the truth."

"Why are you telling me this now?"

"I thought we'd make a little arrangement of our own, Miss Shawn." He reached out to touch her arm, but apparently thought better of the gesture. He pulled away. In the mill the closing bell rang. "You meet me in private and I'll say nothing of what I know. You can organize your little friends for all the good it'll do you."

Behind her Lucy heard the thundering sound of hundreds of feet on the stone stairs. Out in the street, there was the clatter of an old wagon. The sound seemed familiar.

"Don't take too much time deciding, miss," McMahon grinned, his eyes crinkling, forming tiny bright holes. "I am not a patient. . . ."

Above, someone screamed. Lucy's head jerked around. The cry was desperate, piercing. More than alarm—absolute despair was in the voice that shrieked. From the top floor came a slow rumble, the almost liquid roar of collapsing masonry and brick. Covering her eyes as the grit rained down on the mill yard, Lucy turned and ran. She tripped, sprawled and rolled over, then looked up in terror, expecting to feel bricks crash down on her at any moment. She was safe. But the horror of what she witnessed seemed like a terrible, inexorable dream. The corner of the mill that supported the weaving room collapsed upon itself, crumbling into the river. The outer walls bowed out, bursting bricks as a portion of the top level collapsed upon the spinning room floor below. The air rained looms, spindles and bobbins. As the disaster gained thunderous momentum, the second floor gave way. There were piercing screams, separate at first, then merging into one, long continuous shriek. All at once the mill yard was thronged, mobbed by women emerging in terror from the stairwell. Cast-off shoes littered the yard, torn from feet as the operatives ran desperately for safety. All about them, bricks and masonry and equipment pommeled the mill yard. And there were bodies, too. Broken, bent and misshapen.

Crouching against the wall of the furnace house, Lucy caught her breath and looked around for McMahon. He had disappeared.

"What happened?" She grabbed at one of the girls stumbling by.

The girl's rain-streaked face was scratched and bleeding. It was difficult for her to speak. "The floor just gave way. In the corner where they put the extra looms. We were in the stairwell. It stayed solid, thank God. But there were others. Others were. . . ."

Lucy embraced the woman quickly. Over her shaking shoulders she saw young operatives hysterically weeping, screaming. Some babbled incoherently, while others stood rigidly. Lucy watched a woman clamber up the iron fence, trying desperately to escape the horror in the mill yard. The woman's skirt caught on the barbed spikes atop the fence. Until the fabric tore, she hung suspended, jerking her arms and legs in an effort to set herself free.

Lucy saw Wiggins huddled nearby. "Where are the keys?" she shouted at him.

Wiggins looked at her as if she spoke a foreign language.

"Give me the keys! We'll all be killed!" As Lucy grabbed at the old man, he stared at her with terror-struck eyes and fought to thrust her away. The keys were held in his tightly clenched fist. Crazily, he tried to hit her with the heavy ring. It struck the edge of her lip. She began to bleed.

"Lucy, you're all right! Heaven be praised!" It was Marie Leveroux. Her face, clothing and dark hair were covered with a patina of white dust, but she was unharmed.

Together the women fought with Wiggins for the gate keys. It took the strength of both to grapple the ring from him. Marie raced for the gate where several hundred operatives pressed against the iron bars, looking back over their shoulders as if they expected the rest of the mill to come toppling down upon them at any moment.

As Lucy looked up and behind, the sight took her breath away. Fully a quarter of the mill was gone. A monstrous pile of rubble lay over most of the mill yard and there was an island in the river where the bricks had crashed down. Looms, spinning machines and the shattered framework of the weaving room lay in the twisted wreckage about her.

And there were bodies—the dead lay scattered about the wet pavement. Women with smashed, twisted limbs and bloodstained faces filled the air with their cries, moans and pleas for help.

Through the veil of rain, Lucy saw a shattered arm and a twisted pair of legs underneath the base of a huge wooden loom. A single, torn-off hand lay at her feet. A slick film of crimson oozed from the body of a dead child. Lucy staggered through the muck toward the body of a woman and began to tear away at the refuse around it. She screamed for help. She screamed until her throat was torn, while her bleeding hands dug away the litter.

"Come away, Lucy." It was Marie, on her knees beside her. "Let someone else. . . . It is too dreadful." She began to sob but Lucy did not stop to comfort her.

"I have to save her. Just one, Marie. Just this one. If I can save just . . ." Lucy screamed, piercing the air with a noise from the circles of hell. Marie stopped weeping. She looked down at Lucy. The girl lay with her face pressed against the torn breast of the dead operative.

"Come away, Lucy." Marie pulled at her friend, dragging at her shoulders to separate her from the corpse. "Help will come. Soon."

"It's Violet," Lucy screamed, shoving Marie away. "Can't you see?"

The face had been crushed in the fall. Her features were scarcely recognizable, but Violet's closest friends recognized the tiny gold locket she always wore.

Lucy wept, burying her face against the blood-soaked dress. Stroking the matted hair, she repeated Violet's name over and over. She finally had to be dragged away.

"Hush, Lucy. Hush, little girl." Strong arms clasped her tightly. She was held against a broad chest that smelled of tobacco. "Hush, my baby. It is over now."

With one smooth, strong gesture, James Shawn picked up his daughter and carried her to his wagon.

Chapter 35

Suzannah saw it all from her bedroom window. For an instant the intense horror left her breathless. The apocalyptic vision was unreal; she blinked and looked again. Through a chiffon of rain, it was too real. Since her window was tightly shut against the storm, she heard nothing. But her head was full of screams; she would hear the screaming for as long as she lived.

"Father!" She raced to the door and wrenched it open. "Father! Come quick!" Sobbing uncontrollably, she hurled herself down the stairs, her stocking feet barely touching the treads, her finger tips skimming the finely polished walnut banister. With all her strength, she threw herself against the study door, entering unannounced.

"What in God's name has come over this family?" Martin Hopewell was apoplectic. This was the third interruption of the morning. Face livid with rage, he awaited Suzannah's explanation.

She could hardly breathe.

"The mill . . . ! An accident . . . !"

"What are you talking about?"

"Half of it . . . collapsed . . . Father!" All at once she realized what the accident might mean. She grabbed his arm. "Lucy! What about Lucy?" She spun around, looking for the door.

He came around his desk and grabbed her tightly by the arms, pressing so hard she cried out from the pain. She cringed, recalling the sting of his hand when he had slapped her months before. "Don't cower, girl!" he yelled, his face just inches from hers. "Explain yourself!"

"The mill has collapsed. I saw it from my window." Her father made for the door. Suzannah clung to him. "Let me go with you. Let me help. Lucy is down there. My friend. . . . She may be hurt, she may be. . . ."

"For God's sake, let me go!" She clutched the sleeve of his coat. Though he twisted and thrashed out at her, he could not break her grip. His hands began to shake with violent rage.

"Let me go with you. Lucy might. . . ."

He struck her face with stunning force. Her eye seemed to explode with the staggering pain. "Let loose, Suzannah!" he bellowed. But even his cruel blow did not force her to ease her grip.

"I must go with you!" What if Lucy died before Suzannah had a chance to make up with her? What if she was in pain? "Lucy. . . ."

"Damn Lucy Shawn, damn them all to hell! I hope she's buried and dead and there's an end to it."

His words burned white-hot, like summer sun focused through a magnifying lens, severing some small nerve in Suzannah that kept her anger suppressed, her temper cool. Now that thread was cut. Frustration with her father, her family, her whole life, came together at that moment. Her reaction to her father's words was a blinding emotion, unlike any she had known before. She gave up all sense of who she was, surrendered all consciousness of what she was doing.

Beyond her fury lived only one thought: her friend might need her. Her friend might be dying! Suzannah snarled like a wild creature. Making a final, desperate dive toward freedom, she ran for the study door. Martin caught Suzannah before she could turn the knob. Trapping her abundant hair in one huge fist, he yanked back with all his strength. The pain shot through her neck.

"I'll see to you, vixen, once and for all." With his free hand, Martin pulled open the wardrobe door.

"No!" Suzannah yelled, but his cruel hand swung back to silence her. Her mouth was suddenly full of blood, her vision went red. She could no more stop fighting now than she could command her breathing to cease. It was no longer simply a matter of Lucy Shawn. Suzannah knew, without formulating the thought, that she was fighting for her own life now. If she gave up, she would be helpless before her father so long as he lived. Her hand reached up and found the whiskery cheek. Her fingernails dug into his flesh and dragged downward, strengthened by the cry of pain she heard. She gloried in his agony.

He had her by the shoulders now. His thumbs pressed on her throat. She was shaken brutally. With each movement of her head the searing pain mounted. Monstrous, suffocating waves of agony wrenched her body. Her eyes saw nothing but red. She was trying to swim, groping through a sea of blood, certain she would never make it to the top. She could no longer find an excess of anger to turn into strength. The rage had disappeared and with it the physical power. Now, all around her, there was only pain and fear.

A long time passed before Suzannah could think clearly again. When she did, she realized she had been unconscious. All was darkness, except a thin band of light that she could see under the doorway near her eyes. She reached up, touching the hem of Martin Hopewell's coat. So he had thrown her in the wardrobe, like so much baggage. She did not have to touch the handle to know the door was locked—yet she tested it anyway, shaking the door fiercely.

She stopped. Her face pulsed with agonizing pain, but she could scarcely recall what had been done to her. Some mechanism of forgetfulness had spread a balm across her memory.

She knew her father had hit her, but she did not recall the look on his face when he pressed his hands to her throat. And yet, even without that explicit memory, the conviction held. She knew with nightmare certainty that her father had wanted her dead.

Her arms were bruised. Any movement hurt. Still, she tried to shift out of her cramped position in the wardrobe. She reached up and her hand touched the inside knob again, exerting a little pressure, more gently this time. Again, nothing happened.

Tears poured from her wounded eye, singeing her cheek like acid. Where anger had surged, demanding release, there was now a gaping sorrow that only tears could express. Had she not been able to cry, she would have burst from the pain and mortification.

Through everything, her mind returned again and again to ask why. Why had her desire to help Lucy Shawn stimulated Martin Hopewell to such an insane, killing rage? Her father had twice beaten her on account of the Shawns. He hated them deeply, but for what reason?

In her cramped position, troubled by unanswered questions, she finally slept. When she awakened, time had passed. How long, she didn't know. The blood on her face had dried into a hard crust, and her battered body ached fiercely.

I must get out, she thought. I will make a noise. Someone will hear.

She was about to bang against the wardrobe door when she realized the study was occupied. Though she heard only a few brief words at first, the conversation inside immediately captured her attention. For a while she was so caught up in listening that she ignored her pain.

"Are you going to let them blame me for what happened down there, Mr. Hopewell?" demanded McMahon. "You and me both know I was just doing as you bade me when I put those extra looms in. You going to let those hoydens make a fool of both of us?"

"What are you worried about, McMahon? The mill or your own hide?" Eben spoke with harsh disdain. His dark brows formed an angry line.

"Hear that, Mr. Hopewell? Your own son don't know whose side he's on." McMahon was nervous. His life had been going perfectly and according to plan. Now it appeared this accident, this fluke, could ruin everything for him. He would be unable to start all over again at another mill. He had given this job his all and knew he did not have it in him to try once more. He would just give up. "I tell you, sir, what happened down there today was an act of God, plain and simple. No one could have foretold. . . ."

"Father, there were twice as many looms. . . ."

"McMahon's right, Eben. It was an act of God."

Martin was sallow-faced and dirty after spending a long afternoon and half the night at the mill. He tugged at his mustache thoughtfully. As he did, his finger tips grazed the three vertical lines where Suzannah's nails had raked in his flesh. There was no pain, however, no sensation at all. Body and mind were utterly numb. He had passed the last ten hours at the site of the mill disaster and it was all that occupied his mind.

Eben laughed softly, as though amused by a private irony. "You can cry act of God from now until Judgment Day, but no operative is ever going to believe you."

"I don't give a damn whether they do or not. We'll hire us new females and fire the others. Then they can accuse all they like. Isn't that so, Mr. Hopewell?"

Martin's reply was curt. "It is not, Mr. McMahon."

"Congratulations on seeing the light of some reason, Father."

Martin's fist came down angrily on the desk, but Eben did not flinch. "Watch your tongue, boy, or I'll show you reason."

"You aren't going to hire more?" asked McMahon, ignoring the family row. "I don't understand."

Martin spoke as if he were addressing a child. "There are not enough women available. We can't restaff the entire mill. Use your brain, if that isn't asking too much. You know as well as I do that for the last six months we've had to send our hiring wagon farther and farther away to find help."

"Word is out, Father. Hopewell Mills is not a good place to work."

Ignoring Eben, Martin addressed his remarks to McMahon. "What would be accomplished with a mill filled with spare hands? Who would train them?" He shook his head, his expression grim. "No. We need all our operatives back. No way around it."

There was a long silence in the study before Eben spoke. "What did James Shawn tell you, Father?"

"You've heard it already."

"I can guess. I'd rather hear it from you." Eben was certain he could find a way out of the quandary Hopewell Mills was in. The solution, as he saw it, would improve both the family's business and its domestic fortunes. Furthermore, Eben's simple scheme was an idea guaranteed to send the angry blood rushing to Martin's face. That flush of antagonism would give tremendous satisfaction to his son.

"He told me he had been appointed to speak for all the mill operatives. He said they wouldn't come back to work unless we could guarantee safe conditions." Martin spoke through clenched teeth.

The situation was intolerable to Martin Hopewell. His business had been paralyzed by a disaster predicted months before by Travis Paine and now Martin was forced to speak face to face with James Shawn, a man he utterly despised. All he truly wished was to order Shawn off his property forever and, preferably, out of his life. But such orders were not easy to give when every operative would follow the rugged farmer. Hopewell would never forget the look of Shawn as the man stood before him, his face and clothing covered with mud, grim-faced master of the rescue operations. Wearing his rough clothes, bearing the look of a Celtic hero about him, he had instantly become the acknowledged leader that day.

"Father, I think you can answer Shawn's demands without much trouble." Eben sat down and crossed his legs. He grinned rakishly. One heavy brow shot up. "Well? Care to hear what I have to say?"

Martin sighed, pressing his thumb and index finger to the bridge of his nose. "I'm listening."

"Don't give Shawn or the operatives the idea that you've lost control of the situation down there. As quickly as possible, get the place cleaned up and the machines working. We'll get new looms somewhere—if we have to beg, borrow or steal them. Hire the old operatives to do the work and put James Shawn in charge of them. Despite your personal feelings against the man, it's clear the operatives like and trust him. I bet they'd work three times as hard for him as they would for, say, our friend McMahon here."

"You know how I feel about Shawn. I don't want him near my mill." Though the words were clear, Martin spoke with a curious lack of conviction, as if he expected to be dissuaded from this point of view.

"And how many times have you told me that personal likes and dislikes have nothing to do with business? When something needs to be done, it gets done. That's all there is to it. Right?" Eben restrained the gloating in his voice.

"Go on."

"Order Shawn to manage the cleanup and the construction of the temporary roof and floors. He can build a shed in the yard for the extra looms and operatives."

McMahon interrupted. "What about rebuilding the mill? What will convince them. . . ."

"Ah, Mr. McMahon!" cried Eben, as if delighted to hear the man speak. But Eben's voice was insultingly artificial. "Since you are not a Hopewell, you do not know the happy news. Allow me to be the first to share it with you. Your employer's daughter, Suzannah, is to be married to Mr. Travis Paine, the architect."

"Paine!" McMahon spluttered. "Damn him. *Damn* him and all his mealy-mouthed. . . ."

"Never mind what he said. Just listen, McMahon." Martin already understood clearly his son's plan. Though the mill owner could never admit it aloud, the scheme appeared to be sound. He twisted his mustache and touched the sore place on his cheek. Suddenly his fingers hesitated along the thin, red lines gashed by Suzannah's fingernails. A questioning look passed over his face and suddenly he blanched. He appeared, for a moment, horrified and his eyes flickered toward the locked wardrobe door.

"I don't need to hear the rest!" he shouted suddenly. "Go on down—you and McMahon both—tell them Travis Paine will be designing the new mill. If you must, make Shawn the foreman." Martin paced before the wardrobe, chewing on the inside of his cheek. The scratches on his face seemed to glow with pain. He wondered why Eben and McMahon took so long to leave the room.

Martin Hopewell's footsteps approached the door of the wardrobe. There was a moment of silence, then the scratch of a key being inserted in the lock. After another moment of hesitation, the handle turned. The door swung open. Suzannah's father loomed in the doorway.

Cowering in the corner amid the jumble of overcoats, Suzannah tried to scream. Only a pitiful, strangled cry came to her lips. She stared at the man who towered over her, the man who had hurt her so cruelly.

"My God," Martin gasped, touching her bruised and swollen face. "Suzannah. . . ."

"No," she uttered in a hoarse whisper. Her hands went out, trembling, to shield her head from further blows.

"I promise . . . I won't. . . ." His mind was a blank. He could think of nothing to say.

Suzannah began to weep softly. The salt tears

stung her cheeks and she whimpered, sounding more like a frightened animal than a woman.

Martin reached into the wardrobe and lifted his daughter in his arms. She was too weak to pull away, and he held her close. She was quaking like a leaf.

"My God," he murmured. As his fingers touched her blood-matted hair, he repeated the phrase again and again, his expression filled with horror and disbelief.

Frightened at first, Suzannah expected at any moment a recurrence of his rage. But as her father rocked her and crooned to her, Suzannah's body responded to the gentleness of his touch. Now it was difficult to remember clearly who had beaten her. Surely, not this familiar, warm man smelling of pipe tobacco, his drooping mustache tickling against her neck as he held her. All past violence began to fade from her memory at that moment. She did not forget what had been done to her, but the details grew less clear every instant—until, at last, the man who had attacked her then and the father who comforted her now seemed like two distinctly different men. And now she clung to her father, her body torn by sobs.

"Rest now, my darling girl," he whispered. "It is finished now."

Like the rescuing knight he had been to her long ago, Martin carried Suzannah out of the study and up the broad stairs to her bedroom. Sarah was there ahead of them.

"This foolish girl insisted on going down to the mill," Martin lied, placing her gently on the bed. "She must have been hit by something. I can't imagine. . . ." He stared down at the scars across his daughter's face, unable to finish his sentence. Already, Martin half-believed the lie he told his wife.

"My poor baby girl," he sighed. "How could you be so foolish?"

"Papa, please." She was almost too weak to speak. "Help me," she pleaded, knowing only that she hurt in every part of her body. "Please."

Her mind was flooded by the balm of gentle memories. She recalled the other times when her father had come to her side—times when she needed him so desperately she could have burst. If at that moment someone had asked her to name her attacker, she could have given no answer. Certainly she would not have blamed her own father. He had rescued her from the wardrobe and now he surrendered her with tender solicitude to the gentle, healing hands of her mother.

Suzannah was grateful. She had never loved him more than at that moment.

Chapter 36

The party where Suzannah's engagement would be announced was scheduled for a day in August. When the day dawned, Suzannah awoke early to see a sapphire sky, its edges bathed in vaporous mists.

There's sure to be rain by late afternoon, she thought ironically. Strolling out in the garden, she admired her mother's preparations. Sarah had put her heart into this party and all her hopes were pinned on the wedding, which would follow after Christmas. For months, the lawn and flower beds, the shrubbery and trees had been meticulously groomed by gardeners hired especially for the occasion. The boxwoods were pruned at perfect right angles. Low-slung branches of the maple trees had been cut off and towed away, and the leaves were swept from the lawn. In orderly beds of gold and crimson, marigolds and mums nodded in the gentle breeze, their colors flashing in the sun.

The garden seemed particularly lovely so early in the morning. Heavy dew spangled every petal, branch and leaf with gleaming, perfect drops of crystal. Suzannah was distracted by a whimsical thought: it almost seemed to her that Aunt Bronwyn had sent diamonds from heaven to celebrate her engagement to Travis Paine.

No, that wasn't likely, Suzannah reminded herself.

Aunt Bronwyn had never cared for Travis. Several times she had implied that he seemed priggish, straight-laced, incapable of enjoying simple pleasures. Then, with scarcely a breath between statement and contradiction, she always added that he was handsome and had a body like the statue of David in Florence.

Suzannah shot a look to the azure sky. "But you never liked him, did you?" She looked guiltily from side to side. It would not do for anyone to hear her addressing the heavens. But no one was nearby. Looking over the hill, she could just see the stacks of the mill. To her left was the whitewashed wall of the kitchen garden and at right was a long green swath of lawn outlined with beds of profusely blooming summer roses. The lawn was empty. Only the servant working in the stables was up and about.

By three o'clock, Suzannah knew, the drive, coach yard and stables would be crowded with gigs and horses. More than one hundred people would come that day to toast the engagement of Suzannah and Travis.

"You never liked him at all." There! She had spoken aloud again. If she kept it up, someone would send her to Cartland House to take Eben's place.

She didn't want to think about Eben. She could not bear to think of what he'd done. But, the trouble was, she did not wish to think about any of the subjects that filled her mind this early morning. Not Martin. Not Bronwyn. Certainly not Travis.

Travis had been back in Amoset for almost a month. Though he was staying at an expensive men's boarding house in town, he seemed to spend every spare minute at the Hopewells'. Suzannah felt as if she had not had a moment to herself since he had arrived. And sometimes, when he was telling her an interminable story, while he piled one detail on top of another without a trace of amusement, she felt she couldn't breathe in his presence. The last time he had burdened her with one of his stories, she had run from the room as if she had been taken ill. In a way, she had.

The very thought of all the years that lay ahead caused a physical reaction in her. The very atmosphere turned leaden. What had happened to the insane, rhapsodic passion she had once felt for him? The thought of their last night in Sicily was a memory she longed to forget. As long as her mind preyed on every minute detail of that night, the reminder of her humiliation would build a wall between them. In clinging to his sanctimonious virtue, he had been cruel in a way she could not forgive. Only two other people she knew had that same capacity for barbed unkindness. Her father and. . . .

She walked along the edge of the long ellipse of springy grass, her little brown slippers making footprints in the dew. Her feet were wet but she did not mind.

Maybe I'll get the sniffles and have to stay home, she thought, laughing aloud. But somewhere near the end of her laughter, wry amusement turned to angry tears. She stood and stamped her feet, wishing that she were a man, wanting to roar at the heavens or throw a punch into someone's face.

Yet she recognized the source of those wishes, the pattern of her tempestuous nature. No matter how much she hated her father, she was very like him in some ways. Escaping him would be so much easier, she thought, if his nature were not so much a part of hers.

She shook herself abruptly and her expression changed from anger to determination. Quickly she dabbed at her cheeks with the eyelit-trimmed sleeve of her grey gingham morning dress. She had no patience with maudlin thoughts. She had to make the best of an imperfect situation. Suzannah had made up her mind. She had tried to convince herself that no matter how much she disliked Travis as her husband, she would make him a good wife.

Women do it all the time, she lectured herself. Romantic love has nothing to do with marriage. Marriage is a business agreement, a contract. A man gives you his name, the security of his home. He promises that when you're old and sick, he will take care of you like your father. In exchange, you promise to bear and raise his children and keep his household running smoothly.

A woman must marry, she repeated to herself. Even Bronwyn married once and it was Lord Kirkhaven's name that helped establish her respectability in Palermo. Of course, his money helped too.

A woman must marry because the men have all the money.

But some women had other wealth, secret possessions handed down through the generations. Suzannah's diamond pendant was safely hidden in her bedroom behind the wall. Since she and Travis would be living in this house at first, she did not even have to find a new cache for her gem.

Sometimes Suzannah wondered if she would ever have agreed to marry Travis had it not been for that diamond. In the still, lonely hours before dawn, she had lain awake wondering whether she would have the courage to build a new life on the wealth of that diamond, in the event that life with Travis proved unbearable. She hoped she would never know the answer to that question. But somehow, just asking the question made her think the process had already been set in motion. Sometime, someday. . . .

No! She was not going to think negatively. She would go back to the house and have a warm bath. Her feet were wet and she was chilly.

She had just begun a mental list of everything that had to be done before the party, when a voice interrupted her.

"So, little princess, I've trapped you at last!"

It was Eben, dressed in his dark brown riding clothes. Sweat from his horse still marked the calves of his leather boots. His dark hair, as thick and coarse as the mane of his mare, was long and untidy. His green eyes shimmered with good humor.

"You've hardly spoken two words to me since . . . God knows how long it's been. You and Mama have scarcely stopped to take a breath, let alone converse with your long-lost brother." She turned to go. "What's the matter, Suzannah? Aren't you going to say anything?"

Without stopping, she walked quickly toward the house, Eben hurrying after. He ran in front of her and blocked the entrance to the kitchen garden. "What's the matter? What have I done?"

She glared at him. "Let me pass."

"Suzannah!"

"What do you want, Eben? Gratitude? Which of your many kindnesses would you like me to thank you for?" He did not budge. "Tell me, Eben, what will you do if you don't like what I've got to say? Will you follow in an old family tradition and beat me up?" The tiny scar at the corner of her mouth would be a lifetime reminder of her beating. She would never forgive her father, nor would she care for Eben again. In the ways of cruelty, he seemed intent on matching his father. "Let me alone, Eben. We have nothing to say to each other."

Above the sea-green eyes, his dark, thick brows knitted together in anger and confusion. Though he reached for her shoulders, he held her with gentle firmness. Still stinging from her sarcasm, he made no movement that might injure her. "You owe me an explanation, Sister. Haven't I made up to you. . . ."

Suzannah laughed. Sneering, she replied, "You are so very like Father, Eben! When you came back from the South, I thought you seemed different, but I was wrong. You still think like he does. You believe it's your right to grind people under your heel and kick away their remains!"

Eben wanted to shake her violently, but he recognized the danger and calmed the electric impulse of his frayed nerves. Why couldn't she love him? Couldn't she see his supplication? Her anger was ruthless, unreasonable.

"Don't pretend to be innocent. You can never fool me again. Never! You set up this wedding just so you could impress Father with what a conniving businessman you are. Well, I will grant you that! Now your mill has a fine new architect. That arrangement should satisfy Lucy Shawn and all the other little gypsies down at the mill. Indeed, I am sure it satisfies everyone except me!"

Astonished, Eben dropped his hands from Suzannah's shoulders. Quickly taking advantage of her freedom, Suzannah fled around him into the garden. For a long moment, he simply stood, staring at the place where Suzannah had been. Her words seemed imprinted in the air before him.

Turning, Eben strode away from the house.

Crossing the velvet lawn, he made his way between the rosebushes back to the stable. A ride on Gaylight, the new mare, was what he needed. That mare liked the rush of the wind in her nostrils. Well, today he'd give her a good taste of the country air.

She never wanted to marry him, Eben repeated to himself in disbelief. She blames me for the arrangement.

Over and over again as he readied Gaylight, he tried to understand how Suzannah could have come to blame him. True, there was an element of expediency in the match. But Eben had involved himself only because he saw an opportunity to please his sister, to give her what she wanted and to win her affections again. How could she have come to a conclusion that was the direct opposite of the truth? What had she overheard and misinterpreted? As he saddled the chestnut mare, Eben reviewed his recent conversations with Martin. But for some reason his memory had obliterated that spring day when the mill disaster had occurred.

Walking Gaylight into the stable yard, he mounted the mare and tugged her reins, urging her toward the river trail. As soon as he reached the broad open meadow, he gave the mare her head. She tore through the tall meadow grass, her mane a ragged banner flying from her neck, nostrils flaring. He hugged her girth tightly with his muscular calves and felt the muscles strain for speed as the mare swung from a canter to a fleet gallop. Hunkered down against her neck, Eben moved in time with Gaylight, horse and rider one being, a mythical creature flying to destruction.

"Where is that brother of yours, Suzannah? The guests will be here in half an hour." Sarah was as

ready as she ever would be for her daughter's
dramatic engagement announcement. The dress was
mulberry-colored polished cotton. It was light as a
feather, but the warm day had made her uncomfortable and beads of perspiration slid down her breasts
and shoulders. "And look at the weather!" Sarah
fretted. "My Lord, if those servants don't remember
to put up the canopy, we'll be humiliated."

From Suzannah's bedroom window mother and
daughter watched the dark clouds scudding by over-
head. The wind, beginning to rise, whistled as it
teased about the eaves and shutters.

Suzannah turned her eyes to her own reflection.
The dark rose-colored afternoon dress flattered her
complexion but, even so, she appeared wan. She
pinched her cheeks hard.

"Don't do that! You'll look like an apple-cheeked
Dutchman." Sinking into a chair, Sarah fanned herself
with her hand. "It is too humid! I will simply have to
change this dress." Nervous as a flea, she hopped up
again and dashed to the hall door. "Oh, by the way,
did I tell you that Lucy Shawn will be here? Your father is all up in arms, but what can he do? She's coming with that newspaperman who wrote the articles
about the mill accident." Sarah cocked her head
thoughtfully. "You know, Suzannah, if she marries
that man and you're married to Travis, there is no
reason why you might not be able to be friends again.
She could never be called your social equal, of
course; but being married to a journalist is respectable, I should think."

Suzannah felt irritable after her mother left. She
did not want Lucy at the party. Her friend was just
one more unpleasant, unresolved problem to think
about. But Eben would be glad.

Where was he, anyway? Was he going to stay

away because of their morning conversation? She didn't care.

Let him stay away forever. Let him never come back, she thought.

Along the riverside Eben slowed the mare from a canter to a trot, and finally Gaylight was willing to walk. For a few moments, the exhilarating chase down the flank of Cooper's Mountain had cleared Eben's mind. Now, however, along the sylvan shores of the river, where the woods were full of the morning sounds of insects and birds, Eben was reminded of Savannah and of his walks among the live oaks hung with festoons of Spanish moss.

It didn't matter what Suzannah had overheard, he decided. If she had loved and trusted him, she would have come to him for an honest explanation. Instead, she had believed the worst without hesitation. It was obvious she didn't love him at all. She saw him only as the mirrored likeness of his father. That judgment stung him like the kiss of death. Far more than his sister, Eben knew Martin was a man without a heart, a shell of flesh and bones that had grown about an inner core of greed.

Much later, approaching the far side of town, Eben dismounted and walked beside Gaylight, holding her reins loosely. Without thinking of where he was going, he walked with a plodding determination. His eyes remained fixed on the ground a few feet ahead of his steps. His hands were clenched behind his back. Thick dark hair hung in his eyes until he brushed it away with the back of his hand. His face showed no emotion.

But his mind was racing. Inner voices clamored against each other. His head was filled with a cacophony of comments, cries and accusations. Finally he had to stop walking. He rested his forehead against the trunk of an elm.

All this had happened to him before. He had known the blinding despair before—particularly on the day after his grandfather's murder. He had gone mad attempting to rid himself of the feeling of total hopelessness. He had smashed things, yelled and caroused, beat his fists against walls he could not remember. Nothing he did made any difference.

This time, he felt no need for action. His limbs had a peculiar leadenness.

Dropping Gaylight's reins, Eben walked off the horse trail toward the river. He found the rocky shore where he had awakened after the debacle at the tavern. Once again, those boulders high above the cataracts exerted a powerful attraction.

There was no use trying to live down his father's influence. He could never be anyone but Martin Hopewell's son. It was a shame Eben could not endure any longer.

He took long strides up to the rocky summit. At the perilous edge, he could see around the curve to where Amoset lay, just upriver. If he could take just one more step, he would be able to see Hopewell Mills rising above its competition at the foot of Cooper's Mountain. He might even see his home . . . if he took just one more step.

He stared down into the green water swirling into the rapids. One more step and he would be spread out on the rocks like. . . .

"I don't want to die!"

He said it without thinking. The cry came so suddenly that he spun around, surprised, to see who had spoken. "I don't want to die!" He said it again, only this time he owned to the words softly.

He laughed loudly, hooting like a raucous school-boy caught in a prank. Stalking like a savage over the boulder, he roared mightily to be heard over the noise of rapids and the thunder of the approaching storm.

"Damn you all! Eben Hopewell is going to live!"

SECOND IN THE POWERFUL NEW HOPEWELL SAGA

Silent Dreams

by

Drusilla Campbell

Soon to be married to Travis Paine, Suzannah Hopewell travels to Savannah, where her brother Eben has taken over his grandfather's business interests.

But happiness does not come easily to this brother and sister, children of a haunted past. Eben discovers that his forthcoming marriage to Amanda White poses a terrible dilemma for him—and Suzannah returns to Amoset still unsure that her engagement to Travis Paine can bring her peace. When she re-encounters James Shawn, the father of her childhood friend, her world is shaken as she realizes that her only happiness lies in a forbidden love.

The destiny of Eben and Suzannah and the fate of the Hopewell family fortune reach a shattering climax in this powerful novel, as Crazy Edythe on Cooper's Mountain exacts her revenge at last.

**DON'T MISS *SILENT DREAMS*
BOOK #2 IN THE**

HOPEWELL SAGA

COMING IN MAY
FROM
DELL/BANBURY

THIRD IN THE HOPEWELL SAGA

Stolen Passions

by

Drusilla Campbell

Striving to rebuild an empire from the shattered remnants of a family fortune, Suzannah takes over the Hopewell Mills even as her brother Valentine tries to seize the reins of power from her grasp. Corrupted by greed and resentment, living in the shadow of a sordid history, he fights recklessly to wrest the fortune from his sister's control. But he is no match for the savage evil that lurks in the underworld of Amoset, where a cruel enemy of the Hopewells seeks monstrous vengeance on the young and innocent, taking his toll in blood.

In her struggle to rebuild the family empire, Suzannah must face her own bitter secret, reminded of her past by the constant presence of her only son, the child of a forbidden love.

LOOK FOR *STOLEN PASSIONS*
BOOK #3 IN THE

HOPEWELL SAGA

COMING IN AUGUST
FROM
DELL/BANBURY